Paws for Christmas

ANNA SWANN

CHAMPAGNE BOOK GROUP

Paws for Christmas

Published by Champagne Book Group
2373 NE Evergreen Avenue, Albany OR 97321 U.S.A.

~~~

First Edition 2021

pISBN: 978-1-77155-444-2

Cover Art by Robyn Hart

www.champagnebooks.com

Version_1

To my family and my pups.

Dear Reader:

Thank you so much for selecting this book. I hope you'll enjoy reading it as much as I enjoyed writing it.

This book is a happy, hopeful story about a woman who works too hard—a situation many of us can relate to—and who dreams of a perfect Christmas vacation. But when work interferes with her holiday plans and takes her away from her beloved dog and her parents, she expects to have a miserable time. She soon learns that sometimes life's biggest disappointments lead to its greatest joys.

Reading for pleasure allows us to take a break from stress, to visit a new place, to meet special people (and in this story, special dogs), and to share their good and bad times. So, relax, get comfortable, read, and enjoy.

Anna

Chapter One
Routines

Love was not on the itinerary.

When the day began, that was the last thing on Emily Saint-Claire's mind.

The alarm screeched, jolting her from a too-short sleep. Immediately, she grabbed the phone from her bedside table. Eleven texts, thirty-seven emails, a dozen comments on her blog post. She adjusted the pillows behind her back and tapped quick replies. *Yes. Can't. Talk later. Tnx. No prob. Let's discuss.*

She got out of bed by 6:30, then barreled through the rest of her day like a fire engine rolling down a crowded street to douse a five-alarm blaze. A quick shower. A few gulps of hot coffee. A bite or two of toast. She rushed to the office, snatched her phone messages from the receptionist, tackled the list of chores scribbled on dozens of sticky notes slapped on her credenza, shoveled one task out of the way, dug into the next, sighed with a sense of failure each time she realized she completed only two, at most three, items on her to-do list by noon.

At lunch, she raced to the food cart downstairs, ran back to her office, wolfed down a cold sandwich at a desk piled high with papers and notebooks. Emily never had time to clear the clutter. She just built higher stacks of paper. Maybe one day she'd have time to conduct an archeological dig and find her missing pens, missing stapler, missing notes. A few years ago, she lost her cellphone. Maybe it was somewhere in there too.

Sometime between 6 and 7 PM, she stopped work, ending the day with a doleful sigh, disappointed once again that she accomplished far less than she planned. She bought a take-out dinner on her way home, hurried down the streets, rushing past people she didn't know, people who kept their eyes straight ahead, who never smiled. *Are they exhausted too?*

After she got home, she answered emails at her computer till her head nodded. Around 10 o'clock, she fell into bed. Promptly at 3 AM, she woke up, worried for an hour or two before drifting back into a restless sleep. When the alarm sounded, she began her day again, stressed and exhausted.

Every morning was the same. Every day was the same. Every year was the same.

Her life could be summed up in three words: work, worry, repeat.

Once her job challenged her, exhilarated her, like an early morning run up mountain switchbacks. Emily breathed in the fresh air, looked back at where she'd been, satisfied, reveling in a sense of fatigue and accomplishment. But lately, she was limping along a rocky trail in the hot, humid August sun, sharp pebbles inside her ill-fitting shoes, gasping for air.

Hang on. Relief is on the way.

In a few hours, she would pack her suitcase. Tomorrow, she'd hop into her car, connect her phone to the car stereo, hum along to her favorite Christmas tunes, and practice the *ujjayi* breathing she learned in yoga class. She hadn't had time for a downward or upward dog in years, but she remembered the "ocean" technique that promised to energize and relax with each inhale and exhale. The Brooklyn skyline would disappear in her rearview mirror, and with each mile she drove, the tensions she carried inside her would melt away. She'd enjoy her first vacation in three years.

For now, she pushed on. There were two more work chores ahead of her, and one of them was *big*.

Emily stared into her closet, hands on her hips, contemplating. She chose two outfits, then stood in front of the bed.

"This is called a sheath dress, and it's red, and it says, 'I am powerful and feminine.'"

She gently placed the dress on the blue and white gingham upholstered chair.

"What about this? Gray is a neutral color. These slacks and this sweater say, 'I'm serious, I'm competent, but I don't want to call attention to myself.'"

Silence.

"What do you think?" She tapped her foot on the hardwood floor.

Gracie cocked her head to the left as if she was carefully considering the two options. Then she barked.

"Right!" Emily exclaimed. "You're always right. The red dress was my first choice too. If I wear this, I can wear my Christmas scarf."

She hung the gray outfit back in the closet and spread the red dress on the bed. Gracie promptly plopped on top of it. Emily would find her lint brush later, but years ago she accepted she would never leave the house without dog hair on her clothes. People just had to understand. She searched through a dresser drawer until she found her favorite Christmas scarf—crimson poinsettias and emerald green leaves printed on black silk, with slim silver threads woven from top to bottom so the oblong scarf shimmered when the light caught it just right.

She zipped the dress, pulled on her black boots, looped the scarf around her neck, then turned to Gracie for approval. "What do you think?"

Gracie barked again.

Emily glanced at herself in the mirror, straightened her dress, adjusted her scarf, picked off a few of the more visible dog hairs.

She sat next to Gracie on the bed, stroking the dog's rough honey-colored fur. That's when she broke the bad news. "I can't take you with me to work today."

Gracie put her chin between her paws.

"I know, I know." Emily rubbed Gracie's head. "I wish I could, but I have an interview at a television station, and I'm not sure there's a good place there for you to rest. This interview is a *major* deal. Once that's done, I'm meeting Sebastian for lunch in a restaurant. I won't have time to come back and get you.

"But don't worry. Tomorrow, we'll head home, and I'll have three weeks off, and we'll spend every day together, all day long. We'll go to the farm. Mom will bake sugar cookies—I suspect a bite might accidentally fall on the floor for you—and Dad will take you on a walk in the woods, and we'll cut our Christmas tree. It will be perfect. It will be the best Christmas ever."

Gracie flipped onto her back, signaling to Emily it was time for a belly rub.

"Gracie, I wish I was as relaxed as you. The interview is making me soooo nervous."

Gracie stretched and sighed as Emily's fingers tickled the little dog's pink stomach.

"Yes, I know. We have a bigger problem. I promise, as soon as Christmas is over, I'll take care of it. I'll have a serious talk with Sebastian. I'll tell him I'm tired, I can't keep working this hard. I've dropped some hints, but I haven't said it directly. You and I know I can't keep going like this. I need a change."

Gracie's eyes closed as she fell into her post-belly rub state of bliss.

"Don't worry. I won't tell him today because we don't need a big drama right before vacation. As soon as we finish lunch, I'll come home and start packing. After Christmas, definitely. I'm definitely talking with Sebastian."

Gracie raised her head, yawned, and rolled onto her side. "I knew you'd understand." Emily sighed. "I just hope Sebastian does."

As she did every morning before she left for the office, Emily took Gracie's leash from the Good Dog wooden plaque on the wall, and they took a quick walk through the park across the street. In the winter, the park offered some welcome patches of green grass, a warm contrast to gray buildings, and a quiet respite from the noisy crowded streets and traffic sounds. But only a few moments of reprieve. There was no time to laze on the benches, to enjoy the sun, to watch the children play on the swings, to chat with the three gray-haired women who brought their cups of coffee and met for morning conversations.

Gracie and Emily sprinted through the park. Without fail, a daredevil squirrel darted in front of them, and Gracie gave chase, dragging Emily with her as they wove a zigzag path through the now-bare oak trees. Gracie barked hello to another dog, a springer spaniel they met each morning. Emily waved to the owner. She'd heard him call his dog Gus. She'd never taken time to ask the owner his name.

On their way home, she and Gracie bumped into their neighbor, Mr. Bertelli. Tommaso Bertelli was one of Gracie's favorite people. Every day, he took time to pet her, to talk with her, to praise her for being "*cane più amichevole del mondo*"—the friendliest dog in the world.

Emily liked Mr. Bertelli. A man who was gentle with dogs was bound to be a good person. Even though they spent only a few minutes together each day, she had gleaned enough information during the past three years to piece together a biography of Gracie's friend.

He was born in Cetara, a small town in western Italy. A few months after his wife, Giulia, died, he moved into the building where Emily and Gracie lived. He told Emily he missed his "dearest one—fifty-four years of *amore*," then added, "God has given me more days. I must live them to the fullest." During one recent conversation, Mr. Bertelli shared he'd celebrated his eighty-first birthday—or was it his eighty-second?

Each morning he came to La Prima Tazza, a corner coffee shop he said reminded him of home, for his morning espresso. He bragged to her that later in the day he walked another mile and lifted weights at the gym two blocks away. His silver hair was always neat, short, trimmed—he had been a barber before he retired. Today he wore a navy down vest, green sweater, pressed khaki trousers, and polished black loafers. As he did every morning, Mr. Bertelli bent to stroke Gracie's furry head.

"*Bella* Gracie," he said gently, wistfully. "Someday you and I will hike in the lemon groves in Cetara, *la mia bellisima città*. The ocean is *blu e luminoso*. The smell of lemons and salt air is *celeste*. And the sun is always *caldo*. You and I, we will be *contento viaggiatori*."

Gracie was bilingual and understood every word Mr. Bertelli uttered. Emily, on the other hand, waited for translations. He looked her in the eye and spoke slowly as if he was talking to a four-year-old. "I said someday I would like to take Gracie to Cetara, my beautiful home town. The ocean is blue and bright. The smell of lemons and salt air is heavenly. The sun is always warm. And Gracie and I will be good travelers together."

Emily's lips curled into a slight smile as she imagined him and Gracie ambling through lemon groves. "Cetara sounds wonderful." She checked her watch.

Emily had never been to Italy. She wanted to go, but she couldn't take time off from work. She dreamed about adventures in exotic places and asked Mr. Bertelli to teach her Italian, in case she traveled abroad one day. She loved the way his conversations floated back and forth between two languages, graceful as a dancer moving from ballet to jazz.

After several weeks of instruction, Mr. Bertelli took off his glasses, laid them on top of the dining room table where the two were studying, rubbed his eyes, and said, "My dear Emily, I believe it is time for you to find another teacher, one with *pazienza*."

She looked up the word when she got home. It meant patience. Just as well. She was so busy with work, she didn't have time to learn another language.

"You will come, too, to Cetara," he reassured her. "Gracie and I cannot enjoy the trip without you."

"One day." She checked her watch again. "My job takes all my time, but maybe you can go back soon."

He shifted his gaze from her to the horizon. The corners of his mouth turned down. Mr. Bertelli's voice quivered as he took a starched white handkerchief from his pants pocket and dabbed his eyes. "I hope."

She patted his arm. "I hope too."

She struggled to keep her face frozen in a neutral expression. The most positive, vibrant person she knew, Mr. Bertelli was never sad or pessimistic, but today... Was his morning conversation about his home town an indicator of nostalgia for a place he left, or was he lonely, or did the holidays stir memories of Giulia? Emily was about to speak, to ask why he was sad. She glanced at her watch. She didn't have time.

He put the handkerchief back in his pocket, straightened his shirt collar, smoothed his down jacket. His voice was steady now.

"Christmas. What will you do for Christmas, *cara* Emily, dear Emily?" He wagged his finger at her. "Will you be working? You work too much."

"No!" Her voice rose an octave, and she talked quickly. "I have some time off—three whole weeks! Gracie and I will drive to my parents' farm. We leave bright and early tomorrow morning. I can't wait! Christmas is my favorite time of year. My parents own a Christmas tree farm, so we'll cut our own tree. This year we're cutting a Fraser fir, and we'll decorate, and we'll bake cookies—snickerdoodles are my favorite—and we'll go to the annual Christmas concert in the town plaza. We have a community choral group, and we also have a hand bell choir. Gracie loves going home because she can run without a leash. And I get to visit with my parents. I talk to them on the phone, but it's not the same as visiting in person. I miss them so much."

She stopped, out of breath. Maybe he didn't want to hear that much detail.

"You are lucky to have your parents."

"Yes, I'm grateful they're healthy and happy."

"My parents died when I was a boy. I came to America when I was twelve to live with my aunt and uncle. They were the only relatives I had."

"I didn't know." She looked down at the sidewalk, hoping he wouldn't see her embarrassment. All the years he'd been her neighbor, and all the times he petted Gracie, and all the daily conversations they'd had, she had no idea he'd been an orphan, that he'd come to the United States out of necessity.

"I miss my parents," he continued, "all these years later. Especially during the holidays."

"Maybe you can do something special to remember them and Mrs. Bertelli."

"Oh, I do. I will." He smiled. "I say a prayer I will never forget them. I light a candle for them."

Emily tugged at Gracie's leash. *Time to go. Past time. I'd love to stay here and chat, but Mr. Bertelli, you are retired and don't have to work, and I have a schedule. A schedule!* She was ready to say goodbye, to turn to leave, when she stopped. Was her neighbor going to be alone Christmas day? If she left now, she could be early for her TV interview. But if she asked, he would answer, and his leisurely reply might make her late. And what if she did learn he was going to be alone? She would feel terrible. Her conscience won.

"I told you my Christmas plans. What are you doing for the holiday?" she asked. *Please make it quick.*

"Ah, it will be wonderful. I will take the train to visit my daughter and her husband in Connecticut. You know I have three grandchildren, two girls and a boy. They are excited about Santa Claus, although in Italy *La Befana* gives the children presents. I make my *pizzelle*—waffle cookies—to take with me. It's the anise makes them special."

He smiled, then stooped to pet Gracie again. "Good day, my *dolce bambina*, you have fun on the Christmas tree farm. I hope Santa is good to you and brings you a new toy." He looked up at her. "I told Gracie she is my sweet little girl. To you I say, may Santa be good to you and bring you some rest."

"Thank you. I'm looking forward to doing nothing."

"*Buon Natale*," he said to Gracie. "Merry Christmas," he translated.

She looked at her watch, then scurried home. As she turned the key in her apartment door, she felt a twinge in her heart. Mr. Bertelli dabbing his eyes—that was something she hadn't seen before.

What did she know about her neighbor? She knew on the days when she was frazzled or sad, he sensed it. He dispensed advice the way grandfathers dispensed butterscotch candies. He knew the right thing to say—first in Italian to Gracie, then to her in English. When she doubted herself, he said, "*Avere sale in zucca.*" It translated to "you have salt in the pumpkin," which he explained meant you have a good head on your shoulders.

When she was homesick, he once told her, "*A ogni uccello il suo nido è bello*"— "to every bird, his own nest is beautiful." When she was struggling with a problem at work, he reminded her "*un buon inizio è metà della battaglia*"— "a good start is half the battle." Once when she'd been uncertain about taking a trip to Hawaii, he told her, "*Mangia bene, ridi spesso, ama molto.*" It meant eat well, laugh often, love much. He offered her good advice, but Emily was too busy working to eat, laugh, or love.

He was her north star, present, constant, shining bright with cheer. He had become part of her morning routine, a happy coda to the walks with Gracie. Emily assumed he would be on the street each morning with his take-out coffee cup, eager to pat Gracie on the head, delighted to offer some encouraging words.

She tossed her keys onto the hallway table and unhooked Gracie's leash. The dog bolted to the kitchen, her little toenails clicking against the hardwood floor, to begin the breakfast stake-out.

Overwhelmed by her thoughts, Emily remained behind.

I don't know Mr. Bertelli at all. Yes, they talked daily, but she never took the time to learn, to ask questions, to understand what life he'd experienced in his eighty-plus years. How blue was the water along the Italian coast? Was it love at first sight when he met his wife? Did he enjoy being a barber or was it a job to make money? When was the last time he visited Italy?

She didn't know. She talked *to* him, not *with* him. He was a ghost; he appeared, disappeared. For her, he didn't exist beyond their quick morning encounters. She welcomed his kindness, but she never gave anything in return. She vowed to do better. Soon. Right after Christmas. Right after she talked with Sebastian and told him she was going to quit working so hard.

First, she had to get through this day.

Chapter Two
Transformations

Gracie barked three times, a signal she was losing patience. Emily cast aside her questions about Mr. Bertelli and joined Gracie in the kitchen. First, she tossed Gracie her morning turkey bacon doggie treat, then filled her bowl with chilled, distilled water and served her a Cock-A-Doodle-Doggie chicken stew breakfast. The label on the dog food package said she was eating "the finest organic chicken, suitable for the most discerning canine palate," but she was the kind of dog who tried to drink from mud puddles and eat pizza she found on the street, so Emily wondered if Gracie truly appreciated a gourmet meal. But Emily's dog-parenting style was all about pampering. What was the point of having pets if you couldn't indulge them now and again—or every day?

Gracie locked her four legs, buried her snout deep in the food dish, and like a lawnmower buzzing through a grassy field, made quick work of breakfast. She gobbled with the gusto of a dog who had not eaten in three days, although supper was less than twelve hours ago, and licked the stainless-steel bowl so clean it sparkled, then tilted her head to ask, "More?"

"No, no more." Emily picked up Gracie and gave her a compensatory hug. "Gracie, you're a great dog."

On a cold, rainy night six years ago, the two had found each other. Emily was walking home from work, a purse full of boulders slung over her right shoulder, a hundred-pound briefcase balanced on her left shoulder, each step ten miles long. She was so tired, she wanted to lie on the street and nap. The dampness seeped right through her raincoat, and her blouse stuck to her skin like a clammy, wet shroud. Her teeth chattered.

Then she saw *her*.

A soggy little ball huddled between two trash cans, her head down, her shoulders hunched, her tiny body shivering from the cold.

Emily stopped and stared. *Is that a puppy? Where is the owner?*

She dropped her purse and briefcase and scooped up the quivering waterlogged bundle. Six weeks old, she guessed, maybe less.

"Are you lost?" she asked, drawing the dog close to her chest, shielding her from the harsh weather.

She looked up the street, then down. People sped by, dodged strangers' umbrellas, splashed through puddles. No one showed concern. No one seemed anxious about a lost dog.

"Is this your dog?" "Have you lost a dog?" "Do you know who this dog belongs to?"

The same brusque answers came back each time. "No." "Sorry." "Can't help."

After an hour confronting strangers, she said, "Enough." She heaved her purse and briefcase back on her shoulders, held the tiny dog close to her chest, and brought her home.

This is temporary till we find your owner.

Emily had rubbed the dog's fur dry with the sage-green towel Sebastian had given her as a housewarming present, lit the gas fireplace, and stroked the puppy's head. There was no dog food in the house, and she didn't want to go out in the storm again, so she scrambled the only egg in the refrigerator. The small dog scarfed it down, then whimpered for more.

"Has it been a long time since you had any food?" she asked. "Hmmm, what do dogs eat?"

She took out her computer, placed it on the kitchen counter, and searched for puppy food substitutes. "This will do," she said mixing a few bites of instant mashed potatoes with a can of chicken, then gobbling the rest herself. The two stared at each other. *What next?*

Puppies were probably like her friends' babies, Emily guessed: They liked to eat and sleep. She took the puppy in one arm, grabbed the navy blue chenille throw she normally kept on the sofa for short naps, then moved on to the bedroom, where she spent a good ten minutes folding, refolding, fluffing, and bunching the throw. *Perfect.*

"There," she said, setting the dog in the middle of the makeshift puppy bed. "Nice and soft. Comfortable. Now snuggle in. Go to sleep."

Waving vigorously as if she were saying goodbye to a best friend on the train platform, Emily climbed into bed. "Sweet dreams. I'll see you tomorrow."

She switched off the light and pulled a blanket over her shoulders. Within thirty seconds, the puppy started to cry—a mewl at first, then a full-blown yowl.

Oh, all right." Emily flipped on the light and threw back the covers, placing the dog in bed beside her. "Just for tonight." The dog snuggled close, burying her nose near Emily's ear. Tiny puffs of puppy breaths gently tickled her neck.

At that exact moment, love bloomed. She had fallen hard off the puppy-love cliff of no return. "Gracie," she said. "I'll call you Gracie because you're a gift of love."

Since then, Gracie had been Emily's BFFF (best furry friend forever). They napped together on rainy Sunday afternoons in winter, cuddled on the sofa by the fireplace on snowy nights. On Saturday mornings, they practiced yoga in their sunny living room, Emily working to balance during the tree pose while Gracie easily perfected downward dog.

Saturday nights in the summer, they met Emily's friends for "yappy hours" at outdoor restaurants where people enjoyed iced drinks and hot appetizers and the dogs lapped cool water in bowls set beside the tables. Gracie accompanied Emily on trips to the beach in the spring and the fall, and while she read under an umbrella, Gracie dug holes in the sand, barking at fiddler crabs who scurried too close to the folding blue beach chair.

Or they used to.

Lately, the only playtime Emily shared with Gracie was their brief morning visits to the park, a few minutes at night before bed. Gracie came to the office with her during the day, but Emily concentrated so intensely on work she sometimes forgot Gracie was sleeping in the corner.

Emily consoled herself that Gracie enjoyed a bounty of love. She had all the food and toys a dog could want. They lived in a nice home, in a pre-war one-bedroom ground floor apartment, with a den where Emily often worked, a tiny, fenced patio that allowed Gracie a small space to run and play. But Emily's job demanded ninety-nine percent of her energy and a hefty supply of her brainpower, which meant Gracie got only leftover time and attention.

This morning, she sat by Emily's feet, begging for a few minutes of outdoor play. She opened the backdoor and watched Gracie run with abandon. How to make her understand? Yes, life was busy now, but vacation was only hours away. Soon there would be time for endless hugs.

Three glorious weeks! The most time Emily had ever taken away from work. She and Gracie would drive to her parents' farm, and after they arrived, there would be no schedule. Emily would sleep late, maybe stay in her pajamas all day, and relish time without plans.

When she considered her life, she was proud she moved to the city and made a good living. She understood spreadsheets, navigated her way through the New York subway system, knew the best bodega (corner grocery) in her neighborhood, gave detailed directions to lost tourists, and managed a successful business. Most of all, she counted her greatest accomplishment as the ability to remain calm and cool in any crisis.

"Ask Emily. She'll know what to do." "Emily's the steady one." "Emily never gets rattled." What those people couldn't know was that inside, Emily's soul was a frayed cloth.

That was why she wanted—*needed*—to go home—to be with people who had no expectations, made no demands. Her parents would treat her like a child, and she wouldn't have to pretend to be competent. Some people might resent the hovering, but Emily daydreamed about the days ahead.

Her mother would cook her favorite foods—fried chicken, black-eyed peas, pecan pie. Her father would take her Christmas shopping and ask if she wanted to stop at the drug store for hot fudge sundaes on the way home. They would sit in one of the booths, in the red upholstered vinyl seats, and laugh and talk as they had when she was a little girl.

Her aunts would visit, show off their knitting or quilting projects, urge her to take up the same hobbies because they would help her relax. (Counting stitches, measuring fabric was math. It looked complicated and time-consuming so she was skeptical). Her uncles would talk about the community toy drive and ask, "What kind of toys do the kids like today?" as if she was young enough to answer with authority. They would ask her to help them deliver the presents, and she'd happily oblige.

Her adult cousins would coax her to the ice skating rink downtown. They would laugh, drink hot chocolate, share memories of growing up together—traipsing through the woods, swimming in Lake Laurel, getting together for Sunday dinners. The younger cousins might grow weary of hearing the stories; the older cousins never grew tired of telling them.

Emily leaned against the door frame smiling as Gracie burned off those last bits of energy before she settled in for her morning nap. *Is there anything more fun than watching a dog play in the yard?* Actually "yard" was too generous a term for the six-foot by three-foot space behind their apartment, but for Gracie, the area was the wide-open spaces where she ran, rolled, and sniffed every blade of grass. Emily learned enough Italian from Mr. Bertelli to christen the space *Giardino di gioia*, the joy garden—the place where Gracie frolicked, and Emily laughed watching her antics.

Today, the joy was interrupted when the phone in her pocket pinged. She was never without her phone because somebody in the office might need her.

Oh no!

When she read the message, she learned this was no work crisis. It was much worse.

Please join us for a reception to honor artist Matthew Thoms, whose playful mixed media works offer a sensory experience of color, emotion, light, and humor.

Thoms has been heralded by The New York Times *as a "soulful, yet whimsical artist whose star is rising in the American Southwest and beyond."*

We'll see you Friday, December thirteenth, 5-7 PM, at the Turquoise Cactus Gallery, Canyon Road, Santa Fe, NM.

Emily groaned so loudly Gracie looked up, her tiny, pointed ears standing at attention. Emily had placed Matt in the mental box labeled "Exes I don't want to hear from anymore. Ever. As long as we both shall live." The text brought waves of memories that crashed over her with hurricane force.

The two met the year after she came to New York, long before Gracie came into Emily's life. She didn't know many people in the city, and Sunday afternoons were endless and lonesome. The day she met Matt, Emily planned to go to a movie, but she reckoned she could watch a film in any city in the world. She decided instead to visit the Museum of Modern Art.

She had visited a museum only once before when she was a child on a school field trip to the state capital. There, she had wandered from one painting to another, mesmerized by colors and brush strokes that transported her to the misty pastel Seine River at Giverny in France, the dark and fiery eruption of Mt. Vesuvius in Italy, or the bold journey of Harriet Tubman as she led six slaves to freedom. Emily might not have artistic talent herself, but she admired others' creativity.

That afternoon at the Museum of Modern Art, she was again fascinated by the paintings—paintings she'd only seen in books. Up close, the artists' emotions flowed from the canvas into her heart. As she examined the paintings from every angle, Emily marveled at Vincent Van Gogh's rich blue, green, and gold swirls in *The Starry Night*. She studied Paul Cézanne's short strokes in *Château Noir,* which created a beautiful stone home peeking through blue-green leaves. Frida Kahlo's self-portrait, a serious woman with a necklace of thorns, filled her with sadness and determination. And Jackson Pollack's frenetic twists and splatters of black and white paint chaos in *Number 1A* made her want to break some rules.

After hours of roaming from exhibit to exhibit, Emily's legs ached from standing. She found a vacant bench, opposite the Andy Warhol painting of Campbell's soup cans—eight cans across, four down, thirty-two varieties in all.

She was reading the soup labels to herself: Clam chowder, chicken noodle, cream of vegetable, onion, green pea…when she became aware someone was standing behind her. She smelled his cologne—fresh, like leaves and snowfall—and heard him jingling change in his pocket.

"What do you think?" he asked. His voice was deep, gravelly, as if he'd been outdoors in the wind ten minutes too long.

Emily had been a city dweller only a short time and was sure her lack of sophistication was a neon sign flashing so brightly people could see it from outer space. She didn't turn around to face this raspy-voiced, fresh-smelling man, pretending instead to study the Warhol images.

After careful thought, she replied, "I read he painted this because he used to eat a lot of soup for lunch. For him, this piece was practical *and* artistic."

"Hmmm. That's what you read, what someone told you. But what do *you* think? How does it make you *feel*?"

"It's supposed to challenge the idea of art as innovation, creativity." Emily was serious as she parroted what she read on the museum website. "To illustrate the banality of human existence and the commercial enterprise. Personally, I like his untitled *Flowers* works better. They take their subjects from nature. The colors are soothing." Emily paused and gestured toward the painting. "How does it make you feel?"

"Hungry, like I want a toasted cheese sandwich."

There was a nano-second of silence until both burst out laughing, so loud people in the museum stared.

The man took a seat beside her. He extended his hand. "Matt. Matt Thoms."

"Emily Saint-Claire," she said shaking his uncalloused hand.

Faded blue jeans, beige Henley T-shirt, worn-leather bomber jacket, sandy blond hair, suntanned face, hiking boots. His appearance suggested he'd just wandered in from Colorado—or a photoshoot for an REI commercial. "Are you an art expert, Emily?"

"No, not at all—I'm sure you can tell. I want to learn more. Are you an expert?"

"No, just a bored guy looking for something to do on a Sunday afternoon. So, Emily, do you come here often?" He grinned and shrugged sheepishly. "That didn't come out as smoothly as I expected."

Awkward but charming.

"This is my first time here," she explained. "I haven't been in New York long."

"Where did you move from?"

"North Carolina. Western North Carolina. In the mountains. What about you?"

"I've been here two years. I moved from Denver, Colorado."

Bingo. His hiker wardrobe was a dead giveaway.

"I'm kind of tired of the museum," he said. "What do you say we go somewhere for coffee?"

Their relationship began that afternoon in a tiny bistro with exposed red brick walls, soft yellow lights—intimate and cozy, the perfect place to get acquainted. They talked for more than two hours.

Emily told Matt she was a book editor who liked her job and hoped it would lead to a full-time writing position, somehow, at some point. She learned he was an investment banker who loved his job, who never imagined himself doing any other kind of work. A self-described type-A personality who relished corporate competition, Matt liked to push himself hard. He worked twelve- to fifteen-hour days. "I thrive on stress," he bragged.

A less-lonely person would have heeded the warning, might have viewed his workaholic intensity as an ominous sign, but she rationalized he was merely dedicated. Passionate. He wanted to be successful. Matt's fierceness was wildly attractive that first day. She wanted to know more. Emily asked dozens of questions. He had dozens of answers, but no questions for her.

"What kind of music do you like?" She leaned across the red checkered tablecloth, her hands close to his, their foreheads nearly touching.

"My favorite opera is Bizet's *Carmen*."

"The best concert I ever went to was the Rolling Stones," she said proudly. "I also saw Aretha Franklin once. Wow! What a voice! What's your favorite book?"

"Reading is boring," he replied.

"My favorite book of all time—if I had to pick one it would be so hard—I'd have to say *To Kill a Mockingbird*. Where did you grow up?"

"Cherry Hills Village Country Club in Denver. My family also has a home in Aspen, so I spent a lot of time on the slopes."

"I grew up on a farm. What's your dream vacation?"

"Chamonix in the French Alps. I went there for the first time when I was twelve."

"I haven't had my dream vacation yet, but I'd like to go to a beach somewhere. Maybe a beach in California. I've never been west of the Mississippi."

Matt took his phone from his shirt pocket and scrolled through his messages. "Hey, you wanna meet for dinner next week? I don't have anything else…"

"Yes, of course!" Emily blurted out her answer before he finished his question, before she took time to realize a man who asks a woman for a date because he has nothing better to do was not issuing an enthusiastic invitation. Nonetheless, she floated home. The soles of her shoes never touched the sidewalk. She was already planning where she'd shop for her new date night dress.

The first few months of their relationship were dizzy, and she was happily off-balance, head over heels in…like.

In the early days, their differences were fascinating. She didn't see them the way she should have, like flashing red lights at a railroad crossing. She was simply grateful to have someone to talk to in this big, bustling city. The people in her office were nice but too swamped with work to engage in conversations that might lead to friendships. The first day she introduced herself to several co-workers. One muttered hello, then went back to his computer. Another nodded but didn't speak. The third grunted. Emily decided she would find friends elsewhere.

Now, she'd found Matt. Whenever her phone rang or pinged, she rushed to answer it because it might be him, calling to ask if she could drop everything and meet for dinner or a movie, texting her a selfie and asking her an opinion of a shirt, tie, or suit he bought. If there was a knock at her door, she ran to answer, hoping he sent flowers. She checked her emails first thing every morning, to see if he'd wished her a nice day or tell her he couldn't wait to see her again. Sometimes her anticipation was rewarded. Most times, not.

When Julia Alvarez, one of Emily's favorite authors, came for a reading and book signing at a Barnes and Noble store, she asked him to go. "Sure," he said. While she was sitting alone in the audience, he texted. *Busy at work. Sorry.*

When she surprised Matt with tickets to *Così fan Tutte* for his birthday, he apologized instead of thanking her. He'd made plans to go home to Denver.

"You go. Have a great time." She asked Mr. Bertelli to go with her instead.

All the disappointments—she shrugged them away or laughed

them off. The frequency with which they happened gave her the evidence she needed to build the case that Matt was a busy man with an important job.

One Saturday afternoon, he took their relationship to a new level. Unfortunately, she didn't realize they were headed to a lower level. Her phone rang, and he said, "Hey, I've got a business trip to Boston in two weeks. Wanna go?"

Boston! She'd never been but heard the city was beautiful in the fall. Indeed, those reports were correct. A lovely town on a river, full of fascinating history, stunning architecture, and public parks. Early the first morning, she explored the city on a hop-on, hop-off trolley, visiting the Boston Common, Paul Revere's home, and the Old North Church. That afternoon, she visited the Museum of Fine Arts for an Ansel Adams photography exhibit of southwestern landscapes. The second day, she took a bus tour to Salem to Nathaniel Hawthorne's house, followed by a visit to the witch museum. What an amazing place.

There was one problem: She did all this by herself.

Matt was so busy, she saw him less than five hours the entire trip. Once they met for dinner, but he was called away to solve a problem at the office. She finished eating crab cakes alone in the restaurant. The next day, they planned an early supper. He called while she was putting on her mascara to tell her he needed to tend to a work issue.

She walked a block to Cetara—a restaurant that shared its name with Mr. Bertelli's home town—and brought back an arugula salad and homemade ravioli with ricotta and pistachios. She and Matt shared one meal, a breakfast of bagels and coffee at the airport while they waited for their flight home.

On the way back to New York, he apologized. His voice was sincere, childlike. Work took more time than he anticipated. He would make it up to her, he promised.

"It's okay," she said. "You're busy. I understand."

But she didn't. Within the next three months, he planned and canceled trips to San Francisco, Austin, and Fort Lauderdale. After the Florida cancellation, which would have been a nice escape from the historic snowstorm that shut down the city, Emily ate a half-pint of Ben and Jerry's Chocolate Fudge Brownie ice cream and called her mother.

"Work will always come first." She sighed.

"I suspect so," her mother said.

"Is it me? Am I not pretty enough? Smart enough? Sophisticated enough?"

"It's him."

"What am I doing wrong?"

"You're spending your time with a man who doesn't appreciate you."

"It's better than being alone."

"Is it?"

That day, Emily answered yes, but she knew she was lying to herself. The sad truth was she was too afraid to make any changes, so she drifted along in a relationship built on a shifting foundation of insecurity. If she or Matt needed a date for a party or a wedding, they called each other. If one had some free time on the weekend, they met for brunch. He was handsome, successful, self-assured. "Jackpot," one woman commented slyly as he strolled by. When Emily heard her and saw the covetous look in her eyes, she decided she didn't appreciate him enough.

She was determined; she would make herself care. When she finally told him she loved him, she wondered why she wasn't happier. Where was the spark, the chemistry, the fireworks she'd read about? She convinced herself he was "the one," but she knew in her heart he was the one she settled for. Maybe he shared her ambivalence. They never talked much, so how could she be sure?

But there was another problem in their relationship. A much bigger issue. An issue that made Emily grit her teeth, clench her fists, and fantasize about Matt falling over a cliff.

He didn't love Gracie.

He didn't even like Gracie. He tolerated her, and even that was a struggle. One Sunday morning in September, Emily invited him over for pancakes. She was in the kitchen, the griddle sizzling and the sweet smell of vanilla—a culinary secret she learned from Sebastian—perfuming the apartment. Gracie usually stayed right by her heels. Today, however, Gracie rested in the living room with Matt, who was checking phone messages.

From her vantage point at the kitchen pass-through window, Emily saw Gracie rest her chin on Matt's knee. He pushed her away. She tried again. Same response. She cuddled with him. He shoved her away. When Emily brought the pancakes to the dining room table, she caught sight of him tossing Gracie off the sofa. *Picking her up and tossing her off.*

So distracted watching his hostility toward the sweetest dog in the world, Emily burned a pancake and saved that one for him.

The end of their relationship began when he flew to Albuquerque a few weeks before Christmas to meet a movie mogul from Hollywood, who wanted to buy several abandoned warehouse buildings near downtown and convert them into studios for her film and TV productions.

Emily didn't hear from him that week. He was supposed to be home by Friday night. They had tickets for the Rockettes at Radio City Music Hall the following day. A few hours before curtain time, he texted. *Need to cancel. TTYS.*

The next week, he send a longer text.

Hello, Emily, Sorry to be out of touch. I've been incredibly busy. I'm breaking up with you. I am moving to New Mexico. I met someone. She is wonderful. I'm in love for the first time in my life. Best of luck, Matt.

Best of luck? She felt like a racehorse sent to pasture.

To add insult to injury, he included a link to the biography of Cordelia Brilliant, creator of *Galaxy 505*, a billion-dollar film franchise, in which heroine Daisy Quinn, a Nobel Prize winning astronaut and part-time model, battles the forces of intergalactic evil.

Emily's knees grew weak. She sat on the sofa to recover, then read the message to Gracie a half dozen times to let it sink in. *He broke up with me by text. And at Christmas.* "Well, he's gone," she said with all the emotion of the six o'clock news report. Gracie's furry little face transformed into one giant question mark.

"Gone," Emily repeated. "For good. Forever."

It might have been her imagination, but Emily thought Gracie smiled as she wiggled closer. From that day on, she remembered Christmas as the season of the Dear John text. Although she never spent Christmas with Matt, Emily knew he was there, somewhere in the background, like an old decoration you didn't put on the tree but knew you'd find if you needed to fill a vacant space.

Six months later, on a lazy Sunday, a rare afternoon when she didn't have work to do, she was relaxing with Gracie. Unscheduled time was such a luxury. As Emily scrolled through her tablet, she came across a photo that made her stop.

Matt.

A little punch in the stomach, a reminder he left her behind right before the Christmas holidays. In the color photo, Matt grinned at the camera from an oversized rough-hewn chair. He didn't have a care in the world, hands folded in his lap, bare feet propped on the wooden railing of a spacious porch wrapped around an enormous adobe home. Behind him, an endless vista of hazy watermelon-colored mountains resting against a brilliant blue sky. The caption read: "Art phenom Matthew Thoms relaxes at his vacation home overlooking the Sandia Mountains in Santa Fe."

There was a second photo of Matt, with orange and purple paint smudged on his cheeks and forehead, a rainbow of paints puddled on palettes strewn before him on a handmade wooden table. The photographer captured him in profile, biting on the tip of his filbert paintbrush, contemplating his next stroke.

This caption read: "Artist Matthew Thoms crafts another masterpiece at his studio in Santa Fe. 'The paintbrush is the greatest tool in the universe for peace,' Thoms says."

Curiosity drove her onward, and she skimmed the article. "Genius." "Once in a generation." "Rebel." "Anarchist." Then, because she hadn't tortured herself enough, Emily clicked on the link for photos of Matt's paintings.

She gasped. "Oh, no!"

Had Matt painted the blue-green agave plants or the purple-flowered prickly pear cacti that sprang from the rust-colored desert sand of New Mexico? No.

Had he painted the jaw-dropping kaleidoscopic sunsets in the endless blue sky? No.

Had he painted the burnt-clay adobes, the turquoise doors, the bright red geraniums or the pale pink hollyhocks growing along the city walls? No.

Matt painted Gracie.

Emily frantically clicked through the twenty-three photos, then she clicked through them again. The dog he pushed off the couch was now the muse for his creative chaos, the chaos that generated a torrent of praise and a healthy bank account.

She stared. There was an abstract painting with short, brisk strokes of bright yellow oils, mixed with sand, depicting Gracie cowering in front of a purple door. There was a deep rose-light pink watercolor with Gracie looking directly at the viewer, with big eyes made from Coca-Cola bottle caps. There was a painting, huge swirls of vibrant gold and aqua acrylics, with her lying supine on a black sofa, a Rolex watch face glued on her stomach. And another with her fur painted as an orange and white checkerboard and real ruby earring dangling from her pointed left ear.

Emily clicked on the audio link, and Gracie's ears perked up at the sound of a familiar voice. She instantly jumped off the couch.

"People ask me, 'What's the inspiration for the *Gracia Transformado* paintings?' The idea grew from a negative experience I transformed into a positive one," Matt said on the audio.

"In New York, I had a trifling acquaintance who owned a little dog—a pesky creature who created turmoil wherever it went. This dog had no manners. It had a sour personality, always growling, snarling at me.

"I was haunted by these unpleasant encounters with this annoying dog and its sad owner, and I wondered, 'Why can't I purge these demons?' I burned some sage for purification and decided to take command of my destiny. I transformed the negative experience into delight—into art that gives millions joy."

Emily put down her tablet. She punched the sofa pillow with both fists.

Pesky? Sour? Growling? Snarling? No manners? The words tumbled around in her head like leaves in an autumn windstorm. She didn't care if Matt reduced her to a "sad," "trifling acquaintance." But now he'd insulted her dog. That elevated her anger to a whole new plateau.

Emily looked at Gracie, hunkered near the fireplace, trembling. She stared at the floor with worried eyes. Emily motioned for the dog to come. Gracie crept toward her, looking over her shoulder repeatedly before she curled up at Emily's feet. She ran her fingers through Gracie's fur.

"Don't worry. He's not coming back," Emily assured her. "You're none of the things he said. You're the best dog ever."

This morning, as she stood in the kitchen doorway watching Gracie play outside, Emily re-read the invitation to the reception in Santa Fe. Probably a mistake. Some office assistant got the numbers in Matt's cellphone and sent the art exhibit invitation to everyone. Yet, accident or not, the message reminded her she spent years in a relationship with someone who never added much to her life. And now, he'd berated Gracie and made her a cartoon.

She texted him.

Remember the good times we had? Me neither because we never had any. Gracie doesn't remember either because you treated her like a dirty towel. Stop using my dog for your art, or I'll do something. PS— Dogs rule.

She punched the send button, then immediately regretted it. She regretted she'd promised to "do something," not the strongest threat, but she was tired of his intrusion in her life.

"Why did this have to happen today?" she asked Gracie. Emily stomped her foot.

"I have so much going on. Doggone it!" She turned to an alarmed Gracie. "It's just an expression."

She put her hand on the kitchen counter, steadied herself, and took a deep breath. She needed to do what she always did in a crisis— bury her emotions. She shoved the aggravation of Matt, the fatigue from her job, and the anger at herself for her role in a dead-end relationship—down deep, deep inside.

There was work to do. She hugged Gracie goodbye, then headed out the door.

Chapter Three
Three Wishes

Emily squinted. The sun-bright lights blinded her, and her eyes struggled to adjust. She shifted from side to side in the leather chair as giant butterflies rocketed through her stomach. A hand reached from behind her throat. She flinched.

"You're late." A young woman fiddled with the microphone attached to Emily's collar. "You were supposed to be here thirty minutes before airtime. Zaya doesn't like people who are late."

"I got a…a text message I needed to respond to."

"No one cares," the woman snarled. "You were late. That's a sin around here. No one breaks the rules in Zaya-land."

The interview was not getting off to a good start.

Concentrate. Keep calm.

"Just speak normally," the young woman ordered. "We'll start in three minutes."

Three long minutes.

Emily had interviewed hundreds of people, and she'd been interviewed by reporters dozens of times, but in a few moments, she would be sitting opposite Rae Zaya. *The* Rae Zaya. The TV host so popular people called her by her last name only. The journalist *People* magazine called "Empress Z." The woman named "America's most trusted public figure" by ninety-two percent of readers in a *Washington Post* poll. The woman, who the day before, interviewed Queen Elizabeth by Skype.

When Zaya's office contacted Emily, she sprinted down the hall to tell Sebastian, then rushed from office to office, shouting the good news to co-workers. On the way home, she wanted to stop people on the street, to tell them too. But twenty-four hours later, and in the thirty-four days since Zaya's call, Emily had developed a knot in her stomach that grew tighter every day. Zaya could be a gentle spring rain or a category five hurricane. *Who would she be today?*

TV hosts who interviewed Emily in the past met with her ahead of time, introduced themselves, chatted to put the guests at ease. Zaya preferred a different tact. *I like to surprise my guests* ☺, her email to Emily said.

No more surprises, please. Not today. The text from Matt was enough.

She fidgeted on stage, untying and retying her Christmas scarf, trying not to sweat under the blazing lights, trying not to faint from the waves of nausea. When the stage director told the audience ninety seconds to show time, the crowd clapped and chanted "Zaya! Zaya! Zaya!" so loudly Emily wanted to put her hands over her ears. Instead, she sat motionless, ignoring the butterflies, which had now multiplied into a mad swirling herd.

Sixty seconds later, when Zaya took her seat in the "living room," with its white overstuffed chairs and bouquets of fresh flowers, the entire audience fell silent in hushed reverence. Rae Zaya gained the stature of a mythical creature. Soon everyone in the audience could say they'd seen a unicorn or dragon, depending on her mood.

Emily swallowed hard.

"Relax." Zaya checked her notes but didn't look at Emily. "I do this every day."

But I don't. I wished I hadn't read that text about Matt. Is it too late to back out?

"In four, three, two, one." A man behind a camera pointed at Zaya, and the interview took off.

She faced camera one and flashed a smile as broad as the Mississippi River. "Welcome, welcome to all my friends in the audience and at home! Today, visiting in my living room, is Emily Saint-Claire, one half the brain trust behind Bow-Wow Enterprises. Emily started her business in her bedroom, and now she and her partner, Sebastian Farrell, run one of the premier nonprofit companies in the country. We're devoting the entire hour to learn more about this fascinating woman and the Bow-Wow phenomenon."

I'm fascinating? Emily smoothed her dress. *Maybe this will be okay.*

"I have to confess I couldn't wait for this interview because I adopted a rescue dog several months ago. This is Ruthie." On the screen behind them, a picture of a grizzly gray terrier mix appeared. Emily's butterflies fluttered less vigorously.

Zaya's a dog lover. Like me.

"So," Zaya turned to face Emily, "your business took off like a rocket."

The photo on the screen backdrop changed to a posed photo of Emily, Gracie, Sebastian, and his dog Rollo on the cover of *Forbes* magazine with the headline, "Entrepreneurs Take their Business to the Dogs." Emily and Sebastian, both in black, sat on a hot-pink sofa, their dogs in the laps, the wallpaper behind them decorated with big green dollar signs.

"You began Bow-Wow as a community newsletter, then you turned it into a magazine, then into a company. You started as a local business, went national, then international. Your list of accomplishments is stunning."

Zaya looked at the audience. "You won't believe all this woman has done. I'm going to describe some of her achievements. You—well, you won't believe it. Emily, I speak for everyone here today when I say the big question we have on our minds in when do you sleep?"

The audience laughed. Zaya turned back to Emily, who had yet to smile.

"Seriously, Emily, I want to start by discussing your nonprofit work. Bow-Wow is all about helping dogs—"

"And people," Emily interrupted. She winced. *Oh, no! I've interrupted Empress Z. Punishment to follow.* Her body grew stiff as she braced for the stomach punch that was sure to come.

But Zaya was gracious. "Of course! Dogs *and* people!

"Now, for the past five years, Bow-Wow has partnered with businesses and organizations to promote special projects to benefit dogs and, of course, people." She pointed to the screen behind them, which now projected an article from the *Chronicle of Philanthropy,* with another posed photo of Gracie and Rollo, sitting at computers, with Emily and Sebastian standing behind. The headline read "Charity Began at Home."

"One of the first helping projects you did was your work with a local school district to start Upward Dogs, a yoga class for first graders. Tell us how that came about."

Emily took a deep breath. Most of the butterflies had vanished.

"At Bow-Wow, we have a saying, 'Ideas follow needs,'" Emily said. Her voice was confident, calm. "Marta, one of our Bow-Wow staff, is married to a schoolteacher, Evan. He worried his students weren't getting enough exercise, that they worked too long at their desks. Marta told us the transition from kindergarten to first grade is incredibly stressful for children. I practice yoga to relax—or I used to before my job got so hectic—and I casually mentioned that to my instructor. Fast forward to a month later. All of us met for breakfast. Sebastian is a great cook, and he made eclairs. While we ate, we brainstormed ideas to get kids moving, and we came up with the idea of a yoga recess. During the first sessions, we brought in dogs from the local rescue center to 'practice' yoga with the children. It made the kids feel calm, it gave the dogs a chance for some hugs—a win-win. The program expanded to other grades, into other states."

"Yes," Zaya said. "Audience, Emily's work won a special citation from ESPN for creating a new generation of health-conscious youngsters. But you've also focused on mind as well as body. You and Sebastian founded the See Spot Read program, another partnership with schools in which dogs 'enrolled' in reading classes, and students read out loud to them. The New York State Education Department's research shows this program improved reading skills, piqued children's interests in storytelling, and helped them lose some of their anxieties about learning. How did you come up with that idea?"

The audience sighed. The photo on the screen behind them changed to a picture from the Bow-Wow website. A girl, dressed in purple tights, a pink paisley top, and pink sequined tennis shoes, sat with her back against a classroom wall, reading *Junie B. Jones* to a big black dog, who rested his furry head in her lap.

"I used to read to my dog when I was a little girl," Emily said. "Dogs are good listeners. They're a great audience."

"You and Sebastian also coordinated Friends with Fur, which involves rescue dogs visiting homeless shelters, correct?"

"Yes, we created that program to remind our community everyone needs and deserves love. At first, the visits happened a couple of hours each week. Eventually, some homeless shelters decided to adopt rescue dogs, to give them permanent homes, to help dogs and people connect. The dogs are there for companionship, but they also sit in on job training sessions, as well as the job application process, to help reduce people's stress."

"You've also organized numerous charitable events to raise money for, pardon the pun, 'pet projects.'" Zaya winked at the audience. They laughed and applauded as if she'd given them a year's supply of chocolate. "Bow-Wow organized Dogs and Drag, a weekly bingo night hosted by local drag groups to raise money for animal shelters. Dogs attend, and I understand there have been lots of adoptions."

The screen behind flashed a photo of a beagle wearing a pink feather boa, and the audience applauded.

"Then you started Pets for Vets, which helps match veterans with rescue dogs to give the pups forever homes."

The screen changed to show a man wearing a U.S. Marine Corps cap, hugging a golden retriever mix wearing a collar embroidered with "Semper fi"—always faithful.

"Also, you founded Rainbones, a program in which dogs accompany guest speakers who talk to young people to prevent bullying, especially bullying of LGBTQ youth. And who can forget the Gray Matters effort, which encourages senior citizen homes to adopt older rescue dogs? Why did you go in these directions?"

"Dogs are the most accepting, loving creatures in the world," Emily said. "They don't care who you are or what you look like, your income or social status. They don't care if you wear sequins or camouflage. They don't care if you have wrinkles. Love—dogs want to be loved, the same as people do, and they can show us how to care for each other."

"How wonderful!" Zaya exclaimed to the audience. "Isn't that wonderful?"

The audience cheered and clapped. Two women in the front row fist-pumped. Two more shouted, "Woo-hoo!" Five people in the second row wore "Zaya for President" T-shirts.

Zaya made Emily feel special, even comfortable. The audience was there to shower love on Zaya, not to scrutinize Emily, so the pressure was off. *This isn't bad.*

The TV host glanced at her notes and shook her head in amazement. "Emily, the list of good work you've done goes on and on— and, audience, I'm highlighting only a few efforts. We only have an hour show."

The audience laughed again.

"You and Sebastian established a charitable foundation called the Gracie/Rollo Fund to help abused and neglected animals. You've also partnered with other charities. For example, you worked with Wagglesome Waifs, an organization that finds forever homes for homeless pets. You worked with Angel Paws, a therapy training program for dogs who work with children with special needs. You organized Bark the Vote, which brings rescue dogs to voter registration drives. At last count, Bow-Wow has helped register more than half a million voters and found homes for more than five thousand dogs. That's incredible, isn't it, audience?"

No butterflies now!

"Our company made a lot of money very fast. We wanted to give back to the community of dogs and dog lovers. We're always brainstorming creative ways to do that."

"You even have some celebrity supporters," Zaya said. "You and Sebastian organized Dogs Rock, a concert with Elton John, which helped raise money for rescue associations. And when fashion designer and animal rights activist Stella McCartney created a new line of vegan dog collars and accessories, she called Bow-Wow first to ask you to help with promotion."

"Yes, we appreciate their support, but I'm sure they'll agree dogs are the real stars."

Zaya laughed, and the audience applauded. *This is going great!*

"Emily, let's shift gears for a moment. I want to talk with you about your magazine. I suspect everyone in the audience has read articles from Bow-Wow. If you haven't, there's a copy under your seat. You have a print magazine, plus an online publication. In this digital age, why both?"

"The online publication allows us to go in more depth, to include videos and additional photos. Nonetheless, we kept the print publication because our research shows us some older readers don't use the internet as much as our younger readers. Also, many people in rural areas don't have easy access to the internet. We believe we need print and online."

"How smart! Isn't that genius?" The audience roared their agreement. "Now, you've created numerous sections for the magazine, or departments as we say in the business," Zaya said. "There's 'Rx: Dogs,' which reports on advancements in health care for dogs, as well as studies that explore how dogs can improve human health. I'm a fairly new dog mom, and that's the first thing I look for when I get my magazine. Audience, the column is 'written' by Emily's dog, Gracie. Isn't that clever? There's 'Stay! Strong!,' a column that profiles dogs who've helped people with disabilities. I loved the recent story about Angelo, the dog who helps his ten-year-old owner, Meghan, open doors, turn on lights, pull on her clothes each morning.

"Now we've talked about the good work you do at Bow-Wow. I want you to take us back in time. How did you get started? When did the light bulb go off to create a nonprofit to help dogs?"

Emily was relaxed now. Every muscle was fluid as if she'd gotten a hot-stone massage. She leaned forward in her chair, regarding Zaya as a newfound friend.

"Bow-Wow came about because of a catastrophe. At least, I thought it was a catastrophe at the time, but it turned into something great. We have a sign in our office that says, 'Sundown leads to sunrise.' That's the Bow-Wow motto."

"Tell us more," Zaya said. The audience chanted, "More, more, more!"

"It began a few weeks after I got Gracie." The audience swooned. Emily turned to see a photo of Gracie, the "mug shot" they used for Gracie's column—pink tongue, black eyes, blonde hair sticking up in all directions as if she'd been put in the dryer and popped out with a bad case of static cling.

"My apartment didn't allow dogs…"

"Oh, no!" Zaya gasped, putting her hand to her mouth. "I hope you got out of there fast!"

"Not right away. I smuggled Gracie in and out for a few weeks. Hid her under my coat, but as she got bigger, smuggling got harder. It didn't take long for Gracie to lose her youthful shyness. She stopped making little puppy-whimper sounds and started barking, and once she discovered she could bark, she barked loudly and often. When my landlord sent me a note I needed to stop by the apartment office… Well, I knew she was going to tell us to leave."

"Your landlord didn't like dogs? What kind of person doesn't like dogs, right, audience?"

People booed.

"Our apartment complex was a no-pets allowed building. Let's just say the apartment manager wasn't a rule-breaker. We tenants nicknamed her The Enforcer with good reason."

"What a sour puss!" Zaya pouted.

"I begged to stay. I asked her to reconsider. I asked her to let the tenants vote on a new dogs-allowed policy. She said no, no, and no. But she told me she'd let me stay if I got rid of Gracie."

"Get rid of your beloved Gracie!" Zaya clutched her chest. "No way! I'd never abandon my precious Ruthie."

"That wasn't an option I ever seriously considered. She told me because she liked me, I could stay for another two weeks instead of leaving that night."

Zaya leaned forward in her chair. Her audience members leaned forward too. "What did you do?"

"I panicked a little, then I panicked a lot, then I got hysterical. That was the first hour. I spent the rest of the week frantic, searching for a new apartment. I'd find ads for 'Studio, safe neighborhood, great view' or 'Cozy, sunny, roomy efficiency near bus line,' but each one ended with 'no pets allowed.'

"One morning, I started my computer search, and after a couple of hours, I looked at Gracie. Her face was so sad—like she was carrying all my anxiety…

I decided we both needed a break, so I took Gracie for a walk. We went to the park near our apartment, to relax in the sun for an hour. I told Gracie, 'It will all work out,' but I couldn't convince myself. On the way home, we passed the Pupcake Bakery…"

"I love Pupcake!"

Zaya and I shop at the same place! How cool! It's like we're sisters.

"I discovered it right after I found Gracie. The owner, John George, became my canine guru because I knew nothing about puppies or nutrition. He gave me lots of good advice. John opened the bakery because he wanted healthy treats for his beagles. Shout out to Petside, an animal rescue group, that helped John George find Paul and Ringo."

"That's where Ruthie came from!" Zaya exclaimed.

How much better could this interview get?

Emily continued confidently, "That day I stopped in for a treat for Gracie, a cup of tea for me. I planned to ask John if he could recommend any dog-friendly apartment complexes.

"While I was waiting for him to come out of the kitchen, I found a flyer tacked to the bulletin board. 'Rent this room! Two-bedroom, two-bath apartment, quiet neighborhood. You'll have your own space, privacy. We'll share kitchen, living room. Must love dogs.'

"I tore off the phone number at the bottom of the page, ran back to the park, and called right away. I begged to come over. Sebastian was so stern, so unfriendly on the phone. I remember he said, 'I'm looking for someone quiet. Someone who loves dogs. Someone mentally stable.' I screamed, 'That's me, that's me! I'm quiet, I love dogs, I'm stable.' I didn't make a convincing case.

"I picked up Gracie and practically ran over there. Sebastian's apartment looked like a page from *House Beautiful*, except for a ragged striped sheet draped over an easy chair where Rollo liked to sleep. Sebastian invited us in, served us some homemade lemon pound cake and tea, asked dozens of questions and took notes—like he was interviewing me for a job as president of a Fortune Five Hundred company. All business."

The audience "ooohed." On the screen behind Emily, a photo captured Sebastian in a black tuxedo and his dog in a red bow-tie. Emily laughed. "Those are my guys! Sebastian introduced me to Rollo right away. He told me about Rollo before he told me anything about himself. Rollo has a complicated lineage. He's a little bit bulldog, a little bit Corgi, a lot we can only guess. He's a rescue dog, like Gracie.

"The dogs hit it off—no problems. They tussled with a rag bone. But Sebastian—I wasn't sure what he thought of me. I answered his questions well, including one about my childhood hero. I told him Lassie, the TV dog, because she was smart and brave."

"What did you do to convince him?" Zaya asked as if Emily was the only person in the world and Zaya could not go on with her life until

Emily answered her question.

"A happy coincidence finally persuaded him I was okay. I helped him clear the dishes, and I followed him into the kitchen, also like a page from *House Beautiful*, granite counters, warm cherry cabinets. He warned me not to trip over Rollo's water bowl and food dish.

"While I was in the kitchen, I saw two magnets on the refrigerator: 'Spoiled rotten dogs live here' and 'Rescue is my favorite breed.' Cute. Then I saw a third magnet for the Sugar Mountain Bakery. My jaw dropped. That bakery is near my home town in North Carolina. I asked Sebastian where he got the magnet, and he told me his parents owned the bakery. He said, 'The smell of flour makes me homesick.' That was the first time he smiled."

Zaya clapped with delight. "You grew up together?"

"Near each other, in towns twenty miles apart, but we didn't meet till we moved to New York. And we never would have met if it hadn't been for our dogs. Sebastian said, 'It was destiny. It was meant to be.'"

"What a wonderful story! Isn't that wonderful, audience?"

Aaahhh. Emily wanted to kick off her shoes. She was soooooo comfortable in Zaya's living room. Emily wanted to hug Zaya, to ask her if they could be best friends. She remembered sleepovers with Hannah Rose, her best friend in elementary school. They would sit by the fireplace, making s'mores and confiding their celebrity crushes. Emily could imagine herself and Zaya doing the same thing next weekend.

"I moved out of my apartment that night."

Zaya rocked back in her chair, laughing like a girl who'd bested the class bully. "Love it! Love it! Good for you for standing up the Enforcer. Now tell us, how did you and Sebastian start your company?"

"That was destiny too. One Saturday, Sebastian and I decided to go out for breakfast, and we took the dogs. There was a new restaurant a few blocks away, and one online review said it served 'the best chocolate croissants this side of Paris.' But when we went in, the host told us the dogs weren't allowed. We walked a block farther to another bakery that advertised croissants 'so buttery and flaky, you'll swear they were made by angels.' No dogs allowed. At that point, we gave up on sweets and decided on savory. I'd read about a restaurant that promised 'fluffy buttermilk biscuits with peppery tomato jam,' but it didn't allow dogs either.

"We finally picked up some doughnuts and coffee at a grocery and took our breakfast to the dog park. While we were eating and watching the dogs play, I said something like, 'I wish there were more dog-friendly restaurants in our neighborhood.' Sebastian guessed there were, we just didn't know about them. He made an offhand comment like, 'We need a dog-friendly map of our neighborhood.'

"Later in the afternoon, he came to my room and said, 'I'm going to post a question on Facebook and ask if anyone knows if there are pet-friendly restaurants in our area.'"

"A week later, he had more than twenty-five replies. A month later, he decided to create a website and publish a list of the dog-friendly restaurants people suggested to him."

"So, you started small," Zaya said. "How did you grow from *Bow-Wow! Bulletin* to Bow-Wow Enterprises. Did you have a business plan?"

"No," Emily confessed. "We didn't a plan or even an *idea* for a business. All we wanted to do was find a restaurant that would let us eat with our dogs. But in a few months, we were publishing information about pet-friendly hotels in our neighborhood, and pet stores, and pet groomers.

"Our first big change in direction came when a reader, who volunteered at the local animal shelter, asked if we'd run photos of pets ready for adoption. That's when we added a section to the website called Love at First Bark. I called it 'a matchmaking service for loving pets and loving people.' That led to another section for the website called Happily Ever After. I wrote follow-up stories about the dogs who found new homes."

"Now, how did you go national?" Zaya asked.

"We started getting requests from advertisers—a pet-food company, a pet-friendly hotel chain. Since, it's been like riding a rocket."

"Now, Emily, you've told us a lot about your business, but I'm sure our audience wants to know about your personal life."

Please don't ask me. Please don't ask me. Please don't ask me…

"Matt Thoms. You used to date him."

The disgust bubbled inside Emily. Her left eye twitched.

If there was one lesson she learned in growing up in the South, it was always, always be polite. And the second lesson: If you can't be nice, state the obvious.

"Matt." She took a deep breath. "He seems happy now."

Emily looked into the host's brown eyes, pleading. *No more.*

"Let's move on," Zaya said cheerily. "Let's talk balance. How do you balance your work and personal life? I'm sure everyone in our living room wants to know how you spend time in *your* living room."

"It's hard. It's very…it's just…so hard. I'm…well, I never…I can't…it's hard." Emily shifted in her chair.

Zaya gestured to the audience, making a sweeping motion with her hand. "It's clear you devote a great deal of time and energy to work. Tell us what you do for fun?"

Emily gazed heavenward. Maybe a happy memory would fall from the sky. "I work so much. Fun...I don't have time..."

"Oh, come now," Zaya coaxed. "You must have *some* fun adventures to report. You play with your dog, don't you?"

"Yes, I take her to the park in the morning for a quick walk. We play ball for ten minutes when I get home at night before I go back to work on my laptop."

"On the weekends?"

"I work then too." Emily hung her head.

"You must travel to interesting places for work."

"Not really. Not lately." Beads of sweat popped out on Emily's upper lip.

"Hmmm, why don't you tell us some local fun place you've been here in New York? Maybe you can give our audience some ideas of places in the city you like, places they should visit?"

Emily tilted her head, put her index finger on her cheek. "I...I'm not sure."

Zaya grimaced.

"Wait, wait. A year ago, my washer broke, and I did go to this cool laundromat."

The other woman muttered under her breath. Emily leaned forward. She strained to hear but couldn't quite make out what Zaya was saying.

"What about your workout routine. How do you stay in shape? You're so thin!"

"I don't have time to eat."

Zaya sighed angrily. Her voice was less friendly now when she said, "Let's talk Christmas. Just a few more weeks. What will you be doing?"

"Sleeping." Emily shrugged. Zaya rolled her eyes. "I mean, I'll go home to North Carolina. I'll get some rest there. I'll visit my parents."

"How nice. There's no place like home, right audience?" They clapped.

Emily suspected the applause was for Zaya, who maintained some measure of composure, not for her, on the verge of falling apart.

"What about New Year's? Will you be ringing in the New Year here in New York City? Or are you traveling to some far away glamorous place? Vail for skiing? Maybe Miami for some sun?"

"No, I'll be at my condo. I'll probably go to bed early."

"More sleep?" Zaya didn't sound as cheerful as she had an hour ago. "Emily, there's a fun game I like to play with my guests."

Excited murmurs rippled through the audience.

"It's called three wishes. I want you to pretend I'm your fairy godmother. This microphone is my magic wand." Zaya waved the mic, tapped it in the air three times, and the audience clapped. "I can grant you three wishes. Now, there are a few rules. Everyone says, 'world peace.' That's a given. Take that off your wish list. Also, second rule. People tend to make wishes for others—I want my children to be happy, or I want to give my spouse a diamond bracelet..."

Audience members whispered excitedly, "Diamonds?"

"These have to be selfish wishes. Wishes for you alone."

Emily pursed her lips. "Okay, I wish I could live on a farm and have lots of dogs—a dog ranch where I can take care of homeless dogs."

"That's one," Zaya said. "All of us can agree it's a great wish. What else?"

"I'd like to travel. I've never been outside the country. I need a change of scenery. I'd like to visit a new place, meet new people, learn about a different culture."

"How nice," Zaya said. "And three?"

Emily squirmed. Her throat tightened. Tears burned her eyes.

"And?" Zaya asked eagerly. Audience members leaned forward in their chairs.

Emily was silent—a tortured silence—the kind of silence in elementary school when the teacher asked if you've read the assignment, and you read the wrong assignment, and you don't know how you'll save yourself. Zaya glanced at Emily, at her crew, back at Emily. Ten seconds ticked away on the clock. For her, it was ten hours.

"Emily, your third wish is—"

"I wish I could run away," she blurted. The words hung in the air like thick black smoke.

Zaya rocked back in her chair and whistled softly.

At this point, Emily realized she still could save the interview. She could laugh and say, "I want to run away and become a beach bum." Or "I want to run away with the man of my dreams." Or "I want to run away and join the circus." Instead, she ran the train off the track. And over the cliff. And into the roiling river below.

"I want to run far, far away and never come back. I'm so unhappy."

Zaya gasped. The audience fell into a state of silent shock.

"I'm exhausted. My job is too much. No one should have to give up her entire life for a company. I'm weary to the bone. And I'm lonely. My last relationship was a mess. How will I ever have time to meet anyone else? I want a change in my life, a big change, but I don't have the energy. I wish my life was different. Better. Different. I don't care. Just not this. Everything is such a mess. I'm miserable."

Emily put her head in her hands and sobbed. *I hate this game.*

Zaya gasped. True pro that she was, she recovered. "We can relate, can't we, audience? We all have those moments when we're overwhelmed. Our jobs. Our families. The holidays. We women particularly experience that. People expect so much, and we feel obliged to please them. We put too many demands on ourselves."

Emily cried harder and louder.

"Emily has given us a lot to think about, hasn't she, audience?" Zaya's exasperation was now clear. "I don't believe we've ever had anyone cry in our living room, but there's a first for everything."

She looked at her crew. She adjusted her earpiece. "What? Okay. Now's a good time to brighten our spirits with some Christmas cheer. It's time for Zaya's Christmas Extravaganza Basket Bounty!"

The audience members jumped to their feet. They thundered with excitement, hugged, danced. A dozen of her assistants, dressed as elves in green and red plaid costumes, skipped down the aisles with giant handmade willow baskets wrapped in bright blue cellophane tied with shimmery silver bows. Meanwhile, a compassionate crew member brought Emily a box of Kleenex as she wept uncontrollably on stage. She grabbed three, wiped her face, blew her nose.

Zaya ignored her soggy guest. "Now you can open these baskets at home, but why keep you in suspense? Let me tell you what you'll find." She rambled through the list: "a new iPhone; gift cards from Apple, Amazon, and Starbucks; two tickets to tonight's Rockettes' performance at Radio City Music Hall; a trip for four to Disneyworld; and, of course, a diamond tennis bracelet."

As the audience members continued to celebrate, they chanted, "Zaya Claus! Zaya Claus! Zaya Claus!" She beamed.

Emily slumped in her chair and blew her nose again. She hoped the audience would be so delirious over the gift baskets, they wouldn't remember her breakdown on national TV.

Zaya held up her hands to quieten the rowdy crowd. "Before we close, I want to thank you for visiting my living room today. And I want to thank Emily Saint-Claire for her stories. Emily, you're a great storyteller!"

"Hu, hu, hu." A series of loud sob escaped from Emily's throat.

"Also, Emily, my charity, the Z-Fund, is making a ten thousand dollar contribution to Bow-Wow charities."

"Thank you." Emily mouthed the words because the giant lump

in her throat wouldn't let her speak. Giant tears slid down her cheeks. She snatched the last of the Kleenex from the box.

"This is Rae Zaya signing off, and what's our motto?" She put her hand to her ear.

"Z positive!" the audience shouted in response, shaking their fists toward the heavens.

"And we're clear," a crew member said.

Zaya jumped out of her chair, tore her microphone off then threw it on the floor. She left mumbling. When a woman came over to unclip the microphone from Emily's collar, her tone was brusque. "This will air next week."

"Do you think you might edit the last bit—you know, the part where I cried?"

The woman delivered a steely gaze. "I certainly hope so."

Emily couldn't remember what happened next. When she came to herself, she was standing outside the TV studio, staring straight ahead. What should she do? What *could* she do? She lost control in public—not only in public but on a TV show with eleven million viewers on a slow day.

Her phone pinged. She read a text message from Sebastian. *Running late. See u soon.*

She'd have to tell him.

Instead of hailing a cab, she decided to walk to the restaurant. She needed to clear her head, get a grip on her emotions.

Why did I crash and burn?

Of course, Emily knew why. New York City was home to eight million people, but she could count her friends on one hand. She lived in a city that manufactured excitement, yet it was a lonely city full of strangers. No one smiled. No one ever met her gaze. No matter how fast she walked, other people walked faster as they shoved her along. To be fair, though, she rushed, never smiled, never looked people in the eye. No doubt, they considered her a haggard stranger who bolted from one chore to another.

Her bones ached. Her head throbbed. And she wondered: Was numb exhaustion her permanent state now?

As she struggled to keep pace with the crowds roaming the sidewalks, she reckoned her big charade had come to an end. The past few years, she pretended to be a competent business executive and, frankly, deserved an Oscar for that performance. Today, she berated herself as a failure; her valiant efforts to bury her emotions had fallen apart. Anger and loneliness spilled out in Rae Zaya's living room in front of two-hundred and fifty guests today and an audience of millions next week. Emily was sorry. She was surprised.

She pulled her red hat around her ears and tucked the scarf into the neck of her gray coat. Her mother knitted both from the softest wool, wool she bought from a neighbor's sheep farm in the mountains and gave them to her for a Christmas present last year. Every time Emily wore them, she thought about home, swaddled in comfort. After the Zaya meltdown, they were especially soothing.

"The sun is the best medicine." That's what her mother used to say when she'd shoo her outside to play. Today, as the warm rays seeped through the cold air and touched Emily's face, they erased a modicum of the humiliation inside.

She admonished herself to shift focus from the Zaya disaster to Christmas, her favorite time of year. Store windows filled with jolly Santas, industrious elves, spirited reindeer. Street after street decorated with garlands of multi-colored lights. The sweet smells of vanilla and cinnamon wafting from the bakeries. The rich aromas of delicate spruce and fresh evergreens in the Christmas tree lots. Hopeful carols from the churches as choirs rehearsed, and the shrill jingle of the Salvation Army bells that echoed throughout the city. Weren't those the most comforting sounds anyone could hear?

Emily reminded herself to enjoy those sights, sounds, and smells, to draw them deep inside, to let them be the healing balm for her wounded spirit. After all, this was her last day of work before she left for her three-week vacation. She might have shamed herself on national TV, but soon she'd be home, where life was easier.

As she dodged aggressive pedestrians and raced to beat traffic lights, she imagined how different life would be in a few days. Soon, she'd be wandering through pine trees, calmed by gentle earthy smells, with Gracie, happy and content, running at her heels. She wouldn't hear the traffic sounds, only bird songs floating on the wind. She'd warm her hands by the fireplace, and every face in Holly Mountain would welcome her. Maybe there would even be a soft dusting of snow on Christmas Eve. Emily longed for life on the farm because, like Gracie, her heart beat free there, and love was abundant.

Chapter Four
Cake

Sebastian suggested they meet for breakfast at one of Emily's favorite restaurants, Gusto Global. "Enjoy global flavor. Take your taste buds around the world," the menu promised. The restaurant changed its offerings daily. Oatmeal from Scotland one day, mandazi, a sweet coconut doughnut from Kenya, the next.

She had sampled every exotic item the restaurant offered—rice porridge with fish from Japan, crunchy baguettes and tangy orange marmalade from France, savory rice-dough pancakes from India called idlis, warm corn tortillas stuffed with eggs from Mexico.

One day, she would have time to visit exotic places, to admire roaring waterfalls, sandy beaches, snow-covered mountains. For now, Gusto Global had to satisfy her travel appetite.

Emily claimed a table by the front door, so she could wave at Sebastian when he came in and so she could people-watch through the window while she waited.

How many meals had she and Sebastian eaten together? Hundreds? Thousands? They had been partners six years, and their careers spiraled in directions they never imagined. He would often punctuate every accomplishment with a broad smile and the pronouncement, "Not bad for a couple of small-town kids."

True, there were a lot of not-bad things in her life. But also true: Her life was one endless to-do list.

She checked her phone. No message. *Where is he?* Sebastian was perpetually late, but today he was even later than usual. She was drumming her fingers on the table, impatient and anxious, when he finally bounded through the door.

"Over here!" She waved to catch his eye.

He bounced—he never really walked—over to the table, shed the purple plaid scarf wrapped around his neck, and unbuttoned the gray wool coat.

"Sebastian, I need to tell you something," she said.

He eased into the seat opposite her.

"Before you say anything, I'm sorry to be late." His cheeks were rosy from the cold, but she could tell he also was flushed with excitement. "I have something to tell *you*. You'll never guess who I talked to this morning."

Before she could answer, he blurted out, "The first lady! Of the United States! She's developed a campaign to promote volunteer work, and she wants to work with us to encourage people to become foster dog parents."

Emily's eyes widened. "That's fantastic!"

"After the holidays, she wants us to come to Washington and meet with her in the White House! You know what a dog lover she is."

"I do." She paused. "I have an idea. Let's write an article for our website about the three dogs they fostered and kept. We could explain how the president and first lady became foster parents, then rescue parents. Maybe we could post interviews with her and other White House staff who've fostered dogs, to have them share their experiences."

"Those are great ideas, but you don't sound very enthusiastic. Aren't you excited we'll get to visit the White House?"

"Sure, sure I am. But I need to tell you—"

"Good. We'll brainstorm with the staff back in the office." Then he added, "I'm in such a good mood!"

"Yes, you are," she said, hanging her head. "That's why what I have to say so painful."

Sebastian dismissed her worry with a flip of his hand. "Nothing you can say will spoil my day."

"Oh, I don't know. This might."

"Nope. No way."

"Today was my interview with Rae Zaya."

"I forgot! I was so excited about the first lady. How did it go?"

"Okay—at first. She gave the Gracie/Rollo Fund a check for ten thousand dollars."

"That's great! Yay, you!"

Emily twisted her napkin. "At the end…at the end, it didn't go well. I…I didn't handle things the way I should have."

He leaned forward, took the napkin from her, and patted her hands. "Did she ask you some absurd question like whether you've ever been arrested?"

"No." She hesitated. "She asked thoughtful questions, interesting questions. She asked about our nonprofit work, how it all started."

"I'm sure you answered her questions like a pro. You're good at interviews."

She looked at her hands, not at Sebastian. "At the end, she plays a game where's she pretends to be the fairy godmother. She grants you three wishes."

"Yeah. It's kind of silly…"

"I think so too! I'm glad to hear you say that. It is silly, isn't it? But that's the segment that didn't go the way I hoped."

He planted both palms on the table and said with mock seriousness, "Tell me more. I'm braced."

"I had a breakdown—a brief one—but it was bad." Emily lowered her voice. "On a scale of 1 to 10, 10-bad." Her voice cracked. She tried not to cry. "I said I wished I could run away from my job. I said it because I'm overworked—broken down. I cried on national TV," she confessed.

He shrugged. "Maybe they'll edit it out."

"I suggested that. I hope they do, but I'm pretty sure I visited Zaya's living room for the first and last time."

"Doesn't matter."

"I didn't want to embarrass Bow-Wow or embarrass you, but what I said during the interview—it's true. I need to talk to you about my job. Sebastian, I planned to delay this conversation till after Christmas, but I need a change. I work all the time, I work days, nights, weekends. I work…"

He held his finger to his lips to "shhh" her. "Emily, don't worry about the interview. For sure, we'll talk about workload after Christmas. Today, nothing you say today can torpedo my good mood, thanks to our wonderful first lady. Besides, I have some more news that will make you forget that crazy interview. You'll be so happy, you'll jump up and kiss me."

Emily leaned back in her chair. "The last time I jumped up and kissed you, you got us backstage passes at a James Taylor concert. He video-called my parents and sang a verse of "Carolina in My Mind"."

"Yeah, after my parents catered those Lots of Lemon cupcakes for his Asheville concert, he's been super-friendly, but this is even better than backstage passes. First, let's get some food."

"Okay," she said suspiciously. "What looks good to you? I'm thinking about the Spanish breakfast—the *tortilla de papa*—the potato omelet."

He shook his head. "I pre-ordered for us."

"You did?"

"It's part of the surprise." Sebastian beamed with the pride of knowing a secret. "You'll love it."

He motioned for a waiter to come to their table. Sebastian asked for a pot of hot Earl Gray tea, then explained he'd placed a special order. Within seconds, the waiter scurried back with the tea and a cake, giving Emily no time to discuss her job woes.

"Dessert first?" she asked.

"A good motto," he said, "especially today."

She studied his face for some clue. Nothing. Just a mischievous smile, the way he looked the time he came into her room to tell her he mistakenly ordered a 70-inch TV instead of a 30-inch TV, but did it matter because it would provide hours of entertainment, and wasn't that the goal anyway?

"Do you know what kind of cake this is?" Sebastian asked as he set a gigantic slice on Emily's plate.

She took a bite. Light, moist, not-too-sweet, flavored with toasted almond, alternate layers of sweet raspberry jam and tart lemon curd. The top and sides were frosted with luscious vanilla buttercream, covered with silver sprinkles.

Before she could answer, he said, "It's a Marisol Christmas cake."

"It's delicious," she said, taking a big bite.

"The sprinkles and icing are supposed to remind you of snow and stars."

"Thanks, Sebastian, this is a nice treat."

He rocked back in his seat.

"What?" she asked. "Why are you smiling?"

"What do you know about Marisol?"

"Hmmm." She took another bite. *Delicious.* "I've read articles in travel magazines. It's supposed to be a beautiful place—at least the photos are beautiful. 'The land where the sea kisses the sky,' right? It's a vacation spot for tourists in the summer because of the beautiful beaches and draws people in the winter because of the mountains and skiing."

"Right. What else?"

"Their baked goods are outstanding." Emily pointed to the cake with her fork, then took another giant bite. *Apparently, having a meltdown on national TV gives one a hearty appetite.* "Don't they have a food and wine festival in the summer to promote local agriculture?"

Sebastian nodded. "And?"

"And?" She shrugged. "Not much else. Wait. I read they have a king and queen and a prince whose wife died a few years ago—some kind of accident? I remember the photos of the royal family in the newspaper. Lots of sad faces."

"Anything else?" He grinned as if he was ready to explode.

She took a sip of tea. She stared at the cake crumbs, hoping they might offer a clue. "Oh, wait! They host an international dog show each year. Of course. How could I forget the Royal International Canine Invitational—the RICI. I've watched the re-broadcast on TV on Christmas Day with my parents and Gracie."

Sebastian's eyes twinkled. His face shone like the sun. "Wouldn't you love to go there?"

"Sure. Who wouldn't? Maybe someday. When I have some vacation time." She glared to remind him she was stressed at work.

"What about now?" He fidgeted like a third-grader who'd been in math class too long and was eager for recess.

She narrowed her eyes. "What do you mean?"

He pulled an envelope from his coat pocket. "You're going to Marisol! You're going to cover the Royal International Canine Invitational! Here's the invitation letter."

She stopped, her teacup suspended in mid-air. "No." She put the cup down and shook her head.

He nodded vigorously, his head bobbing the way a child does when you ask if he wants an extra cherry Popsicle.

"No. No. No."

Sebastian ignored her. "You leave tomorrow. You'll write a special daily blog on the competition, and you'll post it on the Bow-Wow site each evening. You'll cover the activities before the competition, the competition itself, plus some special events after. There's something called the Fetch! Play Ball, a big whoop-de-do at the royal palace for dogs and owners, and there's an even bigger whoop-de-do, the Holly and Ivy gala for owners and handlers, and you'll cover that. Think about it! Very old Europe. Waltzes. Tuxedos. Evening gowns. Elegance!"

"No," she said firmly. She grabbed her coat, hat, and scarf then slid out of the booth.

He held on to her sleeve. "We'll post every article you write. You can take some photos and videos. We'll post those too."

"No." Emily stood beside the table, trying to wiggle away from Sebastian. If she sat, she reasoned, she'd signal she was willing to negotiate. She was not.

"It's a dream assignment. Nobody can do it better than you."

"No!" Her voice was loud enough he slowed down.

"No? Why not? You've said for months you want to write more, manage less. This is three weeks of writing. Nothing to do but write—

maybe take a few pictures."

She scowled. "I planned to leave tomorrow for my three weeks of Christmas vacation."

"Full-time writing," he repeated.

"Yes, I've wanted to do more writing, but I've wanted time off from work too. I worked overtime to get my management chores done before the holidays. You know how important Christmas is to me. I can't believe you did this." She folded her arms across her chest, stomping her foot. "I'm not going."

"You have to go."

"No, I don't."

"Yes, you do." He was pleading, not dictating, but Emily didn't care. "I promised the Marisol government you'd be there. I promised the RICI president you'd be there. The RICI is selective—they don't allow many journalists to come."

"Well, un-promise them!" she shouted. The other diners stared. The wait staff turned around. The restaurant manager peered from behind the bakery case.

"Emily, calm down," Sebastian whispered as he smiled at the people in the restaurant, an effort to assure them the situation was under control.

It wasn't. She took a step away from him. "I don't care what you promised. Did you tell me here, now, because you thought I wouldn't make a scene in the restaurant? Well, I am going to make a scene! Right here, right now. Look, everyone, I'm making a scene!"

She glowered—the glower she reserved for people who supremely irritated her—like people who cut in line in the grocery store or people who talked out loud on cellphones in movie theaters.

"Emily, this happened so fast. Yesterday afternoon, I got a call from the coordinator of the Royal International. They practically begged for Bow-Wow to cover the event."

"They should have contacted us months ago."

"They did—or at least they tried. They sent us a formal invitation and wondered why we never got back in touch. Someone at their end sent us—or thought they sent us—a package of materials through DHL. A few days ago they found the invitation lying on a desk in one of their offices. It never even went out for delivery. They emailed us several times, but the email went to the wrong address. Finally, they called."

"The wrong address? Our email is <u>bow-wow@bow-wow.com</u>. How can anyone mess that up?"

"They left out the hyphens. You always say punctuation is

important. This proves your point."

Emily groaned. "Just because they're inefficient doesn't mean we have to accommodate them."

"When they called yesterday, they were beyond apologetic. I *promised* them we'd cover the RICI."

"You knew yesterday? Why didn't you tell me then?"

"I wasn't sure it would come together. You need a visa to get into Marisol."

"That means I can't go, right?"

"They've expedited a visa for you."

"There's no way I can get a flight this late. Even if I could, it will cost a fortune."

"The RICI president arranged a flight for you. She's sorry about the mistake. To make it up to you, she got you a first class ticket." His eyes twinkled. "First class." He repeated it slowly for emphasis.

"What about a hotel? There can't be any rooms left at this point."

"The Royal International sets aside a block of rooms for the dog show. They reserved one for Bow-Wow."

Emily could feel the tears threatening. She bit her bottom lip and turned away from him. First the invitation from Matt, then the disaster with Zaya, now the surprise from Sebastian. *Could there be a worse day?*

"Look," Sebastian said as he fished around in his briefcase. "Here's the itinerary. Fun every day! Extreme fun!"

Emily snatched the schedule from his hand and scanned the pages. *Pages!* The blue and gold crest of Marisol was printed at the top left of the first page—a dolphin leaping from the sea with a mountain in the background. At the bottom right corner, there was a line drawing of a shaggy white dog sitting by a little girl dressed in a coat, mittens, and a hat. In dark blue type were the words, "RICI Day-by-Day."

There was a note underneath: "We want to give you maximum time to meet with show participants. We hope this schedule will allow you time and flexibility to develop your own stories and pursue ideas that will interest your readers and viewers. Check daily emails for updates and specific meeting times."

As she read, her eyes grew bigger. Her mouth formed a large "O." Her jaw dropped lower with each line.

December 8—Arrive in Marisol, attend news conference with Prince Alexander, royal RICI ambassador.

December 9—Spend day with dogs and owners in the hound group.

December 10—Spend day with pastoral/herding group.

December 11—Spend day with working group.

December 12—Spend day with toy group.

December 13—Spend day with sporting group.

December 14—Spend day with utility/non-sporting group.

December 15—Spend day with terrier group.

December 16—Spend day with agility dogs and owners/trainers.

December 17—Morning: Blessing of the animals. Afternoon: Visit with local officials and royal family representatives to learn about the nation's Good Dogs program, a charitable effort to help humans and animals provide emotional and physical support for each other.

December 18—Agility dog competition. No trophies. Just fun.

December 19—Meet the most "promising pups" and junior handlers—champions of the future—and watch practice competitions.

December 20—Meet and interview RICI judges. Learn how they evaluate each breed and learn what it takes to become a judge.

December 21—First night of competition: Hounds, pastoral, working, toy groups.

December 22—Second night of competition: Sporting, utility, terrier groups. Royal International champion named.

December 23—Afternoon: Fetch! Play Ball event for dogs and owners/handlers in the Royal Palace garden. Evening: Gala Holly and Ivy Ball in the Royal Palace Grand Ballroom, for owners, handlers, and their guests.

December 24—Pack your suitcases and your great memories. Say goodbye to beautiful Marisol and return home.

December 25—Merry Christmas!

No days off. Emily gasped as if someone had knocked the breath out of her. The workload was staggering. She would have to write several stories each day—and she would need to shoot photos and videos to accompany each blog entry. She looked at the itinerary, then at Sebastian, then back at the itinerary, then she fixed her stare on him.

"Why aren't you happy?" he asked. "I know you want a change. I know you miss writing. I thought this would send you over the moon."

"It might have. Another time. Yes, I want to write, but I want less work, not more. You made all the plans without even talking to me. Sebastian, you're not only my business partner. You're my best friend. How long have we been a team? I deserved to know. You didn't even ask."

She wanted to cry, but she refused to cry again because 1) she'd already shed buckets of tears on Zaya's program and 2) one of Emily's mottos was no tears at work; tears in the bathroom, in the car, on the bus, but not during work meetings.

"And because I'm your best friend, I wanted to do something

nice for you." He took both her hands in his and kissed them.

"It's Christmas." Emily was surprised at how whiney the tone of her voice was. She was so exhausted, she struggled to string the words together. "I planned to take off three weeks. Christmas is my favorite time of year, and I wanted to spend the holidays with my parents on the farm. You knew that."

Sebastian took the printed itinerary from her hands. "The Holly and Ivy Ball is December twenty-third. You can fly home Christmas Eve and drive to your parents' house on Christmas Day. Problem solved."

"Problem not solved. The drive takes twelve hours, if the traffic is light. Sometimes, I spread the trip over two days. By the time I get home, Christmas will be over. Even if I wanted to drive, I'll be too jetlagged to drive safely."

"You could fly in," he suggested.

"Sebastian," she said, her voice rising with exasperation, "Holly Mountain only has that tiny airport for private planes. Even if I could get a plane reservation at this late date, I'd have to fly into Charlotte, rent a car, and drive three hours to get home."

She frowned, hoping he felt guilty. "Besides," she said, "the best part of Christmas is the anticipation, the excitement. Buying presents. Wrapping presents. Hiding presents. Going downtown to oooh and ahhh at the window decorations. Baking cookies and cakes. Waking up in your own bed and hoping there's snow on the ground. I'm going to miss that. And what happens to Gracie? I can't take her with me to Marisol."

"She can stay with me."

"When are you leaving for Christmas?"

"In two weeks."

"Great. I only need to find doggie care for the third week, Christmas week." Emily threw up her hands. "I'm guessing every doggie hotel in the city is booked."

"Emily, I apologize." His voice was somber, remorseful. "I thought I was doing the right thing. I wanted this to be a surprise but a happy surprise."

Both were silent. Sebastian stared out the window while she looked at the bakery counter because she was too angry to face him.

"I am truly sorry," he said.

"Can we tell the Royal International it's too late—we can't send anyone?" She was desperate. "We can promise we'll come next year. Please. I have my heart set on going home."

"That would be hard. It's a big deal for Bow-Wow if we come. We've worked to wrangle press credentials for the RICI for years. They limit the number of journalists who attend. Because we're not a news organization, like Reuters or BBC that usually get credentials, they've made an exception for us.

"They made mistakes that caused us not to get the invitation in time," he finished, "but they've gone out of their way to accommodate us. First class," he repeated, stretching his arms to mimic airplane wings.

"Can't you go instead?"

"I'm not a writer," he reminded her.

"Can we send someone else?"

Sebastian's face clouded over.

Then she answered her own question. "Of course we can't because everyone else is busy or already has Christmas plans. You won't ask them to change their plans, yet you'll ask me."

He withdrew a large manila envelope from his backpack. "Look at the silver lining. Here's a packet of information the dog show officials sent us. There's a press pass, airport transfers, a map of Marisol, a list of restaurants. There's a brochure on the top ten things to do during the dog show. Look at the pictures. Did you ever see a more scenic country?"

"Yeah, well, I'm guessing I won't have time to do even one of those top ten things."

"Don't go away mad. Sit down. Please. More cake?"

Emily shoved the invitation letter, the massive itinerary, and information packet into her green nylon satchel. "I don't have time. I have to pack."

Sebastian stood up and put his arm around her shoulder. "I am so, so sorry," he said. "Can you forgive me?"

"Sebastian, we've been friends for years. I'm sure, in a few centuries, I'll get past this. Right now, I'm disappointed I won't get to go home, and I won't get my time off. Please, let me be angry. Don't try to convince me to be happy."

She brushed his hand off her shoulder. She wanted to make some dramatic gesture, one that would show she was truly furious. She wanted to throw a plate, throw a tantrum, slam the restaurant door on the way out, but she was too polite to do those things. After looking at the uneaten Marisol Christmas cake, she angrily drew a frowny face in the icing with her index finger. "There!" Not much of a protest statement but the best she could do at that moment.

She headed for the door, her boot heels clicking and clipping against the wooden floor.

"Call me when you get to Marisol," Sebastian yelled.

"Sure. I'll call in my hours of spare time," she growled.

Emily shoved her gloved hands into her pockets and stormed down the sidewalk. She hadn't planned to go into the office, but now she had to, to collect her computer, some notebooks, and pens for her trip. Usually, she was pushed along by the crowds. Today she pushed back, elbows out as she gouged her way forward like a hockey player. A woman turned the corner and bumped into Emily, almost knocking her over.

"I'm sorry," she apologized.

"Watch it," Emily snarled. She rolled her eyes and walked faster.

A bell ringer called, "Merry Christmas."

"I don't think so," she snapped back.

The reality of the disastrous lunch with Sebastian fell on her like an anvil. She wasn't going home. Home was salvation, like coming up for air after a deep dive to the bottom of the ocean. *How will I get through this?*

Using the full force of both hands, she pushed open the glass doors of her office building, and they slammed so hard one of the wreathes fell to the ground. She pounded the elevator button to the tenth floor three times with her clenched fist. She shoved open the double oak doors of Bow-Wow. As they shut behind her, the jingle bells, hung to bring Christmas cheer, rattled furiously as if a hurricane wind was blasting through.

On any other day, she enjoyed coming into the office. The mood was perpetually upbeat, the way she and Sebastian designed it years ago. They promised each other their business would be a no-drab zone. Both had worked in places where the walls were the color of winter fog, the furniture comfortable as prison cots, the mood reminiscent of a funeral, the work tedious as a nineteenth-century assembly line, and the workers weighted down with the temperament of zombies. They made a pact they would do things differently.

When they moved their office out of their apartment and into the vacant building that now housed Bow-Wow headquarters, they pledged to create a cheerful workplace. The first day, he spray-painted in bold red letters, "No dreary allowed!"

Of course, they painted over it, but she never forgot the words were underneath, a promise they both made to never again work in a boring place.

They started by creating what he called "a joyful outside that will lead to a joyful inside." Midnight blue carpet with bright orange paw prints led from the elevator to the entrance of Bow-Wow headquarters with a ginormous hand-painted rainbow-colored logo outside the doors. The Bs were red and orange, the Os were purple, the Ws were yellow and green, the hyphen replaced by a horizontal blue bone, the exclamation point replaced by a vertical orange bone with a green paw print underneath. Inside, the office walls were happy reds and blues and greens, decorated with the yellow and purple paw prints of employees' dogs.

As Bow-Wow expanded, Sebastian and Emily hired dozens of staff with one common quality: They loved dogs. People could learn how to do a job, they reasoned, but love—that was something that could never be taught.

"No one can be jubilant every minute," she remembered telling Sebastian, "but if they love dogs, they'll forget to be sad for a few minutes."

"Agreed," he had said. "I want anyone who comes in here to feel as if they've gotten a big, warm hug."

She wanted a big, warm hug, but today, she wanted a vacation even more.

As she approached the receptionist's desk, the melody of laughter, punctuated by the occasional barking of the dogs, greeted her. Today, as every day, Bow-Wow staff ran in and out of each other's offices, rushing to finish one chore and start the next, answering the endless ringing phones, clicking away at their keyboards. Some dogs rested beside their owners' desks, snoring, and dreaming. Others romped in the playroom, chasing each other and chewing on tennis balls, as a group of children visiting from the church daycare center next door sang "We Wish You a Merry Christmas" with the special holiday gusto only preschoolers can muster.

"Emily!" Peter, the receptionist greeted her with a smile. "I didn't expect to see you today."

Emily didn't smile back. "I didn't expect to come in."

"Why are you here? You leave tomorrow to go home, right?"

"There's been a change in plans," she said, careful not to show any emotion in her voice or on her face. *Don't take it out on Peter. This is not his fault.* "I'm not going home. I'm going to cover the Royal International Canine Invitational in Marisol."

"The RICI! Oh, my gosh!" He gasped, then swiveled round and round in his chair in celebration. "We've wanted to cover the RICI for years! So few journalists get to attend. This is great news! Lucky you! You'll have so much fun with all those dogs. Dogs from around the world. And Marisol is a gorgeous country. Paradise."

He typed "Marisol" into his computer then turned the screen so she could see the landscape of sun-sparkled blue seas, lush pine-covered mountains, and white-washed buildings with turquoise roofs. "Wow!" he said.

He was the most positive person at Bow-Wow, the perfect

person to work at the front desk. He laughed easily, smiled non-stop, and his exuberance was infectious. Today she was immune.

"When did this happen?" he asked. "How come I didn't know?"

"Sebastian surprised me." Again, she kept her tone even. *Don't air your grievances with Sebastian here.* "I need to get my work laptop, maybe some note pads, pens."

Peter nodded. "Can I help?"

"No, thank you. I'll get my computer and go. You have a merry Christmas."

"Oh, I will," he said. "I won't be going anywhere as glamorous as Marisol. I'll be home in Kansas City. My parents and brothers and I will have an old-fashioned Christmas. We'll have a big family dinner with roast turkey. We'll go to the Plaza to see the Christmas lights. We'll watch Christmas movies on TV. But Marisol! The RICI! You're living a charmed life."

She didn't feel charmed. She felt cursed. A pang of jealously stabbed her from inside, so sharp she almost bent double. *I want a family Christmas.*

"Your Christmas plans sound wonderful," she said. "Have a great time, Peter."

She trudged to her office. She and Sebastian had designed Bow-Wow so each employee had a small office with some privacy, and under each name plate, there was a photo of the person and his or her dog. Her photo showed she and Gracie on a boat at Lake Laurel, near her parents' home. A brimmed straw hat and sunglasses shaded Emily's eyes as she held a soaking-wet Gracie in her arms, coated with sunscreen and beaded with lake water. She squinted at the sun, and Gracie, with her mouth wide open and her tongue lolling out, flashed a smile, in her doggie way.

Before she could open the door, Nora, who worked as the executive assistant for both Emily and Sebastian, tapped her on the shoulder.

"I didn't think you would be in today," she said.

"I didn't plan to, but I have to leave town tomorrow."

"For Christmas, right?"

"No, for work. I'm going to the Royal International Canine Invitational in Marisol."

"The RICI!" Nora exclaimed. "Lucky you! Bow-Wow has fought to get credentials for the RICI for years. I can't believe it. It's so exclusive. They don't allow many journalists, you know."

"I've heard that." She tried not to grit her teeth. "I need to get my laptop, some pens, some notepads, then I'm gone."

"Do you need me to help with any arrangements? Flights?

Hotel?"

"No, thanks. Sebastian took care of all that."

"How did Sebastian keep all this from me?" Nora put her hands on her hips in frustration.

Emily was surprised too, because Nora knew *everything*. She could tell you when the next shipment of coffee was due to arrive and which farm in Costa Rica harvested the beans, where the recyclable paper towels for the kitchen were manufactured, and, if you woke her from a dead sleep, she could recite how much money the company took in last month and how much it spent, to the penny. Her brain was an encyclopedia of office information, earning her the nickname Nora Plethora from Sebastian and Emily. She delighted in the title and even signed office memos "NP."

"Before you go, you asked me to go over the pitch letters for story ideas from freelancers," Nora said. "They're pretty good. I put the most interesting ones on top. You'll want to review them and decide. You said you'd get back in touch with the writers this week."

Oh, no! "I forgot. I planned to write everyone before I left for Christmas. Now I won't have time. Nora, I don't..."

"Say no more. I'll email everyone and tell them you've gone out of town for the RICI—they'll all be envious—and you'll email them after Christmas."

"Thank you. This trip was so unexpected. My mind is reeling."

"No worries," Nora said. "I'll take care of everything. Wonder why Sebastian didn't mention this to me?"

"He wanted it to be a surprise."

"How wonderful!"

Not wonderful. Tragic. Emily opened her office door and slumped down at her desk, then called after Nora, "Have a merry Christmas."

She poked her head inside Emily's door. "I will. There's no place like San Antonio at Christmas. Luminarias along the Riverwalk. Tamales. I can't wait to visit with my family."

Again, jealously sliced through Emily's chest.

On her way out, she ran into Javier, one of the graphic designers.

"Hey, Ems. Headed home for Christmas?"

Emily shook her head. "Change of plans. I'm going to the Royal International Canine Invitational in Marisol instead."

"The RICI?" His eyes widened. "Oh, my gosh! That's the most prestigious dog show in...in the universe. You'll have a blast. And Marisol is magnificent—at least that's what the pictures showed in the July issue of *InStyle* magazine. Lucky you! Have a great time."

"You have a good Christmas too, Javier," she said.

"I will," he assured her. "It won't be as exciting as yours. I'm flying home to Louisville. My cousins live close by. We go to the church cantata, then come back to our house to open presents."

She choked on the lump in the back of her throat. She told herself to be brave. "It sounds nice. You and your family have fun together." "Have fun in Marisol. I can't believe it. The RICI! You must be living right to pull an assignment like that."

Despite the envy her surprise work assignment generated among her colleagues, Emily didn't feel very blessed.

She came home to find Gracie at the door, her short tail thumping against the hardwood floor. Emily never needed to force a smile with Gracie. "How's my sweet girl?" Emily hugged her tight.

She collapsed onto the sofa, holding Gracie in her lap. *How to break the bad news?* The direct approach was best, she decided.

"Gracie, there's no good way to say this. I have to go away, and I can't take you with me."

Gracie, whom Emily was convinced was the most intuitive dog on the planet, whimpered. She stroked Gracie's fur, realizing she wouldn't have this comforting pleasure for several weeks. She missed Gracie already.

"I have to go out of town," Emily repeated, "for work."

Gracie sighed heavily, reinforcing Emily's belief that her dog could understand human words, and, on the off chance she didn't understand every word, she could read people's moods.

She petted Gracie a few moments, trying to figure out who would take care of the dog during her trip to Marisol. Emily had taken less than a half dozen business trips since she worked at Bow-Wow, and Sebastian had always been Gracie's sitter. When he traveled, Emily took care of Rollo. She and Sebastian even coordinated vacation plans, so neither would be gone at the same time, and the dogs would have a familiar guardian. Since the two pups were roommates at one point, all four were content with the arrangement.

There were a couple of doggie hotels nearby, but she guessed rightly both the Wagmore and Tails of the City didn't have room for Gracie during the holidays. She was secretly glad because she worried Gracie would be lonely, even though Bow-Wow staff gave both pet hotels the top five-paw rating. The Wagmore offered doggie massages; Tails featured a pool and dog-themed movies. But Gracie needed *her*.

In her research for Bow-Wow, Emily read dogs had no sense of time, but Gracie was exceptional, and Emily suspected her pup could read clocks. This was a dog who woke every weekday morning at 6:30, began supper watch promptly at 6:30 every night, pawed at her leg at 10 to remind her to come to bed. Gracie understood weekends were for sleeping late—maybe till 7:30—but that was the only allowance she made for variance in their schedules.

Who would keep track of Gracie's schedule while Emily was gone? Would they remember to feed her on time? Would they take her for a morning walk in the park? Would Gracie's tiny heart break during their separation?

Emily rested her head against the back of the sofa and closed her eyes. Who could she call? Maybe one person could take Gracie for a few days, another could take her for a week—but everyone was going away for the holidays. The ones who weren't were in a frenzy, baking, decorating, shopping because their families were coming to visit.

She wondered if she could get Gracie a ride to her parents' farm. She'd once written an article about big-rig truckers who transported a lost dog from Ohio back to his home back in Wyoming. They'd driven a relay. One trucker traveled along Interstate 80, then passed the dog to a trucker on I-25, but those drivers were doing a good deed to return the dog to its permanent home, not helping a woman with a demanding job and a business partner who liked surprises.

Emily was lost. What to do?

Her phone rang, and she was relieved that Georgia Davies was on the other end of the video call. Georgia had been Emily's friend since their first day together in a thousand-person college chemistry class when the male professor announced, "Most of you are going to fail this class, especially you girls."

Emily and Georgia had exchanged startled glances. Georgia put her head down, scribbled on a piece of paper, then passed it to Emily. "Marie Curie and I disagree." She slid a note back. "It seems not all dinosaurs are extinct." Georgia smiled.

Both took advanced chemistry in high school, and neither was about to be defined or defeated by a teacher with a lot of degrees but not much sense. His low expectations motivated them, and Emily and Georgia got As in the class. By the end of the semester, they were bonded tighter than a chemical compound. They studied together, visited each other's homes during holidays and breaks, and became roommates in their junior year, splitting the costs of a 500-square foot apartment on the edge of campus.

Both lived in New York now, yet their lives were radically different. Emily's work filled all her time; Georgia's two pre-school children were the center of her life. After the children were born, she left her job with a high-powered property company. For the past five years, she managed her own residential real estate business—a boutique agency, she called it—and worked part-time, specializing in the sale and purchase of historic homes. She had helped Emily find her condo.

"I'm glad you called," she said as she answered the phone. She curled her legs under her as she sat on the sofa, Gracie's head in her lap "What a day!"

"Me too." Georgia took a sip from a king-sized glass of Diet Coke, her favorite beverage. "Christmas is ruined."

"What?" Emily was so wrapped up in her own drama, she never imagined someone else might have a holiday problem too.

"Ruined," she repeated. "Ruined. Ruined with a capital R."

"What's wrong? Is it Quinton? The kids? Your parents?"

"No, nothing like that. Everyone is fine, fine," Georgia assured her. "Maybe ruined is too strong a word, but Christmas is a mess."

"What happened?"

"The maintenance people for our apartment building came today. Each year, they make a routine visit to check on the boiler in the basement, but now…"

"There's a problem," Emily finished the sentence.

"A *big* problem." Georgia sighed. "The boiler heats all the apartments, but it's shot. The apartment managers had been talking for some time about replacing it and decided to wait till the summer when we don't need heat. Now, we don't have a choice. During their routine visit, the maintenance people discovered the boiler had broken and flooded the basement, including our storage closets. Now, the management company has to replace the entire heating system. They said it could take two, maybe, three weeks for us to have heat."

"Oh, no!"

"Oh, yes," said Georgia. "Can you believe it?"

"Why so long?"

"First, they have to pump the water out of the basement. That will take a least a day. It will take a couple of days more to dry the area with industrial fans. After that, we tenants have to go through our belongings to determine what's salvageable. Then, finally, a repair company will come to replace the system because it's so old. The apartment building was constructed in the early 1900s, and it's beautiful with the wood parquet floors and crown molding, but a 100-year-old building has character, a 100-year-old boiler does not."

"I'm sorry."

"A lot of tenants will be gone for the holidays, but for those of us staying in town, it's a headache. We got emails from the apartment management company. They'll help us find hotel rooms and check whether insurance will pay any of the 'displacement' costs. So, money may not be an issue, but there's the bigger problem of finding a room in this city at Christmas. It's impossible."

"When do you have to leave your apartment?" Emily asked.

"As soon as we can. Today, tomorrow afternoon at the latest. My apartment is on an upper floor, so it never gets too cold here, but all the tenants have to leave. The goal is to have us back before Christmas Eve. It's so disruptive, and I know this is silly, and the kids will be happy wherever we are, but I was looking forward to decorating and baking and making costumes for their Christmas play. I have a long to-do list."

Emily was sure there was no domestic project Georgia couldn't tackle—and couldn't complete in record time with a flourish. She cooked, she sewed, she decorated. Plants, even temperamental African violets, thrived in her care. She never gave anyone a Christmas present unless it was handmade. Last year she presented Emily with three jars of strawberry jam from berries she picked at a farm upstate. The year before, Georgia quilted a pillow cover for Emily. The year before that, she gave Emily six "coupons" for homemade meals, with the menu of her choice.

"I planned to do so much." Georgia sighed again.

"Let me remind you Christmas isn't an endurance test. You don't have to be best at every single thing. There's nothing wrong with a store-bought gift instead of a handmade one. There's nothing wrong with mac and cheese from a box instead of making it from scratch. You're super-organized. Maybe you have to be flexible now."

"I enjoy the Christmas 'chores.' That's fun. But the first 'chore' I've got to deal with is finding a place to live. I'm going to have to pack enough clothes for me and the kids, because they may not let us back in the building once the replacement work starts. Plus, I have to pack the materials to make the costumes for the Christmas play. Oh, and I need to pack tablets and games and books and videos to keep the kids occupied."

Emily sat up straight. She realized: Her problem was Georgia's solution. "Georgia, I may be able to help."

She explained her unexpected business trip, her dilemma in finding care for Gracie, her disappointment in not being able to be at home with her parents.

"Oh, Emily, I sorry," Georgia said. "I knew you were leaving tomorrow for home, and I assumed that was still the plan."

"Plans change. You know what my mom says: 'If you want to make God laugh, tell Him your plans.' God must be rolling on the floor."

"I'm sure He's laughing *with* us not *at* us." Georgia chuckled. "Would you really lend us your apartment? We'd love to take care of

Gracie. If we stay at your place, it's close by, so we can get to Jack and Harper's pre-school and their Christmas play rehearsals. I can set up my sewing machine on your desk by the window. It's portable—easy to get it in the taxi."

"Let me remind you, you can do all your holiday cooking here because I have a kitchen with lots of cookware and baking supplies," Emily said.

"Which I bought you, and you never really use."

"I love to cook, but I don't—"

"Have time because you work so much. I know. I worry about you."

"I told Sebastian today I want to cut back, and I'll talk more with him after Christmas. All I can think of right now is packing for this trip. Once I get to Marisol, there's so much to do. But when I come home, I'm going to make some changes."

"I hope so. Working this much isn't good for you."

"Yes, but first things first. If you can take care of Gracie…"

"No problem. I'm happy to do it. Jack and Harper love playing with her. I hope Gracie won't mind wearing doll clothes and captaining the *Millennium Falcon*. I tell you what, we'll plan to come over tomorrow afternoon, and we'll stay till you get home, even if the repairs are done early. It's the least we can do. You leave Gracie plenty of food and water tomorrow morning when you go to the airport, and I'll take it from there. We'll be there by noon. I'll make sure Jack and Harper go easy on the treats for Gracie."

"I usually decorate," Emily apologized. "This year I planned to be gone for most of December, so I only put up a calico tabletop tree— the one you made for me a couple of years ago. The apartment is, um, bare."

"Don't worry. My house is already decorated. I'll help get yours ready for the holidays." Emily once teased Georgia she set an alarm for 12:01 AM the day after Thanksgiving to leap into the official holiday decorating season. "I'll bring leftover ornaments to your house and that way, you'll come home to a Christmas-y apartment. The kids will be thrilled to decorate a tree twice, and we'll be happy to have a nice place to stay."

"I'll call every day to check in," Emily said. "I should be home late Christmas Eve."

"Don't worry about us, and don't worry about Gracie. She'll have three dog lovers caring for her. She'll be spoiled—or I should say more spoiled—when you get back. The day you come home, just text to let me know you're on your way. I can stay till around 3 PM. I've got to work for a couple of hours late Christmas Eve, but I'll take care of Gracie till then."

"I thought the real estate business was slow in December," Emily said.

"Usually, it is, but I got an email from a client, a man named Jackson Harp—how weird his name is similar to my children's—who wants to see a listing Christmas Eve. Can you believe it? He's flying in from somewhere—he didn't say where—and he has one afternoon for house hunting. I told him we could visit several houses, but he said, no, he only wants to look at one. That's never a good idea, to fall in love with pictures of a house before you see the inside and the neighborhood, but he says he's sure it's the house he wants."

"Is he buying it for himself or for a family?"

"He didn't say," Georgia replied. "I asked, but all he told me is he can't meet any other day but Christmas Eve."

"Normally, I'd offer to babysit," Emily said.

"Normally, I'd ask you to. I'll email Mr. Harp that I have to bring my children."

"I owe you, Georgia. I do."

"No, you don't. You're helping me." Georgia paused. "I'm sorry you won't get to go home at Christmas."

"I'm sorry too. And I'm sorry Quinton won't be home this year. I know you miss him."

Georgia traced the outline of Quinton's face in the photo on the table beside her. "Every day, but when you're a doctor in the military, you go where they send you."

"He'd rather be home with you and the kids."

She nodded. "The good news is he'll be here after the New Year, at the end of January. We'll celebrate our Christmas a little later."

Emily was ready to say her goodbyes when Georgia asked, "Wait! Didn't you have your interview with Zaya today?"

"Yes, but let's not talk about that now. I need to pack."

Georgia didn't press the issue, and Emily was glad she didn't have to relive the catastrophe.

She hung up and looked at Gracie, who was now at her feet. Gracie sensed change; Emily suspected Gracie could smell it. She stroked Gracie's fur, a feeble effort to comfort them both, then made the call she dreaded.

When her mother answered, she was sitting in front of the fireplace, logs blazing, the stockings hanging on the mantle. Christmas music played softly in the background. Emily recognized the tune and felt a twinge in her heart— "I'll Be Home for Christmas." A perfect recipe for homesickness.

Emily explained she would miss Christmas.

"Don't you worry." Her mother was cheerful. "Dad and I are disappointed, of course. We'll miss you, but we understand. You have to work. That's the way it is."

"Mom, when Sebastian and I started this business, I had no idea work would be this demanding. He loves it. He likes the planning and the managing and the money-raising. I don't. I want a change. I told him today—we need to have a big heart-to-heart discussion when I get back from Marisol."

"What do you want to change?" her mother asked.

"Lots of things. I want to write full-time, not have administrative responsibilities, but it's more than that. I'm restless for…something…something different. Something big. Something new. A new job. A new city. A new life."

"You want a lot of changes. Maybe try one at a time."

A tear slid down Emily's cheek, despite her best efforts to keep her emotions in check.

"Sebastian sprung this on me," she said, her voice cracking. "He meant well. I just wish he'd talked to me before he decided to take charge of my life."

"Do you have to go?" her mother asked.

"I can't figure an easy way out. Bow-Wow has been trying to cover this event for years. It's a big deal to be invited."

"So, it's good for business," her mother said. "Is it good for you?"

"It will give me a chance to write and report full-time, but I'll be away from you and Dad and Gracie. I wanted to help Dad with the Christmas tree sales. That's why I planned to take off three weeks. I wanted to help the customers find the perfect trees. I wanted to help you sell apple cider and doughnuts. I wanted to give out candy canes to the kids."

Emily loved ambling through the Christmas tree fields, describing the benefits of fir versus spruce, wearing hiking boots instead of high heels, snuggling in a bulky sweater and jeans instead of zipping up a business dress.

"We'll miss you, but don't worry." Her mother smiled sweetly. "Your dad and Uncle Frank will manage the Christmas tree farm. Maybe you can come home in January. We'll celebrate then."

Emily couldn't bring herself to tell her mother that January's calendar was full—the magazine to write for and edit, the New Year, New Pup rescue event to match homeless dogs with owners, the Canine

Courage Fun Run, which raised money for veterans' housing. Work was never-ending.

"We'll see." Emily hoped she masked her discouragement but realized her mother read her mood. "I love you, Mom. Tell Dad I called. I'll call every day from Marisol."

"Be sure to take pictures. It's supposed to be a winter wonderland."

She nodded.

"Wait!" her mother said. "How did the interview with Zaya go?"

Emily shrugged. "Okay. She asked a lot of questions. I stumbled through."

"I'm sure you did an amazing job," her mother said. "Zaya was lucky to have you as her guest. You have fun in Marisol."

Emily pushed the red button to end the video call. Fun? That wasn't possible, given the lengthy itinerary of RICI activities. *I'll check the schedule again, but I'm pretty sure fun isn't listed there.*

She walked into the bedroom and set a timer on her phone. Then she stretched out on her bed and cried. She'd already cried several times today, but she allowed herself ten more minutes for intense pre-trip crying. This day would go down in history as a trifecta of disasters: Matt Thoms's betrayal of Gracie with his gaudy artwork. Rae Zaya's stupid three wishes game. Sebastian's unwelcome surprise that would send Emily on the worst trip of her life.

The timer beeped, and she dried her eyes. She pulled her suitcase from under the bed—the navy blue one with the big white polka dots—dots because it made the suitcase easier to see on the luggage carousel. Gracie's pointed ears perked up. She understood what a suitcase meant. The dog lowered her chin, resting it between her paws. Her big black eyes brimmed with sadness.

"Georgia and Harper and Jack will stay with you. You love them, and they'll take good care of you," Emily said in her most chipper tone.

Gracie turned her head away.

"I'm sorry," Emily said. "It's not like I want to go. I have to go." *Don't I? Or am I too timid to stand up for myself?*

She re-read the itinerary, studied the list of activities, then checked the weather forecast for Marisol. Three weeks away from home would require a warm coat, business slacks and sweaters, and—unbelievably—a ball gown. A groan escaped from deep inside.

A ball gown was not part of her current wardrobe, and she didn't have time to shop for one today. *It's not like there's a ball gown store on the corner, between the diner and the dry cleaner's.* Even if she bought a ball gown, she'd never need it again, so she packed the outfit she wore at last year's Bow-Wow Christmas party. It would have to do. She would never see any of these people again. What did it matter?

As Gracie moped, Emily begrudgingly folded her clothes between tissue paper—a trick she learned from Sebastian to help prevent wrinkles—then sorted through toiletries, imagining every item she might need the next three weeks, from shampoo to Band-Aids. She packed her jewelry, a pair of gold hoop earrings, a pair of silver hoop earrings, and a rope necklace—one side gold, the other side silver—that she bought many years ago at a flea market where she and Sebastian had gone to search for furniture for Bow-Wow offices. Last, she tossed in dressy black leather shoes, plus "clunky" walking shoes for comfort. Done.

The sooner this ordeal is over, the better.

Emily spent the rest of the afternoon, alternating between sniffling and hugging Gracie.

After she fixed Gracie's dinner, she tortured herself with a toasted cheese sandwich and a can of tomato soup. Of course, the soup-sandwich combo brought back bad memories of Matt, but she didn't have much food in the house.

At 9:30, Emily climbed into bed, determined to rest for the flight. But she didn't sleep. She tossed. She turned. She checked the clock. A year passed between 11 PM and midnight, two years between midnight and 1 AM. As she lay on her back, then her side, then her stomach, she counted sheep, took deep breaths, and read a few pages in a book, but her mind whirled.

What if I can't find any good stories to write? What if I can't find my way around Marisol? What if I get lost? I haven't had time to do any research. What if I don't have enough background to ask good questions? What about Gracie? What if she gets sick? What if she won't eat? What if she doesn't get enough exercise? What about my parents? This is the busiest time of the year for them. What if they need me? What if this trip is a major waste of time? What if this job is a colossal waste of my life? What if I'm too much of a coward to change?

Emily didn't have answers. When she drifted off the sleep around 4 AM, she had *the dream*. The one where she was in a classroom, and the teacher gave a test, and she panicked, not only because she hadn't studied, but because she didn't know there was a test, and she didn't even know what class she was taking.

The alarm buzzed at 5:30. Emily sat on the edge of the bed, mustering the energy to take a shower. Gracie was snoring, head on the pillow.

"This is bound to be the worst holiday ever."

A random thought drifted through her mind, like a cloud in the midday sky. Mr. Bertelli told her once, "See life from a flower's point of view. Wake up every morning knowing marvelous adventures are in store."

Emily put on her robe and headed to the bath. "Mr. Bertelli, this morning I am the weed, not the flower. This will be a bad day, a terrible day, and all I have to look forward to is three weeks of bad days. No marvelous days are around the corner. I'll wager you money."

Chapter Five
The Journey

"Where you headed?" the taxi driver asked.

"To the airport."

"Then?"

"Out of the country. To Marisol."

The driver's eyes meet Emily's in the mirror. "It's supposed to be spectacular."

"So I hear," she replied glumly.

"First time there?"

She nodded.

"Travel is such a blessing," the driver said. "You visit someplace new. You meet interesting people. You make great memories. You are so lucky. How excited you must be—and grateful!"

"Uh-huh." *I'm not excited. Not blessed. Not lucky. Why do people keep saying that? No merry Christmas or happy New Year for me. Just work, work, more work.*

She pretended to stare out the window, to study the skyline, as she sulked. Her phone pinged. Sebastian texted: *Hey, E. Got this in my morning "Thoughts for the Day." Might help you. "Be grateful, even when you don't know the reason."*

Emily silenced her phone. *Please don't try to make me feel better.*

Deep in her heart, she had many reasons to be thankful. Georgia, Jack, and Harper would provide Gracie with endless hugs. Her mother and father were happy and healthy. They would manage their business fine without her, as they had every year. True, she wouldn't be home for Christmas, but her parents were only a phone call away. And she was visiting a place many people dreamed of, a place that, any other time in her life, she would be thrilled to explore. Yet, at this moment, her heart wanted to be in familiar and comfortable Holly Mountain, not exotic and strange Marisol.

She crossed her arms in the back seat and made up her mind: *I refuse to like it there.*

As she hopped out of the car, the driver handed Emily her suitcase. "Have a safe flight. Enjoy your trip."

She tipped him but didn't thank him for the good wishes. She checked her bag, got through security faster than she expected, bought black coffee and a plain bagel with butter, then settled in the waiting area. She looked at her watch. Sixty minutes till boarding. *Let's get this nightmare over with.*

"Ladies and gentlemen, we're sorry to tell you your flight to Marisol is delayed." The mournful voice of an airline desk agent echoed through the waiting area.

A chorus of moans followed, with Emily's moan the loudest.

"The plane from Marisol is on its way, but we expect it to arrive an hour later than scheduled."

More moans and sighs, with a sprinkle of profanities.

"Once the aircraft arrives at the gate, we'll need to de-plane passengers, service the cabin, then we'll be ready to board. Our new boarding time is 11:45."

A baby wailed. Emily knew he wasn't crying because of the flight delay, but she shared the baby's frustration.

She pulled her phone from her satchel and checked *The RICI Pupline* then clicked on the animated white furry dog, skiing and wearing sun goggles, which took her to daily updates so she could skim the first-day schedule. She'd arrive in Marisol in time to get a few quick interviews with dog owners before the prince's press conference but, with the flight delay, there was no time to check into the hotel and relax. She'd have to go directly from the airport to the Seaside Center, the site of the dog show.

Emily left the waiting area to buy an apple (her healthy snack), a chocolate bar (her medicinal snack), and a few magazines to pass the time before takeoff. *No news magazines. Nothing sad.*

Back at the gate, she thumbed through *InStyle*, enjoying the celebrity news, the photos of spacious ocean-view homes in Malibu, and the gossip about which wealthy movie star was dating which wealthy real estate developer. When she came to page one hundred and twelve, she stopped at the headline, *Star Power in Monsaraz: New Home for Newlyweds.*

She scanned the article and learned that Matthew Thoms and wife Cordelia had purchased a two-million-dollar vacation home on a hillside in Portugal.

The superstar couple, known to fans as CoMa, furnished their palatial but cozy abode with antiques they bought at local markets and, of course, Matt's spectacularly subversive artwork. When asked why they bought another new house, he chuckled. "We have so many magnificent homes, I've lost track of the number and where they are, but Cordelia and I love beautiful things, and we can't help treat ourselves when we find a new house that speaks to our spiritual well-being. Fortunately, we have enough money to keep our souls nourished."

Emily turned to the woman in the chair next to her, a solo traveler in her early twenties. "Would you like this magazine?" she asked. "I'm finished. Really. Finished."

"Oh, thank you," the young woman said. "I appreciate it."

Emily shuddered. Matt was her ghost of Christmas past.

She opened her copy of *People* and read an article about a Marine who came home from a deployment, surprising her children at their school Christmas play. Emily thought about Quinton and how his happy reunion wouldn't be with Georgia, Jack, and Harper until after Christmas. *Christmas is hard when the people you love are far away.*

Next, she scanned a recipe from celebrity chef Bobby Flay for the perfect Christmas brunch of eggnog waffles and cranberry compote, and she glanced at photos in a story about Jennifer Lopez's plans for a mellow Christmas in Hawaii. When she got to page eighty-six, she paused. "Christmas in Marisol: Another Heartbreaking Holiday for the Prince?"

Emily studied the small photo of Prince Alexander with Lady Charlotte van Amsberg, dressed like a couple ready to walk the red carpet at the Oscars. He was dapper in a black tuxedo, and she, radiant in a shiny silver strapless gown and emerald jewelry. His short hair was dark, curly, and his beard was neatly trimmed. Mountains of white-blonde hair cascaded over her bare shoulders and almost hid her long sparkly earrings. She smiled broadly, her hands draped around his neck, gazing at him the way Gracie gazed at the Milk-Bone box. He faced the camera, eyes hidden behind sunglasses, hands clasped in front of him, the corners of his mouth turned down. Emily read the article with curiosity.

The snow is falling, and shoppers are crowding the city markets as Christmas rapidly approaches in the idyllic country of Marisol. But this holiday promises to be less than merry for the lonesome Prince Alexander.

The rumored romance between the prince and socialite Lady Charlotte van Amsberg appears to be off—although some speculate it was never on. The couple had been spotted at several charity events, but royal watchers say the two no longer seem as friendly as they once were.

"The prince came to the recent fundraiser for Marisol's music education program alone," Marielle Famston, a local resident, remarked. "We were hopeful perhaps Lady Charlotte would be a romantic interest, at least a special friend, but apparently, that's not the case."

"They were school chums," said a palace insider, who asked not to be identified. "Nothing more. There was never any romantic attraction between the two."

Prince Alexander has been alone since his wife died five years ago in a hiking accident in the Swiss Alps. People dubbed the prince and princess "the world's perfect couple" when they married. The two were deeply in love, according to friends.

Yet, their fairytale romance ended tragically, leaving the royal and his young son and daughter grief-stricken.

"The prince is focused on his children," said palace spokeswoman Sarah Donegal. "There is always a great deal of speculation about his romantic life, but it's only speculation. The prince is not interested in a romantic relationship. He is committed to providing his children with a stable, loving home."

Emily hadn't had time to do any research on Marisol, its dog show, or the prince whom she'd encounter in a few hours at the press conference. She tore the page from the magazine, then stuffed it into her satchel. Once she on the plane, relaxing in first class, she'd have time to learn more.

"Paging Emily Saint-Claire. Emily Saint-Claire, please come to the check in desk at gate twenty."

Oh, please, please, please. Let them give me a free trip somewhere because they delayed my flight.

"I'm Emily Saint-Claire." She was face-to-face with a buoyant redhead, who greeted her with a toothpaste-ad smile that gave no indication of the bad news she was about to deliver to an already weary, anxious traveler.

"Ms. Saint-Claire, we have a problem." She said it so gleefully, Emily wondered if she misunderstood.

"We do?"

"Yes, our first class cabin is overbooked, and we need to change your seat. Yours was the last seat purchased, so we need to reassign you. We don't have another seat in first class, and we don't have a seat in business class either. Marisol is a popular place this time of year. You'll have to fly coach unless you want to postpone your flight. We have another plane leaving at 9 tonight."

Emily frowned.

"Don't get upset." Her bubbly tone made it sound like a suggestion, not a command.

"If I fly coach, isn't there a difference in price—and amenities?" Emily asked.

"Don't worry. The purchaser's account will be credited."

Emily leaned across the counter, looked the agent in the eye, and said in her most desperate voice, "Listen, I'm on a business trip, and I need to work, and I didn't get any sleep last night, and I was on Zaya's TV show yesterday, and I didn't even want to go on this trip, and my ex-boyfriend keeps turning up like a bad penny, and did I mention I need to work? Can you assign me a seat where there won't be any people near me?"

The agent diligently studied the computer screen, then turned her sunny eyes toward Emily. "No can do. We have a full cabin today. Sorry." She continued to smile.

Maybe it won't be too bad.

But it was.

If there was a worse seat on the plane, Emily couldn't imagine it. Wedged between two teenage girls, who watched YouTube videos of boy bands and social media influencers with great enthusiasm, Emily heard the continual clicking of keys, the pinging of phones, and the shouting as they talked over her to make sure one had gotten the other's text.

If Emily had felt less tired and less tense, she might have remembered herself as a teenager, how much fun life could be when you're young. She might have appreciated the girls' excitement, traveling outside their home country, an opportunity Emily had never had until this trip. She might even have ignored the man behind her who jabbed his knees into the back of her seat a dozen times an hour. Or not been aggravated that her seat was only a few feet from the galley where industrious flight attendants popped tops on soft drink cans, rattled bottles, and stocked and restocked food carts all night as they prepared, served, and cleared away snacks and meals.

But she was at the point of fatigue where every sight, sound, and smell irritated her, the way crowded grocery store aisles and slow Internet connections irritated her.

Give me strength.

If only she'd brought headphones or earplugs, but she'd forgotten both. She tried to listen to music through the plane's earphones. They didn't work. She pushed the call button. "No spares," the courteous flight attendant told her. "Full flight. Sorry."

Why does everyone on this airline smile when they give me bad news?

After more than an hour scrunched between two giggling seatmates, Emily concluded catnapping was pointless. She decided to use her time for work. Once she got "in the zone," once she began her research on Marisol and the Royal International Canine Invitational, she'd tune out the distractions. She hoped.

She kept her elbows close to her sides as she tapped the keys on her laptop. She Googled "Marisol" first. Dozens of articles popped up on her screen. One from *Condé Nast Traveler* called Marisol "a tiny country of enormous beauty." The article continued: "Marisol has everything the discerning traveler could want: Exquisite beaches, magnificent mountains, breathtaking views, a charming city center, and stunning architecture. Add to this friendly people, and you have the perfect travel destination."

Travel & Leisure described Marisol as "the most magical place on the planet." The author wrote: "Do you want to spend your night listening to soft ocean waves? Gazing at the stars? Or do you prefer cool evenings in the deep primeval forests listening to the songs of nightingales, thrushes, and crickets? Or would you rather dine on the balcony of a luxurious hotel and fall asleep to city sounds that include the clip-clop of horses' hooves along cobblestone streets? If you come to Marisol, you won't have to choose. You can have it all."

Emily looked next at the country's official website. Again, the photos showed one spectacular scene after another: a sunny white-sand beach dotted with blue and yellow striped umbrellas, the waterfall frozen into a lace sculpture on the mountainside, and hills blanketed with wildflowers in every color in the rainbow. The website said:

Welcome to Marisol, a land where the sea kisses the sky.

With its warm golden sun and clear turquoise waters, Marisol is a summer destination for travelers around the world. And with its powdery white snow and beautiful evergreen-covered mountains, Marisol is also a destination for travelers who crave winter fun.

No matter, what the season, you'll love Marisol.

In spring, the flowers bloom.

Marisol has been called the most colorful country in the world. In spring, the hills are bright with brilliant red poppies, rich purple columbines, sunny yellow buttercups, and pale blue forget-me-nots. The city streets are lined with pink and white cherry blossom trees, and Marisol's unique sea-blue tulips decorate gardens and window boxes. This "natural riot of vibrant color," as National Geographic Traveler *called it, offers a feast for the eyes. The perfume of thousands of flowers will intoxicate you as you wander through the town and countryside.*

In the summer, the sun shines.

As the weather gets warmer and the days grow longer, relax on Marisol's famous cloud-white beaches, sandy, soft and lustrous. You can surf, sail, swim, or simply doze under an umbrella, in a comfortable beach chair, with a cold drink close by. You'll watch brown pelicans dive for fish dinners in the ocean, marvel as blue herons glide above you, and catch a quick glimpse of the brown sandpipers as they scurry along the shore.

In the fall, the colors glow.

As fall arrives and the leaves change colors, you'll be awestruck by the rich patchwork of crimsons, golds, ambers, and oranges sprinkled among evergreens in our deep forests. Hike in the cool woodlands. Fish in the crystal clear lakes. Snap photos of the jeweled mountain panoramas. With warm days and crisp nights, sunny afternoons and starry evenings, Marisol is a fall paradise.

In the winter, the snow falls.

As the weather turns colder, Marisol transforms into a winter fairyland. Enjoy endless vistas of blues and whites. Downy snowflakes fall in the morning, covering our mountains and hills with a sugary layer of beauty. The sun typically shines in the afternoon, making the snow sparkle like a field of endless diamonds. Marisol is perfect if you want to ski, snowboard, or sled.

Don't enjoy a day outside in the cold? No problem. If you'd rather curl up by the crackling fire and sip a steaming cup of peppermint hot chocolate, Marisol offers that as well.

Come in winter, and you can visit the Christmas markets to buy unique gifts, including brightly colored wool scarves, artisan glass ornaments, or handmade wooden toys. Sample crispy cinnamon waffles and delicious dark-roast coffees. Buy fragrant candles to remind you of the scents of Marisol's oceans and forests.

So, come to Marisol, a country for all seasons. No matter when you visit, we're confident you'll fall in love with our beautiful country.

Come, play, stay.

We're waiting for you.

Emily took off her glasses and rubbed her eyes as her two seatmates squealed over Jonah or Justin somebody. *Either Marisol is truly gorgeous or some writers have gotten pretty creative.* Emily didn't expect to visit any sights. She figured she'd see the inside of the Seaside Center during the day and the ceiling of her hotel room before she collapsed in bed each night. *Maybe one day I can come back to take a look at the waterfall. Or eat one of those waffles. Or wiggle my toes in white sand and feel the sun or my face and... Wait. Research. More to do.*

She searched the Marisol website and found a link: "Follow me to RICI!" She clicked on a cartoon of a big cream-colored shaggy dog with coal-black eyes and a neon-pink tongue, who barked three times and galloped away once she hit the mousepad.

She tapped the sea-blue paw link.

Welcome to the Royal International Canine Invitational, the most exciting dog show in the world!

The RICI is more than a competition. It's a jubilee. The RICI is merriment. The RICI is joy. The RICI honors dogs and the people who love them.

Come. Sit. Stay. Celebrate.

The first photo to pop up on the website was Zeus, the rust-colored Hungarian Vizsla, who won the previous year's competition. A video showed the last few minutes of the competition as he leaped two feet off the ground when his name was announced as best of show champion. "Zeus captures the spirit of RICI—happiness unleashed," the caption read.

She scrolled through the list of winners in each breed category, then examined photos of the auditorium exterior and interior. There was a map, and she studied it in an effort to memorize the location of the press center, the information booth, and the grooming area. Then she read about the dog show.

Champions come in different shapes and sizes. The Royal International Canine Invitational—the RICI—is an opportunity for the best of the best to come together, to vie for the coveted crystal trophy symbolizing excellence.

Dogs from around the world compete at the RICI. Our first event took place one hundred and forty-five years ago when a half dozen Marisol dogs and owners gathered for an afternoon of fun to claim bragging rights as to who had the "best" dog. The popularity of an event showcasing dogs' fidelity and nobility grew, and Marisol soon became home to the premier dog show in Europe, then the world.

This year, we've added a new category: Most Promising Pup. This event allows dogs under twelve months old to gain experience in the competition. Also, it gives audience members a chance to witness cuteness in its fuzziest form ☺

The RICI wraps up with fur, fun, and frivolity. After the champions receive their trophies, and Prince Alexander presents the best of show award, dogs, owners, and handlers are invited to the Fetch! Play Ball, held in the Castle Sol garden. Dogs can run till their hearts' content chasing tennis balls and chasing each other. The prince will toss the first tennis ball, which signals an afternoon of tail-wagging delight.

Emily smirked, imagining Gracie running around the palace garden, chasing a tennis ball tossed around by some snooty prince. Gracie marched to a different drummer. Rules weren't rules to her; they were suggestions she felt free to ignore. She might chase a ball, or she might curl up and take a nap as dogs wandered around her. Emily wasn't a strong disciplinarian. Her life was so structured and ordered, she felt stifled and couldn't bear for Gracie to feel the same way. She read more.

Later in the evening, the prince will host the Holly and Ivy Ball, a dazzling event full of old-world glamor and charm. The Castle Sol is decorated in its most spectacular Christmas finery. The delicate smell of forest greenery and roses, the silver shimmer of candlelight, the rich sounds of chamber music as couples waltz in the stunning Seascape Ballroom—all promise a magnificent evening.

"Give me a break." She spoke so loudly her seatmates turned away from their phones. A formal ball. They ought to call it the Stuffy and Pretentious Ball.

The website contained a link to press materials, including a list of contacts for more information. Emily keyed the names and numbers into her phone—the six press officers who would be available "round the clock to answer questions and facilitate your work on stories about our fascinating event."

As she researched, she wondered how she might find *any* unique story angles. This dog show existed for nearly a century and a half. What could she write than hadn't been written already? What photos or videos could she take that hadn't been published before?

She massaged her aching temples, dreading the landslide of work ahead, then stretched and craned her neck, peering out the plane window, to give her mind a rest. The squealing from her teenage seatmates interrupted the few seconds of quiet time Emily planned, as they viewed a YouTube video of K-something or other, a thin young man with curly blond hair, who wore a bathrobe over his jeans and pretended to sing into a hairbrush microphone. She wanted to laugh along, too, but she didn't have the energy.

Finally, she searched for information on Marisol's royal family. She learned King Phillip and Queen Lilianna ruled together for more than thirty years. They were a couple happy with their jobs and happy with each other. They were less pleased with Prince Alexander, their only child and, apparently, a source of worry for many years.

Emily sifted through photos of Alexander when he was young. There he was in church, sticking out his tongue at press photographers;

lying on the floor, red-faced, kicking his feet in anger, during a knighting ceremony in the palace; triumphantly ripping a page from a schoolbook.

As he got older, he earned the title "Prince of Trouble" from one magazine and "The Royal Pain" from another. His father was caught on a hot mic, exasperated, telling a friend his son was "a train wreck inside a tornado."

While his parents were embarrassed, the prince eagerly embraced his reputation as rogue and radical. When he was thirteen, he repeatedly skipped school and proclaimed to his teachers "school is a waste of my time." He showed up late at a formal royal tea wearing a red baseball cap with the words "I Hate Beowulf" stitched in black, ripped dirty jeans, and a Freddie Mercury T-shirt, with the singer's silhouette shouting into a microphone, one arm stretched toward the sky, one leg bent as if he might spring into the air. Emblazoned across the shirt were the words, "I want to break free."

And the prince did break free, momentarily, when he "ran away from home" at age fourteen, boarding a train for a twelve-hour trip to Amsterdam to the annual Comic-Con festival for "a lark." He managed to get an autograph from *Spiderman* creator Stan Lee before he was forced to go home. As his parents led him away, he screamed at the press, "My superpower is indifference."

She read article after article describing Alexander as "aimless," "lost," "adrift," a "child with no inner sense of direction and no appreciation for his privileges."

To be fair, that could be true of any teenager, but as he grew older, he didn't mature. The prince moved onto college, even though he proclaimed education was for "sheep," and the news articles and celebrity magazine stories described him as "His Surly Highness," "Alexander, the Ingrate," and "Alex, the Terrible." Reporters branded him petty and immature. His professors said he lacked motivation. Other students described him as aloof and arrogant.

After two miserable years in college—miserable for Alexander and anyone acquainted with him—the prince discovered science, specifically veterinary science, and found his passion. His attitude and his life changed. "Science was the only thing that made sense to me. Science was logical. It required facts. It was love at first equation," he told *Hello* magazine.

There were photos of Alexander at a game reserve in South Africa, where he developed a special bond with an orphaned rhino named Essie. More pictures from Australia of a weary prince tending to koala bears burned in a bush fire. And finally, a wistful prince in Scotland, at the Loch of Strathbeg, helping introduce the rare Konik horses back into the marshlands.

Emily studied the look on the prince's face—a man who was simultaneously seeing freedom and seeking freedom. Sometimes, she longed to run free too.

Then the prince fell in love. He met his wife at a fundraiser for homeless animals in Marisol. The new princess Clara, who had been his classmate in secondary school, confessed she was not a fan during the prince's adolescent years. During their two-year courtship, she changed her mind. He was, she decided, a caring person despite his self-absorbed past.

In one photograph, the couple strolled along the shore, hand-in-hand, engaged in an earnest conversation, their eyes soft and kind. In another, the prince lifted his baby daughter above his head, both laughing with delight, while Clara played peek-a-boo with the little boy.

The camera doesn't lie, Emily reckoned. They must have been a happy couple. And deeply in love.

But the prince's sublime family life ended abruptly. Princess Clara traveled to Switzerland, her favorite childhood vacation spot, to appear in a film promoting European tourism, with plans her husband and children would join her in a few days. The last photo showed the princess on the tarmac before she boarded the plane. Clara held her son in her arms, and her daughter, a sheepish grin on her face, hid behind her mother's skirt as she kissed the prince goodbye. Two days later, a frantic prince, who'd left dozens of unanswered phone messages, learned his wife had slipped down a rocky incline and died while hiking alone.

Although Emily scoured the internet, she found less than a half dozen articles that mentioned the prince after his wife's death, and the articles she did locate focused on his presentation of the RICI trophy. In recent months, however, the press reports became more frequent as the prince eased back into public life, and the paparazzi sought to document his every move. Photographers followed him to concerts, plays, and charity events, and so did wealthy, willowy women with jobs such as "equestrian" and "designer brand ambassador."

Emily's gut instincts told her despite his best efforts to smile pleasantly, to pose nonchalantly, the prince wasn't happy. The media confirmed her hunch when they described Prince Alexander as "the forlorn prince," "the lost royal," "the melancholy monarch."

She closed her computer and fished through her purse for a tissue. *Why am I crying? Again? For someone I haven't met.* When one of her seatmates looked up from YouTube, and asked, "Are you all right, ma'am?," Emily lied, "Of course."

She didn't know the prince, but she did understand loss. She understood longing for someone you loved, the eternal struggle to adjust to a life emptier because they were no longer with you. Years ago, she learned life's hardest lesson: After someone you love dies, life goes on, pushes you forward to a new unfamiliar place, whether you want to go or not, but grief stays with you; it ebbs and flows like the tide, some days more difficult to navigate than others.

As the girls next to her continued their marathon of giggles, and the man behind her shoved his knees deeper into the back of her seat, Emily shut her eyes, hoping for a short nap. She felt she was floating, almost asleep, when the dimmed cabin lights brightened, then flashed, disrupting her minutes-long rest. The flight attendants rolled noisy carts down the aisle to serve a breakfast of yogurt, sweet rolls, and scrambled eggs.

"We'll be on the ground in less than ninety minutes," the pilot announced through the microphone static. "It's been snowing in Marisol this morning, but by the time we get there, the sun will be shining, and you'll enjoy a temperature of forty degrees Fahrenheit, four degrees Celsius. We're expecting a beautiful afternoon. Enjoy your time in paradise."

Paradise? Paradise is not here. Paradise was in Holly Mountain with Gracie and her parents.

The flight attendant handed her an orange juice. "Can I get you anything else?"

A ticket out of here. A few days of rest. Some purpose in life.

"No thanks. I've got more than I can handle."

Chapter Six
A Misunderstanding

Silver hard-sided suitcase. Lime green duffle bag. Blue backpack. Skis. More skis.

Emily tapped her foot as she waited for her suitcase to tumble onto the luggage carousel. Finally, she spotted her bag, the second from the last piece to be unloaded, and breathed a sigh of relief that she and her luggage arrived in Marisol at the same time.

The digital clock in the baggage claim area reminded her she had approximately three hours until the prince's press conference. No time to stop by the hotel to relax, freshen up, change clothes. She needed to go directly to the dog show to work on her first-day story, which meant she would have to drag the heavy suitcase with her.

Outside in the cold sunny air, she took a deep breath. Fresh. Crisp. The RICI organizers had arranged a car to transport her to the hotel, but she was late, and the car was nowhere in sight. The line for a taxi was twelve-people deep, and as she edged her way to the back, she tried not make eye contact with anyone. Why make her bad mood worse with superficial conversation?

When her taxi came, twenty minutes later, she slid into the backseat and snarled, "I'm going to the Seaside Center for the RICI."

"You and everybody else." The driver smiled as they sped away.

On the thirty-minute drive through the mountain roads, Emily checked her phone to find a well-intentioned "bouquet" of texts from Sebastian.

Hi, Ems. Hope you have a good flight. Text me when you get in.

Hi, E. Me again. Enjoying first class? Text me.

E, you're probably sleeping on the flight. Maybe that's why I haven't heard from you. Text me, K?

E, I'm sorry I ruined Christmas. Text me.

E, I'm really, really sorry. Text me.

Hi, E, here is a cute pix of Rollo to make you smile. Don't be mad. Do text me.

Hi, E, you should be in Marisol by now. Here's an article that says it's not good to carry anger too long. Text me.

E, Good news! I found a photographer who can help the first day. Text me.

E, since you haven't texted, I'm texting to let you know photog is a freelancer from University of Marisol journalism. Good recommendations. Text me.

E, photographer will be waiting for you by entrance to press room. Text me.

E, why aren't you texting? Text me.

Sebastian may not have been the most considerate with this surprise assignment, but he was persistent in his efforts to smooth over any hard feelings.

Emily wrote back. *S, phone off during flight. Now in Marisol. Headed to Seaside Center. TTYS.*

She glanced at her wristwatch again. Not much time—a little more than two hours until the prince's news conference. She'd have to find the photographer, some dog owners to interview, and a solid first-day story idea before she had to break to hear the prince's welcome remarks. Press briefings were notoriously dull, as they typically featured rehearsed comments from a drab, humorless speaker, and they didn't yield any useful information or great action shots. The reporters all got the same dry speech and the same stilted photos and wrote the same stale story.

"Maybe I'll skip it altogether," she said.

"Did you say something?" The driver's eyes met hers in the mirror.

"Just thinking about work."

"Are you one of the dog owners?"

"I have a dog back home in the United States, but I'm not one of the dog owners at the RICI."

"I wondered. Most of them got here last week. So, why are you here?"

"I'm reporting on the RICI."

"What a fun job. Most reporters got here last week too."

Emily didn't respond.

"First trip to Marisol?"

"Yes."

"It's a wonderful place. I moved here ten years ago. Came for a vacation and never left. There's a saying, 'If you come to Marisol, you're bound to fall in love.'"

"That won't happen to me. I'm here to work. I have a lot to do."

"Don't be so sure," the driver said with a sly grin. "Everyone who comes here falls in love. They fall in love with the sea, or the mountains, or the forests. Or they fall in love with the friendly people and the relaxed lifestyle. Or, sometimes, they meet someone special, and they fall in love with her or him." A brief pause.

"True love," he added for emphasis. "It happened to me. I fell in love with the country, then I fell in love with the people, then I fell in love with one person in particular."

She shook her head. "I don't have time for love. I assure you, I won't fall in love with anything or anyone."

The car stopped at the Seaside Center, and the driver took Emily's suitcase from the trunk, pulled up the handle, and rolled the bag toward her.

"True love," he repeated. "It can happen."

He sounded so certain, she wished she believed him.

"True love," he called after her.

She turned and waved before she climbed the steep steps. *I don't think so.*

When she walked through the enormous blue glass doors, she understood how Dorothy felt those first few minutes in Oz. Would Glinda, the good witch, descend in a pink bubble? In only a few hours she had traveled from an ordinary place to someplace extraordinary.

Emily read the plaque at the entrance: "This building is dedicated to the people of Marisol, who make our scenic country even more beautiful through kindness." A huge welcome banner stretched across the lobby—giant white letters on a turquoise background— "Time to pause for paws."

Dozens of people scurried past her, chatting, shouting, laughing. Their dogs raced alongside them. Elaborate silver chandeliers, each with hundreds of lights shaped like tiny, floating crescent moons, glowed blue-white, giving the lobby a dreamy quality. Silk and wool turquoise carpets embroidered with images of shells—white, beige, brown, rose, coral, gray—covered the floors.

Across the room, floor-to-ceiling windows framed a dramatic view of waves crashing against the rocky cliffs of Marisol Bay. The windows were tinted a warm gold, designed to give the impression the sun was shining, no matter what the weather outside, no matter whether day or night. Paintings by local artists—bright abstracts, gentle landscapes, and seascapes, still life's of pastel flowers and muted shells—lined the walls.

She struggled not to become hypnotized by the building's architectural grandeur.

Focus.

She found a coat-check room, gave the clerk her suitcase, asked for directions to the press room, got lost, then wandered till she found the sign: "Contestants and owners enter here."

Even though she was neither, she went in. She walked through a bright hallway to discover a mammoth grooming area. Dozens of dogs stood on towels draped over silver metal tables. Owners bathed, clipped, dried, and spritzed their dogs' fur into curls, or waves, or straight styles—a huge, upscale canine beauty salon. The excited owners' conversations created a pleasant, happy hum, and pups barked with excitement or restlessness.

Her phone pinged again. Another text message from Sebastian.

Saw your plane arrived. R U at the Seaside Cntr? Freelancer photog should be there now. PS—Pls don't be angry with me.

Emily texted back. *At the Center. Waiting for photog. Still angry. Will take time.*

She texted again. *What does photog look like?*

IDK, Sebastian texted back for I don't know.

She sighed. *M? F? Old, young? Tall, short?*

M. Youngish. Don't know height. Will meet you outside the press room.

She shoved her phone into her satchel and groaned. *Male. Great. Now you've narrowed it down to half the people in the building. Didn't you check this guy's website when you hired him? Does he even have a website? Does he even exist?*

She left the grooming area and positioned herself in the hallway outside the press room. People and their dogs hurried from one meeting to the next, making the narrow corridor feel like a busy highway at rush hour—but a happy busy highway. She scoured the crowd for the mysterious photographer.

Where is he?

She concocted a plan to find the man who resembled the photographers she knew at Bow-Wow—pleasant, eager, disheveled, rumpled, slightly lost because they weren't concentrating on their surroundings but instead saw the world as one giant prospective photograph. The obvious giveaway would be if he had a camera slung around his neck, but he might carry his equipment in a backpack. She would look for a man who was serious but confused.

She studied the crowd. One man with a backpack walked toward her.

"Are you the man I've been waiting for?" she asked.

He smiled and eased away.

A second man came to the press room door, and she tried the direct approach. "Are you a photographer?"

"No," he replied.

She approached two more men who passed. Neither was the photographer. *Am I in the wrong place?* She re-read Sebastian's text message again. *Nope, right place.*

She would give the photographer five minutes more. If he didn't show up, she'd roam the grooming area, find a good first-day story, and take the photos herself.

She peered up and down the hallway, pacing and looking at her watch in twenty-second intervals. No photographer.

Enough.

On her way from the press room to the grooming area, she went past a man, bedraggled but thoughtful, a well-worn backpack slung across one shoulder. He was talking to a slim woman with stylish pink cat-eyeglasses, short spikey white hair, and a badge that said, "RICI Organizing Committee." Emily turned her back toward them and pretended to study the carpet while she eavesdropped on their conversation.

"Yes, yes," the man said. "I can do that."

"And photographs?" the woman asked.

"Yes, of course. I can definitely do photographs."

That was all Emily needed to hear. She wedged her way in between them.

"You're here," she said to the man. She didn't try to hide her exasperation. "I've been waiting. Where were you?"

"I just arrived," he replied calmly.

"I've been wandering around, trying to find you."

"You have?" His eyes widened.

She turned to the conference organizer and waved her away. "You can run along now. I'm taking him with me."

The woman started to protest. Emily held her palm to signal "stop." "He needs to come with me. *Now.*" She took the man by the elbow. "Let's go."

She left the woman in the hallway, her mouth open as if she might speak but was too afraid.

On an ordinary day, Emily would have been pleasant, possibly, charming. Not today. With less than five hours sleep during the last forty-eight hours, she was exhausted, surly, and impatient. She was in a place she didn't want to be, doing a job she didn't want to do, and the volume of work that lay ahead was mind-rattling. *Patience is the first casualty in social interactions when you're tired. And there's a cultural gap. The RICI woman is a polite European. I'm an assertive American. I had to interrupt her and take him with me.*

"I waited for you by the press room," Emily said to the man, "but I gave up."

He started to speak. She "shhhed" him.

"I don't have time to listen to excuses. I need to get a good first-day story. You need to get some interesting photos. Move it. Let's go."

"There's a press conference…"

"Yeah, yeah, with a boring prince giving a boring welcome talk. What kind of story will we get from that? A boring one. We can find a better story. We need a story that's unique, special."

The man didn't move.

She dug her fingers into his elbow and pulled him along until they reached the grooming area. She let go and walked twelve paces before realizing the photographer wasn't beside her. He was still standing in the doorway, glancing around the room like a child lost in the mall.

"Oh, for Pete's sake," she yelled. "Move!"

The man arched his eyebrows.

"Now!" She gritted her teeth. He rushed to her side.

The two of them entered the grooming area—a sea of tables supporting all sizes and shapes of dogs, sporting shaggy, curly, wavy, smooth, and rough coats. Dogs barked in soprano, baritone, tenor, every pitch in between. She took in a deep breath—apple-scented shampoo and wet fur.

"This must be what heaven is like," she said to the photographer.

She eyed him up and down. Walked behind him. Came back around and folded her arms. *Something's missing.*

"Where's your camera?"

"Here," he replied taking a cellphone from the pocket of a tattered brown corduroy jacket.

"Great." Emily slapped her palm to her forehead. "A photographer without a decent camera. What kind of journalism schools do they have in Marisol? Apparently, not very good ones."

"My phone takes nice pictures." His voice was defensive.

"Nice isn't good enough," she snapped. "I could have taken pictures with my phone. I thought you were here to help. I expected you'd bring an actual camera with some wide angle or telephoto lenses. Maybe some lighting equipment. But no, I got you, and all you have is a cellphone. Hold on."

She took her phone from her satchel and texted Sebastian. *Who is this bozo photog you sent?*

She put the phone away and motioned to the photographer. "Come on. These pictures aren't going to take themselves."

Emily had a mission and a deadline, and she was determined to find the best story possible before she was herded into a room with the other reporters, forced to listen to the lame news conference. Afterward, she'd weave whatever interesting bits of information she gathered from her interviews into a story, then finally, finally, get some sleep. Her body ached for a hot bath and a good night's rest.

The photographer followed her, trying to match her brisk pace. She waited for him to suggest a shot or speculate about a unique angle. Nothing.

For a professional, he seems woefully uninspired.

Her patience wore thin, and she took charge, suggesting photo possibilities—a shot of a white poodle and owner sporting similar bouffant hairstyles, a sheepdog with its white-gray hair pulled on top of its head and tied with a neon green scrunchy, a super-chill beagle getting its teeth brushed.

If she recommended it, the photographer snapped a picture, but initiative was not his forte.

After her third forceful "suggestion," the photographer got the idea, but his choices seemed random—and foolish. When he shot a picture of a red water dish, she rolled her eyes but kept quiet. When he aimed his camera phone at leopard-print leash hanging on a peg near a grooming table, Emily asked him, "Why?"

"It's a juxtaposition of presence and absence," he replied. "The leash is waiting for the dog."

"Right." She groaned. *Did you read that in some intro to photography book?* Inside she screamed and banged her head against the wall.

She couldn't manage to be a writer and an art director at the same time, so devised a new plan. Lower, really lower, her expectations for the photographer and focus on the story she had to write.

"Follow me," she ordered. "I'm going to do some interviews. Try to get at least one candid shot of a dog and one shot of its owner."

"I'll try."

In her mind, she collapsed on the floor, cried, and kicked her feet like a two-year-old. In reality, she squared her shoulders. "Stick with me," she said evenly.

She talked to at least a half dozen dog owners that afternoon.

"Where are you from? Tell me about your dog. Why did you

come to the RICI?" She learned in college a good reporter could ask a few general questions, keep quiet, and interviewees would open up.

Today, she didn't have much time, but she did what she always did—listen, bury the stress. She furiously took notes, used her phone to record conversations, got contact information in case she needed to check a fact or ask an additional question later on.

The photographer spent most of his time petting the dogs.

How does this guy earn a living? He certainly isn't a ball of fire.

As they walked to the next grooming table, the photographer tickled a gray and white schnauzer under the chin. "Who's a good boy?" he cooed. "Who's the best boy in the world?"

Good grief.

She studied him for a moment, in part because she wanted to be able to relay the details about this clown to Sebastian when he asked how the photographer worked out. The man didn't act like a professional; he certainly didn't dress like one. Gray plaid flannel shirt with one pocket partially ripped and dangling, and dirty jeans rolled up to expose hiking books caked with mud. Surely, he'd dug that jacket from the bottom of a rag bag. He needed a shave. His shaggy black hair peeked from under a gray flat cap and wandered down the back of his neck—and not in a Brad Pitt sexy way. And he smelled like a horse barn. Like a horse barn that hadn't been cleaned in three days. Moldy hay, sour oats, and manure.

She shuddered. Despite hours of travel and a noisy flight across the ocean, she managed to look neat, albeit casual, as she made her way around the dog grooming tables. With some fresh lip gloss, a little blush, and a quick coat of mascara, she could look neat even though she was a weary wreck inside. But this guy…what a mess.

After an hour in the grooming area, she decided to write her first day story about a series of firsts. Adairia, a sixty-two-year-old retired schoolteacher, had come to the dog show for the first time. She had taken her first flight on her first trip away from her home country, Scotland, and she'd never shown a dog before. "I'm trying to keep my head, but my nerves are getting the better of me." Daffodil, her border collie, who spent her days on their farm herding a small flock of sheep, was the first dog in the canine family line to compete in a dog show.

Adairia was talkative—a reporter's dream. She answered every question Emily asked and added her own unsolicited observations.

"A lady in my village told me I was too old the start showing dogs, and I told her you're never too old to take a chance, so here I am. I'm trying to enjoy myself and not get anxious about the competition. At home, we say if you're failin', you're playin.' The most important thing for me to remember is I'm in the game.

"So many beautiful dogs. But, frankly, some owners and handlers aren't as beautiful as the animals," Adairia finished with a wink.

In addition to her colorful comments, Daffodil was a giant bundle of love, so making them the focus of Emily's first-day story would provide a good introduction to the RICI. Once she had her good idea, she relaxed. A bit. There was still the problem of an incompetent photographer. He spent most of the time with Adairia and Daffodil brushing the dog's shiny black and white fur as Emily took notes.

Emily had to drag him away. She ordered him to peruse the grooming area one last time with her.

"I enjoy seeing all these dogs," the photographer said, plucking clippers from the grooming table, clicking them on and off several times. "Dogs are such happy creatures."

She shrugged. "I don't know. These dogs are too…too perfect. Dogs ought to be free. They ought to run on the beach, or roll in the mud, or play with kids in a park. They shouldn't be gussied up like contestants in a beauty pageant."

"I'm sure they act like real dogs when they're not 'gussied up,' as you say."

"Maybe, but look at them. They're so…artificial." The words left a bitter taste in her mouth.

"Do you have a dog?" he asked, now snapping scissors open and shut, pretending to cut an imaginary dog's coat. "Or do you just write about them?"

She detected a snide tone and shot him a sideways glare. "Oh, I have a dog. She's a rescue dog. She wasn't bred to perfection like these beauty contestants. She's a great dog. Great dogs don't have to have a pedigree."

"I suspect the owners think these dogs are great dogs too," he said as he shot a photo of a gray hairdryer on a gray table.

"Whatever." Emily sighed.

The photographer glanced at his watch. "I have to leave now."

"You're not taking photos at the press conference?" she asked, amazed.

"No, I can't." He extended his hand. "I've enjoyed working with you."

She wanted to tell the truth. 'You've been a colossal disappointment, and you've wasted Bow-Wow's time and money.' Instead, she shook his hand and muttered, "You're welcome."

She turned away, searching for a sign to direct her to the press conference site. When she turned around, the photographer had vanished. *Where'd he go?* She had never even asked his name. Just referred to him as "you." Oh, well. Sebastian had his contact information, so the incompetent photographer would get a check. *It's good we're paying you for your time because the quality of your work is pretty sad.*

She returned to the main lobby, with the beautiful ocean view, gold-tinted windows, and turquoise carpet, and asked directions to the news conference. A woman with a "RICI Usher" badge directed her to the Kings Crown Room.

As Emily dashed to the press conference, she debated with herself: Cover this stale prince or spare herself an hour of dullness? What she desperately wanted was to go to the hotel, write Daffodil and Adairia's story, soak in a hot tub, then fall fast asleep. Maybe the hotel would have bubble bath. But a sense of responsibility overwhelmed her, and she stayed. At least, she could end her story with a sentence, "The prince welcomed guests to Marisol, blah, blah, blah."

She took her seat in a folding chair near the front of the room— the chairs in the back that would allow her to slip away unnoticed were taken—and waited for the prince to bore them to death. She anticipated his comments: "Welcome, Marisol is great, the RICI is great, and you will have a great time." *Lame.*

Her phone pinged. She saw a text message from a Marisol number she didn't recognize.

Hello. I was supposed to take photos for you today. Sorry, I can't make it. Car trouble.

She stared at her phone. *Can't make it? But you did make it.*

She started to text back, but Marva Delano, the Royal International president, took the podium. Emily recognized the white spikey hair and the pink cat-eyeglasses. She was the woman talking earlier with the slovenly photographer.

"Welcome, welcome." Marva bounced with glee. "I am pleased to welcome so many journalists to the one hundred and forty-fifth Royal International Canine Invitational, the RICI. As you know, this event brings together dog lovers from around the world, and we believe it brings people together too. We see the goodness of dogs—they are companions, they are workers, they are helpers, they are our loyal friends. We humans can only aspire to be as devoted as they are."

The reporters murmured agreement.

"You'll note from our itinerary, we have nearly three weeks of events ahead of us. We hope you'll take time to get to know the dogs and their owners and handlers. Please don't hesitate to contact me or any RICI officials directly if you have questions."

Emily stared at her phone again as the rest of Ms. Delano's words faded. *Car trouble? Car trouble? But you were here.*

"Now, it's time to introduce our host, His Royal Highness Prince Alexander. You'll have more time to talk with him later today at a reception next door for journalists. Welcome, Your Highness."

Her confusion melted away, replaced by embarrassment, followed panic, then utter and complete humiliation. She stared in horror as the bedraggled man in a plaid shirt, corduroy jacket, dirty jeans, and muddy hiking boots walked from behind the turquoise velvet curtain to the podium. Her mouth gaped open. Her stomach flip-flopped. Her face caught fire.

"Hello," he said with a shy smile. "It's my pleasure to welcome each and every one of you to my home. I have to begin with an apology for my appearance. I'm sure I don't look like the photos you've seen in the RICI program or the celebrity gossip magazines. Earlier today, Mrs. Delano asked me if I was in disguise. As many of you know, I studied veterinary medicine at university. This morning, there was a small emergency at the stables. Della, one of our mares, gave birth. We had a difficult time, but I'm happy to report mother and foal are fine. I'd like to think I helped, but when it comes to giving birth, mothers do the hard work."

The audience laughed politely—except Emily who was frozen in shock.

My photographer is the prince? That incompetent klutz is the prince of Marisol?

"I planned to shower and change clothes before I came on stage," he continued. "I also planned to get a haircut. In fact, one of the palace assistants was to meet me here with a suit, but when I arrived at the Seaside Center, I was delayed with an unexpected work assignment that came my way, so I didn't have time to change."

He winked in her direction. She didn't wink back.

Maybe the floor will open and swallow me. A long shot, yes, but a possibility.

When that didn't happen, she took matters into her own hands. As quietly as she could, she fished through her satchel for her red scarf, wrapped it around her neck and stretched it to cover her nose and mouth. Then she found her red hat and tugged it low over her forehead. Her eyes were the only part of her face showing. *Of all the times not to have a superpower. Invisibility would be a good one right about now.*

"Today, you're here for the RICI, and I'm pleased you have come to this phenomenal event in the world of dog shows. I'm the official host, and it's a job I thoroughly enjoy."

The reporters laughed and applauded politely—except Emily whose mortification grew exponentially. She hunched her shoulders and tried to make herself as small as possible.

"I'll be here throughout the RICI, and although I have a good many behind-the-scenes responsibilities, I also want to be accessible for interviews and questions. The press officers can help you get in touch with me. I'll do my best to accommodate your schedules.

"The RICI generates several million dollars annually, and the money goes to fund children's education programs, health care services, and animal welfare organizations. We are committed in Marisol to make sure all dogs have loving homes, and one of our important charities is the Rescue U program, which provides education about the need for foster care and adoption and provides training for new pet owners to help them give the best homes possible to animals. You have financial details in your packets, and our press officers can put you in touch with representatives of these charitable organizations, many of whom will be on-site for the next few weeks. These are important causes, and I'm proud RICI can support them.

"But the RICI does more than raise money. It generates goodwill. It enlightens people about the special bond we have with our pets.

"Journalists often ask me what the chief export is here in our country, and I tell them kindness. When tourists come to Marisol, they meet local residents at the beaches, in the town square, in the shops, on the slopes, and they learn this country is more than a tourist destination on a map. It is home.

"I realize you have a great deal of work ahead, but please make time to enjoy this lovely country where the sea kisses the sky. I hope you'll want to come back and experience our other seasons as well. There's something here for everyone, no matter age or interests. Again, let me welcome you. As the days pass, I hope you will feel at home here too."

Very poetic. For a moment, she became entranced by the sound of his deep voice and almost forgot her embarrassment.

He smiled, took a deep breath, and asked Ms. Delano, "Do we have time for a few questions?"

No, no, no.

"Of course we do," she assured him.

Why are these people so accommodating? Don't they understand I need to get out of here?

The prince and Ms. Delano answered ten thousand questions from reporters. Or maybe a half dozen. Whatever, Emily's insides were twisted into one giant solid figure-eight knot. If she hadn't embarrassed herself by commandeering the prince and berating him for his poor photography skills, she might have been a curious reporter too, asking for details about the charities, about the role the royal family played in planning and executing the dog show, about new programs at this year's RICI. She would have asked whether the royal family had a dog or whether they only talked about animals, as Prince Alexander said so sarcastically in the grooming area. Instead, she lowered her head, pulled her scarf another half inch higher and her hat a few centimeters lower, and prayed once again to disappear.

To her dismay, she didn't disappear. Instead, she squirmed in her seat, knocked over her water bottle then dropped her phone on the floor, whispering, "I'm sorry, excuse me, my apologies," to every reporter as she crawled over loafers, boots, and high heels, searching for it.

This is the most humiliating moment of my life. Worse than the time in high school when I was in assembly and the principal called the name of the winner of the Award for Academic Excellence, and I bolted up on stage only to learn the winner was Emily Simpson, not Emily Saint-Claire. More humiliating than the time when I went to a job interview and my prospective boss asked about my organizational skills, and I told him they were superior. His pen ran out of ink, and I volunteered to find one. I dumped my purse out on the table, and there were three partially eaten chew sticks, a Milk-Bone, a squeaky dragon toy, and a two-day-old sandwich. No pen. No new job either. This is much, much worse.

"We need to bring the questions to a close," Ms. Delano said as she stepped to the microphone, pleasant as ever. "I want to invite each of you to come next door to the Sea Glass Room for our press reception. You'll be able to mingle with RICI officials, as well as the dog owners and handlers. And there will be plenty of Marisol Christmas cake!"

Emily developed a new plan: Skip the reception, go straight to the hotel, grieve privately in her room over the shame of it all.

Despite the temptation of food, the crowd seemed to be in no hurry to leave. Writers and photographers shook hands, hugged, chatted, and crowded in the doorway, blocking her exit.

"Excuse me. Pardon me. I'm in a hurry. Leaving now," she said as she elbowed her way past them.

What's wrong with you people? There's cake in the next room.

Once out the door, she started speed-walking down the hall, searching for the closest building exit, talking out loud to herself, planning her evening.

"Write the blog as fast as I can. Have a light room-service supper, take a hot bath, turn off the lights, go to bed. Tomorrow will be a better day. If there's an all-night hair salon, maybe I can dye my hair so the prince won't recognize me. Maybe I won't run into him again. Maybe he'll be stricken with amnesia and won't remember me."

"Wait! Wait!"

She pivoted.

Him.

"I want to talk with you."

Emily pretended not to hear, then broke into a sprint.

"I warn you. I can run pretty fast."

Rats. Almost out of the building. She stopped, gasping for breath, and faced the man who, a few minutes ago, she mistook for an inept photographer. The prince ran toward her, out of breath too.

"Why did you leave?" he asked softly.

Her plan was to answer calmly, casually, to say she had a deadline and needed to check into her hotel to start writing, but her voice trembled. "You humiliated me! I'm so embarrassed. Why didn't you tell me who you were?"

"You didn't tell me who *you* were. I still don't know," he said.

"Your name?" he asked.

She adjusted the band holding her ponytail. "Martha Washington."

"I know that's not true. I studied in America."

A long sigh. "Emily Saint-Claire."

"Where do you work? You never told me that either."

"Bow-Wow Enterprises."

"Bow-Wow!" The excitement in the prince's voice was clear. "Your efforts in matching rescue dogs and owners are impressive. Your organization does great work to help animals—and help people. What do you do there? You're a writer?"

Emily raised an eyebrow, surprised he was familiar with Bow-Wow. She considered saying "yes, I'm a writer," because that answer would lead to fewer questions, and she could escape. Instead, she told the truth. "I started Bow-Wow with my partner Sebastian."

"Your husband?" Prince Alexander asked.

"No, no, my friend, my business partner."

There was a silence, then they both spoke at the same time. "I have to go," she said as he asked, "Aren't you coming to the reception?"

"My flight was late, and it was a long, noisy trip, and I haven't even checked into the hotel yet. I left my suitcase in the coat room. I need to start writing." She paused, her voice tinged with hurt. "I'm too ashamed to go."

"No one knows what happened but us two," he said. "And I won't tell."

"Please. I can't put into words how upset I am. I need to go."

"Let me make it up to you."

"You can't. I'm here as a reporter. I'm not supposed to assume, but I did. Now, I feel foolish. I assumed you were my photographer. This is my fault."

"No, it's mine. I should have told you who I was, but I was having so much fun, I kept going." His tone went from apologetic to princely. "Let's not assign blame. Let's put this behind us."

"I want to leave." Emily inched closer to the door.

"Here's what I think we should do," he said. "You're writing your first story tonight? About the Scottish lady with the Daffodil dog?"

She nodded.

"I'm sure it will be a fascinating story, but imagine how much interest it will generate if it's accompanied by pictures taken by the Prince of Marisol. Wouldn't that be something unique and special? Wouldn't that draw more readers, generate some clicks, as your journalists say?"

He does have a point.

"You're afraid the photos won't be any good, aren't you? Don't worry, I'll have my office assistant go through them, pick a few that aren't completely terrible, and email them to you. I do believe I got one suitable shot of Daffodil on the grooming table."

"Thank you. That would be nice," Emily said, although she was pretty sure her definition of suitable was different from the prince's. "Now, I have to leave. I have a lot to do. I need to work. I need some peace and quiet."

"You're at the Marisol Royal Hotel in the city center?"

"Yes."

"It's a lovely hotel, but most journalists and dogs and owners stay there during the show, so it can be quite busy and noisy. I know a better place where you can have all the peace and quiet you want."

"A bed and breakfast?"

"Sort of," the prince said, reaching into his pocket for his cellphone.

An hour later, she was standing outside the Castle Sol, the royal palace and city home of the prince and his family. The prince arranged for a car to collect her at the Seaside Center. The driver brought her through the huge black iron gates, decorated on top with gold lion's paw shells, up the long, winding cobblestone street, through the circular drive, and to the palace's ancient dark oak doors. The cream colored-stone exterior, with its steep-pitched turquoise roof, arched windows, and decorative turrets made her wish Georgia and Sebastian were with her. *They would love decorating this house.*

A guard, pleasant but serious, in a light blue uniform with gold braids over his right shoulder, welcomed her, pushed open the heavy door, and nodded for her to enter. Emily was sure she spent at least ten minutes slowly turning round and round, enthralled by the splendor. The palace interior glistened the way the ocean did when the sun shone on a late summer afternoon. A huge bell-shaped crystal chandelier shimmered in the foyer, and the white marble floors sparkled with flecks of gold.

She ran her fingers over the pale, sea-blue colored walls, so calming and soothing, and she took out her phone then snapped a photo of the mural of angels and animals on the ceiling. A grand staircase with a polished mahogany banister and wrought iron spindles, each spindle with a gold scalloped shell in the center, led, she imagined, to dozens of rooms, equally as ornate as the entry.

"Madam?" a gentleman called.

She extended her hand. "I'm Emily Saint-Claire. I'm supposed to be here."

"Yes, Ms. Saint-Claire. I'm Anton Halliman. I'm Prince Alexander's secretary. He told me you would be with us during the RICI. Welcome."

"Thank you." She set her foot on the first stair, prepared to lug her suitcase to the top. "I need to check in to my room."

"There's no need to check in. This is your home for the next few weeks. You can leave your luggage here, and someone will bring it to your room," he said. "In the meantime, if there's anything you need, let us know, and we'll get it for you. We understand this is a working trip."

Too overwhelmed to speak, she could only nod.

"Your room is on the third floor. There are elevators." He pointed down the hall.

"I don't mind taking the stairs."

"Let me lead the way."

She tripped once staring at the ceiling mural, caught herself, and apologized for her clumsiness.

"Of course, you're tired." Mr. Halliman's voice was kind, but Emily wondered if he was thinking, "Bumpkin."

She felt ill at ease in this spectacular palace, but, at the same time, oddly relaxed and at home thanks to Mr. Halliman's courtesy.

He opened the white double doors to her room, and she drew in a deep breath. She expected a nice room with a comfortable bed, and she hoped there would be a window. Instead, she was stunned to find a small suite, as large as her apartment in New York—a living area with a large overstuffed cream colored sofa, peach and turquoise silk pillows propped along the back; a dining area with a glass table and two chairs upholstered with sea-blue fabric embossed with lighter blue images of starfish; a king-size four-poster bed covered with a luxurious peach silk duvet; and, an en suite bathroom with the lushest turquoise cotton towels she'd ever touched and a plush white terry cloth robe hanging on a silver seahorse hook on the back of the door. The bath had a spa steam shower, like one she'd seen in a decorating magazine and envied. There was an office area with a white wooden desk that faced a floor-to-ceiling window.

Emily peered out. She had a view of the palace courtyard, now dusted with snow. In the distance, the sunset—rose, gold, teal—colored the sky above the jagged hazy blue mountains. To her right, she saw a window seat with blue and white plaid cushions, peach-colored pillows, and a neatly folded coral-colored cashmere throw for relaxing and napping on a cold day.

On the desk, she spied a bouquet of white roses, decorated with sprigs of green holly and red berries, and accompanied by a handwritten note. "Welcome. Hope this room inspires you to write special and unique stories. A."

Emily bit her bottom lip and tried not to smile. Prince Alexander was a gracious host, and perhaps, a guilty host after the photographer incident.

She turned to Mr. Halliman, standing patiently with his hands behind his back. "Satisfactory?" he asked.

Her first impulse was to throw her arms around his neck and hug him tightly to show her amazement and gratitude. But she heard Europeans viewed Americans as too forward. Instead, she replied, "I'm certain I'll be happy here."

Her suitcase arrived, and Mr. Halliman offered to help her unpack. She thanked him and told him she needed a few minutes to herself. He pointed to the desk and an antique white phone with a heavy receiver, an earpiece, and blue morning glories painted on the handle, the kind of phone movie stars from the 1930s used to invite each other to nightclubs.

"Ring zero for anything you need, no matter how small. The palace operators are on duty from 7 AM till 9 PM, and they'll be more than happy to help you. I'll leave you my personal phone number, in case you need anything."

"Thank you, Mr. Halliman."

"Anton," he corrected.

"Anton, thank you. What a beautiful room."

"I hope you'll be happy here."

Who wouldn't be? Emily unpacked her computer first. She placed it on the desk so she could look out the window and daydream while she wrote, as she did at home. The courtyard below was busy with human and animal activity—palace officials darting from one side of the yard to the other, clutching folders and briefcases; people in turquoise and gold uniforms, carrying baskets of fresh vegetables, talking and laughing with each other; squirrels and rabbits scurrying under bushes; and brown wrens and yellow chickadees flying from snow-covered tree branches to bird feeders. *Gracie would love it here.*

Emily opened her computer and was about to sit down at the desk when she heard a soft knock at the door. She opened it to find Prince Alexander, his hair cut and combed, his face clean-shaven, dressed now in a dark suit and smelling like woods and warm spice, nothing like the horse barn fragrance he sported earlier.

"Are you're getting settled in?" he asked.

"Yes, thank you. What a lovely room. Oh, and thank you for the roses. They're beautiful."

Not sure what to say next, not sure what he expected her to say, Emily stood frozen in the doorway.

"May I come in?" he asked.

"Oh, sure. Of course. This is your house. I'm sorry. I had a long flight, and it's been a hectic day. I must have left my manners somewhere over the Atlantic Ocean."

He strolled past her, surveying the suite. "I thought this room suited your personality. It's…casual."

"Thank you for not saying messy." She grimaced at her reflection in a circular mirror framed with bleached driftwood. She smoothed a few stray strands of hair that had fallen from her ponytail and tucked them behind her ears.

He frowned. "That's not what I meant. I thought this room would be more comfortable. Some of the other rooms in the palace are too formal. They're furnished with antiques. It seems my ancestors were more interested in style than relaxation. But this room is different. It feels 'warm' to me. The colors are soothing, like the inside of a seashell. It suits you."

"Thank you," Emily muttered, wondering how the prince could think she was warm after she had been rude to him a few hours earlier.

Alexander looked out the window at the courtyard below. "This room has a nice view too," he said. He motioned for her to come to the window. A green wooden cart came to a halt in front of the palace doors, and two men unloaded a ginormous Christmas tree.

"That will go in the grand ballroom, for the gala on the last day of the RICI," the prince said. He added, "We're in the middle of ball season in Marisol."

"What kind of ball do you play here?" she asked earnestly. "Football? Basketball?"

"Not that kind of ball," he replied. "I was referring to dancing. Formal dances. Our ball season begins in November and continues through February. There are grand balls throughout Marisol every weekend."

"Oh." Her cheeks heated, grateful he hadn't laughed at her. "Where I'm from, ball means sports, and sports is a big deal."

"When I visited America, I went to some sports events in your country. Very entertaining."

I need to travel more.

He nodded toward a phone on the table. "I'm sure Anton told you this old-fashioned phone will connect you to anyone in the palace. If you need something, pick up the receiver, dial zero, and talk with an operator. There will be a driver available to you each day. Call at least ten minutes before you need to leave. The driver will give you a phone number, and you can ring him when you're ready to come back to the palace. It's best to catch a ride to the Seaside Center. It's several miles away. But you can walk to the town center from here if you decide you want to see the sights. If it's too cold, you can ask for a car to take you there."

"You're too kind, especially since I wasn't kind to you today."

"History." He smiled as walked back toward to door. "Did Anton tell you about meals? Dial zero if you want something to eat or drink. The palace operator will connect you with the kitchen staff, and they will fix you breakfast and dinner—lunch if you want it. I realize you will be working during the day, and you may take lunch at the Seaside Center—there will be food catered in for the press, but there's a nice café in the building. If you prefer, you can ask the kitchen staff to prepare a box lunch to take with you. Also, you can call the kitchen staff if you want tea or coffee or a snack. They'll bring everything to your room."

"Wow! Sometimes I'm too tired to cook when I get home, so I eat chips and hummus."

"And your little dog? Does she get chips and hummus?"

Emily grinned. "No, she has her own food—usually more nutritious than mine."

"You take better care of her than you do yourself."

He stood by the door, started to turn the cut crystal knob, then pulled away. "Now, the cooks usually prepare one meal for everyone. Tonight, they're serving broiled trout. Is that all right for you? Are there any foods you don't like?"

"As long as it's not a can of soup and a grilled cheese sandwich, I'm fine," Emily said, remembering Matt and his opening line at the museum.

Alexander's face wrinkled with confusion. "We make our own soup here."

"Never mind. A long, unimportant story."

He glanced at his watch. "I'd like to stay, but I'm due downstairs."

He placed his hand on the doorknob again. Emily called after him. "Thank you for stopping by. I'm grateful you invited me to stay here. The room is lovely—stunning, actually. I appreciate you arranging transportation and food. And thank you for the roses. Such a sweet touch of spring on a winter day."

"It's the least I could do. Please accept my hospitality—and my apologies for the misunderstanding earlier."

"History," she said, said waving her hand dismissively.

"Let's agree there will be no more apologies tonight. I suppose you need to get to work," he said, eying her open laptop.

"Yes. I do have to write now. I'll unpack later."

"Good luck with your story. My assistant sent you some photos."

"I'll take a look. Again, thank you for this gorgeous room, the lovely flowers."

"I hope you can use some of the photos. I mean, I hope they're serviceable."

"I'll make sure you get your name in the photo credits," she teased.

Was that a giggle? Did this man giggle?

He cleared his throat and straightened his tie. "I hope I see you tomorrow." This time, he twisted the doorknob, opened the door, and was gone.

Emily took a deep breath and exhaled. *I thought he'd never leave.*

She sat at the desk and put her fingers on the computer keyboard.

Firsts can be sweet and special. First days of school. First dates. First jobs. First kisses.

For Daffodil, a black and white border collie from Scotland, and Adairia, her owner/handler, this is a week of important firsts.

It's the first time they have participated in the Royal International Canine Invitational, the first time they've traveled abroad, and the first time they've visited Marisol.

She stopped typing. "He really did stay a long time," she said.

Today, at the Seaside Center, Adairia discussed how the duo is prepping for their first competition together.

"We are both overjoyed to be here," Adairia said. "We have a wee case of the jitters because it's all so new, but what an adventure for me and my pup!"

Competing in the RICI marks a huge change in routine for Adairia, a retired elementary school teacher who now volunteers two mornings a week at the Dalbeattie Museum, and Daffodil, whose typical day involves herding sheep on the small family farm. To give Daffodil some semblance of home life, Adairia packed three stuffed toy sheep in her bags so this hard-working border collie can herd animals at night in their hotel room.

Emily stopped typing again and murmured, "Why did he stay so long?" She continued her article but it wasn't long before she stopped typing again. "Hmmm," she said. "He did stay here an awfully long time. Why did he do that? And he sent those flowers."

She stood up to stretch and glanced out the window. The Christmas tree cart was gone, and the only activity in the once-busy courtyard was a white horse, with a sweeping gray mane and tail, pawing at the snow, nibbling on the grass beneath. Out of the corner of her eye, she saw Alexander tromping through the snow until he stood alongside the majestic creature. He flipped up the collar of his wool coat, to shield his neck from the cold, then took carrots from his pocket and fed them to the horse as he rubbed its nose. The prince was talking. Emily opened one of the windows and strained to hear.

"Stable...moon...oats...crunchy...wave..."

The odd word drifted into her room when the wind blew just right. She started to close the window when the wind carried the prince's laughter into her room. A rich laugh. Warm. Like velvet. Emily smiled at his one-way conversation with the horse. *Like Gracie and me.*

She sat down again, studied her notes, and wove in Adairia's comments about the neighbor who told her she was too old to try something new, the adage that even if you're failing, you're playing the game, and the comment about beautiful dogs and less-than-beautiful owners.

Emily re-read her story, then added a few quotes from the press conference—Ms. Delano's comments about how dogs were our companions, workers, helpers, and loyal friends and how "we humans can only aspire to be as devoted as they are." And Emily added the prince's assertion that he loved his job as royal ambassador to the RICI and mentioned the charities that benefitted from the dog show. She ended with a shift in focus.

Adairia, Daffodil, and I share a common bond. This is also my first trip to Marisol and my first visit to the Royal International Canine Invitational. Each day, I'll write about the competing dogs and their owners and handlers to give you a glimpse inside the RICI, what's been called the most prestigious dog show on earth.

Dogs from around the globe are here, and each one has a unique, special story. I'll share more stories, plus photos and videos, tomorrow. Please come back to our website!

Emily drew a deep breath and checked her electronic mailbox. The moment she dreaded: Time to look at the prince's photos. Were there *any* that weren't truly atrocious? She needed at least one to break up the text of her story. She didn't want to hurt the prince's feelings, but her expectations for his work were not high. She debated whether opening the email was a waste of time, then decided the prince would ask her for an assessment of his work, and she'd need to be ready with an honest answer.

She clicked on the email and opened the three photos Alexander's assistant sent. Emily blinked twice, surprised to find one perfect for the blog—Daffodil licking Adairia's nose, and Adairia tilting her head back, laughing. Emily had been so caught up in interviews, she didn't see Alexander snap that picture. She posted it, plus a second one, not as good a composition, of Adairia brushing Daffodil's fur. There was a third one—an orange towel, crumpled on the floor by the grooming table. Emily let that one go. Readers didn't need to see a photo juxtaposition of presence and absence.

Next, she texted the Marisol photographer. *Sorry we missed each other. Hope car is working now. Temporary photographer helped today. Can u come tomorrow?*

He texted back: *Sorry, can't. Covering RICI for Marisol newspaper. Next year?*

Of course, at this late date, he had other commitments. She was on her own.

Next year, she wrote. Emily added a 😊 emoji, but she wasn't happy. This meant she'd write, photograph, and shoot all the videos. *Work, work, more work.*

Emily sent a text to Sebastian to tell him she'd posted her story online. Next, a text to Georgia to check on Gracie. *Arrived safely. Hope you're settled in. My home is your home. Thanks for taking care of my sweet Gracie. All is well. Tired. Will call tomorrow.*

Georgia's reply included a picture of Jack and Harper asleep at opposite ends of the sofa in their matching red Christmas pajamas with Gracie, lying on her back between them, her legs stretched as far as they could go.

Finally, Emily contacted her parents, admonishing them not to worry and wishing them sweet dreams.

With all her work done and messages sent, it was finally time to relax. She stood and stretched her arms and legs, then rubbed the back of her neck and yawned.

I need to rest my eyes.

The bed looked incredibly inviting. She lay on top of the peach silk comforter. *Soft.* Then, she put her arm over her eyes to block the lights in the room and sighed, exhausted from anxiety, travel, and work.

Two hours later she woke, not sure where she was, but the delicate perfume of white roses helped her remember. A few minutes past 9 PM. The palace operators would be gone, and she was hungry. She could walk to the city center, but she was too tired.

A quick search through her purse turned up a pack of pretzels left over from the plane trip and a few bites of her medicinal chocolate bar. She peered into the refrigerator in her room, looking for a bottle of water. *Gold mine!* Shelves stocked with still and sparkling water, milk, soft drinks, fruits, cheeses, yogurt.

In the freezer, she found a half dozen cups of chocolate chip ice cream, another half dozen of strawberry, and a small cheesecake. Her refrigerator at home had never been stocked like this. She looked in the cabinet to the right of the fridge—cookies, chips, nuts, granola bars, cereal, snacks galore.

Emily fixed a plate of cheese, fruit, and crackers, then curled up on the window seat. The courtyard was quiet now. In the distance, the multi-colored Christmas lights from the town center twinkled, and above, the stars glimmered blue-white in the deep indigo sky. *So peaceful. So pretty.*

As she took a bite of orange slice, she watched the snow fall gently, and her mind drifted back to her awkward meeting with the prince, his conversation with his horse as he stroked the creature's nose, the flowers he sent. And she smiled.

Chapter Seven
An Adventure

After her first good night's sleep in two days, Emily was ready to face work again. As she did at home, she checked her text messages from bed. The first one was from Sebastian.

Great first day story! Photos by prince! How? No one else has those!

Emily texted back. *Thanks. Photog had car trouble. Couldn't make it. Mistook prince for photog.*

What??!? 😱

Don't worry. All good. 🙂

Is prince upset? Will they kick you out? 😨

No. All is well. Relax. 😎

She waited for a barrage of questions from Sebastian. When the phone didn't ping anymore, she guessed he must have been on his way to a meeting because there was no follow-up text demanding details. What a relief—she didn't have to explain the whole embarrassing incident again.

She picked up the palace phone and asked for the kitchen.

"Ms. Saint-Claire?" a pleasant woman responded. "Breakfast this morning? We're serving cinnamon waffles and bacon. Would you prefer something lighter?"

"No, waffles are perfect," Emily said. At home, she would have scarfed a piece of toast and gulped a cup of coffee or, once she was in the office, wolfed a protein bar and washed it down with a bottle of juice. *This is much better.*

As she waited for breakfast, she gazed out the window. Two deer wandered leisurely through the courtyard—an ordinary day at the palace, an extraordinary day for her.

She gave herself a hug. "I may never leave."

~ * ~

After spending all morning and most of the afternoon with the hound group, Emily decided to write her blog report on Pascal, a two-year-old petit basset griffon vendéen, who lived on a lavender farm in southern France.

At her desk in Castle Sol, she rifled through her pages of written notes. *Where to begin?* She'd gleaned such a wealth of fascinating information about Pascal, she could have written three stories. Emily thought, squirmed, wrote, deleted, got up to stretch, sat down, thought some more. She searched the refrigerator for a snack. *Better not.* Tonight's menu featured beef stew with seasoned tomatoes and paprika, and she didn't want to spoil her dinner. Back at her desk, she put comfort before creativity. She kicked off her shoes, then pushed up the sleeves of her green sweater top. Next, she took off her earrings, necklace, and watch. Now, she was ready to write.

Pascal rocks.

Once a week this two-year-old petit basset griffon vendéen (PBGV) brings baskets of lavender soaps and sachets as gifts for residents at the Connexion senior home.

They reward him with some freeze-dried chicken treats, lots of belly rubs, and a hearty chorus of "Hound Dog."

"Pascal's visit is the highlight of the week for everyone at Connexion," said owner Etienne. "The love from the residents is the highlight of Pascal's week, as well. The residents look forward to his visits—petting him, hugging him, and, of course, singing. Pascal loves to howl along. He's a PBGV, but surprise, he's also a rockhound."

Emily leaned back in her chair and studied the introduction. Change it? Leave it alone? She read, re-read, then stopped for a second. She put her head on her desk to give her eyes a rest from staring at the computer screen.

Behind her, she heard muffled conversation. She glanced in the mirror to her right. No one. She went back to writing. Giggles. She looked in the mirror again.

Nothing.

She began typing again.

A bark, followed by a "shhh!"

In the mirror, she saw two children—a boy and a girl—peering into the room, trying to hide behind the door they'd partially pushed open. The girl gripped the collar of a pony-sized dog with cream-colored curly fur.

Emily smiled to herself and pretended not to notice her visitors. Acting as if she was engrossed in work, she adjusted her glasses, then typed a few sentences.

The children whispered loudly to each other and to the dog. At last, the dog broke free from the girl's grip. He bolted into the room and jumped on Emily, almost knocking her out of the chair.

"Who do we have here?" she asked, standing up, patting the dog's head.

"This is Stefan," the girl said, then added, as if Emily wouldn't know on her own. "He's a dog."

"Well, he's a beautiful boy." She continued rubbing his head and massaging his long floppy ears. "And what are your names?"

"I'm Isabella." The girl took the boy's hand then pulled him to her side. "This is Lukas. He's my brother." Both children extended their hands. Stefan offered his paw.

Emily was impressed with their manners. "I'm pleased to meet you. I'm Emily."

"I know," the girl said proudly.

"You know?"

"Yes, our father told us."

"Your father?"

"Yes. He told us last night at supper."

"Your father works here? What does he do?"

"He's a prince." Isabella shrugged as she studied Emily's computer screen. Lukas climbed into her chair and spun around.

Emily remembered from her research the prince had children; she never expected to meet them. On TV, royal families sent their children to boarding schools. "Your father is Prince Alexander?"

Isabella nodded. "You ask a lot of questions."

"It's my job," Emily replied. "My job is asking questions so people will tell me stories."

"What a fun job." Isabella read Emily's story. "How do you pronounce this?" She pointed to the dog breed name.

"Now who's asking questions?" The playful tone in Emily's voice earned a smile from Isabella.

Emily told the children how to pronounce petit basset griffon vendéen. She showed them a short video of Pascal delivering gift baskets and another of the seniors singing a rocking version of "Hound Dog" with a rollicking piano accompaniment that would have made Elvis Presley proud.

With two children and a dog in her room, Emily was forced to take a break from work. Stefan sniffed every corner, Lukas swiveled around and around in her work chair, and Isabella talked nonstop, providing Emily with detailed biographies. Isabella was nine years old—

nine years and two months. Her brother was seven and a half. They spent their day at school, her favorite class was history, and Lukas's was art. The two walked to school every morning, and their father went with them, but sometimes he worked, so their grandmother or grandfather came instead to walk them back home.

"Papa says we're too young to go alone," she said, although she sounded skeptical her father was right.

Stefan napped at the palace while they were in school. As soon as they got home, all of them went to the kitchen for a snack of fruit, cookies, and milk.

"But none for Stefan," Lukas said. "Only dog treats."

Isabella told Emily her favorite color was yellow, Lukas liked apples, and Stefan had a new bed that was very soft. They asked Emily what her favorite food was. Spaghetti, she replied. Did she like to snow ski because they might go this weekend, and would she like to come too? Skiing was fun, but work was the reason she'd come to Marisol. Why was she writing? Emily explained she was telling a story about the dog show, then showed them a photo she snapped of Pascal getting a haircut.

"He's fluffy, like Stefan," Isabella said. Then she whirled around and shrieked, "Ohhh, nooo!"

Emily caught sight of Stefan out of the corner of her eye. He was on the bed, one of her shoes in his mouth. He shook his head furiously and growled a warning: "This shoe has met its match."

"He's going to kill your shoe!" Isabella exclaimed.

She darted toward Stefan, and Lukas ran after Isabella. Stefan jumped off the bed with the shoe clenched firmly in his jaws then bolted down the hall. The children chased Stefan and Emily, barefoot, chased the children as Isabella and Lukas screamed some of the time but laughed most of the time.

"Stop, Stefan! Come back!" they called.

The four of them dashed through the long, long hallway, past the portraits of stern-faced former kings and elegant queens, Stefan leading the way, his ears flying back, clutching the shoe in his mouth like a trophy. Without warning, Alexander walked out of a door and into the hallway, and Emily slammed into him with such force, he spun around and nearly fell to the floor.

Both apologized, but Isabella interrupted, yelling over her shoulder, "Papa, Stefan's got a shoe!"

"Not another one!" Alexander cried as he joined the chase.

The second collision was between Stefan and Jenine, the housekeeper for the third floor. She dropped the stack of towels she was carrying, and they scattered over the marble tiles. Momentarily distracted by the falling towels, Stefan stopped and she grabbed his collar then wrestled the slobbery leather scraps from Stefan's mouth and inspected them.

"Another shoe, sir?" she asked the prince.

Alexander took the mutilated mess from Jenine's hand. "I'm afraid so." He shook his finger at Stefan. "You have to stop this. You have toys. You have chew sticks. No shoes!"

Stefan cocked his head, a puzzled look on his face that said, "No shoes? Why not? Especially when they're so tasty?"

Alexander brought what was left of the shoe to Emily as the children and Stefan followed.

"I'm sorry," Alexander said. "I think this is beyond repair."

What an understatement. She stared at the lump of wet shoe bits in his cupped hand. "You can toss them," she said sorrowfully.

"I'll replace the shoes," he assured her.

"Oh, it's not that. They weren't expensive."

"I promise I'll make it up to you."

"No need. Dogs will be dogs." Although she did marvel that Stefan made such quick work of her shoe. He had demolished it in mere seconds. If there was a world record for shoe destruction, she was sure Stefan shattered it.

"Please, let me take care of this," Alexander insisted. He turned to the children. "We need to remember to keep Stefan away from shoes."

"You're making much too big a deal out of this," Emily said.

"He's eaten three of my shoes and two of Lukas's," Isabella volunteered. "He ate one of Grandpa's slippers last week."

"He certainly has a hearty appetite," Emily joked then laughed. But her laughter subsided. The prince fixed his gaze on her. She clasped her hands behind her and backed up two steps. *Why is he staring at me?*

"I should get back to work," she said. His stare was so intense, it made her uncomfortable.

"Can we come with you?" Lukas asked.

"No," Alexander said. "Emily needs to do her job, the way I have to do mine sometimes. She can't take time to play now." He looked at her. "Maybe later?"

She grinned. "Maybe later."

~ * ~

After dinner, she was hard at work, polishing her story about Pascal and Etienne, when someone knocked at the door. She answered. No one was there. Instead, she found a green and white striped silk shoebox, tied with a gold velvet ribbon, and a handwritten note inside.

"Please accept these with Stefan's apologies."

Emily opened the box to find a pair of black suede shoes—stylish with low heels, practical for work. She looked down the hallway. Alexander, Isabella, Lukas, and Stefan peeked around the corner. Emily tucked the box under her arm then walked to meet them.

"Thank you, Stefan," she said as she rubbed his shaggy head. "These are much nicer than the shoes Stefan ate," she told Alexander.

"I called a friend who's a cobbler. We've given him quite a bit of business since Stefan arrived. He found the size on one of the shoe scraps, and he had these in his shop. I hope they will work for you."

"They will. Thank you," she said. "I appreciate this."

"Ask her," Isabella nudged her father with her elbow.

"Can you come with us to eat cupcakes?" Lukas blurted out.

"That *was* what we wanted to ask you," Alexander said. "The children and I would like to invite you to join us for dessert—if you have time. We can walk from here. The bakery is about ten minutes away. It's in the opposite direction from the city center, so we won't get to see the Christmas lights, so you may not be interested. I understand you're working. You may be too busy…"

Emily smiled. "I'd love to. I can see a new part of Marisol, and I can wear the new shoes. I'll be right with you. For future reference, I never refuse cupcakes."

~ * ~

The next day, after Emily spent the morning and most of the afternoon with the herding group, she took a break. She poured herself a cup of coffee in the press room, then decided not to work there because it was too noisy—reporters shouted to editors on their phones, talked to themselves as they wrote, chatted about dinner plans.

She found a cushioned bench by a window with a view of the sea. She read through the notes she scribbled about Jesse, a Cane Corso, and his owner Christina, from Seattle. She stopped short.

What's different? What's missing?

She stared out at the ocean. Smooth water, small waves today, splashed happily against the rocks. *There's no knot in my stomach. Where is the fear I'll never get my work done?*

Gone. All gone, like the mist that rested on the mountains in the morning, then vanished as the sun grew warmer. She took a deep breath, then slowly exhaled. Sebastian was right: This was her dream assignment—if only it hadn't spoiled her plans for a perfect Christmas.

~ * ~

Emily was amazed at how little time the transition took. She quickly settled into a new routine, one in sharp contrast to her routine back home. Each morning, she woke to the sound of cheerful conversation in the courtyard below her window or the melody of church bells chiming in the city center. No screeching alarm. She took a leisurely shower, enjoying the steam and the rosemary and mint-scented soaps. No rushing. She ate a hearty breakfast the kitchen staff prepared— omelets, pancakes, or oatmeal with fruit. No gulping. A palace staff member drove her to work. No shoving her way through crowded streets.

Each morning, she strolled through the Seaside Center and talked easily with owners and handlers to learn about their dogs. As she asked each owner the same question, "What makes your dog a champion?" she prepared to hear bragging about bone structure and superior bloodlines, descriptions of silky coats, even temperaments, or lengthy histories of blue ribbons and trophies.

Instead, she learned about Bridgette, the corgi, who "herded" two toddlers to bed each night in their Dublin apartment. She heard stories about Marco, the dalmatian, who loved opera and "sang" along when his owner played recordings at their home in Rome. Betina, the golden retriever, was a champion "snorer," who never hesitated to take over owner Angela's bed in San Francisco, and Bernardo, a chihuahua, practiced yoga with his owner every morning on their apartment terrace in Mexico City. Rolfe, a German wirehaired pointer, once ate an entire apple strudel, meant to be the dessert when his family welcomed the new pastor to their house in Dresden. Andres, a black Labrador, lived with his owner and enjoyed barking at pigeons that flew by their rooftop apartment in the historic Alfama district of Lisbon.

"What makes Andres a champion?" Juan Pablo stroked the lab's big head as he and the drooling dog exchanged adoring glances. "He makes my heart delight."

Emily spent her workday wandering through the grooming area, asking that question and others, taking notes, visiting the press room to make small talk with the other reporters. She returned to the palace around 3 PM to write another "tales of the champions" profile.

An hour later, she'd hear a knock at her door, which she now left wide open while she worked. Isabella and Lukas, Stefan in tow, politely asked to come in, although they were well inside the room before they asked permission. They plopped on Emily's bed, asked what she was writing, begged to see pictures of the dogs she'd met that day, and told her about their day at school.

The children brought their schoolbooks, their electronic tablets, and their toys and settled in for the rest of the afternoon. Long ago, Emily had learned to write, no matter what her environment, no matter how many distractions, so the children's talking and laughing and Stefan's panting and barking didn't hinder her concentration. In fact, the noise became pleasant background music.

As she wrote, she'd occasionally call over her shoulder, "What are you doing?" One of the children would reply, "Studying my math" or "Working a puzzle," and Emily would continue working until Alexander came to collect them for dinner between 6 and 6:30.

When he visited, Emily struggled to concentrate on work. Instead, she studied his interactions with the children. Even though he had dropped the youngsters off at school a few hours earlier, their evening reunions were filled with running, jumping, hugging, laughing.

He kissed each child on the cheek, rubbed Stefan on the head, and nodded hello to Emily. One child clasped his left hand, the other his right, and they pulled him onto her bed amid their books and games. He'd start to speak, but before he uttered a word, Isabella gave a full report on her and Lukas's day at school—the games they played at recess, the foods they ate at lunch, the lessons they learned, the friends they talked with.

After she finished, Alexander would turn to Stefan. "And you? Did you nap all day?" Stefan would bark as if to say, "Yes, of course, I'm a dog, that's what I do best."

Then Alexander asked Emily how her work was coming along, and she eagerly summarized the profile of the canine "champion" she wrote that day.

At least, that was what she intended to do. A simple, "Today, I interviewed a woman who owns a Doberman. The woman's name was Carol Sue. The dog's name was Max," would have been an adequate answer. Yet, when she talked to Alexander, Emily struggled to construct a coherent sentence. She stammered. She babbled. She forgot words. Her cheeks burned. Her palms grew cold and clammy. Her breath was shallow. She wondered if Alexander noticed, and if he didn't, how he could be oblivious to her nervousness, on full display.

After the updates, and after Emily rambled enough to embarrass herself, Alexander wished her a goodnight and ushered the children off to dinner. A normal person would have said "thanks." Instead, she uttered a few disjointed phrases. "You. Sure. You, um, you, you have a night. Goodnight. Okay?"

After each encounter, she sat down at her computer, banged her head on her desk, then took a half dozen deep breaths to regain her composure. Once she reclaimed her focus, she continued her work with occasional breaks to berate herself. "How foolish," "What's wrong with me?" "Could I have acted any sillier?" She'd mutter until a cart arrived with her meal around 8 o'clock.

Before she went to bed, she'd text Sebastian an update on stories and photos coming his way, then she videoed with Georgia, who pointed the camera toward Gracie so Emily would see her little dog was fine.

"Hello, Gracie!" Emily would wave, and Gracie would stare lovingly into the camera. "What did you do today? Did you have fun? Mommy misses you so, so much. I'll be home soon. I love you." Emily hoped Gracie understood she didn't want to leave her behind—her job forced her to be gone.

After the call to Georgia and Gracie, Emily phoned her parents for a video chat. "How are the Christmas plans coming?"

"Fine, fine," said her father, who held his nighttime mug of tea. "The fields are getting bare now because people are coming to cut their Christmas trees. Business is brisk."

Her mother stood behind her father, holding up a red sweater she'd knitted. "What do you think? Do you think Uncle Frank will like it?"

Her father updated her on rehearsals for the church Christmas pageant; he was a choir member. He sang a few lines from "The First Noel" or "I Heard the Bells on Christmas Day" or whatever song the choired rehearsed the day before.

"I miss you." Emily sniffled.

"We miss you, too, hon," her father replied.

He and her mother blew her a goodnight kiss.

As she lay in bed at night, she'd replay her day, plan for the work tomorrow. But she also marveled at her happy new routine.

Then, as she was getting used to it all, the routine shifted. Emily still went to the Seaside Center in the morning for her RICI interviews and stories, but the children were out of school for the Christmas holidays. They stopped by her room in the mornings to say hello, then came in the afternoon for longer visits.

Instead of chattering about school, now they reported on what Lukas called "our Christmas adventures." Helping bake cookies, shopping for presents, hanging stockings, decorating trees. Isabella and Lukas were rehearsing a Christmas play; Lukas played a snowflake, and Isabella was a Christmas bunny.

She practiced daily in a hand bell choir, and she would soon perform "Deck the Halls" in a lunchtime concert in the town square. Their adventures were not unlike Emily's childhood exploits.

As they reported each activity, she balanced listening with writing, dividing her attention between the children and her work. At times she found it taxing, but there was an unexpected pleasure in juggling.

~ * ~

Computer. Pen. Notebooks. Phone. Eyeglasses. Emily gathered the "tools" she needed for her work day. Today, journalists were scheduled to spend time with RICI judges.

She found her favorite lipstick, a rosy shade called Winter Kiss. She stood in front of the mirror and was applying a second glossy coat when Lukas knocked on the door. He bounced in and jumped on the bed.

"I'm on my way to work, honey," Emily said, glancing around the room, checking one last time for any missing items. "I'd like to talk, but I need to work."

Lukas folded his arms across his chest, stared straight at Emily, and asked, "Why do you have to go to work?"

"It's my job. I have to write about the dog championship."

"Why?"

Rather than tell a child, who was living from one Christmas adventure to the next she needed to earn money to support herself, she decided sometimes reality was more than a seven-year-old should handle. "I made a promise I would write about the royal dog competition. I have to go to the Seaside Center so I can do my job."

"But you've worked every day," he protested. "You didn't come to our Christmas play. You didn't come hear Isabella play hand bells."

"I'm sorry. I wanted to, but I needed to work. And I'm late now. I have to leave." She moved a few steps toward the door and motioned for him to follow.

He didn't move. "Why can't you go with us? Today we're having a play day. All day. We're going to the Christmas market, and we're going to sled on the big hill, and we're going to drink hot chocolate. Papa is taking the day off. Why don't you?"

"I can't. Remember, I have to work."

He folded his thin arms across his chest. "Do you have to work *all* the time?"

Emily was quiet for a second. She sat on the bed beside him and took his hand. "Lukas, I ask myself that question every day."

"Please, please, please come with us," he begged.

"I would like to, I would…," she trailed off. What explanation could she create to satisfy a small boy?

"Pleeeeaaasseee!" He wrapped his arms around her waist. His hug surprised her.

"Lukas, your dad may want to spend time with you and your sister. He may not want someone else to come along."

"You would be welcome to join us." A deep voice came from behind her.

She turned to face Alexander.

"I'm sorry," he said. "I didn't mean to eavesdrop. I went looking for Lukas. I suspected he might be visiting you."

"Please, Papa," Lukas said. "Make her go."

"I can't make her go, Lukas. Emily can do what she wants, and we must respect her decision. Emily, we would be happy for you to spend the day with us. The children would be happy to have you come with us." Alexander took a deep breath. "*I* would be happy to have you come with us."

She tried to read his face. Was he asking to be polite? Was he inviting her to please Lukas? Did Alexander want to spend time with *her*?

Lukas clasped his hands together in front of his chest as if he were praying. His eyes were closed, and he mouthed the words, "Please, please, please, please, please…"

She glanced at Alexander. He whispered, "Please."

"Okay," she said, her voice brimming with excitement at the prospect of a play day, an entire day off, and if truth be told, time with Alexander and the children. "Give me ten minutes to get ready."

Lukas clapped his hands and cried, "Yay!" He ran down the hall, shouting the news to Isabella.

"Do you want to go?" Alexander asked. "I shouldn't have pressured you. I understand you have to work. I can explain to Lukas. He has to realize he can't always have what he wants."

"I'd like to go, but you don't have to invite me because Lukas put you in an uncomfortable spot."

"I think we both may be trying to be too polite here. There's more to Marisol than the Seaside Center and the palace. Marisol is a charming country. I'd like to show it to you."

"I'd like that. I really would."

"Then, it's settled. We'll have our 'Christmas adventure' together today. I'll meet you by the elevator. Take your time."

Alexander left the room, and Emily listened for his footsteps. When she was sure he wasn't coming back, she jumped up and down with delight. After a quick change from her work dress to slacks and a sweater, she dumped her satchel upside down on the bed and got rid of her pens and notebooks. No need for them today. When she draped the bag across her shoulder, it felt ten pounds lighter. She grabbed her coat and hat and rushed out the door.

Her heart raced but not from running. Each encounter with Alexander left her flustered, blushing, breathless. Every time he visited, she wished she could spend a few more minutes with him. Now, she would have an entire day.

As she waited for him and the children to meet her at the elevator, she texted Sebastian. *S, No stories today. Taking a day off.*

Seconds later, he texted back. *What? We need a story!*

I need a day off. You can manage.

Nooooooo! Please write something.

Nooooooo! Not today. Sorry.

She turned off her phone, then stuffed it deep inside her satchel.

She heard a bark. Stefan ran toward her, jumped on her, and knocked her backward. "Stefan!" she patted his white curly head. "You're coming with us?"

"Of course," said Alexander. "It wouldn't be a true Christmas adventure without Stefan. He's part of the family, aren't you, boy?"

He held the elevator door open, and as she walked in, Isabella grasped Emily's hand. The tenderness of those small fingers resting in her palm, the spontaneous show of affection—sent a burst of warmth through her entire body.

"Everything okay?" he asked as he pushed the elevator button to the ground floor.

"Absolutely." She squeezed Isabella's hand.

The foursome, plus Stefan, strolled past the palace gates, crossed a stone footbridge spanning a narrow frozen river, then strolled a few blocks to the town square. Alexander and Lukas led the way with Emily and Isabella following behind. Stefan wove in and out, as if each person were an agility pole, with the two bells Isabella tied to his collar jingling joyously.

They talked about the cold weather as the snowflakes softly swirled around them; about Stefan's old plaid collar—he was getting a new one with yellow dolphins on it for Christmas; Lukas's loose tooth; Isabella's bright blue coat and the red cardinal pin her grandmother gave her last Christmas; Alexander's accident at breakfast—he'd knocked over a glass of orange juice; Emily's watch, which not only told time but tracked the number of steps they took. The conversations about the smallest things, the melody of their voices, the ease among them would be stitched together in a special memory for Emily. *Like a Christmas quilt.*

When they entered the town square, she stifled a delighted gasp. They walked through a lighted archway, and the image on the website brochures became real—the centuries-old white stone church with the turquoise roof, a spire towering toward the dove gray sky, jeweled-stained glass windows on either side of the building. The fountain in front of the church was frozen now, the water transformed into an icy bridal veil sculpture. Smaller cream-colored stores and houses, all topped with the blue-green roofs so common in Marisol, dotted the cobblestone streets surrounding the church.

In the distance, snow-covered mountains soared above the town. Emily took a deep breath—the same luscious wood-smoke scent that reminded her of home blended with the buttery fragrance of fresh-baked pastries from nearby restaurants. The air chilled her face, and she clapped her gloved hands together to keep warm.

Winter had never been her favorite time of year. The days were short, dark, and gloomy, the wind harsh, and the snow a constant barrier to outdoor ventures. The people she passed on the streets scowled more than usual as they hurried to get home, their faces cheerless. But winter in Marisol was different. People laughed as they ambled along the cobblestone streets, stopping to chat with neighbors and friends.

As they approached the Christmas market, Alexander cautioned Isabella to hold tightly to Stefan's leash.

"He likes to sample baked goods from the booths," Alexander explained. "He once got away from us and ate four iced cinnamon star cookies before we found him."

Isabella gripped Stefan's leash so firmly, her knuckles were white. Lukas took Emily's hand. "Don't get lost," he told her.

They wandered under a canopy of tiny white twinkling lights, strung from one side of the street to the other. As children from the local church gave candy canes to shoppers, amateur quartets played Christmas carols. "Hark the Herald Angels Sing" flowed happily into "Joy to the World," which blended perfectly into "Good King Wenceslas." The aroma of hot apple cider and sweet waffles perfumed the air, and a small bonfire gave shoppers an opportunity to warm their hands and feet.

"What do you think?" Alexander asked.

"It's amazing. I didn't expect this." Emily turned to face the prince. "I'm glad I didn't work today. I would have missed so much."

"The day's just starting," he reminded her.

"Papa." Isabella tugged at his coat sleeve. "May we buy Christmas presents? *Alone?*"

"You may," he replied. "Don't be gone long. Do you have your watch?"

She held up her wrist to reveal an orange band with pink flowers.

"One hour," he told her. "Then meet me, and we'll have lunch." He gestured toward rows of tables, covered with red tablecloths, where shoppers sat in white folding chairs, resting, visiting, and eating.

Alexander and Isabella synchronized their watches. "Look after your brother," he called as the children and Stefan scampered away. "And don't let Stefan near the food booths."

Alexander's booming voice caught shoppers' attention. They crowded around him, shaking his hand, wishing him a merry Christmas, and asking questions on assorted topics. He shook hands, laughed easily, scribbled notes to get in touch with those who had concerns. He posed for photos. He called people by their first names, asked how their children fared in school, promised he'd chat with them at the RICI and the ball, and wished them a merry Christmas.

Emily was surprised at the familiarity. He regarded the people who talked to him as neighbors, not royal subjects, definitely not as strangers.

When she caught his eye, she motioned toward the Christmas market booths and mouthed the word "shopping." He nodded, and she set off on her own.

Scurrying from booth to booth, she bought one-of-a-kind presents to wrap and give well after Christmas—pale blue knitted scarves, soft pink wool mittens, luscious dark chocolates, soaps scented with lavender, sandalwood and sea salt.

Children, giggling and clutching candy canes, raced past her, and couples kissed under mistletoe boughs. Bakers wearing white jackets over their winter coats twisted fresh dough into pretzels, grilled sausages, and fried potato pancakes. The tempting savory aromas mingled with the sweet warm smells of pumpkin loaves, butter cookies, and raisin breads.

The stalls stacked full of Christmas decorations—jolly Santas in red velvet robes, carved wooden angles with elegant white wings and silver halos, gold paper-star lanterns, and nutcracker soldiers with rouged cheeks—made her homesick for the store windows in Holly Mountain.

I wish I could be home.

As she paid for frosted gingerbread cookies to take to Alexander and the children, a quartet of carolers strolled by singing "We Three Kings," and Emily was taken aback by a realization. Christmas was happy, jolly, joyous in Marisol—just as it was back home. She'd been so busy sulking, she hadn't noticed. The holiday market was full of anticipation and wonder, the same as the downtown streets of Holly Mountain. *The Christmas sparkle isn't limited by geography.*

The warm-cookie perfume permeated the air as she searched the crowd for her lunch companions. She heard Stefan bark.

A short, brisk walk across the square took her to Alexander and the children, whispering and laughing. Her heart fluttered when the prince smiled at her and motioned for her to join them.

"What's going on?" she asked suspiciously as she took a seat beside Alexander. Suddenly, she was conscious she sat only a few inches from him.

The children, sitting across from her, mumbled to each other.

"Go ahead," Alexander told them.

Isabella presented Emily with a small sea-blue box tied with a gold satin ribbon.

"It's a Christmas present!" Lukas shouted.

"Oh, my! You shouldn't have done this." Emily's throat tightened. She clutched the gift to her heart. "This is so special to me. Thank you. I'll treasure it forever."

"Open it." Isabella wiggled with excitement.

"Shouldn't I save it till Christmas?"

"No, no! You won't be here at Christmas, so open it now!"

Emily stared at the box to avoid the eyes of anyone at the table. Reality stung her. On Christmas Day, she would be back in the city, alone with Gracie in her apartment. She'd be far from Marisol, a place she never wanted to come, but now... Isabella's simple statement of fact made her realize a thorny truth: she'd miss Isabella, Lukas, Stefan—and Alexander. How was it possible they'd become dear to her in such a short time?

"Open it!" Isabella insisted.

Emily glanced at Alexander for a cue.

"The children bought this for you with their allowance. You can open it now."

She untied the ribbon, opened the box, and unwrapped the delicate silver paper.

"It's a snow globe," she said as she held it up for him to see. "I don't have one of these." She shook it. The silvery-white flakes whirled around figures of a girl in an ankle-length blue coat and a white dog that could have been Stefan's twin. The girl carried a wicker basket filled with pine cones, and the dog wore a red scarf and bell around his neck instead of a collar.

"Do you like it?" Lukas asked, his voice anxious and excited.

"I love it." Her voice quivered. *Please don't let me cry.* She steadied herself, then said evenly, "Honestly, I love it."

"The children wanted you to have a souvenir of your visit here," he said.

"Thank you, Isabella. Thank you, Lukas," she said. "This will remind me of my trip to Marisol."

"It's Saint Angelina and Nicholaj," Isabella explained.

"Do you know the legend?" Alexander asked.

Emily shook her head. None of her Marisol research uncovered stories about Saint Angelina or Nicholaj.

"Let me tell, let me tell!" Isabella insisted. She faced Emily and clasped her hands on the table, sitting up straight as if she was ready to deliver a school lesson. "Angelina was a little girl in Marisol, living right here, in a house near the town center. It was Christmas Eve, a long time ago, and Angelina didn't have any presents for her family. She decided to take a walk into the forest nearby to gather some pine cones. Her family didn't have much money, and she couldn't afford to buy presents. Instead, she went to the forest to find a present from nature—from God."

"Those are the best presents," Lukas added, "the presents from nature."

"That's right," the prince said. "You both are telling the story very well."

Isabella and Lukas beamed. Isabella continued, "Angelina searched for the perfect pine cones for her mama and papa and brothers and sisters. She looked and looked until she found the best ever pine cones. She decided to add some branches and holly leaves and berries to make her present even prettier.

"She was so busy, she didn't realize the sun was going away, and the sky was getting dark. She tried to walk home, but she got lost, and she was afraid."

"Very afraid," echoed Lukas.

"When her parents couldn't find Angelina, they worried. They knocked on every door, and they asked neighbors if they knew what happened to her. No one knew, but they offered to help search for Angelina. The neighbors took lanterns and torches for lights, and they searched for Angelina in the town, then in the forest. That night, it snowed, snowed a blizzard. The people had to stop looking, and Angelina's parents cried.

"When Christmas morning came, everyone was sad. Angelina was gone. No one wanted to open Christmas presents. Instead, the people gathered at the church to pray." Isabella pointed in the direction of the church spire. "They wanted Angelina to come home badly. They prayed very hard. Then they heard a bell, far away, and the sound got closer. Someone said, 'It's Angelina!' And there was Angelina. And Nicholaj."

"Who was Nicholaj?" Emily asked.

"He was a dog," Lukas explained.

"Angelina's dog?"

"No, a miracle dog," Isabella said as she clapped her hands with glee. "An angel dog. Nicholaj was a homeless dog. The shopkeepers used to shoo him away when he would come to the doors to beg for food. No one wanted him. But Nicholaj was in the forest when Angelina got lost, and he heard her crying, and he stayed with her all night. He kept her warm with his furry coat, then he helped her find her way back home because dogs have the best sense of smell."

"He rescued her," Lukas said, for emphasis, to make sure Emily understood.

"Sometimes we rescue them. Sometimes they rescue us," Alexander said sweetly.

She remembered their first conversation in the grooming area when she bragged to him she rescued Gracie, that she didn't care much for "gussied up" show dogs. *I guess all dogs are rescue dogs. Sometimes we rescue them. Sometimes they rescue us, maybe from getting lost in the forest, but maybe from boredom, or sadness, or solitude.* Daffodil rescued Adairia from loneliness following her husband's death, and Pascal rescued the senior citizens from boredom and isolation.

"What happened to Angelina—and Nicholaj?" Emily asked.

"The town was happy," Isabella said. "That Christmas was the best ever because Angelina came home. Even though her family wasn't rich, they adopted Nicholaj. Then, when Angelina grew up, she wanted to help others because the people in the town helped her family, so she started a hospital and a school."

Alexander nodded toward the west. "The children attend Saint Angelina's School nearby, and Saint Angelina's Hospital sits on the outskirts of town."

Stefan rested his head on Alexander's knee, and the prince rubbed the dog's ears. "Stefan is a Marisolian snow hound, the same breed as Nicholaj. Snow hounds are our national dog."

Emily patted her leg and called Stefan to come. He obliged, tail wagging.

"One of the traditions here is we gather pine cones and greenery to put in our houses at Christmas," he said. "We're going to do that later today."

He then assumed a father-teacher tone of voice, "Now, what can we learn from this story?"

"There are three lessons," Isabella said. "We must always try to help others." Lukas held up one finger. "We should never give up hope." Then a second finger. "We must always have love and respect for all people and all living creatures." Finally, finger number three.

"What a beautiful story," Emily said. "It makes me sad and happy at the same time."

"Me, too!" Isabella exclaimed, her tone amazed as if she found it impossible to believe anyone else ever felt the same way she did. She jumped from her chair and hugged Emily. She kissed the top of Isabella's head.

"The children wanted you to have the snow globe," Alexander

said. "They're sold every year at the Christmas markets. I think every home in Marisol has one. It will be a nice remembrance of your trip here."

She grew quiet. The children had given her a gift she didn't expect, and it came with emotions she didn't expect either. The gift touched her heart, but her soul was shaken by the realization she would be sad to leave Marisol in a few days—and sad to leave this family. Then Lukas changed the subject, and her mood shifted from serious to light.

"Do you like pancakes?" he asked.

Alexander laughed. "Lukas is always hungry."

He nodded vigorously.

"Let's get some lunch for this starving boy," Alexander said. He and Lukas left the table and brought back sausages, potato pancakes, and hot apple cider. Emily shared the gingerbread cookies from the market.

As they ate, Isabella, the more inquisitive of the two children, peppered Emily with a series of random questions.

"Do you have a dog?"

"I do. Her name is Gracie." She showed the children and Alexander pictures on her phone.

"She's cute," Isabella observed. "What does she like to eat?"

"She has some dog food with chicken, but she eats anything—carrots, green beans…"

"Shoes?" Isabella asked.

Emily laughed. "No, she never developed a taste for shoes. She did chew up a pair of fleece gloves once."

"Have you ever been sailing?"

"I have. I enjoy it."

"We do that in the summer," Isabella said, then added, "It's too cold now. Do you like horses?"

"Yes," Emily said. "We have a horse on the farm where I grew up."

"What's his name?"

"Her name is Tess. She's a golden Palomino."

"Can you drive a car?"

"I can, but I don't have a car where I live. I take a bus or a taxi or a train."

This must be how people feel when I interview them—overwhelmed.

"Do you have a boyfriend?"

"Isabella!" Alexander said sharply. "Don't ask such personal questions."

"It's okay," Emily assured him. "Isabella is a lot like me. She asks lots of questions. Maybe she'll be a reporter and cover the royal dog show one day."

Isabella folded her hands on the table and smiled, giving her father a look of supreme satisfaction. Emily looked at Isabella's young, innocent face. She was waiting for an answer.

I did have a boyfriend. He didn't like dogs, and I was too afraid to be alone, so I didn't toss him out, which I should have done years before. I did nothing—just drifted along—until one day he texted me he was in love with some other woman, who apparently is the most beautiful, richest, and smartest woman in the world, and the two of them have a perfect life.

Emily decided to keep those thoughts to herself. "No, I don't have a boyfriend," she said quietly. She gazed straight ahead, avoiding Alexander's eyes.

Isabella continued without drawing a breath, "Do you have any brothers and sisters?"

Before she could answer, he said, "Enough questions for today." He urged the children to finish their meals. "We have lots to do this afternoon."

He bought two paper cones filled with gingerbread almonds— roasted salty nuts rolled in sweet cloves, cinnamon, nutmeg, and ginger—to share with her and the children, and they talked, laughed, and munched as they made their way back to the palace to drop off their packages.

He went to the barn, took two red sleds from a storage room, and the four of them, plus Stefan, walked to Palace Hill outside the castle gates. Today, the hill was covered with children and adults wearing bright scarves and mittens, sailing down the snowy hillside in a blur of color.

"It's like a box of paints." Emily laughed. "A supersonic box of paints."

"It is, and in the summer, it's even prettier. This hill is covered with wildflowers—every color you can imagine."

"Papa, let's go." Lukas was impatient. He dragged one sled uphill. Isabella, Stefan, and Emily followed with the prince towing the second sled, then they took turns hurtling to the bottom, scrambling back up, swooping down again.

"Girls against boys," Isabella declared at one point. She and Emily raced against Alexander and Lukas, while Stefan loped and barked behind them. At times, Stefan squeezed onto the sled with the "boys," his white ears flapping in the wind, his pink tongue drooping out of one side of his mouth.

Emily loved going fast—speeding along, the cold air stinging her cheeks and the bright sun warming her face. She loved the smell of fresh snow and evergreens, the bursts of color as they rushed past other sledders. Stefan's jubilant bark, Isabella and Lukas's frenzied giggles, and Alexander's deep, hearty laugh filled her ears—and filled her heart.

After Emily took a spill, fell off the sled, and rolled partway down the hill, she decided to take a break. Alexander and the children worried she was hurt, but she was only embarrassed at her clumsiness.

At the bottom of the hill, she gathered with the other spectators, cheering the sledders and shouting. "Faster, faster!" Emily loudly encouraged her "team" as they laughed and barked its way down the hill. Sometimes Alexander rode with Isabella, sometimes with Lukas, sometimes the children rode together, sometimes Stefan rode with them on the sled, other times he chased behind.

At one point, Alexander stood upright on the sled, balancing as if he was riding a surfboard, and "wiped out" at the bottom of the hill. The children applauded, their faces shining with delight. Each time they dragged the sled up the hill, they waved to Emily. She took pictures with her phone and promised herself she'd share them with Alexander and the children, but she also wanted to save the memories of today for herself.

As the afternoon slipped away, the temperatures grew cooler. When Alexander, the children, and Stefan came to find Emily, they were out of breath, their cheeks flushed.

"That was super fun!" Lukas exclaimed. "Sledding makes me hungry."

Alexander laughed as he tousled Lukas's dark curly hair. "What doesn't make you hungry?"

Emily assumed their adventure day was done as they walked back to the palace, but her eyes widened as they entered the palace gates. A white horse with a gray mane and tail stood by the front doors, harnessed, ready to pull a red sleigh. The horse shook his head, and the bells on his harness jingled.

She stroked his forehead. "What a handsome boy. I think I saw you the first day I was here. You were with Alexander in the courtyard."

"I'm sure that was us," He patted the horse's flank. "He and I have lots of good conversations, don't we, boy? Today, he'll take us into the forest to collect our pine cones."

"Like Saint Angelina did," Isabella said.

"We won't go far," he assured Emily. "It will be dark soon, so we'll stay close to home, but there's a special place in Marisol I'd like you to see."

Isabella and Lukas scampered onto the rear bench of the sleigh, with Stefan in the middle. Alexander tucked red and green wool blankets around the children's legs, then helped Emily into the front seat, climbed in beside her, and gently flicked the reins.

Silence. Only silence. She was hypnotized by the stillness. No traffic noises, no car horns, no sirens, no pedestrians screaming into their cellphones or shouting at each other on the street. Not today. The peace was broken only by the children chatting with Stefan, the bells jingling on the horse's harness, the horse's hooves padding through the snow. Gentle and light, like leaves rustling in a breeze. She tried to memorize her mood. *This is what contentment feels like.*

Alexander guided the sleigh through a small meadow blanketed with fresh morning snow, fine and soft, like sifted sugar. The rugged mountains covered with vast evergreen forests—waves of green, dusted with white—made Emily feel small, like a child safe in an embrace.

They stopped near a cluster of pines. Snow hugged the gray tree trunks and lay in huge mounds on the pine limbs, the boughs dipping gracefully toward the ground. The sound of the wind whispered through the forest. Then the quiet shattered as the children and Stefan jumped from the sleigh, squealing with anticipation.

Alexander helped Lukas and Isabella get their wicker baskets to collect pine cones. He adjusted scarves, hats, and mittens. "Run along. Don't go too far. Stay where I can see you."

They dashed away, leaving Alexander and Emily alone. *Just us two.*

"Come with me," he said. "There's something I want you to see."

He led her through the trees to a small wooden bridge that spanned a creek. The clear water, which she imagined danced fiercely over rocks and moss most of the year, was now reduced to an icy trickling stream. The two of them stood on the bridge, opposite the clearing where the children ran, chattering as they searched for fallen pine cones. A few seconds before, the silence surrounding Alexander and Emily was soothing. Now, the silence between the two of them felt awkward.

She and Alexander exchanged nervous smiles.

She spoked first. "The children are having so much fun."

He rested his elbows on the railing. He looked toward the children and concentrated on the stream below. "Yes, they are. But my question is: Are you? Are you having fun?"

She stood with her back against the railing, her gaze fixed on the distant snowy mountain peaks. For an instant, she considered acting nonchalant, shrugging, replying, "sure" because one life lesson she learned was that you take a giant risk when confessing your true feelings. But she ignored what she'd learned and declared what was in her heart.

"This has been one of the best days of my life." The words tumbled out. "Really. It has been one of the best days ever. It's been so long since I had a day like this. I wondered if I was permanently mired in a bleak place, whether I was even capable of enjoying myself anymore, but I found out I am, I can.

"I work too much, too hard." She spoke faster, her voice rising with excitement and nervousness. "I never get much time off, and if I do, it's a few hours here and there. And I'm tired, incredibly tired. I used to love my job. Now my job rules my life. I don't like it. I want it to stop. My life is way out of balance.

"I planned to take three weeks off this month and go home for Christmas, then I had to do this assignment and cover the dog show. I was sure my holiday was ruined. But you and the children and Stefan—meeting all of you—it's been wonderful. I never imagined such a special time in this wondrous place. The children are amazing, and Stefan is so funny, and you..."

Take a deep breath. Too much information shared with a man who asked one polite question.

"Sorry," she said. "That was a long answer to your question. Yes, I am having fun."

"A long but a thorough answer." He turned toward Emily, who was too nervous to meet his gaze. "It *has* been wonderful."

Her cheeks warmed. *Why am I so nervous?* She changed the subject. "How old is Stefan?"

"He acts like a puppy, but he's actually an adult dog, four years old. He's lived with us since my wife died."

She faced Alexander for the first time since they'd stood on the bridge. "I'm sorry about your wife."

"Thank you. Her death was the most difficult time of my life. I didn't know how I would cope. Of course, I worried more about the children. Isabella was only four years old. She had been a talkative, outgoing little girl, but her personality changed overnight. She totally shut down, built a wall. She didn't cry much—at least not in front of me—but she lost interest in everything. Before my wife died, there was no trip Isabella wouldn't take, no place she wouldn't go, no activity she didn't want to try—water skiing, ballet, science club, children's choir. She once asked if she could fly to school in a helicopter.

"After Clara's accident, Isabella didn't want to leave her room. We used to have big sleepovers at the palace with her little friends—movie nights with popcorn—I learned every word to every song in

Frozen—but she didn't want those anymore. She liked to go with me to the barns to feed the horses. She didn't care about that. She loved the beach. I used to tease her she was part dolphin. She would have lived in the water if she could. After her mother died, we'd go to the beach, and Isabella would sit on the shore. She wouldn't talk or smile or laugh or play. Instead, she'd just stare at the water. If I talked to her, she wouldn't answer.

"With Lukas, the reaction was different. He was two and a half, and he cried *all* the time. I could never comfort him. He didn't want to eat, and as you've seen, he's a boy with an appetite. He had been shy and quiet—Isabella talked enough for both of them—but he became aggressive. He shoved another boy at pre-school. He'd never done that before. The other boy got fourteen stitches in his forehead. Fourteen. I still remember that number.

"Every day, the situation with Lukas got worse. He liked to ride the tram to the mountains. I remember one day I tried to get him on the tram, thinking it would cheer him up. That turned out to be a terrible idea. He had a complete meltdown. He'd been fascinated by boats—his first word was 'boat'—and I'd try to take him sailing, and he'd get as far as the edge of the dock, then sob to stay home.

"My parents tried to help. They were incredibly kind and patient, but we were so lost. I worried I wasn't a good father. I was at the point where I pretended every minute of every day. Pretending to be cheerful so the children wouldn't know how devastated I was. Pretending to cope so my parents wouldn't worry about me. Pretending I enjoyed my job. I was living in a nightmare, and I was exhausted from bluffing my way through.

"Then entered Stefan." Alexander smiled. "We adopted him the first Christmas after my wife died. I couldn't imagine how we were going to get through the holidays that year. I forced the children—and myself—to go to the Christmas market. None of us had any interest in the holidays, but I tried to keep up some kind of routine for Lukas and Isabella.

"They weren't excited about the food, or the toys, or the decorations. But there was a man from Sonola, a town ten miles from here, and they were keen to talk to him. He had a basket with three puppies, and he said he found them in his barn. He suspected someone abandoned the dogs but left them in the barn so they'd be safe and warm.

"The children were instantly—what's the word?—smitten. They begged and begged for a puppy, but they didn't need to beg because I knew I'd take at least one. Of course, the children wanted all three. I did go back later to ask about the other two. The man told me they had been adopted by a couple who lived on a farm in the mountains, who had two small children as well.

"We took Stefan home, and none of us slept. We played all night long. I remember looking out the window and seeing the sun come up. The time flew by. Lukas didn't cry himself to sleep that night, and when Isabella finally drifted off, she woke up a few hours later and immediately asked for Stefan—the first thing she'd shown interest in in months. After one night, Stefan was part of the family. I started taking Stefan with me when I went to the barn. I took him on walks. Stefan *made* me leave the palace. People talked to us, and those conversations helped me move outside myself. The people I met might not think a prince was approachable, but they knew they could approach a dog, so I started interacting with people again. One lesson I learned is sometimes, when you're troubled, if you focus on others, that can help you, too. Does that make sense?" Alexander stopped. "I guess I gave you a long answer to your question too."

"A thorough answer," she said with a smile. "Was Stefan your first dog?"

"Oh, no, we had dogs when I was a child. My wife and I planned to adopt a dog after the children came. We never got around to it. I was always waiting for the perfect time. I like to say, 'I was between dogs' before we got Stefan."

Emily's nerves got the best of her. She began to babble. "Once I wrote a story about a sheriff in Texas who opened a ranch for homeless dogs. He said—I remember this quote— 'I haven't always had dogs, but when I have, the quality of my life has been greatly enhanced.'"

"Stefan has certainly enhanced the quality of our lives," Alexander said. "He didn't make our grief go away, but he helped us find some joy again. As I said at lunch, sometimes we rescue them. Sometimes they rescue us. Stefan was a rescue dog, and he definitely rescued us."

Emily continued to babble. "I wrote another article about a study in Germany that showed people with pets are healthier than those without. The researchers wondered if owners were healthier *before* they got their pets. In this study, they controlled for factors associated with health, and scientists found the pet owners made fewer visits to doctors than non-owners."

"And I wrote another story about veterans returning from combat and how service dogs can help them—the dogs offer emotional support and give the vet someone to care for. Some studies show dogs can help people who've undergone any kind of trauma."

What's wrong with me? Why can't I stop talking?

"I read those stories. In the 'Rx: Dogs' column, correct?" Alexander said.

"You read those stories?" she asked.

"I told you the first day at the Seaside Center I was a Bow-Wow fan," he replied. "I was familiar with the site before I met you, but if my photographic work was going to appear with your blog, I wanted to make sure I was working for a quality publication." He winked.

"I'm still embarrassed about that meeting." She grimaced. "I should have asked if you were the photographer, not strong-armed you into a job."

"I meet a lot of people through my work," Alexander joked. "Believe me when I say that meeting you was the most interesting first encounter I've ever had."

"I'm not sure that's a compliment." Emily frowned. "When we were at the market this morning, I watched you meeting people, interacting with them. You were so relaxed. They talk with you, and you talk to them as if you're friends."

"Most are my friends. It's a small country, and I grew up here. I went to school here. I went to university here before I went off to do some special studies in other countries. Now I'm back for good."

"You said at the press conference you were a veterinarian."

"Yes. I studied veterinary medicine at university. I wasn't naïve enough to think I could do that work full-time. I understood my life's work was determined for me centuries ago, and my job would involve helping people. But I loved animals so much, especially dogs, and I wanted a job that would allow me to help them, too, so that's why I became a veterinarian. Obviously, I have lots of responsibilities with public service, but I try to work with our animals when I can. We have a stable with horses. We have farmland with sheep and cattle."

"Papa!" Isabella called. She lifted a basket of pine cones.

Alexander waved back and called, "Awesome work."

He pointed to Stefan romping with the children, then sighed. "I once wondered if Stefan might be good at herding, but no. Stefan is good at playing. He excels at it. I suppose we should all excel at playing, shouldn't we?"

She looked away. Playing was not an activity she had mastered.

"You've said you're not happy with your job," Alexander said.

"I consider myself a writer, but more and more, I'm a manager. I don't enjoy it. My business partner, Sebastian, loves planning new projects. He's a real entrepreneur. His mind never shuts off. He's restless—in a good way. Every day, he blazes a new frontier.

"When we started the business, we only wanted to connect with local dog owners. We ran Bow-Wow for fun—something we did on the side in addition to our regular jobs. We never imagined it would become full-time work, much less an international business.

"Early on, the work was simple. Sebastian generated ideas. I put them into words. Now, we have a staff of sixty-five full-time people, plus freelancers and part-time workers. I don't write as much I used to, and I miss it. That's what this trip was supposed to be. He wanted the trip to be a surprise, a way to give me a chance to write full-time."

"But the timing was wrong," Alexander observed.

"I won't be able to get home for Christmas. I know I'm being foolish. I can take time off later. I can visit my family another time."

"Christmas can be lonely when your loved ones aren't closed by. I've been away from home at Christmas. I do understand."

"Please don't think I'm not grateful to be here. The RICI is such an important event in the dog world. I'm pleased to have a chance to cover it, to come to Marisol. It is a fascinating country."

"We're the land where the sea kisses the sky," Alexander reminded her.

"Yes, I heard that slogan many times, but the scenery is more spectacular than I imagined. The photos don't do it justice."

"Did you also hear the saying that 'everyone falls in love in Marisol?'"

Her cheeks warmed again, but she didn't answer.

"The summer is the best time to be here, in my opinion," he continued. "The seas are the most amazing color—they change from blue to green to blue. The sand sparkles—the locals call it 'diamond white.' I take the children out on the boat to relax. Sometimes we see dolphins leaping through the water. It's peaceful on the sea. Come. I want to show you something."

"We're not going out to sea now, are we?" she teased.

Alexander shook his head. He held out his gloved hand. "We'll be able to keep an eye on the children." He called to them. "Isabella! Lukas! I'm climbing to the top of the hill with Emily. Stay where you are."

Lukas called back. "Yes, Papa!" He pointed to his basket of pine cones, and his face beamed with pride. "I got more than Isabella."

At that point, Stefan stole a pine cone from Lukas's basket and tossed it like a ball.

"Maybe not." Alexander laughed. "Remember, it's not a contest."

He was still stretching out his hand to Emily. She placed her hand in his, and they walked, their breath coming in frosty puffs.

"Here," he said, as he led her to the top of the small hill. "I wanted to show you this."

There, in the misty distance, through the milky winter sunlight, was the seven-story waterfall she'd seen during her internet search on the plane, the water frozen in a wide silver lace ribbon cascading over the cliffs. She gasped and put her hands to her mouth.

"Pearl Moon Falls," he said.

A flock of snow geese flew above them, calling from the sky. Their white feathers glistened in the last rays of light as the sun slipped behind the mountains. Their wings rustled like silk.

"I love that sound," she said, hugging herself. "I imagine it's what angel wings sound like."

He pointed to the right then put his fingertips on her waist to guide her. "Look there."

A herd of a dozen elk grazed in the distance, near the falls, their golden brown coats shining, their heads bowed as they searched for grass.

Such spectacular sights—if only she had been able to concentrate. The warmth of Alexander's gentle touch distracted her. He kept his hand on her waist, and they were silent for a few seconds. She wanted to speak, to say something, but what could she say? *My heart is reeling, just so you know.*

"Papa!" Isabella called.

"Coming." Alexander waved. "We should get back," he said to Emily. "The sun's going down."

He held out his hand again. Emily wrapped her fingers around his and didn't let go. The snow crunched under their boots (Jenine found Emily a pair), and the two made their way down the hill in what she decided was the most blissful moment of her life.

When they reached the bottom, they found the children hurling snowballs at each other.

"It's a shame we have to go," she said. "Children can make anything fun."

"Yes, they can, but one nice thing about being an adult is you can slide back in time—you can act like a child anytime you want." He scooped up a handful of snow and packed it between his hands.

He tossed the snowball at the children, who were delighted their father was now part of the game. They pelted him with snowballs. He clutched his heart and pretended to collapse on the ground until Stefan licked him the face to "revive" him.

He scrambled to his feet, brushed the snow from his jacket. "Are you up for this?" he asked Emily. Then he tossed a snowball squarely at her. It landed with a splat on the front of her coat.

"Up for this? I've got a great pitching arm from tossing balls to Gracie. You better hope you can run fast enough to get away from me." She made a snowball of her own and hit him in the back.

The children shrieked with excitement. Stefan jumped in the air and barked, and what ensued was a storm of white, as snowballs flew fast and furious.

Isabella collapsed first, giggling as Stefan licked her face. Emily and the other two crumpled on the ground in a heap, her laughter mixing with theirs and echoing across the mountains. They ended the snowball fight by making angels in the snow—Stefan wriggled and rolled too, to create his own special dog angel.

Alexander jumped to his feet, extended his hand to help Emily, then lifted Isabella and Lukas.

"That as the epic-ist snowball fight ever," Lukas declared. "We made snowballs as big as hamburgers."

Everyone brushed away snow, straightened their coats, adjusted their scarves and gloves. Alexander pointed to the sky. The sun was gone, and the sky was streaked with blue-gray, rose, and lavender.

"The gloaming," he said.

Twilight. Not quite day. Not quite night. The beautiful in-between time. From busy to restful. That's where Emily was: in-between. Her life had been frantic and was now calm, but she sensed this peace was the middle, a transition, but she couldn't imagine—*a transition to what?*

The children gathered their baskets, filled to the brim with pine cones, and scrambled into the sleigh. Alexander poured them cups of hot chocolate from a thermos, then wrapped blankets around their legs, as Stefan scarfed down a treat. Alexander helped Emily into the seat beside him and pulled a blanket over her lap.

"Let's go home, Marshmallow." He tapped the reins.

"I named him," Isabella called proudly from the backseat.

"It's a perfect name," Emily told her.

"I thought so. It's perfectly perfect," Isabella said.

Emily looped her red scarf around her neck. She shoved her hands deep inside her coat pockets to keep warm. The children laughed in the seat behind her as they told Stefan plans for tomorrow's Christmas adventure. The dog panted, recovering from the romp in the snow. The bells on Marshmallow's harness jangled as he trotted along, his hooves making "woshhhing" sounds in the snow. A few snowflakes fell gently, clinging to her face, chilling her. She tucked the blanket tighter around her legs.

Warmth spread through her body, not because of the blanket, but because of Alexander's smile as he glanced at her from time to time. She smiled back. A genuinely happy smile. A smile that said, "I am delighted to be here with you." A smile for a perfectly perfect day.

As they approached the palace, the lights gleamed from the windows, and the golden glow from inside illuminated the green wreaths and red bows. When the sleigh came to a stop by the huge oak doors of the palace and everyone exited the sleigh, Emily rubbed Marshmallow's nose, patted Stefan on the head, then said goodnight to Alexander and the children. She floated back to her room. *Today was like a dream. A wonderful dream.*

The dream quickly melted away when she sat at her desk to check phone messages. Sebastian texted a half dozen times.

Where R U?

What R U doing?

Are you writing something?

R U okay?

Worried. 😞

Did you get my other five texts?

She texted back.

Back in my room now. Resting. Not writing today. I'm fine. Back at work tomorrow. Needed a day off.

Emily answered a few more work emails, ordered her dinner (tonight, the kitchen served roast chicken with dumplings). When she called Georgia, she learned Gracie had chased pigeons with Harper and Jack in the park then taken an extra-long nap. Next, Emily called her parents. When they asked about her day, she replied, "Oh, you know, a regular day."

She didn't tell them about the fresh smells of the Christmas market, the exhilaration of sledding downhill, the serenity of the sleigh ride to the snow-covered meadow. She didn't recount the wonder of geese that flew overhead or the delight of watching the elk graze. She didn't tell them about the snow globe or the legend of Saint Angelina and Nikolaj. She definitely didn't mention Alexander held her hand. How could she blithely recite the day's events without sharing the bewildering emotions attached to those events? How could she describe feelings she didn't quite understand herself?

Emily glanced at the clock. Nearly 11. She didn't want to fall asleep because she didn't want the day to end. Her body was in the palace; her spirit lingered in the snow-covered forest with Alexander.

She brewed a cup of peppermint tea, curled up in the window seat, and pulled her knees into her chest. The cashmere throw around her shoulders, she rested her head against the window. The almost-full moon shone, casting silvery-blue shadows on the snow-covered ground.

So peaceful.

The snow globe the children had given her was within arm's reach. When she shook it, the tiny white flakes flew around Saint Angelina and Nicholaj. *What a sweet gift. The children are incredibly kind. And Alexander. He's gentle with Isabella, Lukas, and Stefan. So playful, funny. And his smile. That smile. Like sunlight.*

Then an idea flickered across her mind. It startled her, disrupting the calm, like distant thunder echoing across a canyon. She sat straight up, almost dropping the snow globe.

If Alexander were an ordinary man, not a prince, if she met him under any other circumstances, not the fiasco when she mistook him for her helper, if she had a less-demanding job, not a job that required every ounce of emotional and physical energy, and if she had the courage to take a chance—if all those ifs were true, she might *care* for him. Perhaps care deeply. Perhaps…love?

She pushed the idea aside. *How silly. He has his life. I have mine. We enjoyed each other's company today, but we have nothing in common. And I'm going home in a few days. Home. Alone.*

Sleep. That would be the best remedy for her unsettled feelings. As she lay in bed, staring at the ceiling fresco painted to look like seagulls gliding through the sky, she planned her work schedule for the next day, tallied her chores. But her mind drifted back to the Christmas market, Palace Hill, the herd of elk at sunset, and Alexander's smile.

Today began as an ordinary day, but it became something quite extraordinary.

Chapter Eight
Midnight

The next morning, Emily was stuffing her computer into her satchel when she heard *tap, tap, tap.* "Come in," she called.

The children, perhaps Alexander, had come visiting but whoever was on the other side of the door, Stefan would be with them. Today, all four came. Stefan jumped on the bed, and the children sat with him, while Alexander stood beside Emily as she continued to pack.

"Good morning," he said. "We wanted to say hello, to tell you what a good time we had yesterday, right, children?"

"The day was glorious," Isabella proclaimed, stretching her arms as far as they would go.

"The day was glorious for me too." Emily laughed, mimicking Isabella's gesture. Breathless with crimson cheeks, Emily turned to Alexander. "A lot to do today."

Tonight would be the first night of the Royal International Canine Invitational best of show program, and she was preparing for a long day that would stretch into evening. She'd gotten up early to compile a lengthy to-do list, followed by a fair amount of handwringing and lip biting as she wondered how she'd accomplish all the observing, interviewing, and writing. The morning was further derailed by a fifteen-minute search for her glasses, which ended when she walked by a mirror and realized they were perched on her nose. Her breakfast of coconut crepes and maple cream sat untouched, and the coffee was now cold.

Anxious, overwhelmed, discombobulated. How would she manage her workload? But, more important, how would she manage her feelings for Alexander, the most attractive man on the planet, who was now standing so close she could see tiny golden flecks in his dark eyes? How would she reel in her emotions? How would she keep from swooning if he came one step closer? How...

Lukas brought her back to the present. "I get to stay up late with the grown-ups," he told her.

"Cool!" Emily said, stepping away from the prince and giving Lukas a fist-bump.

"I get to wear my princess dress," Isabella said.

"I bet it's pretty." She tapped Isabella playfully on the nose.

"It is! It's pink and white and comes down to here." Isabella pointed to her ankles.

"What is your day like?" Emily asked Alexander. "Are you as excited as the children?"

"I have to work on my speech for the welcome tonight. I'll spend the day at the Seaside Center, then come back here to collect these three and my parents for this evening's events."

"Long day for you," she said as she searched for her computer charger.

"Yes." He paused, shuffled from side to side, whistled under his breath.

She now realized the charger was in her hand then looked at Alexander. "How are you feeling? You seem a little uneasy."

"I realize it will be a full day for you...for me...for us...but...would you have time...if you're not too busy...if you have some free time...Would you like to meet for tea this afternoon? At the Seaside Center around—"

"I'd love to." She didn't wait for him to finish the sentence. The anticipation in her voice was evident. *Why am I so...obvious?*

Since childhood, she had worked diligently to keep her feelings in check. She took immense pride in her public image of cool, calm, and collected even when inside she felt she might fly apart. But that façade shattered the day before she left New York. The wave of red hot anger when she read the text about Matt's art exhibit. The disastrous interview with Rae Zaya that left Emily a tearful wreck. The emotional scene in the restaurant with Sebastian when he told her she was on her way to Marisol.

Now, there with Alexander, she struggled to maintain even the smallest measure of composure. She felt unsteady. Yet, this was a thrilling kind of uneasiness—a feeling anything could happen, a feeling something spectacular was coming her way.

"It's a date," he said as he helped her on with her coat.

A date. I like that.

"There's a restaurant in the Seaside Center," he said. "It can be crowded in the afternoon on Best of Show days. I'll call and ask them to reserve a table—maybe one by the window so we can enjoy the sun if it peeks out later."

"Sounds wonderful!" She was certain she sounded eager.

"Meet you at 4?"

"I'll be there," she said, grateful she repressed her urge to turn a cartwheel.

~ * ~

When Emily arrived at the restaurant, Café Délicieux, (French for delicious), Alexander was sitting at a table by the window, as he'd promised. He waved, and she tried to walk nonchalantly across the room, but her brisk pace made her enthusiasm for their meeting transparent.

He pulled out her chair. "I'm glad you could join me."

"The sun did shine after all. What a spectacular view—the light sparkling on the water."

"I love the sea," he said. "Do you?"

"I grew up in the mountains. I've never spent much time at the beach, just a few vacations here and there. After visiting Marisol, I understand why the taxi driver told me everyone falls in love in Marisol. The ocean is beautiful."

"It's constant but mysterious. It looks peaceful, but it can be exhilarating. So many secrets under the beauty of its surface. So much to discover. So much to learn if one has a lifetime to explore." Alexander's voice deepened, his eyes narrowed.

Her cheeks caught fire. She suspected they were not *really* talking about the ocean anymore.

She held a menu to hide her face and changed the subject. "What looks good to you?"

He ordered hot tea, scones with currants, and clotted cream, and they discussed their workdays. No more conversations about exhilaration and mystery, simply recounting events. She told him she'd spent the morning interviewing the night's Best of Show competitors.

He reported that he'd polished his speech and helped Isabella and Lukas make Christmas cookies. "We saved you some. Let me warn you the children decorated them, so they're a somewhat abstract representation of Christmas."

"I like abstract art." She laughed. *I don't like Matt Thoms and the fact he stole my dog for his garish paintings, but I like abstract art.*

"Do you like to bake?" he asked.

"I do. Baking—really, any type of cooking—relaxes me, but I don't have much time to spend in the kitchen."

"Cooking is one of my favorite hobbies."

"You cook?" She lifted a brow.

"Now and then. When I was a child, I was always visiting the kitchen because I was like Lukas—I could never get enough to eat. Also, there was a big brick fireplace there. The kitchen was the warmest, most restful place in the palace. I remember coming home from school, and that was my first stop. My grandmother and my mother would meet me, and we'd have a snack. That's such a happy memory."

"You became interested in cooking because you like to eat?" she teased.

"Partly. My mother got sick when I was ten years old. She had appendicitis, and the doctors performed an emergency surgery—pretty serious at the time. I was insistent my mother needed a get well present. My father told me what my mother needed was rest, that I shouldn't cause a ruckus around the palace. I was always into mischief—there were quite a few broken bones and trips to physician's offices. My father ordered me not to pester my mother and to find a quiet activity while she recovered. I decided to bake her a get well cake. Cake made me happy, so I reasoned it would make my mother happy too.

"I'd watched the cooks bake cakes, and I was sure I could manage it. I snuck into the kitchen—I waited till no one was there preparing a meal—and I made a disaster of a cake. When the cooks found me, I was covered in flour. There were broken eggs on the floor, cake batter spilled in the oven. I was only alone for fifteen minutes, but I created a culinary catastrophe in quick order.

"Even though I made a gargantuan mess, I enjoyed it. I begged my parents, and they let me take some cooking classes when I got older. I still enjoy puttering around in the kitchen. At least twice a year, I bake cookies for the children's school."

"I'm amazed you do this," Emily said. "You have someone to wait on you, to do any chore you want for you. I would never imagine a prince doing anything so…"

"Normal?"

She nodded.

"Emily, I inherited this job, and it can be overwhelming at times. People treat you as if you're someone special, not as another human being, struggling along, trying to make sense out of life. It can turn your head if you believe what people say. You think you're more important than you are. I want—I have—to stay tethered to the real world. How can I do my job if I don't understand what life is like for people I serve?"

"Your life will never be ordinary."

"No, but it can be extraordinary. I want to live the best life I can, to give the children the most love I can. To me, that means giving them as normal an upbringing as possible. I love my children, but I love them no more or less than any other parent. We parents all want the same thing, for our children to be happy and healthy. I see that wherever I travel. It doesn't matter if you live in a tent or a mansion. If I'm a good parent, my children will have an extraordinary life, I'm certain of it, and I will have an extraordinary life as well because I took care of the people I loved."

He took a sip of his tea. "Now, I've told you a funny story about my childhood. Tell me one about you."

"Hmmm." She thought for a moment. "There are dozens to choose from, but I'll limit it to early childhood. Once I played a sheep in the church Christmas play. All I had to do was pretend to sleep peacefully by the manger, but I really got into the role. I didn't just pretend to be asleep. I fell asleep—fast asleep. I was so relaxed, I tumbled off the stage. In my defense, I was only four."

His face contorted with laughter. He wiped away a tear.

"The story isn't that funny," she said flatly.

"Yes, it is. Besides, it shows me we have a lot in common. Neither of us was well-behaved when we were children. I wish I'd known you then." His voice was wistful, as if he was dreaming of their childhood adventures.

Taken aback, she pretended to study the crumbs on her plate. Was this the time to admit she dreamed the same thing?

He glanced at his watch. "I hate to cut this short…"

Saved. "No apologies necessary. I need to get back to work."

"This has been a most pleasant interruption in a busy workday." His words were polite and formal, but his tone was one of delight. "I understand you have work to do and you're incredibly busy, and I hope this isn't too presumptuous and feel free to say no because it may put too many demands on you, but tomorrow? Same time, same place?"

"I'll make time." *Did that sound too eager?*

"Good," he said with a broad smile. "It's a second date." He pulled her chair out and helped her gather her belongings.

She was certain her feet never touched the ground as she left the restaurant.

Pull yourself together.

Fifteen minutes later, she stood in the middle of the grooming area, closed her eyes, took a few deep breaths. *Focus on the dog show. Stop thinking about the prince. There's work to do, and soaring on a cloud won't get the job done.* Emily opened her eyes, squared her shoulders, and mustered all the strength she had. *Stay grounded in reality. You can do this.*

The grooming area was now a familiar space, and Emily wandered from table to table, interviewing owners in the hound, pastoral, working, and toy groups, snapping photos, and asking her now-favorite question, "What makes your dog a champion?"

She wrote two short blog entries before the evening competition began. One focused on Romeo, a border collie from New Zealand, who liked to fly in his owner's small private plane when they traveled from one farm to another. Romeo had his own goggles, which made for a cute picture.

She also wrote about Daisy, a pug from Canada, who enjoyed rides on the streetcars of Toronto, and posted a picture of Daisy sitting in her owner's lap as they traveled along the Queen route, from Neville Park to Long Branch.

And the entire time she wrote, Emily dreamed about Alexander.

~ * ~

The first night of the championship, the Seaside Center arena was packed with dog lovers from Marisol and around the world. Sitting shoulder to shoulder, people from the top echelons of the dog-lover world chattered eagerly, waiting for the program to begin. Most wore the lapel buttons sold outside the Seaside Center: "Pause for Paws." "You had me at woof." "Dogs=Love."

Emily sat in the press section, talking and laughing with the other reporters, silently reminding herself she was there for one reason: to cover the competition, not to nurture her infatuation with Alexander.

When the prince stepped into the blue-white spotlight at the center of the ring, Stefan trotting beside him, her wild heart turned a somersault.

"Good evening and welcome," he said told the audience. "Tonight we celebrate dogs. And we celebrate the people who love them."

The enthusiastic crowd applauded.

"Dogs are wonderful companions. They are hard workers, helping us on our farms and in our offices. They listen to us in our homes, when we need a friend to talk with, and they keep our secrets. They lift our spirits when we're sad. They nurse us through our illnesses, staying by our sides, and reminding us they will care for us, they are loyal. They are good playmates, and they remind us it's important to have fun, and it is good to be joyous every day."

He turned his face slightly to the left, and his eyes met Emily's. Her minded raced back to their snowball fight, their walk to Pearl Moon falls, the electric sensation when he held her hand. Her heart thumped, thumped, thumped so loudly she wondered if the reporters sitting next to her could hear.

"In a few moments," he continued, "we will meet some wonderful dogs as they compete in this program. Tomorrow night, I will present an award to the dog who is judged best in show, and I will be honored to do that.

"Soon, we will have a new RICI champion. However, I hope we can all agree the dog sitting next to us on the sofa, or the dog snoring at the foot of our bed, or the dog resting his head on our knee as we watch this program on our televisions—that dog is our champion."

The audience roared, and when Stefan jumped and barked as he and Alexander left the arena, the applause was deafening. The show was underway.

Emily dutifully reported on the winners in each category—the hound, pastoral, working, and toy groups. She took copious notes about the dogs' behavior, the handlers' skills, the crowd's reactions to each dog when it pranced, ran, padded, or strutted around the ring.

In the minutes after one group of dogs left the arena and before the next group entered, she turned her gaze toward the royal box. During the first break, Alexander chatted and laughed with visitors. Isabella practiced her ballet poses behind him when she was bored with sitting still, and Lukas, who had been thrilled at the prospects of staying up late with the grown-ups, fell asleep in Alexander's lap as the evening wore on. The other reporters used those breaks to check emails, to buy refreshments, to make phone calls. They seemed oblivious to the activities in the royal box. *How can they not be fascinated by him?*

During the second break, Alexander joked with his parents, the same way she did with hers. The king and queen whispered to each other, the same intimacy she observed in her own parents' interactions as they sat across from her at the kitchen table. At one point, the queen's face grew somber, and the king kissed her hand, the way her dad comforted her mom. Stefan slept on his back, with his feet in the air, the way Gracie did at home.

Then lightning struck. Emily sat motionless in her chair. *It is possible? Do Alexander and I have more in common than I realized?*

She shifted in her chair. Nothing in Marisol was going the way she planned. This was supposed to be a miserable trip, not an adventure that made her eager to wake up each morning. Covering the RICI was exhausting but, at the same time, writing full-time sparked a creative fire in her, something that gave her energy, inspired her to work without fatigue. The solitude and disappointment she brought with her from New York had vanished, replaced now by the much-anticipated daily visits with the children, Stefan, and Alexander. Companionship, and joy, and the quiet promise that each day would more amazing than the next overtook the dread she once felt.

How can I ever go back to my ordinary life?

"Ladies and gentlemen, let's welcome the working group to the ring," the announcer's voice boomed through the arena.

Emily opened her notebook and picked up her pen.

"I can't wait to see what happens next," one of the reporters whispered to her.

"Me neither," she replied. She suspected they weren't talking about the same thing.

~ * ~

On the last day of the competition, Emily was getting ready to leave for the Seaside Center when a cream-colored envelope slid under her door. *An invitation?* The excitement affected her coordination; her fingers fumbled to tear open the top fold.

Inside she found a card, trimmed in turquoise blue, with a large gold script "A" at the top. "Late supper tonight?"

She closed her eyes as she clutched the note to her heart.

Yes, yes, yes!

Time alone with Alexander. She glanced at her watch and calculated the hours till their dinner.

As she rode to the Seaside Center, texting Sebastian her story plans for the day, she warned herself to temper excitement with realism. Her heart had become unruly, but her brain kept wondering: How does this end?

The prince, the children, Stefan made this trip amazing. Yet, in forty-eight short hours, she would leave Marisol. She needed to grab hold of some perspective. This trip to Marisol was a surprise, a pleasant interlude in a hectic work trip, nothing more.

These feelings have to stop.

But I don't want them to stop.

She joined Alexander again for tea at Délicieux, and the two shared details of their work.

The previous night's winners had talked eagerly with Emily about their preparations for tonight's Best of Show competition, and that night's contestants explained how they were preparing. Georgia had sent a picture of Gracie, Harper, and Jack lying in front of the TV watching *A Muppets' Christmas.*

Alexander had met with last night's winners, handlers, and owners, posed for photographs, then talked with the palace staff about last minute planning for the Fetch! Play Ball and the Holly and Ivy gala the following day. Stefan had knocked down a Christmas tree in the third-floor hallway while playing a game of tag with Isabella and Lukas. "When I asked what happened, Isabella said, 'Things just got out of control. You know how it gets at Christmas.'"

Emily laughed until she remembered something her mother told her years ago: "Details are the building blocks of intimacy in a relationship."

Are we in a relationship?

"You seem distracted," Alexander observed.

"Hmmm? I was thinking…"

"About tonight? Dinner?" His voice was excited. "You won't forget?"

"I won't."

As if I could. It would be like forgetting to breathe.

~ * ~

Emily spent her afternoon in the grooming area, the now familiar commotion of dogs barking, scissors snipping, and hairdryers humming in the background as she interviewed owners and handlers about preparations for the big night.

Once she had the materials she needed, she found a quiet space to write. She didn't go to the press room, which was cheerful but noisy, filled with reporters trying to meet deadlines and writers trying to procrastinate by striking up a conversation. Instead, she found a table and chairs by a window with an ocean view. She sorted through her photos, organized her handwritten notes, wrote her lead paragraph, then wrote her story, using her recordings to double-check quotes.

Dogs from around the world will put their best paws forward tonight as the Royal International Canine Invitational presents its Best in Show trophy.

Owners and handlers are doing all they can to keep their dogs happy and calm, from playing flute music to packing liver treats. All are anticipating a memorable evening…

Her mind drifted to her midnight supper with Alexander. *Will my evening be memorable?* She shook her head. *Back to work.*

Tonight, one special dog will go home with the coveted RICI trophy. With so much anticipation, are owners and handlers nervous?

No, they say. Some admit they're apprehensive, but all are more excited than anxious, and their dogs pick up that excitement.

"Penka is a French bulldog," explained her handler, Margarita, who hails from Sophia, Bulgaria. "They were bred to be companion dogs, very popular among lace makers in Europe. Unlike many of the dogs here, Penka isn't a working dog. She's a couch potato. Once I took her to a friend's farm, and the sheep chased her. *The breed is sweet-tempered, gentle, very chill, but Penka reads my emotions. It's up to me to keep myself positive during the competition."*

What strategies do owners use to keep their dogs calm before they enter the ring?

Marianna from Denver, Colorado, plays flute music to calm Chester, her wire fox terrier, whom she characterized as "part excitement, part exuberance, one hundred percent love wrapped in fur."

For Giancarlo from Buenos Aires, it's food that keeps Bombón, his Spinone Italiano, relaxed. Before they enter the ring, Giancarlo stuffs his pockets with freeze-dried liver treats.

The Spinone is a muscular dog, bred to stalk game, but Giancarlos says Bombón isn't a hunter.

"He's easygoing," he said as he nodded toward Bombón, who dozed on the grooming table. "My bigger challenge is how to keep that beautiful white fur clean. Bombón has never met a mud puddle he didn't like."

Owners hope they'll be going home with the champion's trophy, but they say they won't be disappointed if that doesn't happen. They're just pleased they had the opportunity to participate in the world-renowned RICI, to have the experience of competing, and to visit beautiful Marisol.

"Winning," said Ichika, the owner of Kotara, a Lhaso Apso from Nippon, Japan, "would be the icing on the cake." She added with a wink, "Or the peanut butter on the dog biscuit."

In a few hours, the best in breed winners will be in the ring awaiting the judge's decision. No nerves, only high hopes. Check the website later this evening for RICI results.

Later that evening, after the winners were announced in the sporting, non-sporting, and terrier groups, the audience murmured and chattered. In a few moments, the Best of Show winner would be crowned. The mood in the Seaside Center was jubilant, the air heavy with pleasant anticipation. One audience member told Emily, "The suspense is as thick as a Tibetan terrier's coat."

The big moment came, and the dog finalists proudly trotted around the ring, confident and boisterous, seeming to relish the spotlight and the exuberant applause from audience members. As the announcer gave the crowd unique details about each competitor, photos, provided by the owners, flashed on the Jumbotron for the eager audience to view.

The dogs made their way around the ring one last time, and the crowd fell silent. The judge studied each breed, then walked to a table on the right side of the arena to sign the champion's book and record the official winner's name. The crowd whispered as the judge came to the center of the arena. Beside her stood the vice president of the competition, who carried a blue ribbon, and the president, who held the crystal trophy. Alexander was there, too. Emily fought to pay attention to the ceremony.

"The winner of this year's competition is," the judge smiled and paused for dramatic effect, "Trella, the field spaniel."

The volcanic eruption of cheers from the crowd shattered the silence. Emily put her hands over her ears; she felt as if she was at a rock concert. The screams were loud and frenetic, and the cameras flashed like bursts of lightning. Trella raced around the ring again with her handler and owner, Mateo, and the spaniel savored the crowd's attention. When the pair got to the royal box, Mateo stopped and bowed his head. Trella put her head down, stretched her front legs out and her back end up—a bow to the king and queen that drew laughs and applause from them and the audience.

Emily bolted from the press box and started writing in the car. Once she was back in her room, she pounded the computer keys, working with the speed of light. She titled her blog post *"Trella to the Rescue"* and wrote:

And the winner is…Trella!

The rambunctious chocolate-colored field spaniel took home tonight's Best in Show award at the Royal International Canine Invitational. A crowd favorite, this happy-go-lucky dog drew cheers and a standing ovation as judges named her this year's top dog.

But long before Trella came to the competition, she was a champion to owner Mateo, who lives with her in an apartment in the historic Barrio Gotico neighborhood in Barcelona, Spain. Mateo struggled for years with depression, and he calls Trella the "medicine" that made his life easier.

"Trella," he said, "is like the rainbow. She gives me help and hope. She 'forces' me to leave my apartment, 'forces' me to meet people, to make friends. I like to call her Profesora de Felicidad, my Happiness Teacher.

"She comforted me when I was struggling. She reminded me I am loved. Now, I think it is impossible to be sad when I see those brown eyes and that wagging tail each morning. Trella will always be my champion.

"Working with her in this competition has given me a sense of purpose, a focus. I'm grateful to her. People say I take such good care of her, but she takes good care of me too."

Emily tossed in the judge's assessment of Trella's bone structure, plus comments from audience members who sported *Equipo Trella* (Team Trella) T-shirts and came from Barcelona to cheer on the hometown favorite. She promised readers a longer profile of Mateo and Trella in the coming months, then slammed her laptop shut before turning her attention to the day's most critical decision: what to wear for her date.

She had limited choices. Nonetheless, she tried on every outfit she brought, in multiple combinations, mixing and matching tops and bottoms, before settling on a gray wool pencil skirt and pale pink blouse. After brushing her hair vigorously, pulling it back into a ponytail, twisting it into a bun, she took it down. Five minutes ticked by as she searched for her lipstick only to realize she was clasping the silver tube in her hand. If only Gracie were there to help her with her fashion choices, the way she did back home.

"Tonight, I'm on my own, Gracie. I hope I look okay."

Emily closed her door, then inched her way through the wide hallway to the prince's suite, the lights glittering through the milk-glass sconces shaped like clamshells, her shoe heels clicking against the stone floor. The palace took on a mysterious nighttime personality, a stark contrast from its hustle-and-bustle daytime temperament.

No staff charging up and downstairs talking about their work, discussing where they needed to be next. No Isabella and Lukas dashing through the halls, jabbering about their day at school, searching for their father. No Stefan running at breakneck speed, skidding to a halt on the rugs. Emily felt like an intruder, someone out of place.

She tapped lightly on the huge double door, honey-colored wood with massive black hinges and handles. For a second, she hoped Alexander wouldn't answer, that she could go back to her room and forget her foolish promise to meet him alone. She remembered her earlier conversations with the dog handlers and the tricks they used to calm the dogs before they entered the arena ring. Her mind traveled in strange directions, as she wished she had a piece of freeze-dried liver or some flute music to settle her nerves. When he answered with a "hello there," warm as summer, her tensions melted away.

His suite was designed much like hers—a work area, a living room, a dining area, a bedroom—although considerably larger. *A house within a palace.* The entryway led to a spacious office with several desks, and he explained that this was where he and his assistants worked during the day. He pointed to his desk, which held a computer, tidy stand-up files, a turquoise glass paperweight, a basket of seashells. Neon-colored sticky notes papered the cherry wood credenza.

"Like my office at Bow-Wow," she said. "Just much, much neater."

He guided her through double doors with images of ocean waves and birds etched in the frosted glass, into a private living area. She tried to memorize the room: A spacious area dominated by a black granite fireplace. A soft bronze glow cast over the room from the dancing flames. The warmth from the fire gave her a sense of safety, even serenity. In front of the fire was a gray suede sofa lined with lighter gray patterned pillows, matching gray suede ottomans, a red oriental rug, and two huge black leather recliner chairs, which faced a television cabinet.

"Faux suede. Faux leather," he said proudly.

She noticed a coloring book and a box of crayons on the huge dark walnut table in front of the sofa, and a chew bone and red dog bed in the corner. There were photos framed in silver on a small bookshelf—Isabella and Lukas dressed in their school uniforms, the children hugging Stefan, the children sitting on a high limestone wall, their father looking up at them, and the three laughing. *It looks like a home. A real home.*

Dozens of paintings, both historic and contemporary, lined the living room walls. No Matt Thoms' works anywhere! One colorful canvas on the mist-colored wall above the sofa caught her eye: an oil painting of another living room, one with yellow walls, red ceiling beams, and a blue chair on an orange-striped rug. There was a green lamp in front of a window, with a black piano in the background, a reddish-brown dog bed in the foreground, and a toy train and a doll lying under a fuchsia-colored chaise lounge.

"I've seen this before," she said.

"I don't know how. This is the only one," Alexander said.

"I guess I should say it's similar to one I've seen before. Before I started Bow-Wow, I liked going to museums. I haven't been in…let me count…in years. I haven't had the time. But I remember a painting like this. Who's the artist?"

He pointed to the signature at the bottom. "ALEX" was written in blue, in block letters.

"You?"

"Yes. What do you think?"

The last man I knew who painted—it did not *end well.*

"The colors are so vivid," Emily said. "Like David Hockney."

"He was my teacher," he said it matter-of-factly. No big deal. This artist, whose images of California hillsides and translucent blue water in swimming pools elevated him to a prominent place in contemporary art, had been his instructor.

"Name dropping to impress me?" She lifted a brow.

"Not at all, because I suspect it wouldn't work. He and my grandfather were friends at University. We went to visit him several times in California. We would paint in his garden—him, my grandfather, and me. He taught me to think of paintings in layers—add blue, then a deeper blue, then a green, then a deeper green. He made me realize I didn't have to include every item to paint a complete picture. That's why there is a dog bed and toys, not animals or children. It's like they've gone to play outside."

"A juxtaposition of presence and absence." Emily grinned, referring back to Alexander's rationale for the photos he took the first day they met.

"Exactly." He smiled. "I like the colors, but I think I may have gone a little overboard, using every paint on the palette. This may be more David's style than mine. What do you think?"

"Impressive."

"Do you like modern art?"

I used to until my ex-boyfriend became an artist and made a fortune painting pictures of my dog, a dog he never liked, a dog whose pictures he's co-opted and is now selling so he can buy mansions and live with his "brilliant" wife.

"Yes, I do, but I can't paint. I don't have time."

She stopped to study a seascape, a watercolor with multiple shades of turquoise depicting the ocean, rippling lines of sapphire, rose, and pale yellow for the sky, and a small red sailboat in the lower right corner.

"Do you like it?" Alexander stood behind her. His breath ruffled her hair.

"Peaceful. Relaxed." She moved closer to the painting to read the name, *LI's Dream*, etched on the boat's stern. "This is lovely. Did you paint this too?" She didn't expect him to say yes.

"I did. The L and the I—Lukas and Isabella."

Emily gulped.

"Are you surprised because you didn't think I had an artistic side?" Alexander chuckled.

Surprised? No, worried. "Yes, that's it."

He continued the tour, taking her into the kitchen—a kitchen nothing like the kind she imagined she'd find in a castle. She expected a giant fireplace with servants turning a spit with roasted meat or stirring a cauldron, something Shakespearean. Instead, there were black and white diagonal tiles on the floor, a white porcelain backsplash above the sink, and a modern stove, oven, refrigerator, microwave, and dishwasher. The appliances were bright red, with rounded corners, reminiscent of 1950s American homes.

"Isabella helped select the kitchen colors," he said.

"It reminds me of my grandmother's kitchen." Emily's voice was wistful. "I spent many happy hours watching her cook."

She followed him through a hallway decorated with more original artwork, showcased in bright red and blue acrylic frames.

"Papa" was scrawled in orange crayon across the top of one. The drawing depicted a man tumbling down a snow-covered hill, his green skis flying in two different directions through the blue sky. The expression on Papa's face was one of surprise, his mouth defined in red crayon as a big red "O!" The artist, "Isabella," signed her work in cursive writing, each letter a different color.

The second was a finger painting—a cornflower-blue sky with a bright yellow sun and four purple stick figures standing among some gigantic pink and orange flowers. There was a man, a girl, and a boy, all with dark curly hair, and a smiling white furry dog, with a long red tongue. Lukas's name was printed in big block letters across the top of the paper in green.

"Your children are very sweet—and talented," Emily said as she admired the pictures.

"They are. I'm lucky," Alexander said. "Of course, they have their bad days too. They cry, they pout, they misbehave. Neither has fallen asleep and tumbled off a stage in a Christmas play yet, but that could happen."

Her cheeks warmed as she remembered their conversation about childhood adventures the day before.

He led her to a dining area, where there were a glass table and turquoise upholstered chairs in front of four floor-to-ceiling windows. The full moon, suspended in the cobalt sky, shone like a gold coin through the window glass, frosted by the snow and cold night air. Crystal glasses sparkled, and the table was set for two, with bright white china, edged with gold, and a small blue scalloped shell in the center of each dish. Ivory-colored tapered candles burned in the center, and a bouquet of dahlias and peonies—pale pink, deep red, and light coral—perfumed the air.

Alexander pulled out the chair for her and placed the cloth napkin in her lap. She couldn't remember the last time that happened, but she was pretty sure any chivalry came before she dated Matt.

"I asked the cooks to prepare a light meal," Alexander said. "There's a green salad with fennel and grilled salmon, and for dessert, forest berries soaked in orange, and a shortbread cookie."

Much more elegant than a handful of cheese fish-shaped crackers and a bottle of mineral water—my usual supper when I've worked late.

Motionless, her hands clasped in her lap, Emily was so nervous, she was barely breathing.

"Is this all right?" he asked.

"It's perfect. As Isabella says, 'It's perfectly perfect.'"

"If you look," he nodded to the right, "you can see the ocean."

Emily peered out the window to glimpse a sliver of deep violet-colored water, illuminated by the iridescent full moon. She could see the ocean white caps, too, and hear the distant sounds of the waves rolling against the rocky shore.

"Just when I think I've seen the most magnificent scenery, I see something even more awesome." She sighed.

"What is it like in your home? You said you grew up in the mountains." He dished salad and salmon onto her plate and filled her water glass.

"Lots of trees, some lakes."

"Do you hike in the forest? Swim in the lakes?"

"I used to. I don't have much time now."

"Emily," he said, his brow furrowed. "I want to learn more about you, but all I know so far is you don't have time to go to museums, to paint, to swim, to hike. I suspect you know about me if you've read any magazines or newspapers, but I know nothing of your life except you didn't want to come to Marisol and you work too hard."

"Yes." Her spirit deflated. "I work all the time."

"May I ask why? Why do you spend so much time at work when you aren't particularly happy?"

She put her fork down, and her eyes met Alexander's. "I want to make a change, but I'm not sure how to do that." Then she stared at her plate. "I don't have the courage."

"Why did you become a writer? Didn't that take courage? Doesn't it take courage to share your ideas with strangers?"

Her eyes met his. "Not really. For me, it's the most natural thing to do. But, to answer your first question, I became a writer because I was a reader. I was raised on a farm. It was a wonderful place to grow up, but it was isolating, at least for a kid. I didn't have neighbors in a house next door. My closest neighbors were my cousins, and they lived at least a mile away. So, books became my 'friends.'

"Every Saturday, my mother and father would drive into the small town near our farm for shopping. While they ran errands, I spent time in the library. I so looked forward to that trip. The library was the most wonderful place I'd ever been. Hardwood floors, big chairs and tables, stacks of books everywhere. I still remember the marvelous smell of books, the ink on paper, what it felt like holding books in my hands, the excitement when I turned the page. There's nothing like the sound when you crack open a brand new book.

"I'd bring home a stack of books after each library visit, and I'd read them as fast as I could, so we could go back for more. I read everywhere—at the dinner table, in bed. I'd even go to the barn and read to our Palomino horse, Tess. I'd curl up on the couch with our border collie, Ranger, and I'd read to him about Trixie Belden, girl detective, or short biographies—they were called Blue Books—about Clara Barton, and Julia Ward Howe, and other famous women in history.

"Every birthday and Christmas I would ask for a new book, one I didn't have to give back to the library, one that was mine to keep and read again and again. One year—I must have been around Isabella's age—my Aunt Edie gave me this beautiful book with a blue marbled cover. When I opened it, the pages were blank. I couldn't understand. 'There's no writing. Where's the story?' She winked at me and said, 'You get to write the story. All those books you've been reading—you can write a story just as good.'

"So, I wrote stories, not as good, but two to three pages, silly stories. One was about a girl who had a magic lunchbox. When she opened it, she could travel around the world. Another was about a bluebird who asked a fairy to wave her magic wand and make his feathers red, but when she did, his friends didn't recognize him. He was sad and asked her to change him back, and he was happy.

"I had a lot of chores on the farm, but when there was free time, I'd write. Writing was relaxing, therapeutic. If I didn't write a story, I'd write what happened that day—a diary. I remember once writing a true story about Ranger and me playing in the woods, and there was a shallow creek I wasn't supposed to wade in, but I went every day after school. So, I'd confess in my book. I'd confess I didn't like going to bed early. I'd confess that after my parents went to sleep, I'd sneak into the spare bedroom on the other side of the house and read with a flashlight. My marbled book was full of stories that were part fact, part fiction."

"What kind of farm did your parents have? Sheep? Cattle?"

"Christmas trees," she said.

He stopped eating, his fork suspended in mid-air. "I never knew anyone who raised Christmas trees."

"My father and my uncle own Candy Cane Meadows Christmas Tree Farm. They supply trees all over the country—I've even found them at lots in New York. It's also a cut-your-own tree farm. In December, people drive to the Meadows to get their trees. My father and uncle will go with them to the fields. Tess leads the way, or my uncle's horse, Danny Boy, goes with them. When the family finds the perfect tree, the horse brings it back to the parking lot entrance on a cart, and my dad and uncle help the family load it into their car. My mom makes cookies and serves hot cider, and I helped on the weekends when I was in school. I hoped I could help again this year."

"How did your father become a Christmas tree farmer? That sounds like a wonderful job." He dished more salad onto their plates.

"I think he enjoys it, but being a farmer wasn't what he planned to do. My dad was in the military. He was wounded and lost his leg during an overseas deployment. He retired soon afterward—I must have been around seven years old when that happened. Before he was injured, he had been stationed in North Carolina—it's on the eastern coast of the United States—and that's where he decided to stay. His brother lived in the mountains, so my father bought a small farmhouse close by, and we settled in a town called Holly Mountain. At first, my dad was happy being retired, but he was a young guy, in his early forties, and he got restless. After a few months at home, he applied for a part-time job in the local hardware store, and he worked there nearly a year. One day at work, he overheard an older gentleman telling the store owner he was moving to California to live with his son. The man owned a Christmas tree farm and wanted to sell it to someone who'd keep it as a farm, not sell off the land to developers. The man and my dad talked, and my dad told him he was interested. He talked to my mother—she taught third-grade science—and she agreed a farm was a good idea. My father and my uncle pooled their money and became the proud owners of the Candy Cane tree farm."

"So, you were a country girl, but you live in the city now. Why New York? Such a bustling spot—different from a Christmas tree farm, I suspect."

"It's *very* different. I like the city. It's exciting. There's never a shortage of plays, or movies, or museums, or restaurants. Lots to do if you have time. There's also no shortage of people, for sure, and more cars, more lights, fewer trees, fewer stars than on the farm. I went to New York for my job..."

"But not for your dream."

"I went to college near my home, and my senior year, I attended a career fair and talked with a publishing house representative from New York. She offered me a job, and I took it. It was the first job I was offered. I worked with authors, and I hoped one day I'd get to do some writing of my own. That didn't happen.

"When Sebastian and I started Bow-Wow, I did get to write—at first—but as the organization grew, my job evolved into more of a management role."

Alexander rested his chin on his hand. His voice was dreamy as he said, "I'm trying to imagine what Holly Mountain looks like, what you're like when you're there. If you were in Holly Mountain right now, what would you be doing?"

Emily looked at her watch. "Well, because of the time difference, I'd be sleeping."

He smiled. "Once you woke up…"

"Playing with Gracie."

"I saw her photos on the Bow-Wow site."

"Then you know how cute she is," she said.

"She is that."

"And she's loving, like Stefan."

Matt thought Gracie was annoying. This guy gets it. He loves dogs.

"Gracie saved me," Emily said, "and I didn't even realize I needed saving. I didn't know anything was missing in my life, but when Gracie came, I wondered, 'How did I ever live without her?' That sweet black nose, those big dark eyes, those tiny soft paws.

"I found her wandering alone in my neighborhood one rainy night, cold and shivering. I took her in, planning to keep her a few days until I found her a new home…" She shrugged. "You know how that goes."

He laughed. "I do indeed. You can fall in love with a dog so fast! I knew I was going to love Stefan when I took him home from the Christmas market, but the moment I knew there was no turning back was two days after he arrived. The children played with him over there." He pointed to the floor in the living room. "They exhausted him. I was pretty tired myself. I flopped down in the recliner. Stefan was sleeping by the fireside. He was so comfortable, as if he belonged—as if he'd always been in that spot and he'd forever be in that spot—like that space was vacant, waiting for him to arrive. The missing puzzle piece. Stefan was already part of the family, but I knew then I would love him forever."

Emily dabbed her mouth with her napkin. "With Gracie, I knew the moment I tossed that yellow squeaky ball. The day after I found her, I bought the ball on my way home, and when I gave it to her, it was the happiest moment in her little life—and one of the happiest in mine."

She looked across the table at Alexander, the candlelight and shadows on his face. *Was he this handsome yesterday?* The ocean waves whispered in the distance as they brushed against the shore. The fireplace warmed her bare arms. When was the last time she felt this comfortable, this happy, this relaxed? Here she was in this beautiful room, the moon and the ocean outside her window, enjoying a pleasant conversation with another dog lover.

Any worries had seeped out of her body and vanished an hour ago. She forgot the next day was a workday, forgot she had to go back to New York, forgot she would miss Christmas with her family. One summer day, right before she went to college, when she and Hannah Rose were canoeing in Lake Laurel. They rowed far from shore, away from the crowds, and pulled their hats over their eyes and drifted. The gentle sound of water lapping against the boat, the sun like a magnet drawing any tensions from Emily's body, the light orange scent of sunscreen on her brown arms. Tonight was as peaceful as that day.

"What are you thinking?" His question brought her out of the lake dream.

"I was thinking you're a pretty good interviewer." She smiled. "You ask thoughtful questions. What else would you like to know?"

He drummed his fingers on the table, then teased, "How are you so remarkably well-adjusted since you were an only child? I was an only child, and I was in trouble all the time. I think my parents must have been glad there were no more like me."

She froze, biting her bottom lip then turned away. An innocent question, a flip remark, an attempt to be playful and funny, but it opened a door to a place she did not want to enter. She was silent for a few seconds before she responded in a voice soft, sorrowful. "I had a sister."

He touched her hand. "I'm sorry. I didn't realize."

She sighed. "It happened a long time ago. She was eleven, I was nine."

"But it still makes you sad."

She blinked back tears. *I hate this—how you can feel steady one moment, then be drenched with a wave of grief, unexpectedly, and it knocks you off balance.*

"Yes," she admitted. "It does make me sad, but I remind myself I have happy memories of Caroline. I remember one Christmas—we had so much fun. There was a Christmas concert at school, and Caroline and I were both in the children's choir." Emily laughed as she told the story, and just like that, the tears were gone.

"Our school was small, so you didn't have to be a great talent to be in the choir. Anyone who wanted to sing, could. When the Christmas concert came round, we sang our hearts out. Of course, we were off-key, and some of us forgot the words, but we were enthusiastic and loud, and our parents thought the concert was the most significant cultural event in the history of the world."

He laughed along with Emily. She grew quiet again. "The next Christmas, she was gone."

A little sob. *I hate this. I didn't even feel this emotion coming on.*

She took a deep breath to try to gain her composure. "I do think losing her changed me. I had been this lively, outgoing kid, like Isabella. I wanted to be the girl who ran the fastest, played the hardest. After

Caroline was gone, I pulled inward."

"You discovered books," Alexander observed.

"Yes. Books could take me away from the heartbreak for a while. Not for long, but for an hour or two, I was in another world."

He studied his plate, avoiding Emily's gaze. "When my wife died, I feared I would never be the same again. I was right. I'm a different person now."

"How?"

"I'm more appreciative of the people in my life, for one. As you may have read, I was a difficult child and an obnoxious teenager. As I got older, I realized I put my parents through so much hardship for no reason. Sometimes I'm not sure what I rebelled against. Against love? Against two people who cared for me? I hope my children don't do the same. My mother often wags her finger at me when the children have been mischievous and smiles and says, 'Karma will find you, Alex.' I pray not."

"You're a good person now. At least that's what I've observed. You like dogs, so you can't be all bad," she said.

"I try." He shrugged. "Sometimes, I'm self-centered. Too cautious. I was always waiting for the *right* time to do something—the perfect moment to surprise my wife with a gift, or the perfect night to take her to dinner, or the perfect moment to go away for a trip. Clara wanted a dog—we both had dogs growing up. I kept urging her to wait, to wait till the children got older, wait till after the holidays, wait till we weren't traveling. Looking back, I wasted precious time. Waiting for the perfect time paralyzed me into doing nothing. I was too foolish to understand now is the perfect moment.

"When Clara died. I was supposed to be on the trip with her, but I delayed it. I told her to go by herself, and I'd join her in a few days and bring the children. I had work to do, Isabella had a field trip with her pre-school, Lukas had a party at his nursery class—a busy time. Clara was fine with that, but if I'd known what was going happen…"

"So you feel guilty?" Emily asked.

"Every day."

"Losing a sister isn't the same as losing a spouse—"

"Grief is grief," Alexander interrupted. "Grief isn't a competitive sport."

"True, but for what it's worth, I watched my parents cope with guilt. Guilt because they couldn't protect Caroline from being sick. Guilt because they didn't pay enough attention to me when she was sick. I struggle with guilt because I wasn't the sick one. Why Caroline? What not me? All I know, after all these years, is guilt doesn't help us heal."

"Thank you." He clasped her hand. He didn't let go.

She and Alexander sat silently, staring out the window at the dark ocean. Her memories of the past filled the room like heavy gray smoke and settled side by side with the present in a melancholy union.

He spoke first. "It's late," he said looking at his watch. "Almost midnight."

"I should go." She suspected he was giving her a polite cue to leave.

"No, please stay longer if you can. Would you like coffee, tea? We can take it in the living room."

She helped him clear the table and put dishes in the sink.

She followed him into the living room as he carried a tray of cups and saucers. When Alexander sat close to her, the same waves that crashed outside the palace window crashed inside her.

The room was quiet as he poured the tea. Her hands shook, and the cup rattled against the saucer so fiercely Emily feared she would break both. Her heart pounded against her chest. She wondered if he could hear the rapid *thump, thump, thump*.

"Lemon? Sugar? Cream?" he asked. "Is the tea too hot? Would you like another napkin? Do you want anything else to eat?"

She lowered her eyes and shook her head. *Too many questions. Please stop. I can barely think.* Then Alexander asked one more.

"Emily, may I kiss you?"

Her soul shot from her body and danced across the night sky—twirling, spinning, the frost glistening in her hair, the cool wind blowing against her face, her heart glowing like embers.

She set her teacup on the table then turned to face him. Holding his hands in hers, she replied. "Yes, I would like that very much."

Alex kissed her gently on the forehead, then on the cheek, then on the lips. Emily was lost in this new ocean, swept out to sea, and she never wanted to return. *Kiss me forever.*

"Papa."

The voice was so faint, she wondered if she imagined it. Lukas stood before them, in pale green knit pajamas and bare feet, clutching a stuffed panda bear, tears streaming down his cheeks.

Alexander rushed to hug the little boy and knelt beside him.

"I had a bad dream." Lukas's voice was choked with sobs. "I'm frightened."

Alexander scooped him up in his arms, held him close, and sat in one of the recliner chairs, rocking back and forth. "I'm here. I'm here."

Emily rubbed Lukas's back and kissed the top of his head. She whispered to Alexander, "I'll go." He nodded, hugging Lukas, whose cries came in gasps.

Poor Lukas. As much as she might want to comfort him, he likely needed his father more than he needed her—a woman he'd known for only a few weeks. Emily turned the iron door handle to leave, but she stopped. Alexander was holding tight to Lukas, who clung to his bear. The prince sang a song she didn't know. "Where do baby hares sleep? They're sleeping, dreaming in the deep grass. Darling boy, sleep well till morning."

Tiptoeing back to her room, she replayed the evening in her head, each unguarded word, every soft kiss. She stopped and steadied herself against the wall. *Did this really happen?*

As she climbed into bed that night, the words of Alexander's song tumbled in her head: *Where do baby hares sleep? They're sleeping, dreaming in the deep grass. Darling boy, sleep well till morning.* The tender lullaby—and the man who sang it—comforted her, made her feel safe.

But then the troubles crept in. She stared at the ceiling and feared the future.

I'm leaving Marisol in two days. What happens then? Will we email each other, then stop because it's too much trouble? Will we video chat a few times until we both get bored? Will Isabella and Lukas remember me? Will Stefan miss the way I rub his ears?

She couldn't tame her thoughts as she watched the moonlight cast shadows in her room. The future was foggy, unclear. She was, however, sure of one thing: One kiss from Alexander would never be enough.

Chapter Nine
A French Proverb

Emily slept late the next morning. She needed the rest after her late night, before her last two RICI events—the balls. The first, held in the afternoon, involved actual balls. Fetch! brought dogs and their owners and handlers to the palace for "an afternoon of merriment and frolic," the invitations said.

Alexander tossed the first ball, then pets ran off-leash, burning away pent-up energy from three weeks of good behavior during the competition, while their owners and handlers enjoyed tea, coffee, home-made cookies, and pastries. Later that evening guests would return without dogs for the Holly and Ivy Ball, a formal dance and supper at the palace.

She sipped her morning tea and planned her day: Attend the "grand romp," the nickname palace workers gave the Fetch ball, dress for the gala, grab a few hours' sleep, catch her flight, and write stories about both events on the trip home. After her steam shower, she stared at herself in the foggy bathroom mirror.

"My last day in Marisol," she said. "I didn't expect I'd feel this sad."

She opened her computer to prepare the list of questions she wanted to ask when she collected information for her stories. She worked in her bathrobe, with her hair wet, drinking a second cup of black tea and nibbling an almond croissant from the palace kitchen. When she heard the knock at the door, she didn't look up.

"Come in, children," she shouted. A visit from the Lukas and Isabella marked the start of an ordinary Marisol day.

The children and Stefan climbed onto her bed. She stopped working and turned her chair toward them. "Did you enjoy the dog show last night?"

Their heads bobbed up and down.

"We got to see so many dogs," said Isabella. "It was spectacular."

Emily continued to be impressed with Isabella's vocabulary.

"We got to stay up late with the grown-ups," said Lukas, who had fully recovered from last night's bad dream. "Tonight we get to stay up late again."

"You're going to the ball?" she asked.

"Oh, yes! I get to wear my Christmas dress," Isabella said. "We get to hear a real-live orchestra, and we get to dance. We have the most fun!"

"And we get to eat two suppers!" Lukas chimed in. "We get to eat our regular dinner, then Papa lets us eat again at the ball."

"You've been to the ball before?" Emily asked.

"Papa always lets us go. Even when we were babies, he would bring us," Isabella explained.

Each day, she and Lukas reminded Emily even the smallest things—a new dress, an extra supper—could excite children, especially at Christmas. "Sounds like fun."

"Will you be there?" Isabella asked.

"I have to write a story about the ball," Emily replied, "so, I'll be there for a while."

"Will you dance with us?" Isabella asked.

"Oh, no!" Emily laughed. "I have to work."

"But it's a ball. Everyone dances. You have to dance."

Emily shook her head. "Even if I weren't working, I wouldn't dance."

"Why not?" The amazement in the girl's voice was clear.

"I don't know how to dance."

"You don't know how to dance?" Lukas hurtled from the bed with a desperate cry, as if Emily had confessed she didn't know how to breathe. "Everybody knows how to dance."

"I don't."

"Why not?" Isabella's brow knitted. She put her hands on her hips.

"I never learned." Emily shrugged.

"Didn't you learn in school?"

"Nope. No one ever taught us in school. I guess they expected we'd learn outside of school."

"And you never did? You never, ever learned to dance?" Isabella gasped in disbelief, then fell backward on the bed, lying motionless as if she'd been struck by lightning. Lukas smacked his palm to his forehead, then fell beside her.

"No, I never, ever did."

Isabella scurried from the bed. "Wait here!" She ran from the room then returned with her electronic tablet. "I can teach you, so you can dance at the ball tonight."

"No, no," Emily said, turning back to her computer. "Now, I have to work."

"If you don't dance, you can't have any fun. Don't you want to have fun?" Isabella's thin reedy voice pleaded, her eyes were wide with desperation.

Emily took a deep breath. "Okay." She stood up and opened her arms. "Teach me."

Isabella clapped with glee, and Lukas bounced up and down on the bed.

"The easiest dance is the waltz," she said.

The easiest?

"Here, watch Lukas and me." She pulled her brother off the bed. "You step like you're in a box, and you count to four."

They did make it look easy.

"Now, your turn." Isabella searched a playlist of Christmas songs. She found "The Christmas Waltz" on her tablet, and the little girl and Emily danced together, while Lukas stood on the window seat, conducting an imaginary orchestra. Isabella counted to four slowly, but Emily's feet didn't follow her brain.

"I'm not good at this," she apologized.

"You have to practice." Isabella played the song again and again as she and Emily waltzed around the bedroom, into the living area, back to the bedroom again. Then, Lukas danced with her while Isabella counted one-two-three-four. Stefan made himself comfortable, rested his head on Emily's pillow, and snored.

After twenty minutes of dance lessons with a patient Isabella, Emily said, "We should stop. I'll practice more today before the ball."

Isabella put her finger to her chin as if she was a scientist puzzling over a problem in a lab. She studied Emily from the crown of her head to the tip of her toes. "You know what the problem is?" she asked. "I think you're just not good at waltzes."

There's a bigger problem. You can't erase a lifetime of clumsiness in one day.

After searching songs on her tablet, Isabella played "Rockin' Around the Christmas Tree."

"Let's bop." She took Emily's hand.

She twirled Isabella, and Isabella, a good foot shorter than Emily, tried to twirl her.

"How do you know all these dances?" she asked.

"Our school. We take lessons once a week. I don't understand why you didn't have dance lessons in school."

Emily shrugged again. She and Isabella danced until Lukas asked to cut in and be Emily's partner.

"It's like I'm on *American Bandstand.*" She laughed.

"What's that?" Isabella asked.

"It's an old TV show in America. Teenagers used to get together after school and dance."

"And you didn't learn from that?" Isabella was incredulous.

"No, but I'd rather learn from you two. Thank goodness you and Lukas are here to teach me."

The three of them bopped, and while the dance was less structured than the waltz, Emily continued to stumble and struggle, prompting Isabella and Lukas to exchange pitying glances.

She whispered to him. He whispered back. They studied Emily for a moment.

"I know a dance you can do. Everybody can do this one," Isabella said as she searched for a song on her tablet. She played "Peppermint Twist."

"I'm not sure this is a Christmas song," Emily said.

The little girl's face knotted in confusion. "It's got 'peppermint' in it. It's right there in the title. We have peppermint hot chocolate at Christmas."

"Oh, okay." Why challenge the logic of a nine-year-old?

Isabella grabbed one hand. Lukas clutched the other.

"Let's twist!" she exclaimed.

Twist they did, by the window, on the bed, in every corner of the room. Stefan was now wide awake, leaping and barking. Isabella played the song over and over and over, and she and Lukas giggled as they moved with Emily, who sang along, carefree as the children. How easy to forget who you are, where you are, how old you are, and dance, as the song says, as if no one was watching.

She was lost in the giddiness, not conscious of anything or anyone outside that room until she vaulted off the bed and whirled around.

Alexander.

She smoothed her wet hair, cinched her bathrobe tighter around her waist. She was too embarrassed, too breathless to speak. *How foolish I must look.* She stared at her bare feet, which she now realized were her most unattractive feature. Why had she never seen that before?

"How long have you been there?" she asked.

Before he could answer, Isabella wailed, "Oh, Papa, Emily doesn't know how to dance."

Then with a seriousness in her voice that stunned Emily, Isabella proclaimed, "This is a *major* catastrophe. I'm teaching her the waltz and the bop, but she needs *lots* of help. For now, I'm teaching her the twist." Then she whispered to her father, "It's easier."

"Well," he said, taking Emily's hand. "Let's twist again."

Isabella squealed with delight and replayed the song.

"I'm not good," Emily apologized to him.

"You don't have to be. It's not a contest. Just have fun."

She closed her eyes, took a deep breath.

An image flashed through her head: A black and white photograph. Her father, parachuting out of a plane, arms and legs spread wide, soaring in the sky. Free fall. That's what he called it. Surely, if he could skydive out of a plane, she could take a risk here, in the palace.

Emily ignored her wet hair, her bathrobe, her unattractive feet and danced with abandon. Forward, then backward. Arms in the air. Toes wiggling in the plush carpet. The children bounced on the bed, twisting and giggling, with Stefan bounded on and off the furniture, his delirious, happy yapping competing with the music.

Emily lost track of how many times she twirled and jumped to "Peppermint Twist." As soon as the song ended, Isabella played it again. When the four of them finally collapsed on the bed, with Stefan in the middle, rolling from side to side, Emily struggled to catch her breath.

Maybe it was because dancing was akin to an aerobic workout. Maybe it was because she laughed so hard the tears streamed down her face. Maybe it was because Alexander's stare was so intense as they looked at each other over the children's heads.

She rocketed from the bed and pretended to be distracted by activities in the courtyard below.

"There's more fun tonight," Lukas said.

"Now that you've had lessons, you can enjoy the ball," Isabella said.

Emily struggled to concentrate on what the children were saying. *Alexander—those eyes.*

"Emily," Lukas said, pulling at her robe, "you'll come tonight, won't you?"

"What? Tonight? Oh, right. Sure, I'll come, but remember I'm still learning, and I have work to do—"

Alexander put his hands on her shoulders and turned her around to face him and the children. "No excuses. There's a French proverb, '*Ce n'est pas la mer à boire.*'"

"Which means?" she asked.

"It's not the sea to drink. The American translation would be: It's no big deal. You don't have to be good. All you have to do is enjoy yourself." Then he winked. "As Isabella says, don't wait to be perfectly perfect."

That ought to be cross-stitched on a pillow somewhere. Maybe if I ever have time, I'll learn how to cross-stitch.

"Please." Isabella bolted from the bed and clutched Emily's free hand. "Pleeease. You can't go to a grand ball and not dance."

The imploring tone of her voice touched her heart, forcing her to abandon reason. "Oh, all right. I'll practice, but don't expect much improvement between now and tonight."

"Good, it's settled." Alexander squeezed her hand. "Children, we have to go. Stefan, let's make sure Emily's shoes are accounted for. Emily, we'll see you later at the grand romp and the gala ball. Is it a date?"

"Definitely," she replied. She waved, closed the door behind them, then waltzed across the room by herself.

I can't wait!

~ * ~

That afternoon, the grand romp transformed the manicured palace garden into a playground for dogs all shapes and sizes. The RICI contestants, who'd demonstrated their best manners, who'd been their cleanest and freshest the nights before, now scampered unleashed through the fresh powdery snow.

Unlike their owners, who shivered in wool jackets, hats, and mittens under outdoor heaters, the dogs didn't mind the cold. They ran and rollicked, clumps of wet snow clinging to their fur.

Waiters, with white aprons over their dark knee-length coats, served hot apple cider, warm butter cookies, and apple strudel slices to the guests and offered fresh-baked peanut butter treats for the pups.

Emily and Alexander exchanged waves and smiles. The prince spent his time talking with owners and playing with the dogs, while she concentrated on her interviews.

She talked with Charlie, a sheep farmer from Queensland, who came to the Fetch ball with his Australian cattle dog, Henry.

"What are your impressions of the RICI and Marisol? What memories will you take home with you?" Emily asked.

Charlie's brow wrinkled for a moment. "Henry's been an exceptionally good boy these past few weeks." He massaged the dog's black-blue furry ears. "Today he gets to let his hair down." He laughed. "Or, I should say let his fur down. We both are having a great time this afternoon.

"What memories will we take home with us? There are too many to count, but for me, the best was the evening we visited the beach. Yes, we have beaches in Australia, but this was special to me because Marisol's beaches are quiet. The sun was setting. I could see the glow on the horizon, and at the same time, the almost-full moon rose in the sky. Henry and I were the only two creatures out and about. Alone in the splendor. So peaceful. Such a special time for me and my pup."

Emily interviewed Emil from Copenhagen, who came to Marisol with his chocolate Labrador retriever, Sannie.

"Our dogs deserve to relax, and now is that time," Emil said as Sannie raced after a tennis ball. "Is there a more wonderful sight than dogs at play? A sense of merriment—that is what I will take home with me. All the dogs had it in abundance at the RICI. They have it here today. I will remember that when I'm back at work in my law office, and it's a stressful day."

Emily talked with Chloé and her schipperke, Enya, who lived in an apartment in Brussel's Ixelles neighborhood, famous for its restaurants, shops, and theaters.

"This is paradise, no?" Chloé said as she watched the dogs playing. "So much joy. So much cheer. Everyone in harmony. I want to take this sense of harmony home with me. There are people here from all over the world. We've been brought together by love. I will remember that feeling when I leave Marisol."

"Happiness is contagious, is it not?" Noah from Saint Julian's in Malta struck up a conversation with Emily as they sipped cups of spiced tea. He pointed to his Boston terrier, Lulu, who chased an Afghan hound. "It's difficult not to be happy when you're around dogs."

Emily took a shortbread and raspberry jam cookie one of the waiters offered. The snow-covered mountains framed the sky, and when the conversations lagged, she heard the roar of the ocean whipping against the rocks.

I love it here.

The moment of tranquility faded, replaced by a swell of melancholy.

I'm not ready to leave.

~ * ~

Back in her room, Emily organized notes for the story she would write the next day, then dressed for the ball. She'd never been to such an elegant affair. *Calm down, butterflies. Every day here has been a pleasant surprise. Why should tonight be any different?*

She made her way down the winding staircase near the palace

entrance, the same staircase she had climbed that first day at Castle Sol. She admonished herself to relax.

When she entered the grand ballroom, she put her hand to her mouth. "Oh, my!" Was there an appropriate word? Magnificent? Dazzling? Splendid?

The floor was polished oak, set in rows of alternating light and dark wood, with the image of a giant conch shell, inlaid in mahogany, in the center of the ballroom. Six enormous waterfall chandeliers dangled from the ceiling on the right side of the room, six more on the left, their crystal beads cascading and glimmering like Pearl Moon Falls.

Lining the walls were cream-colored wooden panels, three feet high, and above them, flocked gold silk wallpaper stretched to the ceilings.

Above her, gray dolphins swam, brown pelicans flew, and white gulls scurried, while peach, white, and rose-colored seashells glistened against a pale blue dome. The ceiling frescos made Emily feel she was diving under the sea.

Opposite the ballroom entrance, a two-story Palladian window framed an enormous Christmas tree, its deep-green branches heavy with hundreds of twinkling white lights, ornaments shaped like crystal seashells, and white and gold satin ribbons. Emily's work at Candy Cane Meadows helped her determine this was a Norway Spruce, at least eighteen feet tall.

Under the tree sat dozens of wicker baskets, filled with pine cones, to honor Saint Angelina and Nicholaj. Fragrant cedar boughs hung round the room, with sprays of ivy, holly, and berries tied below the clamshell shaped wall sconces.

The room was a colorful blur as couples whirled around the floor—men dressed in sophisticated black and gray suits and white dinner jackets, a few in tuxedos, and women in exquisite gowns of pale pink satins, ruby-colored velvets, forest-green silks, and starry silver brocades.

The sounds of happy conversations and laughter blended in harmony with the music. *Allegro*—cheerful, Mr. Bertelli would say.

Emily studied the room, trying to take it all in as she had the first day when she walked into the palace.

A wave of insecurity quickly replaced awe. Her short-sleeved black velvet jacket with faux pearl buttons down the front couldn't compare with the evening gowns. Her bubble skirt was gold and shimmery—the most stylish outfit she owned—but her skirt was knee-length, and the other women wore floor-length gowns.

Emily fingered her flea market necklace—gold on one side,

silver on another—conscious that the other women wore spectacular jewelry—necklaces, earrings, bracelets dripping with diamonds, sapphires, emeralds.

I should leave right now.

She squared her shoulders and reminded herself she was there to work, not to compete for best-dressed party-goer. Strolling around the room, smiling, she fell into her professional mode and interviewed dog owners about their final impressions of the competition, the grand romp earlier in the afternoon, the ball this evening, the country of Marisol.

As good reporters did, she recorded conversations and took thorough notes, but her mind wandered. *Where is he? Is he searching for me?*

At last, she spied Alexander, talking to a woman with bright red hair piled high on her head and a man stroking a pencil mustache. The children were at his side. Lukas held his father's hand, impatiently scuffing his feet on the polished wooden floor, and Isabella swayed to the music, holding the skirt of her dress between her index finger and thumb.

Emily stood motionless; her feet were glued to the floor. *Should I speak? Maybe he's too busy. Maybe this isn't the best time.*

She didn't have to make the decision. Lukas pointed to her and called, "There's Emily!"

She waved, and the children scampered toward her, weaving their way through dancers. They hugged her around the waist as if they hadn't seen her for days.

"Emily, you're beautiful!" Isabella exclaimed. "You're the most beautiful girl here."

She took Isabella's chin in her hand. Such adoration in those bright brown eyes. "Thank you, Isabella. *You're* the most beautiful girl here too. And Lukas is the most handsome man, don't you think?"

Isabella giggled and dragged Emily onto the dance floor.

"We've been waiting for you," Lukas said. "You have to dance with us, just the way we taught you."

They joined hands and improvised an awkward three-person waltz. Emily was counting out loud, "one-two-three-four," when a gentle tap brushed her shoulder.

"May I?"

She faced Alexander, sure her cheeks flushed a deep scarlet.

Why do I keep blushing?

"My skills didn't improve since this morning."

"I don't care. Remember, you don't have to drink the whole ocean." He nodded toward Lukas. "Dance with your sister. I want to dance with Emily."

Alexander put his left hand on her waist, clasped her fingers in his right hand, and they waltzed, stiffly at first.

"Don't look down," he whispered. "Look at me."

She obliged, but the dance was graceless, painfully awkward. He was patient as she limped along, stepped on his polished shoes, waltzed left when he waltzed right, tripped over her own two feet. When the music ended, she pulled away. He gently drew her back.

"Not yet."

As the next waltz began, he drew her closer and buried his face in her hair. Her knees buckled. Fortunately, he mistook this for clumsiness.

"I realize you don't go dancing often…" he said.

"I don't go dancing ever," she corrected.

"Ever, but I hope you're enjoying this."

"I'm enjoying being with you." They waltzed across the ballroom, past graceful couples in chic suits and dresses. "This is not what I expected."

"Is that good or bad?"

"Good. It's formal, elegant, but it's more relaxed than I imagined. I didn't think there would be children, but there are dozens. And the adults—they're young, old, in between. There's a gentleman standing by the tree who must be in his nineties. And some people are dancing in wheelchairs. I thought everyone would be serious. It's less, less…"

"Boring?"

"I was going to say stuffy, but that too."

"When I was a child, these formal dances were agonizing. The adults were wretched. The children, if we were even allowed, marched in. We were forced to stand around the room, stiff as planks, afraid we'd spill a glass of punch or break some priceless china plate, afraid we'd make a wrong move, afraid we'd violate some etiquette rule we didn't even know existed. After all that misery, we filed out, and the pain finally ended. I swore if I ever was in charge, I'd make sure any palace events were festive, maybe even enjoyable. You ought to leave with a happy memory, not a death wish."

She laughed, and Alexander held her tight. She imagined gliding across the dance floor, graceful as a ballerina, elegant as a sea bird skimming the blue water's surface. His comfortable embrace—she wanted to remember what this felt like, to retrieve it on a rainy day when she was back in New York, alone and tired.

The orchestra's abrupt change in tempo shook her from her

thoughts. The waltz stopped, and the orchestra played "Peppermint Twist." Isabella and Lukas rushed toward her.

"Let's dance!" Isabella clapped her hands.

"Let's rock!" He pumped his fist in the air and spoke with such surprising fervor, the other dancers stared.

"I believe they're playing our song." Alexander twirled Emily.

The four of them twisted round and round and up and down, as the song lyrics instructed, Alexander took Emily's hands in his, laughing as Isabella and Lukas danced around them, in between them. Free falling, Emily thought, and she laughed too, unable to keep the joy inside. The other party-goers danced with them, whooping with childlike delight.

When the music stopped, Isabella yelled, "Encore!" The orchestra dutifully played the song again as everyone danced, twirled, and whirled a second time.

The song ended, and Emily put one hand to her chest, gasping for air, still laughing, while her other hand firmly clasped Alexander's arm. Lukas spun in circles, not ready to stop. Isabella was ready to shout "Encore!" again, but Alexander raised his finger to his lips to "shhh" her.

"I need to catch my breath," he told her.

"But, Papa, I'm not tired," she protested.

"The adults are," he assured her as Emily nodded vigorously. "You two dance together. I'll be with you in a moment. I want to talk to Emily."

He put his hand on her back and guided her to the buffet table. "You may need some sustenance after all the dancing."

He offered her a piece of Christmas cake, the official cake of Marisol, the rich almond, lemon, and raspberry confection Sebastian used to sweeten the news of her surprise overseas trip to cover the royal competition.

"Good," she muttered.

"The cake?"

"The cake. The dance."

Silence.

"Snow. Today. At the romp. With the dogs," Emily volunteered.

Silence.

"The room," she gestured with her fork. "Nice. Pretty."

She had disintegrated into a thirteen-year-old girl standing in the line for punch at the school dance, her vocabulary failing as she struggled to utter words with more than one syllable. She didn't want to make small talk. What she wanted was to throw her arms around Alexander, kiss him wildly, and tell him her heart was free falling and ask him if he felt the same way. Instead, her hand shook so hard, she dropped her fork, which left a trail of icing and crumbs on the front of her dress. As she brushed the food off with her napkin, she hoped some fairy godmother would swoop in with a ball gown. *This man must think I'm such a fool, such a klutz.*

Alexander's voice brought her back to reality. "So, what unique and interesting stories will you write from today?"

"I'll write how much fun everyone had this afternoon at the grand romp and the gala ball tonight. I won't write until tomorrow, on the plane, on the flight back."

"When will you leave?"

"Early in the morning, before daybreak."

More silence. She was sure it lasted twelve hours, although, in reality, the silence was less than thirty seconds.

"Emily," he said, "I am genuinely glad we met, even though the first day was somewhat awkward. The children have enjoyed having you here, as have I."

"Do the children understand I'm leaving tomorrow?"

"I've told them you have to go back to your home."

"The past three weeks have flown by. I never wanted this work assignment, but I'm happy I came. Truly. I enjoyed getting to know the children. I especially enjoyed playing with Stefan because I was homesick for Gracie."

Emily took a deep breath, summoned her courage. "I enjoyed getting to know you. I'll cherish the time we've spent together. When I interviewed people at the grand romp, I asked them what they'd take home with them. I'm grateful to take the memories of you, the children, and Stefan with me. Our 'adventure' day, the sleigh ride in the woods..."

Alexander started to speak when a giggly dog owner from Seattle, a woman with a sweeping black skirt and strapless gold embroidered bodice, interrupted their conversation and asked him to dance.

"It's been a pleasure," he said to Emily and bowed slightly. With those words, he was gone.

It's been a pleasure? A pleasure? That's it? That's all you have to say?

But what else could he say? They both acknowledged they were glad they met. They both acknowledged how special the past three weeks had been. Now, the prince would go back to his life, and she would go back to hers. Hadn't she always known it would be this way?

She found the children. In a counterfeit cheerful voice, she told them she would fly home the next morning, that it was time to go back to Gracie. Emily wouldn't be able to say goodbye before she left because they'd be sleeping after their big night at the ball, but she wanted them to know how much fun she had, how they made her feel so welcome, how she would remember them every time she looked at her snow globe. They both hugged her at the same time, then ran off to find their father.

She drifted toward the doorway and stopped to look back. Isabella, so angelic in her pink velvet dress with white lace collar, danced with her father, her small feet planted on top of his shoes, the way Emily did with her dad around the living room.

Isabella was smiling up at Alexander, so handsome and so different from the disheveled mess she encountered that first day. Lukas tugged at Alexander's hand, and the three swung together in a circle. Emily's bottom lip trembled. She longed to be part of the tenderness.

She ran back to her room, her shoe heels clattering fiercely on the stairs, echoing through the vacant dark hall. She slammed the door behind her. Despite her best efforts to stay in control, a sob escaped from deep inside. Then another. Then one more. Then a flood. Emily stood with her back against the door, tears streaming down her cheeks. They came so fast, she wiped them away with the back of her hands.

The irony. I dreaded coming here. Now I dread going home.

She sat on the bed staring heavenward, her hands clasped in her lap.

Why did I have to come to Marisol? Why did I have to meet him?

Tears. More tears. Oceans of tears.

She sat alone and wept until she was tired of crying. Finally exhausted, she went to bed.

But she didn't sleep. As she did before the trip to Marisol, she tossed and turned as the hours till morning crept along. Around 2 o'clock, she clicked on the television to watch the news. Nothing but tragedies. She turned off the TV.

Alexander must be sleeping by now.

The app on her phone, the one with ocean sounds that were supposed to relax a person into sleep, did little to calm her. The chapters from a book she downloaded on her tablet, the deep breathing exercises. Useless.

Nothing gave her comfort.

Staring at the ceiling, she took stock of her life. What was she going back to? Gracie, of course, her darling puppy. But what else was waiting for her? A job that was more drudgery than creativity. An overwhelming workload. A boring routine. A Christmas alone. A new year the same as the last year, the same as the year before, the same as the year before that.

The alarm buzzed, but Emily was awake, having memorized

every painting on the ancient ceiling. After a quick shower, she checked her phone, took a few sips of coffee. Time to rush again.

She left Castle Sol before the sun rose. No visit from the children, no barking and jumping with Stefan, no crooked smile from Alexander. There was no note from anyone, telling her they would miss her, suggesting she might come back for a visit, asking her not to go.

She remembered her interviews at the Fetch ball.

What will I take home with me from Marisol?

A broken heart.

Chapter Ten
Reunions

Emily fastened her seat belt and settled into her window seat. She was in first class, finally. Extra legroom and orange juice before takeoff, an empty seat beside her, no teens texting and talking over her during the return trip. Definitely an upgrade. She opened her computer and wrote her first story.

They came. They barked. They fetched.

Several hundred rowdy dogs gathered yesterday afternoon in the Palace Sol gardens to run, leap, and play their way to exhaustion, the happy conclusion to three weeks of competition and good behavior at the Royal International Canine Invitational.

The annual Fetch! Play Ball is the final event for dogs participating in the RICI. The afternoon romp gives dogs a chance to unleash their puppy spirit. It offers owners and handlers time to relax.

Prince Alexander, Fetch host, threw out the first tennis ball, which sent several dozen dogs scampering across the palace courtyard, while other dogs chose to frolic in the fresh snow, to wag their tails, or stick close to their owners' heels.

José Luis from Ensenada, Mexico, attended with Alejandro, his Ibizan hound.

"This has been a spectacular event in the most beautiful country in the world. The dogs have worked so hard to be good. Now it's time for them to cavort. Look at Alejandro. He's a champion cavorter, is he not?"

When asked what he would take home with him from Marisol, José Luis, replied, "I snuck away from the competition early one morning to buy some presents for my family at the Christmas market. But I am taking some other gifts with me—some special memories. I had a most enjoyable time getting to know other dog owners. I made many friends, whom I will keep in touch with when I return to Mexico. I met some fellow surfers from California, and we plan to take our dogs to the beach soon. So, my adventures will continue."

Emily dropped in the comments from Charlie from Queensland, Emil from Copenhagen, Chloé from Brussels, and Noah from Saint Julian's, then wrapped up her story.

Each dog left with special souvenirs—a sea-blue tennis ball with "Marisol" printed in gold on one side and a white seashell embossed on the other. Also, dogs received a dozen carrot and peanut butter treats, baked by the palace kitchen staff and packaged in turquoise cellophane bags with gold paw prints, neatly tied with a white ribbon decorated with gold bones.

And each owner and handler left with a heart full of memories.

"The taxi driver who drove me to the Seaside Center told me everyone falls in love in Marisol," said Pam, who lives with Dylan, her chocolate lab, in Virginia. "I fell in love with Marisol—the mountains, the sea, the people. I can't wait to come back."

Emily fell in love *with* Marisol, and as the plane hurtled through the sky, putting thousands of miles between her and Alexander, she wondered if she had fallen *in* love in Marisol.

After the flight attendants served a breakfast of herb and cheese omelets and seasoned potatoes on real plates with real flatware, Emily wrote her second blog post, which began with a description of the grandeur of the Holly and Ivy Ball: the graceful waltzes, the suave men in smart tuxedos and the sophisticated women in stylish gowns, the twinkling Christmas tree lights, the gleaming chandeliers, the woodsy perfume of the pine cones and greenery in the ballroom. She added comments from other attendees, who were as dazzled as she was.

One of the owners who danced at last night's gala was João, who came from Lisbon with his dog, a Portuguese Podengo named Adao. João's comments mirrored the mood of many palace guests.

"I would stay here all night if I could. So many beautiful women. So many handsome men. The room itself is a work of art. The paintings on the ceiling make me feel I'm in a museum. And this ball—it's sophisticated but not pretentious. Tonight has been immense fun. There's no better way to end our time here. All of us want to come back to Marisol."

Adele, who came to the RICI with her Maltese, Shing, agreed another trip to Marisol is in their future.

"We live in Singapore, in a high-rise apartment directly across from a park. We love our home and the beautiful green space we see each morning as we sit on the balcony and begin our day. Several times a week we take a stroll along the beach at East Coast Parkway. I live in

a lovely country.

"But Marisol is unlike any place I've ever been. It's enthralling, especially at Christmas with the snow, which, of course, we don't have at home. I hope we'll come back to the RICI next year to enjoy the winter landscape. I may extend my time here, maybe learn to ski or snowboard."

For Adele, the Holly and the Ivy Ball was a fantasy come true.

"When I was a child, I read stories about magnificent dances in majestic palaces in faraway lands. I never dreamed I would be inside such a fairytale. I hope to return soon to this heavenly place."

Emily sipped rich, dark coffee in a china cup and stared out the window. Snug and comfortable in the huge leather seat, listening to Christmas carols on headphones, she watched the cloud-mountains float beneath her. The flight attendants waited on her as if she were the most special person traveling that day. First class was a nice distraction from her fears.

I may never go back to Marisol. I may never see Alexander, the children, and Stefan again. If I don't, there will be a hole in my heart.

As Emily typed -30-, the journalistic signal for the end of the story, she mentally stamped a -30- at the end of her time in Marisol.

Time to move on.

~ * ~

Emily arrived home after dark on Christmas Eve. The taxi dropped her at the front door, now decorated with a fresh green pine wreath and bright crimson bow—Georgia's handiwork. Emily turned the key and crept inside.

Delirious barking. Frantic jumping. Joyous panting.

Gracie flew around the room—Sebastian would call it a "puppy frenzy," even though her puppy days were past. She bounced on and off the furniture, scurried from one side of the room to another, yapped hysterically, retrieved her favorite yellow squeaky ball and brought it to Emily. She tossed the ball and tossed the ball until her arm was tired and Gracie happily collapsed at her feet.

Emily sank into the sofa, put Gracie in her lap, and hugged her tightly.

"I'm so glad to see you, sweet girl." She kissed the top of Gracie's head.

Gracie looked at Emily, her bright eyes twinkling.

"I think you're as happy as I am," Emily whispered and hugged tighter. "Were you a good girl? Did you have fun with Jack and Harper? Was Georgia good to you? Did you eat enough? Did you go to the park?"

Gracie yawned, worn out from the excitement.

"Never mind. You can tell me later." Of course, all the conversations with Gracie were one-way, but Emily pretended they weren't.

As Gracie curled up for a quick recovery nap, Emily looked around her living room, which had been transformed from the barren space she'd left to a scene from a Christmas department store window.

A small artificial green tree decorated the table by the window, trimmed with blue lights, silver pine cones, and gold garlands. In the corner stood a large live Douglas fir, topped with a glittering star, shimmering with white lights, gold berries, white silk magnolias, and rose-colored satin ribbons. The mantle was draped with a green magnolia leaf garland. White LED candles glowed, and tiny ornaments—toy wooden soldiers, red and silver Christmas balls—peeked through the greenery.

She held Gracie in one arm, careful not wake her, and touched the delicate wings of the porcelain angel in the center, a gift from Georgia's husband when he was stationed in Germany. A silver hook held a white velvet stocking with a red cardinal appliqué in the center and "Emily" cross-stitched with green thread across the top. Beside it was a much smaller stocking with "Gracie" cross-stitched vertically. New handiwork from Georgia. She'd left the radio on, and Nat King Cole's mellow voice crooned "The Christmas Song."

What a wonderful place to come home to. Except...

Relaxing on the sofa, admiring Georgia's decorations, Emily decided she needed to assign Marisol to the past. This was her home. Yes, this was where she belonged. She put a pillow behind her head, closed her eyes, and took a deep breath, inhaling the Christmas tree fragrance, which mingled deliciously with the cranberry-scented candle Georgia placed on the coffee table among a centerpiece of fresh eucalyptus leaves. She fell asleep stroking Gracie's fur.

When Emily woke from her nap, Gracie was snoring contently. Emily gently lifted the dog from her lap, leaving her snuggled on the sofa in a tiny, furry ball.

On the kitchen counter she found a vase filled with red and white roses and carnations. She opened the card.

"Welcome home! I missed you, but I think Gracie missed you more. These flowers are from Gracie, Rollo, and me. Happy holidays. XOXO, Sebastian."

She smiled. Yes, Sebastian had sent her thousands of miles away, forcing her miss Christmas with her family, but what if she'd never gone to Marisol? *What if I'd never met him? And never seen that smile or gazed into those eyes?* She'd call Sebastian and thank him. Later.

Next to the vase, she found a Christmas card from Georgia in her elaborate cursive handwriting with its loops and flourishes—perfect, as if each letter were drawn by an artist, not scribbled in a hurry.

"Welcome back! Thanks for loaning us your home. Gracie was a dream, and we enjoyed playing with her. There's lasagna in the freezer. Not a traditional Christmas meal, but it's what I cook best. You'll also find two dozen Christmas cookies in the cookie jar. I restocked the fridge. You have milk, eggs, and juice. I bought you some cereal, and there's a fruit and cheese gift basket from your Aunt Edie. Hope you enjoy the decorations. Off to show the house to my mystery client. Talk with you tomorrow.

Merry Christmas. Hugs, G."

Emily glanced through her mail, which Georgia stacked neatly on the dining room table. In true Georgia style, the mail was organized—four stacks with different colored sticky notes on the top of each, labeled for content: yellow for junk mail, pink for magazines and catalogs, green for bills, blue for personal letters.

Oh, Georgia, I couldn't have a better friend.

Emily thumbed through the blue stack first. There were several dozen Christmas cards from friends and relatives, which made her feel loved but guilty. Sending Christmas cards was one of her favorite holiday tasks, but there was no time before the Marisol trip. Tomorrow, she would address envelopes—it would help her pass the time on what she suspected would be a long Christmas day.

After unpacking and showering away the "travel," she sat on the bed, drying her hair, struggling not to think of Marisol.

What is Alexander doing tonight? How is he spending Christmas Eve? Are Isabella and Lukas excited waiting for Santa? Is Stefan roaming the palace looking for shoes? Are they having a big celebration with family and friends? Or is this a quiet evening? I wish I didn't miss you all.

Gracie's bark jolted Emily from her daydream. Suppertime. Gracie had a way of re-ordering Emily's priorities.

The whirring sound of the can opener spurred Gracie to do her happy dance—jumping up on her hind legs, spinning around once. Then she firmly planted her four feet on the floor by her food dish, head lowered, gaze fixed on the empty bowl, ready to plow through her meal in record time. Emily was spooning the last of bites of the Let's Talk Turkey canned dinner into Gracie's bowl when her phone chimed.

"Hey, you!" Emily greeted Georgia with a broad grin. She curled up on the sofa, tucked her legs under her, eager for a long video chat. "The apartment looks beautiful. I can't thank you enough for taking care of Gracie. And for the lasagna. And the cookies."

"I'm glad you made it back safe and sound," Georgia said. "You look tired."

"I am. I didn't sleep well last night, so tonight I'll go to bed early. I can rest all day tomorrow. You're back in your apartment, right? And you have heat?"

"Yep. The four of us are getting settled in. We have a fire burning. Christmas music playing. It's warm and cozy."

Emily paused. "Wait. The four of you?"

"That's right," Georgia beamed. "The children and I got our Christmas present early. Quinton came home!"

"Oh, Georgia, I am so happy for you! When did this happen? Did you know he was coming? How—"

"It was a complete surprise. The best surprise we could have had. When I left your house earlier today, I had an appointment to show a house, remember?"

"The guy who only wanted to look at one house?"

"Right. Oh, was Gracie okay when you got home because I left Christmas music on the radio so she wouldn't be lonely—"

"Georgia! She was fine. Get to the big story. Quinton. Home. How did it happen?"

"Okay, okay, but I wanted to make sure you knew I took good care of Gracie."

"She looked well-fed and tired. So, the house?"

"The house the buyer wanted to visit was ten miles outside the city, the most beautiful old Victorian home—yellow clapboard with a steep gray slate roof and white shutters. Huge windows, a wrap-around porch. Original marble fireplace mantle. Four bedrooms. Three bathrooms. Completely renovated—new plumbing, new electrical wiring. Move-in ready. It took my breath away. And when I walked in, I could imagine myself in that house.

"I was daydreaming about baking bread in the kitchen and reading by the fireplace, when I heard someone come in. I looked around, and there was Quinton. He was the mystery buyer."

"And it took your breath away," Emily said quietly.

"Yes, it did. He was supposed to be thousands of miles away, and there he was, right in front of me, after all these months. When he hugged me, I cried and cried and cried. Tears of shock. Joy. Relief. Finally, I pulled myself together and asked the obvious question."

"What are you doing here?" Emily laughed.

"Exactly! He explained he's on leave for a month, he'll go back overseas for another month, then he'll come home for good. He'll work at the veteran's hospital at New York Harbor after that, so we're buying this house. A new year, a new home! And the guest room downstairs— that's yours whenever you want it. The backyard is fenced, so Gracie and Jack and Harper can play all they want."

"What a great Christmas present!"

"It is, but Quinton is the best Christmas present ever," Georgia corrected. "The children are beside themselves with joy."

"I'll bet. I remember what it was like when my dad came home from deployments."

Quinton appeared behind Georgia and kissed the top of her head. Then he waved to Emily.

"Has Georgia caught you up on everything?" he asked.

"Yes, I'm so happy for you. Welcome home."

"I'll go fix us some coffee," he said, "and you two can finish catching up."

"I want to hear all about Emily's trip," Georgia said. "So, tell me everything—Marisol, the dog show, the palace, the prince. He looks awfully cute in those magazine pictures."

Emily had shared only sparse details about the trip with Georgia. Although they video chatted every day, with two small children and a dog in the apartment, she didn't have free time for casual conversation. Their talks were hasty exchanges of information and instructions: Don't forget Gracie's vitamins; the children walked Gracie to the park today; the children went to play practice; Gracie barked at the mailman. Emily's replies were sixty-second news reports. "Today, I covered the hound group." "I spent the day with the toy dogs."

When Georgia asked about her elegant room, Emily admitted she was staying in the palace. "There's was a misunderstanding, so I ended up here," she told Georgia, then quickly changed the subject.

Emily never told Georgia about her day off, her adventures with Alexander, Isabella, Lukas, and Stefan. She hadn't mentioned tea in the Café Délicieux or the midnight supper or the dance at the Holly and Ivy Ball. Definitely not the kiss. Emily was afraid to tell anyone. *If I put it into words, it might disappear like a dream.*

"Let's not talk about it tonight." She dismissed Georgia's curiosity. "Quinton's home, the children are excited, it's Christmas Eve. Let's talk later."

"Why don't you and Gracie come over tomorrow? I'm baking a ham, and there will be more than enough for all of us. We'll have leftovers for days."

"Oh, no. You should spend family time together, but thank you."

"I don't want you to be alone on Christmas Day." Georgia

frowned.

"I'll be fine. All I want to do is rest."

"If you change your mind… You can even just come over in your robe and pajamas."

"Thanks, but I'll be on the phone all day—my parents, Sebastian. You enjoy your family time. I can't wait to see the new house."

"I can't wait for you to see it. I think this is my best Christmas ever."

They said their goodbyes, and Emily pressed the red button to disconnect their call. She yawned, tired from airplanes, tried from work, but there were still a few connections to make before she called it a night.

She texted Sebastian first.

Home. Tnx for flowers. Merry Xmas to you, family. 🎄

He texted back. *Opening presents!* *Call u tomorrow.* 😊

Finally, Emily made a video call to her parents.

"Merry Christmas Eve," she said cheerily. Her parents were in their bathrobes, sipping cups of tea in front of the fireplace. She longed for the smell of the wood smoke, the warmth of the cozy room, the company of people she loved.

"Glad you're home safe and sound," her father said. "Mom and I miss you and Gracie."

"Was Gracie happy you were home?" her mother asked.

"She was, but I think I was happier."

"Did you have fun in Marisol? I want to hear about your trip. Daddy and I read your blog every day. We both agree it was excellent. No one could have done that job better than you. Did you enjoy yourself? Did you see lots of cute dogs? Did you meet any interesting people?"

"Marisol was busy. Lots of work."

"Are you tired? Did you have a good flight? Do you have anything in the house to eat?" Her mother had more questions than a *Sixty Minutes* reporter.

"I am tired, the flight was fine, and Georgia left me dinner." Emily yawned again. "I have so much to tell you…"

"You get some sleep first," her father said. "We miss you. We wish you were here, but you look like you can barely hold your eyes open. We'll talk with you tomorrow, first thing."

"Wait—don't go yet," Emily hesitated. "Can we listen to a couple of Christmas songs together, then we'll hang up?"

Her father nodded. He turned up the stereo volume, and she listened to an old vinyl recording of Bing Crosby's "White Christmas" and "God Rest Ye Merry Gentleman" with her parents.

"Thanks, Dad. I miss you and Mom," Emily said when the songs ended. She waved goodbye, then put away her tablet and sighed with the pain of homesickness.

The apartment was so quiet—nothing like the palace with all the hustle and bustle of RICI and Christmas preparations. Gracie strolled into the living room. She usually fell asleep by her food dish after supper, woke refreshed, then demanded more playtime before bed. Emily found the squeaky ball and tossed it until both fell asleep cuddled on the sofa.

She slept till 11 AM Christmas day; jet lag finally got the best of her. While she was still in pajamas, she video-called her parents to wish them a merry Christmas. Talking with them, seeing them in front of the Christmas tree, decorated with the ornaments her mother had kept for years, filled Emily's heart with a sense of comfort.

"I can smell the turkey roasting from here," she told her mother.

In New York, Christmas day was cold but sunny, a perfect day to play fetch. Emily and Gracie had the dog park to themselves, so Gracie ran free, inspecting every blade of grass, memorizing new smells. Emily tossed a Marisol souvenir tennis ball for more than an hour, and Gracie chased it as if retrieving was the most important job in the world. When her dog grew tired, Emily hoisted her onto the bench beside her, and they both relaxed in the sun. Gracie snoozed, and Emily shut her eyes as the rays warmed her face. *Stay in the moment. Don't think about Marisol.*

When she got home, she returned a phone call from Georgia.

"The Christmas lasagna and cookies were delicious," Emily said. "I ate some for lunch."

"Don't you want to come over for dinner? I made pecan pie."

"My favorite, but tempting as that is, I'll stay here."

"I hate for you to be alone," Georgia said. "It's just not right."

"I'm fine. I appreciate you're only a phone call away. And I have Gracie."

"What if I bring you some leftovers tomorrow?"

"No, just put some in the freezer. You enjoy your time with Quinton and the kids."

"I can enjoy time with you too. This isn't either-or."

"I'm fine, really. I'm a military kid, remember. I know how important it is to get reacquainted."

"But, we have presents for you."

"And I have presents for you all. We can open those next week."

"But…"

"I'm hanging up now. Enjoy your family time. Merry Christmas."

Within seconds, Sebastian phoned.

"Merry Christmas, sweet Emily." He brimmed with love and enthusiasm, even when it wasn't Christmas, and the holidays boosted his energy level even higher.

"Merry Christmas to you. Thanks again for the flowers. They're mighty pretty. What are you doing?"

"Sitting here with my family, eating an afternoon snack. I made spice cake." He took a bite and rolled his eyes toward heaven. "It's delicious, as usual. Everyone says it's the best I've ever made."

"You say that about everything you cook."

"Because it's true. Why be modest? Hey, I wish you were here."

He turned his phone camera to focus on his parents, his brother, and a houseful of aunts, uncles, cousins, friends, all eating giant slices of cake on the Spode Christmas china Sebastian bought his parents several years ago.

"Wave to Emily," he instructed. They obeyed, and Rollo barked hello.

"Your articles were great by the way," he said. "I want to hear about Marisol, all the stories behind the stories."

"I'll tell you each and every one, but not now. Go. Enjoy your family."

"Are you lonesome? We can talk longer."

"I'm fine. I'll check in with you tomorrow. Go. Eat cake." She disconnected the call.

Then silence. Overwhelming, unpleasant silence. Her friends were worried she was lonely, and she assured them she wasn't, but that might not be true.

I will not be sad today.

No pining for family and friends. They were only a phone call away. She wouldn't think about Marisol. That was the past.

For years, Emily had longed for free time. Now she had hours of it but wasn't sure what to do. After pacing from the living room to the kitchen a few times, she addressed some belated Christmas cards, read a chapter in *The Mystery of the Golden Spaniel*, a book she'd started before she left home, watched the end of *Miracle on 34th Street* on television.

4:30 PM.

Maybe another quick trip to the dog park? No, Gracie was snoozing by the fireplace. *Let sleeping dogs lie.* Eating was a good way to pass the time, so Emily wandered into the kitchen to make herself a cup of tea and munch on another one of Georgia's cookies.

Emily brought her snacks to the living room table. There was the snow globe the children gave her. She shook the glass. The flakes swirled, and the storm brought a tempest of memories: the bumbling first encounter with Alexander, the children's visits to her room, Stefan and the great shoe robbery, her day off during their Christmas "adventure," the afternoon teas and conversations, the late night supper, the soul-altering kiss.

In disbelief, she shook her head. She never wanted to travel to Marisol, and now she longed to be back there—with them, with him. How to douse those feelings?

Gracie was awake now, standing guard against any enemy squirrels who might be foolish enough to encroach on her backyard territory. Emily rubbed her arms. The house was chilly, so she turned on the gas fireplace, then lit the cranberry candle. The tart berry aroma filled the room, a soothing Christmas perfume.

Gracie remained on squirrel patrol, not ready for dinner, so Emily called her parents again. Her mother answered. "Hi, sweetie. I have the house to myself. All the relatives have gone home, and Dad went to the barn to feed the horse." She added, "We missed you and Gracie today."

Emily forced a smile. "I missed you too."

"You look sad. Are you sad? Don't be. Daddy and I will visit with you soon. If you're too busy to come home, we'll come there."

"I'd like that," she said.

"How was your day? What did you do this afternoon?"

"Not much. Took Gracie for a walk, ate some lunch, talked with Sebastian and Georgia."

"I hope you weren't too lonesome."

"Oh, no. It was fine." Emily's voice quivered. She didn't even convince herself.

Silence, then tears. One or two at first, then oceans. Emily hid her face in her hands. She didn't expect to cry, but her mother's voice, the house at Christmas—triggered an emotional avalanche she didn't expect.

"Oh, honey," her mother said. "I realize it's been a tough day, but try not to cry. We'll visit as soon as we can. When Dad comes back, we'll look at flight schedules."

The tears kept flowing.

"Emily," her mother said, her voice changing from soft to serious. "This is about more than Christmas homesickness, isn't it?"

Emily blew her nose.

"What happened in Marisol?" her mother asked. "Emily," her mother said.

An all-too familiar tone. Her mother possessed what Georgia called "the gift of maternal perception." All mothers had it, she explained. Children spoke, moms deciphered. And when moms uttered a child's name, their tone indicated they had figured out any child's secrets.

Her mother might say "Emily," and it was a term of endearment. It translated into "I love you more than anyone in the world." Or it could be a declaration of exasperation. "Young lady, I've lost patience with you." She heard that tone daily when she was a teenager. Or it could be a flashing yellow light. "Think hard before you take the next step." Today her mother meant, "There's more here than you've told me."

"Mom, I'm going to tell you something, and I don't want you to tell anyone, even Dad."

"Okay," her mother said hesitantly, "but I don't like to keep secrets from Dad."

"This isn't a forever secret, but for now... What I'm going to say may not be true tomorrow, so if you wouldn't tell Dad, at least today..."

"Okay," her mother repeated, the reluctance clear in her voice.

Emily took another breath. "I'm embarrassed to tell you this—it's silly—and as I said, I may not feel this way tomorrow—and I can't believe I'm even saying this, but I sort of have a crush on Prince Alexander."

Before her mother spoke, Emily held up her hands to stop her. "I know, I know, it's foolish."

"A crush—that's not foolish, and it's nothing to apologize for. We can't control our hearts."

"I wish I could control mine. It's like I'm twelve years old," Emily said, exasperated with herself. "You remember the time we went to the beach at the Outer Banks and we saw the wild horses running in the dunes. That's how my heart feels. I try not to think about him, but I do—all the time."

"Crushes are intense, but they usually go away pretty quickly." Emily scowled.

"Maybe," her mother said quietly, "this isn't a crush."

No reply.

"Emily." That tone meant, "I'm right, aren't I?"

"Oh, Mom, I'm so confused."

"When did this start?"

"Not right away. I didn't like him much when I first met him, but gradually... His children and their dog came to visit me in my room while I was working. I enjoyed having them around. I even looked forward to seeing them. The children were so curious, so full of joy about the smallest things—baking cookies, decorating the tree. And the dog was sweet and goofy. They'd stay in my room for a couple of hours each day, and Alexander would collect them for dinner. Each time he did, I watched him with the children and the dog, and he was so attentive and affectionate and patient, and I thought, 'He must be nice if he's a good father and he likes dogs.' When he picked up the children, he'd talk to me. At first, I thought he was being polite, but he started coming earlier and staying later. Each visit was longer than the one before. One day, I timed how long he was there, and he stayed an hour and a half.

"But everything changed for me the day I took off from work…"

"The day you went to the Christmas market," her mother guessed.

"Yes, that day. We had such an amazing time. We took a sleigh ride, and we played in the snow, and we saw wild geese fly over a waterfall and elk graze in the snow. The scenery was dazzling, but not just the scenery—the mood. This sounds ridiculous—I'm embarrassed to say this—it was magical, enchanting. He was easy to talk to. I could be myself with him. My true self. Not the competent person everybody thinks I am, but the insecure mess I am deep inside and the loving person I want to be. I realized that day I had a crush on him, but I told myself it would go away."

"But it didn't."

"No! It got worse. Much worse. A thousand times worse. He asked me to meet him for tea one afternoon. I can't even remember what I ate or drank because I was lost in a dream. The attraction was so strong. Then he asked me to have dinner, and he kissed me…"

"You didn't tell me that," her mother said.

"When we danced at the ball—"

"*You* danced? You don't know how to dance."

"The children taught me," Emily said. "Let's not get distracted from the big problem here, Mom. I didn't say I danced well, but I did dance with him, and I was comfortable even though I did something I never do. Whatever I did was okay. He wouldn't judge me. He just enjoyed being there with me. He made me feel…safe."

"There were times, Mom, I could imagine… Georgia bought a house, and she said she knew she'd found the right place because she could envision herself in the kitchen cooking or reading by the fire."

"Wait, Georgia bought a house?"

"Yes, and Quinton came home early. Mom, I'll fill you in later. Let's stay focused. What Georgia said about envisioning the future, I did that with him. I could imagine myself taking walks with him on the beach and or talking with him late into the night. I could imagine myself helping the children with their homework every day. I could imagine Gracie and his dog running through the woods together. I've tried so hard to bury my feelings."

"You do that too often."

"I rationalized I was caught up in the moment. I was in this beautiful country, with this handsome man, in this luxurious home. I had a break from my old routine, and my new routine was different and glamorous."

"So, you left Marisol behind, but not the attraction."

"Oh, Mom, what's wrong with me?"

"Nothing's wrong with you."

"I'm beyond frustrated." Emily shook her head in disbelief. "My life is here. His life is there. We live on different continents, separated by an ocean. When we said goodbye—let's just say it was less than passionate. It was like, 'See ya.' Besides, we have nothing in common. Nothing."

"I'm not sure that's true," her mother said. "You're both smart, you're both kind, you're both caring. You love dogs."

She reached for another tissue from the almost empty box. "I just met him. A month ago, I didn't even know who he was."

"There isn't a time limit for when feelings become serious," her mother said. "Sometimes, there's a connection right away. I knew your father six weeks before we knew our relationship was special. We got married three months later. I left everything familiar and moved with him to Germany when he was transferred there. That was a big leap of faith. And your grandmother—she only knew Grandpa for a few weeks before they decided to get married."

"So, I come from a long line of impulsive women?" Emily said, half-joking.

"You come from a long line of women who listen to their hearts. There's nothing bad about being attracted to someone. Maybe you and Alexander will decide you want to get to know each other better. Or maybe he will simply be a good friend. Or maybe you'll decide he's a sweet memory. I can't say for sure, but I do know one thing. Today is Christmas, and it's one of those days that stirs up all kinds of emotions. It's a day when we look forward to time with people we love, and it's a day when we miss people we love if we can't be with them. Why not wait and see?"

Emily rolled her eyes.

"I know, I know," her mother said. "For all your good qualities, patience is not one of them. Trust me when I tell you, if this is only a crush, those feelings will ebb and disappear. If it's something more, the feelings will grow deeper."

It made sense. Her mother's words were logical, calming, but...

"What makes me the most uneasy," Emily said, "is I wanted a change. What I thought I wanted was a change at work. Then I met him, and the children, and the dog, and I realize *they're* the change. Now that I've met him, I'm not sure what to do. It's like with Gracie. I didn't realize I was missing anything, but I was, and now I can't imagine life without her. And I'm having a hard time thinking about life without him."

"Just wait," her mother said. Then, she burst into laughter. "Do you remember when Caroline was little, and she wanted to be a fortune-teller? Your other friends wanted to be scientists or bank presidents or chefs or teachers, but Caroline wanted to be a fortune-teller. I don't know where that came from, maybe a TV program, but she would stop anyone she could and promise to see the future. She would read palms—I remember she sat at the dining room table and read palms for my entire book club. She concentrated, studied people's hands, said, 'Hmmm. Very interesting.' Then, she'd wave her hands and say in this mysterious voice, 'All will be revealed.'"

Emily laughed as she remembered Caroline's predictions— Emily would be a ballerina, an Arctic explorer, a horse trainer in Wyoming—Caroline's visions of Emily's fate changed every day.

"Well," her mother said as she waved her hands and mimicked Caroline's deep, wise voice. "All will be revealed."

Emily dried her eyes and chuckled. "Yes, I'll try to remember."

She thanked her mother for the kind words, and they said their goodbyes. Emily and Sebastian constantly compared who had the best parents, and tonight, she was convinced she won the mom jackpot. As the sun set in a beautiful orange and violet sky, she held the snow globe Isabella and Lukas gave Emily at the Christmas market. She shook it vigorously, and Saint Angelina and Nicholaj were momentarily lost in a snowstorm. As the snow settled, the two were visible again.

She opened her laptop and placed the snow globe beside it. There was one more Marisol story to tell: the legend of the little girl who was lost, the neighbors who joined to search for her as they feared the worst, and the homeless dog who saved her.

But the townspeople hoped. They hoped even when their faith wavered. They hoped even when the future was uncertain and the outcome looked bleak. They hoped with a recklessness that defied all reason. And, in the end, their hopeful spirits were stronger than their fears.

The townspeople learned hope manifests itself in unexpected ways. That day, hope came in with four paws, in the form of a dog no one wanted, a dog no one loved.

In Marisol, a kind gentleman explained the deeper meaning of the legend. Sometimes we rescue dogs; sometimes they rescue us.

Two wise children told me there are three lessons we can learn from the legend of Saint Angelina and Nicholaj: We must show love and respect for all people and all living creatures. We must always try to help others. We must never give up hope.

Christmas is a time for anticipation, a time for love, and most important, a time for hope. Yet today, for some of us, faith, hope, and love seem far away. We are alone. We miss family and friends. We long for people from our past, but the present finds us separated, physically apart or emotionally distant. We hope there will be love in our future, but we aren't certain, and we are overwhelmed with the fear of loneliness.

This Christmas, let's remember even in the harshest storms, even on the coldest nights, even when the sky is the darkest and the stars are buried deep in the clouds, even then, there is reason to be optimistic. Let's remember when we are lost, someone may find us, or we may find them. Let's remember kindness begets kindness. Let's remember we have the ability to help, to care, to expect the unexpected.

This is the season for miracles.

May your miracle find you.

Emily uploaded the article to the Bow-Wow website and told readers she decided to write a postscript to her RICI stories.

She took off her glasses and rubbed her eyes. A wet nose nuzzled her leg. Gracie now sat by her feet, wearing her did-you-forget-supper face.

"I'd never forget you," Emily assured her. She obeyed Gracie and headed for the kitchen, with the dog following close behind.

"I'm glad to be back home," she told Gracie. "I missed our routine. I missed you!" That was true. She had counted the days till she could come home. Now she longed to be back in Marisol. *What if I never see them again?*

Then she remembered Caroline and chuckled. She waved her hands and said, "All will be revealed."

Gracie cocked her head from one side to the other, puzzled as to why Emily laughed when she should be getting supper. She rubbed Gracie's ears and spooned a can of Let's Meet for Meatballs stew into her dish.

"You never got to meet Caroline," she said to Gracie, "but she would have loved you." She scratched Gracie behind the ears as the dog gobbled her supper.

Emily took the snow globe from her desk and placed it on the bedroom nightstand, next to the silver frame with the photo of her parents and the smaller porcelain frame with a school picture of Caroline. That was exactly the right place. Emily would see the snow globe every morning when she woke up and every evening when she came in from work. It would remind her to hope.

Wondering if she might see a star to wish upon on this clear night, she looked out the window.

"Oh, Caroline." Her voice was wistful. "Thanks for reminding me everything will be okay."

~ * ~

The day after Christmas, the sky was a milky white. Snow was on the way. Emily dashed to the market down the street to replenish her marshmallow and hot chocolate supply, then she bundled up Gracie, and they walked to her office.

Emily opened the door to Bow-Wow, today a dark, vacant place, a stark contrast to the bright, busy office she left. She stopped to admire the Christmas tree at the reception desk. Amid the twinkling lights on the evergreen branches were small silver frames—each one with a photo of a dog adopted by a Bow-Wow staff member. She found Gracie's photo—there she was wearing a burgundy velvet ruffled Christmas collar.

"Frosted windowpanes. Candles gleaming inside." The office was quiet except for the Christmas music playing through the building's sound system, Doris Day singing "The Christmas Waltz."

Emily picked up Gracie, hummed along, and danced down the hallway, smiling as she remembered her lessons with Isabella, Lukas, and Stefan. And remembering her dances with Alexander, his hand gently resting against her back, his cheek close to hers, the feeling they were the only two people in the world.

Stop. Pack those memories away.

She unlocked her office door and flipped on the office lights. Immediately, Gracie climbed into her bed, curled into a tight ball, and snored while Emily looked through her mail. She opened a few more Christmas cards, then wrote New Year's greetings with apologies she'd been out of touch.

Today, her main task was to complete the work she left unfinished before she went to Marisol—reviewing ideas from freelancers who pitched stories to Bow-Wow. Reading story proposals was one of her favorite chores.

Some were inspirational, such as the idea from Josh, a writer from Utah, who rescued a mixed-breed dog who suffered years of abuse. He tried for several weeks, but the dog wouldn't let him touch her. Now, a year later, he and Suzy hiked trails around Bryce Canyon, and the dog had become so calm, she welcomed pats and hugs from other hikers. "A little love goes a long way," Josh wrote. He included a photo of himself resting against a boulder, a walking stick in his hand, and an orange backpack on the ground. Suzy sat at his feet, an orange backpack of her own beside Josh's.

Some story ideas were cute. Dara from Virginia suggested a story about her greyhound, Grady, the "blueberry ambassador." She owned a farm, and each morning during blueberry season, Grady carried empty baskets in his mouth and delivered them to customers who came to pick berries. Later in the day, he worked in the gift shop, greeting people who needed jams and jellies, scooping up any stray blueberries that rolled on the floor.

Some story ideas were poignant. Ben, a journalist wanted to tell the story of the Port in a Storm Society, a collection of international volunteers in coastal areas that fostered dogs whose owners couldn't take care of them after hurricanes. He included some reunion photos of owners and animals—images of hugs, tears, laughter.

And some ideas were stories of love. Donley proposed a feature on Elroy, a rescue dog who became the shared pet at an AIDS group home in San Francisco in the 1980s. "In a time when many residents were abandoned and unloved by their families, their friends, and society, Elroy provided the loving touch, the emotional connection many were missing." He lived till the ripe old dog age of seventeen, and neighbors planted a garden in his honor.

She wrote the freelancers, thanked them, told them she liked their ideas, and assured them she would contact them with publication details after the holidays. The process took longer than she planned. When she peered out her window, she saw the sky was dark, and snow was falling. She woke Gracie and got her leash.

Emily pulled on her scarf, hat, and coat, and she and Gracie made their way back home. She'd called her parents earlier in the day and texted Sebastian and Georgia for an update on their Boxing Day plans, so she anticipated a quiet night: re-heat some lasagna, have a cookie, watch *It's a Wonderful Life.*

The Christmas lights sparkled through the falling snow, but the holidays hadn't slowed the city's pace. People rushed home from work or after-Christmas bargain shopping. They dashed to movies or restaurants, hurried to meet friends and loved ones, ran to catch a bus or a train or a cab. Emily was pushed and shoved along, squeezed and jostled by the crowd. She picked up Gracie and carried her in her arms to make sure she wouldn't be stepped on or tripped over.

As Emily navigated the crowded city streets, the wet snowflakes fell on her cheeks and melted on her skin. Hot coffee, pretzels, roasted chestnuts—warm delicious aromas wafted from the street vendor carts. The traffic sounds—horns, car engines, sirens—were all around her, competing with the sounds of voices, chatting, laughing, shouting. Sounds and sights so familiar. She was back in her routine. *My life is back to normal.*

That realization did not make her happy. The city was her home, but sometimes—and today was one of those—she was keenly aware she was alone. Loneliness kept her in the dead-end relationship with Matt, long after she realized they shared few mutual interests, few common values, no genuine affection for each other. She wondered if her fear of loneliness allowed work to dominate her life. Without work, what would she have to fill her days and nights?

What should I do next?

She pulled Gracie closer and kissed the top of her head. That wouldn't give her an answer, but it made her feel better.

Did someone call me?

She listened. Nothing. She shook her head and kept walking toward her apartment.

I heard my name.

There were lots of people named Emily in the city. She shrugged it off.

"There she is! It's her! It's her!"

It took her a few seconds to comprehend what was happening. Isabella and Lukas rushed toward her, with Alexander holding onto Stefan's green and red plaid leash, running behind. Emily put Gracie on the sidewalk beside her. The children flung their arms around Emily's waist and hugged her so tightly she couldn't move.

"We missed you! We missed you!" Lukas cried.

She knelt to hug him again, then Isabella. "I missed you both, too! I really did." She rubbed Stefan's head. "I missed you, too, fella."

Alexander extended his hand to help Emily to her feet. She grasped it and held tight.

"We all missed you," he said. "*I* missed you."

The children jumped up and down, chattering like little birds, talking so fast, she couldn't decipher what they said. Usually protective and quick to growl when anyone got too close, a calm Gracie curiously sniffed the children's shoes, Stefan's paws, the hem of Alexander's wool coat.

Then, on the street where Emily so often felt invisible, lost among crowds of strangers, completely alone, she was, at last, safe.

She threw her arms around his neck and whispered, "I missed you more than you can imagine."

When she pulled away after a long embrace, she looked at him, then at the children. *Are you really here?* She pushed her snow-covered hair from her eyes and blinked. "How did you get here? Why did you come? How did you know where I lived?"

"Reporters who cover the Royal International Canine Invitational have to complete applications for press credentials, and they have to include a home address. Your office provided that. It wasn't difficult to find you."

"I can't believe you're here." She turned, opened her arms, and the children hugged her again. Alexander stood behind her, his hands resting on her shoulders. He kissed her neck.

When the hugs subsidized, she faced him.

"After you left," he said, "it didn't take long to realize we wished you'd never gone. The palace was empty without you, and there was nothing to look forward to. Christmas wasn't as happy because you weren't there. Late last night, I read your story on the Bow-Wow site, the one about Saint Angelina and Nicholaj, to the children. You wrote about hope and the unexpected, and we decided we missed you too much to wait another day." His voice was shaky. "We hoped you'd be glad we're here. Are you?"

"I am, but when I left all you said was it had been a pleasure to meet me. That wasn't very…emotional."

"I wasn't sure what to say, whether to say anything. I was waiting for the right time."

"I was afraid I might never see you again." She rested her head on his chest.

"No," he said firmly. "That wasn't going to happen."

He took her hands in his. "Emily, I want…I feel…What I want to say is, are you sure? Is this too much? Maybe I should have waited till the holidays were over, until the children were back in school, until…"

She held her index finger to his lips. "I'm sure. Absolutely, positively sure. Eternally sure. This is the perfectly perfect time."

~ * ~

Two days after they arrived at her doorstep, the children and Alexander sat with Emily at her small oak dining room table, putting together a jigsaw puzzle of puppies in the snow, a puzzle Harper and Jack accidentally left behind. Isabella announced she wanted more popcorn and left for the kitchen with Stefan and Gracie trailing behind, their noses working overtime, trying to determine what wonderous crumbs she might drop.

She didn't come directly back to the table but wandered around the living room, munching from her giant bowl, "accidentally" dropping a few pieces of popcorn now and then. The dogs made sure no scraps were left behind. She spied a framed photo on Emily's desk. The posed shot was one of Emily's favorites.

She was thirteen years old, wearing a red jacket and a white knit cap with a pom-pom on top. She was looking down, grinning at her dog, Ranger, and patting him on the head. Her parents stood beside her, smiling too, their arms around each other, staring into the camera. Behind them was a green sled, pulled by Tess the Palomino, loaded with a freshly cut pine tree. A blanket of new snow lay on the ground. Emily remembered her Uncle Frank took the picture, and her mother used it as a Christmas card photo.

"Who is that?" Isabella asked.

"That's me when I was a little girl," Emily replied.

"Who's that with you?"

"Those are my parents." She returned to the puzzle, searching for a missing piece that would complete one puppy's ear.

"Where were you?"

"Isabella," Alexander chided. "So many questions!"

"But, Papa, you told me it's good to be curious. You said Emily's job is to ask questions."

She cast a sideways glance at him and mouthed the word, "Touché." She answered Isabella, "That picture was taken on the farm where I grew up."

"You didn't grow up in this house?"

"No, I moved here after I finished college and got a job. When I was younger, I lived with my parents on a farm."

"What kind of animals did you raise?" Gracie and Stefan gobbled up a few more pieces of popcorn Isabella quietly dropped.

"No animals." Emily bit her bottom lip, focused on completing the puppy's ear. "We raised Christmas trees. I grew up on a Christmas tree farm."

Isabella's eyes widened. Lukas looked up from the puzzle.

"A Christmas tree farm!" His little boy enthusiasm bubbled over. "That must be a wonderful place! I bet it's the best place on earth."

Emily and Alexander exchanged glances.

"You read my mind," he said.

The next morning Emily and Gracie boarded the small private plane that had flown Alexander, the children, and Stefan to her then traveled to Holly Mountain, landing at its tiny private airport early enough for lunch at Emily's house.

~ * ~

Emily tiptoed through her parents' living room, past the brick fireplace, the wooden rocking chair, the blue chintz sofa that looked like an English garden. A cup of steaming black tea in hand, she carefully opened the door, relieved her father had oiled the squeaky hinges so she wouldn't wake the others, and stepped onto the front porch. Because she was still in her robe and pajamas, she'd wrapped herself in the quilt from her bed, adding an extra layer of warmth against the winter chill.

An overnight snowfall had turned the ground white, and the western breeze carried the smell of distant pines through the air. Along the horizon, a slender band of sunlight glowed gold against the sky, and the clouds rested in layers of orange, red and indigo. The hazy blue mountains towered before her, and she sighed with the contentment of being home.

She leaned against the white wood railing and took a sip of her tea. This was the porch where she and Caroline played, where she curled up on the wicker sofa with Ranger and read, where she sat in the summer and listened to rain play on the tin roof.

Strong arms circled her waist, and Alexander kissed the top of her head. "Why are you up so early?"

She snuggled against him. "Couldn't sleep. Too excited."

"To be here?"

"And with you."

"It's quite peaceful in these mountains. And quite lovely."

"Over there." She nodded toward a distant peak. "That's Mount Aster. In the summer, it's covered with a zillion blue and purple flowers. And beyond that is Primrose Peak, and the furthest point is the Rosebay Ridge."

He kissed the back of her neck. She pretended not to notice.

"Geologists believe these mountains formed a billion years ago. They're called the Blue Ridge Mountains because the forests release hydrocarbons into the air, and that's why they're such a lush color."

No words from him, just small soft kisses.

"I'm trying to educate you about the ecology of my homeland, and you're distracting me," she giggled.

"I'll read about it later on the National Park website," he whispered.

Emily turned to face him, and they kissed deeply.

"Is there anything better than morning kisses?" he asked.

"Morning tea?" she asked playfully, bringing the cup to her lips. "Morning light? Morning air?"

He shook his head and drew her close. His voice was soft but tender, his eyes serious. "Emily, I want to tell you something."

"Something about morning kisses?"

"Please, something serious. I'm in l—"

"Papa!" Isabella burst through the door, Lukas, Stefan, and Gracie trailing behind. "We were looking for you and Emily. Why are out here? Aren't you cold?" She was barefoot, wearing her pajamas, and the little girl shivered.

Wrapping the quilt around Isabella and Lukas's shoulders, Emily gently nudged them back into the house. "Papa and I will come inside in a moment."

"I need to talk to Emily," Alexander added patiently.

"Okay," Isabella said, standing in the doorway.

"Alone," he said quietly.

"We are alone, together," she replied.

He rolled his eyes. Emily wasn't going to argue semantics with a nine year old. Instead, she tried a different strategy. "Aren't you hungry? I'll bet Lukas is hungry." He nodded eagerly. "We'll be in soon to fix breakfast. I think we're having pancakes, and maybe you two can stir in the chocolate chips."

Isabella clapped with delight, grabbed Lukas's hand, and scurried back inside.

"No chocolate chips for the dogs," Emily called behind them. She turned back to Alexander. Clad in pajamas and a fleece jacket, he shivered. "Are you cold? It must be twenty degrees warmer here than in Marisol. Let's go inside."

"First, there's something I want to say."

"I'm listening."

"Emily." He pulled her close again. "We haven't known each other very long."

"Less than a month." She turned up the collar of his jacket. "There. Warmer?"

He nodded. "In the short time we've know each other, in those few weeks, I've come to realize something, something very important."

"Yes?"

"Very important." His voice rose.

The front door flew open again. "There you are!" her mother said. "Isabella said you two are starving for pancakes."

"Not exactly what we said," he muttered.

"Well, you come inside out of this cold," her mother said. "Right now! It's freezing."

"You need a good breakfast," Emily's father said over her mother's shoulder. "We're going out to the Christmas tree farm, and I'm going to tell Alexander all about seeding, soil content, cutting, erosion. I promised Isabella and Lukas they could ride on the tractor."

Isabella and Lukas squeezed through the Saint-Claires and stood in the doorway again. Gracie trotted out and pawed at Emily's leg for breakfast, while Stefan sat behind Alexander, barking.

Emily took his hand. "We'll talk later," she promised.

~ * ~

"'For goodness' sake keep your fingers crossed,' Trixie went on. 'I think I hear Mr. Stratton coming down the hall. He just has to let us do it. Just think, we'd be doing something to help all those children and maybe save the Bob-Whites, too!'"

Emily closed her copy of *The Mysterious Code*, one of her favorite Trixie Belden stories in which the girl detective fights back after the principal threatens to end all the school clubs, including the Bob-Whites, unless students can prove they help others.

"More," yawned Lukas.

"I want to know what happens," Isabella mumbled, her eyes heavy.

"Tomorrow," Emily said.

"Emily will read to us again," Alexander assured them. He stood and helped her to her feet. "Thank you, Mr. Saint-Claire. It was very kind of you to set up this tent in your living room."

"Well, the next time you come, I'll take the children camping for real. But, for tonight, this will give them a taste of adventure."

"And thank you, Mrs. Saint-Claire, for roasting hot dogs and making s'mores in the fireplace."

"My pleasure," Emily's mother replied. "I'm sorry Stefan ate that pack of graham crackers I dropped. I thought I could pick it up in time."

"No problem," Alexander assured them. "He once at hefty slice of spice cake, and he survived that."

Emily's mother excused herself to read in her bedroom, and her father unrolled his sleeping bag to "camp" with the children. They said their good nights, and Emily pulled the doors shut behind her.

"I'll fix us some hot chocolate," she volunteered.

"I'd like that," Alexander said. "I want to finish our conversation from this morning."

As she stirred the milk on the stove, Emily wasn't sure what Alexander wanted to talk about, but she was sure he'd been distracted all day. While the children played hide and seek among the Christmas trees, he watched but didn't join in. He didn't seem enthusiastic when Isabella learned how to play a few verses of "Away in A Manger" on her father's hammer dulcimer, and he didn't laugh when Lukas started to pick up some of her family's Southern phrases— "Will y'all pass me a biscuit?" and "It's cold as the dickens out there." After supper, when they watched "A Charlie Brown Christmas," and Lukas and Isabella danced to Schroeder's piano solo, Alexander barely smiled.

Emily placed the mugs on a tray and brought them into the den. "Alexander—" she called, but he was sleeping in her father's recliner, Gracie in his lap, and his hand resting on Stefan's head.

Quietly, she set the cups on the cherry wood blanket chest her parents used as a coffee table. Her gray hiking boots were resting beside his brown ones near the hearth, and that sight made her feel warm inside, warmer than the hot chocolate. She sat crossed-legged on the braided rug, staring at the flames as the fire popped, savoring the smell of burning oak, and comforted that he was just a few feet away.

She felt a hand on her shoulder and when she looked up, she saw his face, bathed in warm firelight. "Sit with me," she said, motioning for him to join her.

"I'm sorry I fell asleep." He sat beside her but didn't meet her gaze.

She smoothed his mussed hair with her fingertips. "We've had busy few days, first in New York, then on the farm—well, a busy few weeks before that with the RICI. It's okay to rest." She started to stand up. "Why don't I heat up your hot chocolate? That will help you get a good night's sleep."

"Emily, I love you."

Her eyes opened wide. *What did you say?*

"I realize it would be presumptuous to say it was love at first sight, but from the first moment I met you, I suspected I was *going* to fall in love with you. I fought it because I thought I can't bear to be hurt again, and that was a tough ten-minute battle, but then I realized I would be hurt if I had to live without you. When I was speaking at the opening press conference, I could hardly concentrate because I was thinking about you. When you ran down the hall afterward, I thought, 'I have to talk with her. I can't let her go.' Every day when I came to your room to fetch the children—I tried to be nonchalant, but, inside, my feelings we out of control.

"The day we had our 'adventure' and we hiked to Pearl Moon Falls, I was certain I was in love with you. I wanted to tell you that afternoon but I thought, 'No, it's not the right time.' And our midnight date in my apartment, I'd planned to tell you then, but Lukas had his nightmare. I made up my mind to tell you the night of the ball, but that woman surprised me and asked me to dance, and I panicked, so I just let you go. How foolish I was!

"When I came to New York, I thought I would tell you that first night. You seemed happy to see us, and I worked up my courage, but I told myself to slow down. Maybe you wanted a friendship, nothing more. And if you did want more, better to wait till I could arrange a romantic evening. In my mind, I planned to ask you to go sailing, and we'd pack a picnic supper, and I'd tell you as the sun was setting over the sea, but then I thought, who knows where I can rent a sailboat in New York City in winter.

"This morning, when I found you on the porch, and the sun was rising, and the sky was so glorious, and you were so lovely, I told myself, 'This is the perfect moment.' Then, the children interrupted us, then your parents came, and we were busy all day. Telling you in the Christmas tree field didn't seem right, and when the children were riding on the tractor, the engine noise wasn't what I wanted you to remember. Then, I had to help you dad set up the tent, and telling you over hot dogs and s'mores wasn't very romantic. I thought about waiting till we got back to New York, maybe have a candlelight dinner catered in, but I can't wait. I love you."

"Alexander—" Emily sighed.

"I don't know how you feel, but this is serious for me. There are so many negatives, though, if you tell me to go away I will. We'll never have any privacy because of the children, as you saw this morning. I love them, they're my beautiful boy and girl, my heart and soul, but as your dad would say, 'They're busy as bees in a hive.' Raising children is hard work, harder than anyone ever tells you. And now, I see how happy you are here, and I wonder can you be happy in Marisol because, with my job, we can't live here, but we could come back for vacations. And your job—I can't ask you to give that up. Bow-Wow does so much good work, and you helped build that. You can't turn your back on that. I should never have said anything. I love you. I'm sorry, but I do."

"Please," she whispered.

He held up his hand. "No, don't say anything. The children and I will take you back home tomorrow, then we'll fly to Marisol."

"My sweet boy," she said.

"Now you're talking to me like I'm a dog," he sighed, "I should never have blurted it out. I rehearsed what I would say so many times— it was always elegant, tender—not this bumbling monologue. But I couldn't keep my feelings inside anymore. So, I'm sorry. There never seemed to be a good time to say what was in my heart, and I was afraid to say anything because you might not feel the same. This isn't at all what I imagined. I wanted it to be so perfect. But I'm saying it now. I love you."

She threw her arms around his neck and hugged tight. "Oh, Alexander, I love you. I wanted to say it before, but I wasn't sure how you felt either. But I love you. Really. Truly. Madly. Deeply. Forever and ever."

For the first time that day, he smiled. His hands caressed her face.

"I love you," she repeated.

They kissed until well after midnight.

This night. His smile. Her heart.

As they watched the last embers of the fire smolder, Emily settled into the comfort of Alexander's arms, sheltered in the mystery and light of love.

~ * ~

Emily was unpacking from the Holly Mountain trip when she got a text from Sebastian.

R U home?

She replied, *Y.*

Baked shortbread. Coming over now.

Her life was changing again and, as was the case in every major moment in her life since she moved to New York, it would involve pastry with Sebastian.

He bounded in with a Christmas tin of cookies, Rollo happily trotting at his heels. She led them to the living room, patted the sofa cushion beside her, and motioned for Sebastian to sit. "We need to talk."

He eyed her suspiciously. "This sounds serious."

"Yes, but good serious, not bad serious."

"Okay." He stiffened. "What's coming next?"

She took a deep breath. "I'm going make a change in my job. I'm cutting back on work."

"Is this about Marisol? Because I'm sorry. I thought you'd love it, but I should have asked you before I made the plans, and I apologize a thousand times. You have to forgive me."

"I accept your sincere apologies, and I forgive you a thousand times, but it's more than that. Sebastian, for the past few years, my life's been out of balance. Out of control, really. I work all the time, and I don't want to do that anymore. That's part of the reason I got so upset on Zaya's show. Please tell me they didn't broadcast my breakdown."

"No, we only saw was the confident you."

"Truth?"

"Absolute truth," he said, crossing his heart.

"Thank goodness. I was soaring along—the best interview I'd ever given—then I fell apart. I won't be on TV for a while, if ever again, but in a weird way, I'm glad it happened. That whole day, including me losing my temper with you in the restaurant, the text from Matt—"

"You didn't tell me you heard from that jerk. Every time I think about those paintings of Gracie—tacky. Art critics may call his work profound, but tacky, that's what I call it."

"Ancient, ugly, unpleasant history." Emily waved her hand as if she were flicking away a gnat. "But that whole day showed me I needed to make a change. I've been in limbo, too afraid to go forward because it might be a wrong step. So, I'm going to change my job. I want to write full-time."

"But you're the best business partner—"

She held up her hand to silence Sebastian. "No." Her voice was gentle. "I've given this a lot of thought—long before Marisol, but the past few weeks, it's crystal clear to me. I don't *want* a change. I *need* one. I can't wait any longer. I want to write full-time for Bow-Wow, so I'm giving up my management responsibilities."

He sat quietly, his hands folded in his lap, staring into space then he looked at Emily. "I don't think anyone will ever do the job as well as you. We started this business from nothing. You're not only my business partner, you're my best friend. I want whatever will make you happy."

"Thank you." She sighed with relief and clasped his hands. "You're *my* best friend. I want you to be happy, and I think you *are* happy managing and marketing Bow-Wow, but I'm not. I want to write. I want you to be okay with that. I realize you'll have to find someone to replace me."

"I can't say I'm a hundred percent thrilled, but we can find a good businessperson to help with management responsibilities. Layton in our office—he's got some great ideas for projects. I'll talk with him. He has an entrepreneurial spirit. If he's not interested, I'm sure there is a dog-loving maverick out there somewhere, anxious to dream up new projects for Bow-Wow."

"There's something else."

"Is this the bad part? I knew something bad was coming. Oh, no!" He put his head in his hands.

"Don't be such a pessimist. This is good." She paused and took another deep breath. "I met someone."

"You met someone? At the dog show? I'm intrigued."

She told him the story of the disastrous first meeting with Alexander—an embarrassment that turned into a blessing, the daily visits from the children while she worked, the "adventure day," the ball. Her voice cracked when she recounted how her heart broke when she left Marisol, then brightened when she told how Alexander came to find her, and how, despite her best efforts not to, she fell in love with him, the children, and Stefan.

"This is serious," she finished.

He took her hand in his again. "This man—is he a good person?"

"He's kind, he's smart, he's gentle, he loves dogs."

"I want to meet him before I pass final judgment, but preliminarily, I approve. He has the four best qualities anyone can have. You have my blessing." He squeezed her shoulders in a big Sebastian-kind of hug.

"And you were so unhappy when you went to Marisol," he chided. "See, the trip wasn't a disaster after all. Actually, I was the one who brought you and Alexander together. It was destiny. It was meant to be." He finished smugly, "I think a thank you is in order."

She gave him a sideways smile. "Thank you."

He kissed her on the forehead. "You know what I think we should do next?"

"Does it involve food?"

"Of course. Let's crack open that tin of shortbread."

She brought tea to Sebastian on a tray with Christmas paper plates and napkins Georgia left behind. As Gracie and Rollo napped on the floor in the late afternoon sun, he told Emily his Christmas included a new niece, dozens of relatives and friends crowded around card tables in his parents' small house, all talking "a mile a minute," and a broccoli casserole disaster when his aunt lost her glasses, misread the recipe and added two tablespoons of sugar instead of a half teaspoon of salt.

She gave him the Christmas presents from Marisol with more details of the "adventure" day when she, Alexander, and the children went to the Christmas market, sledded down Palace Hill, and took a sleigh ride into the forest. She reported behind-the-scenes descriptions of the dog show, the Fetch ball, and the gala, and she showed photos from her phone of the ocean and the mountains, as well as the pictures she took of Alexander and the children.

As they said their goodbyes, Sebastian hugged her. "I'll miss having you as a business partner, but more than that, I'll miss working with you every day. Let me know your plans. I'll support you whatever you want to do."

"We'll still work together, and I can't imagine we won't talk every day. It's just that you'll be my boss instead of my partner."

He smiled. "Emily, no one will ever be your boss."

She kissed him on the cheek. "Except Gracie."

"That goes without saying!" He called Rollo to his side and clipped the leash to his Christmas collar, dotted with holly leaves and berries. "Now, I need to take my boss home and check some work emails."

A few hours later, Sebastian texted Emily.

Check our bios on the Bow-Wow site. Made some changes.

Emily opened her computer and read her bio first. Previously, the short description listed her as "expert on all things canine. Juggler of multiple tasks. Rescuer of Gracie. Bow-Wow impresario." Sebastian had rewritten: "Full-time writer. Dog-lover extraordinaire. Fearless traveler. Adventurer in life and love. Optimist. Gracie's mom. Genius and co-founder of Bow-Wow Enterprises." *Maybe a little hyperbole.*

She clicked on Sebastian's link. His bio was mostly the same: "Idea guy. Risk taker. Head honcho. Dog dad to Rollo. Brain trust and co-founder of Bow-Wow Enterprises." Yet, there were two additions. "Royal matchmaker. Instrument of destiny." *No hyperbole at all.*

Chapter Eleven
A Full Heart

The door latch clicked softly.

"Are you asleep?" Alexander whispered.

Emily was reading in bed. "No, no. I was waiting for you."

He collapsed face down on the bed.

"Are the children asleep?" she asked, laughing.

"Finally. For a while."

"Christmas Eve is the most exciting night of the year. You really can't blame them for wanting to stay awake."

"I know. I was the same way when I was younger. I've been reading to them since 8 o'clock. *The Night Before Christmas. How the Grinch Stole Christmas. A Tale of Three Trees. Bear Stays Up for Christmas*, which may have only inspired them keep their eyes open. Each time I'd finish one book, one of them would beg, 'Again,' and they were so cute, how could I say no?"

"Catch your breath," she cautioned. "They'll be up at daybreak to see if Santa came."

Turning to face her, he took her hand. "When did you get back from the emergency room?"

"Hmmm, maybe fifteen minutes ago."

"Is Sebastian okay?"

"He'll be fine. He only sprained his ankle. It wasn't a broken bone this time. Last summer, after he fell out of that elm and fractured his arm, I instituted a no-tree-climbing rule. Now, I need to issue a no rowdiness indoors rule."

"What happened?"

"For Christmas, he bought the children a karaoke machine. He gave it to them after supper and told them to open it because the wrapping paper was torn—"

"Because he tore it?"

"Right, so he and the children were singing 'Santa Claus is Coming to Town', and Sebastian started dancing, and one jeté lead to another, and he tried to leap over a chair. Just didn't clear it."

"Ah, I see. When I asked Isabella how he got hurt, she told me, 'He did something silly.' I didn't ask further."

Emily knelt behind him and rubbed his shoulders. "Thank you for inviting Sebastian to visit us this Christmas. And Rollo. And Georgia. And her husband. And their children. And my parents. And my Uncle Frank."

Alexander kissed her hand. "Your first Christmas here should be happy and memorable."

"I want this Christmas to be special for you too." She put her arms around his neck and kissed his cheek. "I need to tell you something—"

"More company? Is Mr. Bertelli coming?"

"No." She laughed. "I invited him, but he always visits his daughter and grandchildren in Connecticut. This spring, I'll meet him in Cetara, and we'll hike the lemon groves with Gracie, just like he dreamed.

"I'll miss you."

"It's only for a few days." Emily took Alexander's hands and placed his arms around her waist. "But I'm here now." She kissed him once. Then again. Then again.

"Do you know what I'd like to do?"

Her heart raced, and she stroked his cheek. "What, my love?"

"Let's take a walk." He hopped off the bed.

"Now?"

"Now."

She looked at the clock on the nightstand. "It's almost midnight!"

"I know, but I need to relax. Think how peaceful it will be if we walk to the city center."

"It's Christmas Eve. The town will be deserted."

"That's what will make it so peaceful." He took her hands and helped her to her feet.

"But it's cold."

"We'll bundle up." He raced to the closet and threw clothes on the bed. Before she could protest, he helped Emily on with her parka, pulled her hat over her ears, and looped a wool scarf around her neck. He quickly donned his jacket, hat and scarf and motioned for her to meet him at the door.

"One minute," she said, taking her phone from her purse. "I want to text your parents and let them know we're going out for a few minutes."

"A good idea, but we won't be gone long, and the children aren't likely to wake up."

"Just in case." Emily tapped a message on her phone but didn't wait for a reply.

As they walked past the pile of sleeping dogs in living room, Alexander put his finger to his lips, cautioning her not to wake them. Gracie, Stefan, and Rollo were curled together so tightly, it was hard to tell where one dog began and the other ended.

The couple crept silently down the halls, and as they walked through the palace gates and into the city center, a light snow fell, tiny flakes fluttering from the cloudy sky. Ropes of twinkling lights stretched across the cobblestone streets, and giant silver candy canes glimmered under the lamp posts. Hand in hand, they strolled past doors decorated with holly wreaths and giant red velvet bows. Occasionally, they stopped to admire the store windows with their winter scenes of skiers gliding down mountain slopes, elves building dolls and trains, and reindeer flying across the sky with toy-packed sleighs.

In the center of the town square, they paused in front of the Christmas tree decorated with multi-colored lights and hundreds or crisp white paper stars made by children from St. Angelina's school. This year, the town council voted to add a Christmas village and staged a competition, inviting local high schoolers to form teams and build miniature chalets. The two stopped to admire an elaborate entry with interior lights that caused the windows glow and a machine that made smoke curl from the red chimney.

"Alone at last." He wrapped his arms around her waist.

"Is that why you wanted to come here? To be alone?" She smiled up at him.

"I warned you once we would never have much privacy."

She shrugged. "We have enough. Yes, it's been a hectic month. The children had so many school activities—hand bells, Christmas plays, school parties. We both had our work with the RICI. You had your administrative job, and I had to write daily blog posts and work with the University of Marisol journalism interns who helped with Bow-Wow's coverage this year. Plus, Christmas decorating, baking, shopping. I didn't really get tired until the afternoon of the Fetch! Play Ball, and by then, family and friends were coming in. The way I see it, what we're missing in privacy, we've made up for in chaos. Happy chaos."

"And we've only lost one shoe this month, if my calculations are correct."

"Only one," she said. "But Sebastian didn't mind. I think he tempted poor Stefan with that old loafer so he'd have an excuse to buy a new pair."

The night breeze caused her to shiver. Alexander adjusted her hat and scarf and placed his palm on the back of her neck, his fingers laced through her long hair. "Last Christmas Eve, I came here alone."

"I didn't know that."

He nodded. "I put the children to bed, then I walked here with Stefan to think. I asked myself could I live without you in my life? Could I love you completely? Could you love me, and if you didn't, could I live with the heartbreak? I told Stefan how unsure I was, and he looked up at me, as if to say, 'I miss her, too.' And I knew, in that moment, I had to tell you my feelings because love is always worth the risk."

"It is indeed." She rested her head on his chest. "Last Christmas, I was so—so lost. I wasn't sure how I felt about you, how you felt about me, what the future held. I hoped we could be together, but I couldn't imagine how that was possible. But we both took a chance, and here we are."

"Do you remember our wedding day?"

"Since it was only five months ago, yes," she replied playfully. "I wore something old—my mother's pearl drop earrings. And something new—a white silk dress. And something borrowed—a diamond hair clip from your mother. Something blue—one of Caroline's hair ribbons for my bouquet."

"What else? Each time we remember, it's as if we're reliving that day."

"Before the ceremony, we had a delicious pancake breakfast in the garden with the children, then Isabella and Lukas picked flowers— peonies, irises, roses—and that was my bouquet. It was just us and our parents. Later, you took the children, and the dogs, and me sailing, and we saw a pod of dolphins as the sun set.

"When we came back to the palace, you showed me a pink dogwood tree that had been planted outside our window. That was Caroline's favorite, and it was like she was with me. Now, when I wake up every morning, I see it and think of her.

"After dinner we were sitting in the living room with the children and the dogs and I told you 'This is the most wonderful day ever.' And Isabella heard me and said, 'For me, too. It's like there's a rainbow inside me.' She was much more articulate, but that's what I felt—something magical and beautiful and full of promise was in my heart. What do you remember?"

He smiled down and her and kissed her on the nose. "I remember

I was a little nervous—I was afraid I'd forget our vows. But when I saw you, when we were standing in the meadow with the mountains around us, all my anxiety melted away, and all I could think is that I wanted nothing more than to care for you and protect you and cherish you. I remember thinking you were the most striking woman I'd ever seen, and I couldn't believe someone with such a generous heart and kind spirit loved me."

The clock chimed—fifteen minutes to midnight. "Almost Christmas," she said.

"Tell me your fondest Christmas wish," he whispered. "What could I give you that would make you smile? I know we promised no gifts this year, but maybe a quiet walk along the beach, a winter picnic?"

"I have everything. I have love." She paused. "I need to tell you something. We did say we wouldn't buy each other presents this year and, technically, I didn't buy one, but I do have a present for you. Or had. I wrote you a letter, and I was going to give it to you tomorrow morning, but I left it on the living room table. Gracie knocked over my cup of tea, and it spilled all over the stationery."

"Hmmm. A tea-stained letter—I've never had one before. You can still give it to me."

"I will, but some of the words washed out. I wrote and re-wrote so many times, I memorized it."

As she cleared her throat, a curious smile spread across his face.

"Dearest Alexander, A year ago, I came to Marisol, unhappy, alone, weary. But in the year since, there have been so many changes. I married the kindest person I know, became stepmom to the two most wonderful children in the world, inherited a 'big brother' for my little Gracie, and I live in a beautiful country where I can see the mountains and the ocean every day.

"Not only has it been a year of changes, but a year of lessons. I've learned some of the best things happen when life doesn't go as planned. If I'd gone on vacation, as I wanted, I would never have met you. If my plane had landed on time, I would have gone to the hotel and never have run into you at the Seaside Center. If the photographer hadn't had car trouble, I wouldn't have mistaken you for him. Sometimes, things have to go wrong to turn out right. I didn't get what I wanted, and that turned out to be very good.

"I love you. That you already know, but what you may not realize is that you helped me find my courage. I was so timid, always afraid, but you helped me learn my spirit is bigger than my fears.

"Merry Christmas, my truest love."

"That's a lovely letter." He kissed both hands, then held her tight. "I'll treasure it when you give it to me, tea stains and all. And I treasure you. Emily Saint-Claire, you opened my heart."

She kissed him, then slipped her arms around his waist. "I love you so much."

"I love you and that's why I wanted our first Christmas together to be special. Extra, super special."

"It is special because we're together."

"True, but I wanted to give you an exceptional gift for our first Christmas together. Yes, yes, I know we said gifts weren't important this year, but I got you a present too. Technically, I didn't buy it, and it's not something I planned. Let's just say your gift found me." He took her hand. "Let's go sit in the church for a few moments."

"Is my gift in there?" she teased.

He didn't answer but led her down the aisle, and they took their places in the first pew. He shed his hat and scarf, then draped his arm around her shoulder. She had expected they'd be alone, but Sister Daniella Marguerite was there, playing the ancient pipe organ— "Angels We Heard on High" and "The First Noel."

"Bravo," Alexander clapped when she paused.

She turned and bowed her head.

"How beautiful," Emily added.

Following a quick prayer, Sister Daniella joined them.

"Let us be the first to wish you a Merry Christmas," he said.

"Thank you, and the same to you two," she replied.

"Forgive me, this is my first Christmas in Marisol, but do you play every Christmas Eve?" Emily asked.

"Oh, no." She laughed. "I come in here often to practice. We don't have formal services on Christmas Eve or Christmas Day, but the church is open for people who want to pray, reflect, meditate. Our local residents are very forgiving during the Christmas season," she joked. "So, when I play, if my playing isn't top form, they're willing to overlook a few wrong notes now and then. How is the Christmas celebration at the palace?" the sister asked. "A busy time for you?"

He nodded. "Yes, we have lots of company—Emily's family and friends—and the children had numerous Christmas activities at school. And I've been working with my father on his annual Christmas Day speech. Of course, we just finished the RICI—"

"I'm so glad you added the Rescue Day event," the sister said. "So many dogs need good homes. Saint Angelina would be so proud."

"Yes, that was Emily's idea," Alexander noted.

"All the dogs were adopted that day." Emily beamed with pride.

He continued, "We've been so busy at the palace, I hardly had time to think about presents."

Sister Daniella smiled.

"I hardly had time to think about presents," he repeated. "Sister, I believe that's your cue."

She jumped to her feet. "Oh, yes! Right! Emily, I have a gift basket for you."

Emily's eyes widened.

"A gentleman brought it by earlier. It's in my office. Wait here."

Barely able to contain her excitement, Emily turned to Alexander. "What's going on?"

"Wait and see," he grinned.

Sister Daniella came back into the sanctuary carrying a wicker basket with a red and white plaid blanket over the top. Alexander took the basket and placed in Emily's lap.

"Merry Christmas."

"A puppy! You got me a puppy!" She took the tiny dog from the basket—a coal-black ball of fur with floppy ears, a fat belly, and a long tail that wagged non-stop.

"Gracie will be so happy! Another dog to love."

"Truly, I had not planned to get you a gift, but a few days ago Sister Daniella told me the local shelter had taken in an abandoned dog and her puppy. It was too late to adopt them at the RICI Rescue event, and she asked if I knew anyone who might want a puppy—someone who was patient, and gentle, with a heart as big as the sky, and I said, 'I know the perfect person,'" he said sheepishly. "I wanted to adopt the mom, but someone else had taken her."

"Oh, thank you!" Emily cuddled the puppy, who wiggled and whimpered happily. "As Isabella says, this is the perfectly perfect gift. Wait, do the children know?"

"No, it will be a surprise to them tomorrow morning. I had to keep it a secret from them. They would have been so excited, they would told you as soon as they knew."

"Sister Daniella, thank you so much for arranging this," Emily said as she tickled the puppy under his chin. "I can't wait to get you home. So much love is waiting there for you."

Holding the little dog close, Emily floated back to the palace with Alexander by her side. "So this is why you wanted to talk a walk tonight?"

"Yes, Sister Daniella and I worked out a plan so the dog would be the first present on our first Christmas together." He rubbed the puppy's ears. "He doesn't have a name yet. The people at the shelter were calling him Oliver, but you may want to change that."

"Oliver is fine," Emily said kissing the top of the pup's head. His eyes were bright and happy. "His name will remind me of an olive branch, of peace, of Christmas. I can't believe you did this."

"Forgive me for keeping a secret from you?"

"Christmas secrets are always okay," she assured him. "I think that's written down somewhere in Santa's book of Christmas rules." She paused. "Alexander, I have something to tell you. I've kept a Christmas secret from you too."

He raised an eyebrow.

"When we get back to the palace, there's going to be a present for you in addition to the tea-stained letter. Her name is Stella—star, our Christmas star. Technically I didn't *buy* you a gift either. But I *had* to get her. When I was covering the RICI, I ran into one of the volunteers at the shelter, and she told me they'd brought in a young dog who'd given birth to a single puppy. Apparently, the mother had several litters in the recent past, and her health suffered. Stella needed a home, and I said I knew the ideal person to care for her. A veterinarian." She smiled shyly. "Merry Christmas."

"Emily! This is the best present I ever had! Thank you, thank you, thank you."

"That's why I didn't want to go for a walk. I asked someone from the shelter to deliver the dog around midnight, so it would be your first Christmas present. But, when you insisted, I had to make other plans."

"So you told Sebastian?"

"Goodness no. He would have woken the children, then posted it on the Bow-Wow website. So, I texted your parents right before we left to let them know. You mom is fixing bowls of food and water, and your father is getting blankets. You said you wanted to adopt the mother, but someone else I taken her already? I think I might be that someone. Stella may be Oliver's mother."

"You hear that, fella? Your mom is waiting for us." He turned to Emily. "How fast can you walk?"

They rushed back through the city center, under the canopy of twinkling lights, and Emily told the puppy about his new life—two older dogs to play with, children who would love him, a prince who would take him on walks to the barn, through the woods, along the beach, and a dog "mom" with a great pitching arm, who could toss tennis balls and never get tired.

As they approached the palace gates, Alexander caught Emily's arm. "We have four dogs now. Have we gone overboard? How many dogs it too many?"

"Four is a good number. The best number. Except maybe five. Five dogs could be—let's not get ahead of ourselves. For the record, we can never have too many dogs. Saying you have too many dogs is like saying you have too much love. It's not possible."

He rubbed Oliver's head. The puppy wiggled with glee. "He's eager to play. No sleep tonight."

"None at all. Won't it be great?"

"It certainly will." He put his arm around her waist and kissed her on the cheek, then they walked through the great oak doors of the palace. "We're home," he said to Emily and Oliver.

"Yes, we're home," Emily repeated. "Our home."

It was Christmas morning, and her heart was full.

~ * ~

Emily's Blog on the RICI Finalists

What a night!

The dogs took center stage at the RICI best of show championship, the culmination of weeks of grooming, judging, and waiting.

First in the parade of champions was the winner in the terrier group, Tibby, a Parson Russell from Cape Town, South Africa.

"Tibby likes to go on picnics at Table Mountain with his owner," the announcer said. "He also enjoys running along the beach at Saint James Bay, chasing kelp gulls and barking at Cape gannets. Parson Russell terriers are known for their friendly dispositions but also for their fearless independence. Tibby once had an encounter with a baboon, who visited the backyard to steal a few plums. Don't worry: Tibby watched safely through a window inside the house, but he barked ferociously, and no baboons have dared come around since."

The audience applauded as an image flashed on the Jumbotron screen: Owner Zane and Tibby were riding in a tram to the top of Table Mountain, Tibby's eyes wide as he peered over the side of the tram carriage. The pair wore matching bandanas with the colors of the South African flag—red, blue, green, white, gold, black.

The winner in the toy group was Nina, a papillon from Rio de Janeiro, Brazil.

"The papillon is the dog with the butterfly ears," the announcer said. "This breed is quick, upbeat, and curious—but also relaxed. When Nina is not sleeping and snoring in a recliner chair on the balcony of her apartment, she enjoys sleeping and snoring on her owner's bed. Nina once starred—actually, she made a cameo appearance—as 'dog with tourist' in the popular telenovela Malhação, Young Hearts. One of her hobbies is dancing with her owner to samba music."

The audience laughed when the photo popped on the screen. It had been taken at Blocao, the doggie version of Carnivale, held in the Copacabana neighborhood. Nina wore a lime green and orange-flowered sun visor with matching tulle skirt over her silky white fur. She rode in a doggie stroller, pushed by owner Juliana.

Trella, a chocolate-colored field spaniel from Barcelona, Spain, was the winner in the sporting group. In her photo, she joined her owner, Mateo, under a canopy of trees along Las Ramblas, the boulevard that runs through the city's center. Mateo was striding confidently, his hands in the pockets of his khaki trousers, and Trella was running beside him, her pink tongue peeking from the right side of her mouth as she cast her adoring gaze his way. The blue, black, white, and yellow mosaic by artist Joan Miró lay under their feet.

"The field spaniel is a sweet, sensitive dog who enjoys frequent playtimes," the announcer said, "and Trella is no exception. She loves chasing tennis balls in her back yard, running among the kermes oaks and plane trees. Trella also loves to travel. She and owner Mateo often take day trips from Barcelona to explore the beautiful Catalonian countryside. Trella's favorite place is Sant Pol de Mar, a scenic coastal town where she enjoys running with other dogs on the beach, barking at the waves, and stealing an occasional sandwich from tourists' tote bags."

The audience laughed. Trella might be an occasional thief, but they loved her nonetheless.

Ellis, a Portuguese water dog from San Diego, California, in the United States, was the winner in the working group.

"This breed, recognized for its immense intelligence, originally worked with fisherman," the announcer said. "Ellis is a working dog, too. When he's not in the show ring, Ellis is the official greeter at Pots Meet Pans, a kitchenware store in the city's Little Italy neighborhood. His job is to welcome customers searching for gifts for others—or themselves. All he expects in return for his hard work is a belly rub. His favorite snacks are turkey bacon and sweet potato treats, and his favorite leisure activity is rolling in the grass in Balboa Park."

The photo showed Ellis, with a red bow-tie, sitting in front of a display of purple and green dishes with owner, Mia.

"The ears have it," said the announcer with a laugh when Fredrick, a white French bulldog with unique bat ears, ambled around the ring.

"These playful dogs are popular among city dwellers the world over. Fredrick, also known as Freddy, lives in Vienna with his owner Annika. Annika coordinates publicity for the Vienna Philharmonic

Orchestra, and Freddy has attended the summer night concert for the past three years. Freddy is a devout Mozart fan; his favorite piece is Piano Sonata Number One in C Major, evidenced by his howling when he hears the first notes. His hobbies are frolicking and making mischief."

The crowd chuckled at the photo of Annika and Freddy standing in front of the Mozart statue in Burggarten. Annika was holding Freddy in her arms. The camera caught her in mid-sentence, her mouth slightly open, her lips curling into a smile. Freddy wasn't looking at Annika. Instead, he gazed, awestruck, at the famous composer's marble likeness.

Enzo, a Bouvier des Flandres from Vernazza in the Cinque Terre region of Italy, was the winner in the pastoral or herding group.

"The Bouvier's ancestors pulled carts, herded cattle, even delivered life-saving drugs during World War II," the announcer said. "Enzo carries on this proud working tradition by participating in a therapy program at a local children's hospital. The children call him Medico Dolce, the sweet doctor, and doctors and nurses say he never fails to bring a smile to the little ones' faces. Enzo can sit, stay, and speak—if he wants to—yet the command he responds to be best is 'love.' When he hears the word, he nuzzles, ready for the children to shower him with affection."

The photo showed owner Ginevra, a doctor, and her patient, a little boy listening to Enzo's heart with a stethoscope. A chorus of "awwws" swelled from the crowd.

Zounds, the beagle, was a dog who needed no introduction. The applause for him started before he paraded around the ring.

"We have a celebrity in the house," the announcer said. "Many of you will recognize our final contestant from Zounds the Hound, his video series broadcast on YouTube. The series features short videos of Zounds exploring England's Lake District, hiking with his owner, Merrill, in the colorful hills in the spring and fall, swimming in cool creeks during the warm summers, and frisking in the winter snows. Beagles possess a merry disposition. As you can see, Zounds is indeed a happy-go-lucky fellow. Wouldn't all of us be happy to live this dog's life?"

The photo showed a wet and mud-covered Zounds in mid-shake, climbing up a riverbank, a stick clamped between his teeth, his brown eyes filled with impish delight.

After the contestants and handlers made their way around the ring, the judge made her decision. Audience members held their breath.

"And the winner is..."

Acknowledgements

I became a writer because my parents and brothers encouraged me. I am always grateful to them. I'm also lucky to have friends and relatives who encouraged me, as well. I learned about writing from my fellow journalists; from my teachers at Swansboro High School, Duke University, and the University of North Carolina-Chapel Hill; and from my former students. Their "teachings" are woven throughout this book.

I also would like to thank Champagne Book Group for publishing this story. I am grateful to Cassie Knight and Kat Hall for their help and encouragement.

About the Author

Anna Swann has loved books and dogs since she was a child. She pledges that every book she writes will always feature smart, strong female characters, hopeful endings, and dogs who are eternally healthy and happy.

Swann has worked as a journalist, a public relations professional, and a professor, and is now a full-time fiction writer. She has published several short stories about women navigating life's obstacle course, an academic book on women and media, and numerous journalistic articles on women's health.

She loves to travel and incorporates some of her favorite real-life places in her fiction writing. She grew up in North Carolina and now lives in Williamsburg, Virginia, with her cocker spaniel, Emma.

Anna loves to hear from her readers. You can find and connect with her at the links below.

Facebook: http://www.facebook.com/AnnaSwann11
Twitter: https://twitter.com/AnnaSwann12

*

Thank you for taking the time to read *Paws for Christmas* and hope you enjoyed reading it as much as we loved bringing it to you. If the story brought you pleasure, please tell your friends, and leave a review. Reviews support authors and ensure they continue to bring readers books to love and appreciate.

A Nutcracker Christmas

Laurie Winter

Suddenly let go from her news anchor position, Aria Roberts heads north to stay at her late Great-Aunt Clara's house. She has many good memories there and wishes to give Clara's Christmas Shoppe, which is located on the first floor of the Victorian mansion, one final holiday season. When Aria arrives, she finds the special gift Clara left for her—an antique nutcracker with a poem hidden under the back lever. Aria reads the poem out loud. At sundown that night, those words magically bring the nutcracker to life.

Kort Zellner awakes inside the familiar surroundings of Clara's house but learns she has passed away and now her great-niece resides there. The curse placed on him three hundred years ago traps him in the form of a nutcracker but allows him to return every December 1st through midnight on Christmas Day—only between sundown and sunrise.

After some convincing, Aria believes Kort's strange story. She helps him experience life as he is gifted so few hours alive and in doing so, falls in love. he knows his curse makes it impossible to give her the constant relationship she deserves. His plan to leave her forever on Christmas Day collides with Aria's desire to build a future together, even if for only twenty-five nights a year.

Can the curse be broken for a happy ever after?

Chapter One

After all hope is lost, that's when magic happens.

With one hand fumbling for the house key tucked away in her coat pocket and the other firmly gripping the leash attached to her misbehaving puppy, Aria Roberts once again questioned her sanity. Coming here to reopen Clara's Christmas Shoppe for the holiday season had been a stray inkling one sleepless night last week. Her brain had stated she should stay home and focus on the next phase of her career. Her spirit, damaged and lonely, craved comfort and connection to the past. Since she was currently standing at the backdoor of the Victorian mansion that served as both the Christmas store and her late Aunt Clara's home, Aria needn't guess which faction had won.

Bingo, the fluffy pup she adopted three days before taking this trip, made a mad dash toward her parked car. Finding the key would wait. She grasped the leash with both hands and anchored her feet firmly on the top step. Despite her best efforts, an energetic Bingo, with the help of a slick layer of ice coating the landing, won the tug of war. After being dragged for several inches, Aria plunged down the three steps leading onto the pathway, landing hard on her backside.

"Ouch!" She ground her teeth, biting back a reprimand to the puppy.

Bingo must have sensed her mood because he stopped his escape attempt and returned to her side. A lick on her cheek earned her complete forgiveness. How could she stay angry at something so cute? Especially since he was her only companion for the foreseeable future. Her solitude had been her choice. A temporary resignation of what was left of her life.

"I'm fine. I'll be fine." Aria slowly stood to a chorus of pops and aches from various joints and brushed off her rear. She squinted from the bright sunlight reflecting off the snow. Despite a cloudless blue sky, the frozen air bit at any exposed skin, and her poor nose had gone numb. "How about you sit still like a good boy so we can get inside and warm up?"

He gazed up at her and cocked his head.

I'll take that as a yes. Back at the top of the steps, she drew out the skeleton key from her coat pocket and slipped it into the keyhole then turned. Once inside with her suitcase, she took a moment to mentally prepare for the memories. A lump of nostalgia swelled inside her chest. Knowing Great-Aunt Clara wouldn't be waiting upstairs to greet her caused hesitation. Could Aria handle more emotional turmoil?

What other option did she have? She'd already run away from one set of problems. Either push forward or retreat. With a grunt, she heaved up her suitcase and ascended the narrow staircase leading to her late aunt's suite of rooms on the second floor.

Bingo pattered behind her, making a few unsuccessful attempts to squeeze around to beat her to the top.

Aria opened the door then switched on the lights. While Bingo charged through the sitting room and down the hall, she set the suitcase on the hardwood floor, let out a sigh, and glanced around. Clara had resided above the store for most of her adult life, and Clara's Christmas Shoppe had been as dear to her as her own child or spouse. She'd never had either, seemingly happy to run her business as an independent woman.

Everything seemed the same, from the antique cream-colored

side and coffee tables to the crocheted rainbow colored blanket draped over the back of the sofa. A grouping of framed photographs lined the mantel. Aria strolled over and studied them before picking up a picture from her wedding day, an event she didn't enjoy dwelling on. She was placed in the center, dressed in bridal whites, surrounded by her mom, grandma, and Aunt Clara. She kissed the glass over the images of her grandma and great-aunt then set it back into place.

Memories of time spent here washed over Aria, slowing her heartbeat. Trips up north to visit over Christmas break—a treat she'd anticipated every year as a girl. Once she'd started college, life became busy, and she didn't come up with the rest of the family. A weak excuse. Her throat grew thick with guilt. Now, herself a mother to an overachieving daughter, she prayed Ella's priorities were better balanced than her own at that age.

A rhythmic thumping echoing from down the hall grabbed Aria's attention. Her pulse spiked then relaxed. How much trouble could her puppy find inside this small apartment? At the sound of lapping water, she sprinted to the bathroom. *Don't ask the question if you don't want the answer.*

"Bingo," she called out, keeping her voice calm. The articles she'd read on puppy training had said not to scold. As soon as he backed away from the toilet, she closed the lid. "I'll get you a bowl of water if you just give me a minute."

Since a cleaning service had come yesterday to tidy the apartment in preparation for her arrival, she'd been spared the job. The shop area downstairs would need most of her attention if she hoped to open by this weekend. She'd come to the city of Appleton, Wisconsin in hopes of giving Clara's Christmas Shoppe one final season before the merchandise and property were sold. The loss of all the history brought the sting of tears to her eyes, but then again, these days almost everything made her cry.

But who'd blame her? Agitation stirred in her gut. Alone for Christmas after being abruptly unemployed, and her daughter, Ella, away at college then leaving for Christmas break with Aria's ex-husband and his wife on a ski trip to Colorado.

She tipped back her head and gazed at the plaster ceiling, reigning in her emotions. Nothing would change while standing around feeling sorry for herself. How many times had she told Ella that very thing when Aria found Ella closed off in her bedroom after teenage disappointments? Filling a bowl with water for Bingo, Aria huffed. Time to take her own advice, buck up, and do something productive.

After a few trips downstairs to her car, she had the remainder of her luggage. As she took out Bingo's food and dish, she smiled. "At least I have you," she spoke to the dog who was currently sprawled out on the floor.

Perhaps that had been Ella's intention when she'd pushed for Aria to adopt a dog from the shelter. Even so, a cloak of sadness draped over her shoulders and weighed heavy. She missed her daughter; she missed her job. She'd gone to work each day believing she was irreplaceable, then one awful day, the axe fell. She was no longer needed, as neither a mother nor employee. Where was her purpose?

With Bingo settled on his pillow, gnawing on a bone, she reached inside her purse and removed Aunt Clara's final letter. The one written before her passing, leaving strict instructions for Aria not to read until she was ready to run the store. Back then, she'd figured the letter would stay sealed forever. She was a prime-time TV news anchor in Milwaukee. Little had she understood how sharply her life would shift twenty-four months later.

She only planned on opening Clara's Christmas Shoppe for a short time but her brief commitment was close enough to Clara's intention. Besides, Aria's curiosity over the contents of the letter was driving her crazy.

After taking a seat on Aunt Clara's favorite easy chair, Aria used her index finger to tear the top of the envelope. She unfolded the paper, and the sight of her great-aunt's neat cursive brought a rush of tender emotions along with the sting of regret. She should have made more time to see Aunt Clara during her later years. Since she couldn't rewrite the past, all she could do was try to honor Clara's memory in the best way she knew how.

Aria read.

Dearest Niece,

When I left my Christmas shop to your mother in my will, I secretly hoped you would decide to take over. If you are reading this letter, it means my hope has come true. I love you, dear one, like my own grandchild.

I have one final favor to ask of you. Remember my favorite nutcracker, the one I kept locked in the cabinet at the back of the store? I packed him away when I knew I was moving into the rest home, wishing to keep him safe. I need you to find him and set him inside the large room on the third floor. It's a strange request, I know, but I trust you'll follow through. He has a special gift for you, hidden underneath the lever in his back, which should be worth your troubles.

You must think these the ramblings of a senile old woman and perhaps you are correct, but I have faith in you my darling Aria that you will honor my request.

Above all, have a merry Christmas and keep your heart open to love.

Aunt Clara

Aria sniffled and wiped the tears off her cheek with the back of her hand. Sweet and silly Aunt Clara. When Aria was younger, her aunt had often tasked her with small jobs to do. Sometimes, she questioned her aunt's reasoning but always followed her directions, not wishing to disappoint someone who loved her deeply.

This time would be no different. Even though Aunt Clara wasn't there, Aria would do what her great-aunt asked. A strange request but what harm would come from unpacking an antique nutcracker and placing him upstairs in an almost empty room on the third floor? Plus, the promise of a special gift piqued her curiosity. Maybe she'd left one of her pieces of antique jewelry tucked inside the nutcracker.

Clara had written that she'd stored the nutcracker to keep it safe. Perhaps she'd boxed it up and placed it in a storage room. As good of a place to start as any other. In reality, this old mansion had dozens of rooms, and Aria might need to search them all. If her aunt really was determined to protect the nutcracker, she could have tucked him away in an out of the way closet or worse yet, in the attic.

Aria cringed. Even as an adult, the thought of going up to the cluttered and dusty attic produced anxiety. Maybe her mom knew where Clara had hidden the nutcracker before she'd moved to the nursing home. Mom had been here to help during that time.

Aria slipped out her cellphone from the back pocket of her jeans and pressed the contact button.

"Hey, honey," her mom answered. "Did you make it up to Aunt Clara's yet?"

"I'm here now." She strode toward the window and stared out. Across the street in the park, a group of children, dressed in full cold weather gear, chased each other through the snow in the park. "It's not the same without Aunt Clara."

"She did embody the spirit of Christmas all year long." Her mom sighed. "Have you changed your mind then about reopening the shop? You're welcome to fly down to Arizona and spend the holidays with Dad and me. Honestly, I hate the idea of you hiding away up there and spending Christmas alone. Especially after what happened at the station. You don't need to be embarrassed, you know. News stories are quickly replaced with fresh gossip."

Having her contract terminated, though no fault of Aria's own, had stung. Knowing that she'd been replaced as lead news anchor by someone half her age felt like a knife in the back. At forty-eight, Aria Roberts was no longer a desirable face for the station's target market. "I'm not hiding. I want to open the shop one last time. Plus, I think it will give me some time to come to terms with the changes in my life. I need to make decisions about what to do next."

"I still can't believe that ancient station manager told you that you were too old to be on the evening news." She huffed. "He should catch his appearance in the mirror."

Aria stifled a laugh. "He never came out and said I was too old." Though she wished he had. At least she'd have a good lawsuit to look forward to. "Plus, he's not on TV so it's okay for him to look like a wrinkled toad."

"I miss you." Her mom's laughter quieted. "Promise me if you get lonely you'll leave the shop and come to Arizona?"

"I promise." Even though she'd already sworn to herself she'd see this venture through, no matter what. "Anyway, the reason I called is Aunt Clara left me with instructions to unpack her favorite nutcracker, the tall one with the red jacket and black hat. Do you know what she did with it?"

A momentary pause quieted the line. "Actually, I remember Aunt Clara carrying it around with her while I helped pack her belongings for the move to the nursing home. She kept talking to it. Quite strange but then again, at that time she was suffering with dementia and her behavior wouldn't be classified as normal."

"Where did she put it?" With so much to get done before opening the shop, Aria didn't want to waste any more time than necessary on finding one nutcracker.

"I think she boxed it up then placed it on the top shelf toward the back of her bedroom closet. She made me promise not to let anyone touch it until you asked for it."

"Thanks, Mom. Give my love to Dad." Out of the corner of her eye, she saw a blur of golden brown fur streak behind the sofa. *Shoot.* As a new dog mom, she needed to do a better job remembering the sweet rascal. "I'll let you know when I open the shop."

"Talk to you later. Bye."

She ended the call. "Bingo, come on. Let's go on a treasure hunt." She'd make him part of the search since he seemed eager to explore anything and everything.

The dog, apparently able to understand English, appeared at her side. As she entered Clara's bedroom, she caught the delicate scent of Clara's favorite perfume. Even after all this time, she'd kept her mark on every part of the house. Aria yanked the cord in the closet to turn on the light. After a brief search, she found a wooden box sitting sideways on the top shelf.

Standing on tip-toes, she reached up and took it down. The box was heavier than she expected, and she huffed with the effort to keep it from tumbling out of her hands and onto the floor.

A bubble of excitement expanded in her chest. Why, though? It's not like the nutcracker held any special significance to her. Aria was never allowed to touch the antique, let alone grow sentimental about it.

She set the box on Clara's bed and raised the top. Tucked inside, wrapped in a velvet casing, was the nutcracker Aria remembered from her childhood. With gentle hands, she lifted the figure then held it in the sunlight streaming in from the window. The painted wooden object appeared relatively plain. What had made this nutcracker so special to her aunt?

As she carried the nutcracker out of the bedroom to take it up to the third floor, a sparkle reflected in the nutcracker's black eyes. She jumped, yelped, and dropped it onto the floor. All the recent stress must be messing with her head. If she didn't take care of herself, she'd start talking to inanimate objects, just like Aunt Clara.

Heart pounding, she held the nutcracker and brushed it off. "Sorry old chap. Don't tell my aunt, okay? She was very protective of you, and she'd never forgive me." Sorrow cramped around her heart, and melancholy washed through her. Her only comfort—the knowledge Clara would be over the moon pleased if she knew Aria was here to reopen her store.

A piece of tightly folded paper dotted the floor from where she'd picked up the nutcracker, and curiosity brightened her mood. The lever on the back of the nutcracker must have been pushed upward from the fall onto the floor. Whatever Aunt Clara had left for her must be hidden in the paper.

She plucked the yellowed paper and found nothing else inside. Frowning, she shuffled into the living room. What had she expected? A magic time travel spell, sending her back to when she had a successful career and a daughter still living at home? Not likely.

She sat on the sofa and placed the nutcracker by her side. "Let's see what secrets you're keeping." Aria unfolded the note with care. The paper felt brittle and strange in her hand. Once upon a time, Aunt Clara told her this nutcracker had been crafted in the mid-1700s. Perhaps this note was as old.

Read out loud, the handwriting instructed through the network of time. So, she did.

A curse to serve as an example,

pride turned a beating heart to wood,
once a year, life you may sample,
change the past if you could.
Love will be denied you,
sorrow will be your friend,
until you offer your due,
and the curse comes to an end.

Weird and kind of creepy. A chill danced over her skin. After grabbing the box, she carried the nutcracker up the stairs leading to the third floor. She'd follow her aunt's instructions then get to work. Today was already December first, and she hoped to have the shop ready for business in a few days in order to take advantage of the Christmas season. Then, when December twenty-sixth rolled around, she'd begin preparing for the sale of all remaining merchandise and the house.

Aria placed the nutcracker on the floor inside the large main room on the third floor and stared at the figure. It remained motionless in a stream of sunshine coming in from the window, and sparks of light drifted like sprites in the still air. A comforting warmth filled her chest.

"See you around," she whispered before closing the door, unsure why she continued conversing with the wooden object.

As she descended the stairs, she pressed a hand to her fluttering heart. Nothing appeared out of the ordinary, yet she couldn't shake the funny feeling something magical had been released into the air.

Chapter Two

Surrounded by darkness, Kort Zellner rose to his feet. He rolled his shoulders and stretched his neck. It felt good to move again, but his mind hadn't made the full adjustment back to life. His thoughts were covered with a thick fog. He rubbed his eyes, hoping to clear his vision.

Moving toward one of the tall windows in the room, he glanced outside. The sky was dark, of course, but electric streetlamps blended with the glow of Christmas lights on the nearby homes. The patches of illuminated ground showcased a covering of snow. No surprise. The month was December, without a doubt. Given the height he gazed down from and the familiar neighborhood, he relaxed with the awareness he'd awoken on the third floor of Clara's home.

Clara. Her name brought clarity to his brain and a jolt of worry. The last time he'd seen Clara Drosselmeyer, she'd grown weary with age and overwhelmed with the responsibility of running her shop. Given the fact she wasn't here to greet him like she did every sundown on December first since initially bringing him to life, he realized something had changed.

Since he was alive, moving and breathing, someone must have read the poem. But who? Either Clara was nearby or she'd passed along the task to someone else.

Inside a closet, he found the clothing left for him every year—blue jeans, flannel shirts, undergarments, socks, and boots. After setting aside his sword and taking off his soldier hat, he quickly changed out of his red coat and black pants and into modern clothing. Otherwise, he'd look like a nutcracker come to life. The truth would never be believed, regardless. People would label him as eccentric instead of cursed.

After a brief debate, he took the winter jacket from off the hanger and put it on. He might need to leave the house in a hurry. Inside the front pocket, he found a roll of money and a house key. Kort smiled. Clara had thought of everything.

He went to the closed door leading downstairs and cracked it ajar. The sound of a dog barking caused him to hesitate. She never owned a pet and at her advanced age, couldn't handle a dog. Which meant someone other than Clara was likely here. Dread weighed down on his chest. Time continued its forward trajectory while he stayed frozen, locked inside a wooden prison.

Even after crossing centuries and continents, he still held contempt for the unknown. Kort carefully lowered one foot on the top step then descended with care. The door leading into her living quarters was closed. Music played inside—an unfamiliar tune. A woman's steady voice sang along. Whoever this was, she wasn't Clara.

Although he understood that some December he'd wake to find she no longer graced the earth, he hoped now wasn't the time. She was as close to a friend as he had since the curse. She'd purchased the nutcracker version of Kort when she was thirty and read the poem that interrupted his slumber. Since then, they'd spend every evening together from December first through the twenty-fifth. He'd come to life at sundown and return to his wooden form at sunrise. A depressing existence if not for her steady company.

She'd taught him about the modern conveniences of the twentieth and twenty-first century and how to manage the grief of losing everything and everyone he loved. Her home had provided stability. Kort owed her more than he could ever repay.

The dog's barks increased in frequency and volume, and soon scratching sounded on the other side of the door.

He hesitated, heart pounding. His hand hovered over the doorknob. Sweat formed on his brow. Should he retreat?

"Bingo, come here," the woman called out. "Outside is this way."

After some more noise, another door thudded shut. The music no longer played, and the room on the other side of the door was silent. He turned the knob, not an easy job with a clammy hand, and pushed the door just enough to lean forward and peer through. No one in sight. He came inside and glanced around. The lights were on in the kitchen, sitting room, and in the hallway. Clara had insisted on turning off the lights when not in the room. "Electricity isn't free," she'd said, "and money doesn't grow on trees."

Her chair sat empty, without indentation and missing the usual blanket draped across the arm. He entered the kitchen, and his vision rested on a card posted with a magnet on the refrigerator door. *No.* Sorrow rose, catching his breath. In the center of the card was a colored photograph of young Clara and underneath were the words—In Loving Memory.

He swallowed hard. "Be at peace."

She'd struggled with her health the last few Decembers they'd spent together. He should have been there for her more than a few evenings a year. But he was cursed, unable to protect anyone he cared for. He'd been stripped of his family, his friends, and his homeland. As the world changed around him, he remained gripped inside the cold hands of magic.

A half empty mug of coffee sat on the counter. He wrapped his hands around it, noting the warmth radiating through the ceramic. The kitchen was filled with the scents of garlic and tomatoes. His stomach clenched with a deep hunger.

The door banged at the bottom of the stairway leading outside. His pulse quickened. Food would have to wait. If whomever was here wasn't expecting him and found a strange man standing in the kitchen, he might be shot on sight. He didn't fear death though, as he couldn't die—at least not in the traditional sense.

Kort darted to the stairway at the front of the house and crept downstairs, into the Christmas shop on the first floor. He strode through the darkened displays—racks empty of decorations. The shop must have closed after Clara's passing. Another loss, but after hundreds of years of saying goodbye, he'd grown accustomed.

Keeping the lights off, he progressed with only the low filtered illumination of the streetlamps to guide his steps. His foot hit a box placed on the floor between two display racks, and he struggled to keep his balance until a flailing arm struck a row of metal hooks. The ensuing crash masked the sound of his body hitting the ground. Pain burned from his shoulder, and a piece of metal pressed into his back.

The dog's barking returned at a frenzy. A muted scratching sounded from behind the upstairs door.

I need to get out of here. The best way to make an introduction would not be catching him creeping around the shop in the dark. Kort jumped back to his feet and quietly navigated to the front door. After removing the skeleton key from his pocket, he slipped it into the keyhole.

The creak of the door at the top of the staircase announced he'd soon have company.

"Hello," a shaky voice said. "Who's there? I have a weapon...and a dog."

Swallowing hard, he turned the brass handle and drew the front door, providing himself with enough room to slip out. Once outside, he relocked the door and traversed the front steps.

The air stung his face. Good thing he thought to bring the heavy coat when still upstairs. Kort crossed the street and found shelter from the wind behind a thick tree trunk. Hidden in the tree's shadow, he watched the windows at the front of the house. After a minute, the interior of the shop radiated with warm light. Likely the woman was searching for the source of the crash. She'd sounded afraid and rightly so. Especially if she was staying in the large house alone.

How to convince her of his history, as crazy as it sounded? He had plenty of experience. He also had memories of the times he'd failed and spent his evenings alive hidden in a cold attic or barn. Wrapping his arms around his body, he shivered. After living with Clara for decades, he'd grown content. Or at least as content as a man in his condition could be.

A woman's figure appeared in the window. She leaned a shoulder against the frame and gazed in his direction. Even though the darkness hid him, he took a step back, closer to the tree.

She was a redhead, like Clara in her younger years. Her posture was similar, too, standing with a straight spine and shoulders back. The resemblance provided some peace of mind. If the woman was a relation to Clara, he might stand a chance at being allowed to stay here during his brief time as a man. If not, he'd spend this December freezing and lonely.

~ * ~

After a search of the first floor, Aria hadn't found the cause of the crash she'd heard down here earlier. Bingo had given chase to several mice in one of the showrooms, finally losing his quarry as they scurried into a crack in the base of a cabinet. When she'd caught sight of the creatures, she mentally noted to put mice traps and a sturdy broom on the list of things she needed from the store.

Now, she halted before one of the large windows and stared off into the darkness that covered the landscape. Despite her intensions for today, she'd only pulled out about a dozen boxes from the storeroom. The many empty display racks and shelves taunted her confidence. Her plan to get the store ready in only a few days might be unrealistic, if she had to do everything herself. If she took too long, Christmas would be over then she'd check another box on her list of regrets.

Bingo's tail thumped on the ground by her foot, capturing her attention. She ran her gaze through the interior of the store, turning her thoughts to the job at hand. *I won't fail you, Aunt Clara.*

At the same time as she turned off the lights in the showroom, the doorbell chimed. The noise echoed throughout the foyer. Her heart leaped into her throat. Who'd stop by after dark? The store had been closed for a little over two years. She considered slipping upstairs in the hopes whomever was there went away. But, this could be one of Clara's neighbors who'd seen the lights on and wanted to check in. Besides, no one from Aria's circle of media acquaintances in Milwaukee knew she was here.

With Bingo pattering along at her side, she went into the foyer, flicked on the lights, and unlocked the front door. She opened it enough to peer out. "Hello?"

A tall, broad shouldered man stood on the porch, several feet away. "Hello." He raised a hand in greeting. "My name is Kort Zellner. I've come to help with the shop. Clara should be expecting me."

She studied him, finding his eyes strangely familiar. His voice held a German accent. "Clara passed away almost two years ago, and the store has been closed since she moved into a nursing home." Her journalist instinct kicked in. What was this man's real story?

"My condolences." He lowered his head and closed his eyes. "I've been away and haven't been able to visit for several years. I hadn't heard the news."

The sadness that had washed over his features appeared genuine, but life had taught her both words and appearance could be very deceiving. What to do? If he came to work for Clara, Aria might convince him to stay and help her. Though, she didn't feel like standing here all night playing twenty questions, trying to discern the truth.

What small fact would only a friend or relation of Clara know? "What's Clara's favorite Christmas song?"

"*Stille Nacht*." The edges of his mouth relaxed in a slight smile. "Better known in this country as "Silent Night". We used to sing it together on Christmas Eve."

Correct. Another crack of grief formed in her heart. Aunt Clara had loved attending church on Christmas Eve to listen to the children's choir sing "Silent Night" in her parents' native tongue. Aria released the door all the way and waved him inside. "I'm Aria Roberts. Clara was my great-aunt."

He extended his hand and shook her own, wrapping it in strength and warmth. "Pleasure to meet you. Have you taken over the business and house?"

He appeared to be in his early forties, with a few creases around his eyes and mouth. A handsome man who owned his age, his brown hair threaded with silver around the temples and short beard. "I'm only here temporarily to open the store for one final Christmas season. With Clara gone, there's no reason to keep this big house sitting empty. In January, my family will put it on the market."

"This town loves Clara's Christmas Shoppe." He stuffed his large hands into the front pockets of his coat. "In December, I'd come to help out during the busy season. Clara let me stay on the third floor as a room and board arrangement."

"I've never seen you around here before." Aria stopped herself from saying more.

When was the last time she'd visited during the Christmas season? If she remembered right—the year after her ex-husband filed for divorce. Ella had been twelve, and Aria had brought her to spend the week of Christmas vacation with Clara. Why had she waited so long to spend Christmas in Appleton again? Her stomach ached.

She'd been so neglectful of someone who'd shown her nothing but love. "Never mind. I hadn't been around much anyway to meet you."

With a bark for greeting, Bingo jumped and set his two front paws on Kort's legs.

"No...down." She took hold of the dog's collar. "I need to teach you some manners."

"He's fine." Kort lowered onto one knee and ran both hands over Bingo's wiggling body. After the puppy seemed satisfied, Kort gazed up at her. "I missed the last several Decembers due to unforeseen circumstances. I'm very sorry to hear that she's no longer with us."

"So am I." Tears burned her eyes. "If you were planning on staying at Clara's house, you'll need to make other arrangements."

With a nod, he rose. "No need to explain. I'd still like to help with the store, if you could use an extra set of hands." Entering the showroom to the left, he glanced around. "Looks like there's a lot of work that needs to be done."

Without a doubt. And the cheerless shop interior was not helping her spirits. "That would be great. I'll take all the help I can get."

He rotated around, his gaze scanning the room. "I remember my first December working with Clara." A small grin formed on his face, deepening the lines around his eyes. "After Christmas Day, I didn't want to leave."

"Why didn't you stay?" Aria examined the man. Despite his air of sincerity, he seemed guarded with his words. His slow manner of speech wasn't only due to English not being his native language.

He let out a quiet grunt. "After the holiday rush, there wasn't much for me to do."

She held his gaze. He left her conflicted—attraction distorting her usual analytical nature. "Can you come again tomorrow morning?"

He went back toward the door. His shoulders sloped downward, and the corners of his mouth drooped. "I've a prior commitment during the day. I'll come later in the afternoon, if that's all right."

"Works for me. I'll be busy day and night until I'm ready to open for business." She watched him return back outside. As he positioned himself under the glow of the porch light, a sparkle flashed in his eyes. She almost let out a squeak in recognition. Her imagination was working overtime now that reality held no appeal. *Stop searching for an escape into fairy-tales.*

He lingered on the edge of the porch. "Good night, Aria. See you tomorrow." After a quick nod, he descended the porch stairs.

She nudged Bingo back and closed the door, sealing off the blast of cold air. If he'd planned on staying at Clara's tonight, where would he go? The temperature was dropping, with predictions of sub-zero lows. Worry gnawed at her gut.

Aria bit at her lower lip. He was a grown man and surely could take care of himself. He wouldn't freeze overnight. Hopefully. She stalled in the entryway, fighting the urge to invite him back. No—she couldn't allow a stranger to stay under the same roof as herself.

As she climbed the stairs leading back to Clara's rooms, a spark of warmth lit inside her chest. Maybe her luck had finally turned. There were worse ways to spend the holidays than working besides a mysterious, handsome man.

Out Now!

What's next on your reading list?

Champagne Book Group promises to bring to readers fiction at its finest.

Discover your next
fine read!
http://www.champagnebooks.com/

~~~

We are delighted to invite you to receive exclusive rewards. Join our Facebook group for VIP savings, bonus content, early access to new ideas we've cooked up, learn about special events for our readers, and sneak peeks at our fabulous titles.

https://www.facebook.com/groups/ChampagneBookClub/
Join now.